I0730639

BOOK THREE OF
THE CROWNED CHRONICLES

# OF REIGN AND EMBERS

ASHLEY W. SLAUGHTER

OF REIGN AND EMBERS
Book Three of THE CROWNED CHRONICLES

Copyright © 2025 by Ashley W. Slaughter

The right of ASHLEY W. SLAUGHTER to be identified as the author of this work has been asserted in accordance with the Copyright, Designs and Patents Act 1988.
All rights reserved. No part of this publication may be reproduced, transmitted, downloaded, decompiled, or distributed, in digital or physical form, including use in AI, without express permission from the copyright owner. Thank you for purchasing an authorized edition of this book and for complying with all copyright laws.

Library of Congress Cataloging-in-Publication Data
Name: Slaughter, Ashley W., author
Title: Of Reign and Embers / Ashley W. Slaughter.
Description: First edition. | Sulphur, LA: AWS Writing, 2025.
Identifiers: LCCN 2025805658 | ISBN (hardcover) 978-1-7369638-6-9 |
ISBN (paperback) 978-1-7369638-7-6 | ISBN (ebook) 978-1-7369638-8-3

First edition, October 2025

Edited by Gina Kammer
Cover Design by Lena Yang
Published by AWS Writing

For more information or to contact, visit ashleywslaughter.com

BOOK THREE OF
THE CROWNED CHRONICLES

# OF REIGN AND EMBERS

ASHLEY W. SLAUGHTER

A MAGIAN PENINSULA NOVEL

ADRIAN ICE SHELF
Pax Pass
Borea
TARASYN
Viridi
Flecte
THE WEST LANDS
Pruin
BERYL FOOTHILLS
SILVER MOUNTAINS
Ferox Pass
Vespost
HIDDON
Vena
THE HAREN DESERT

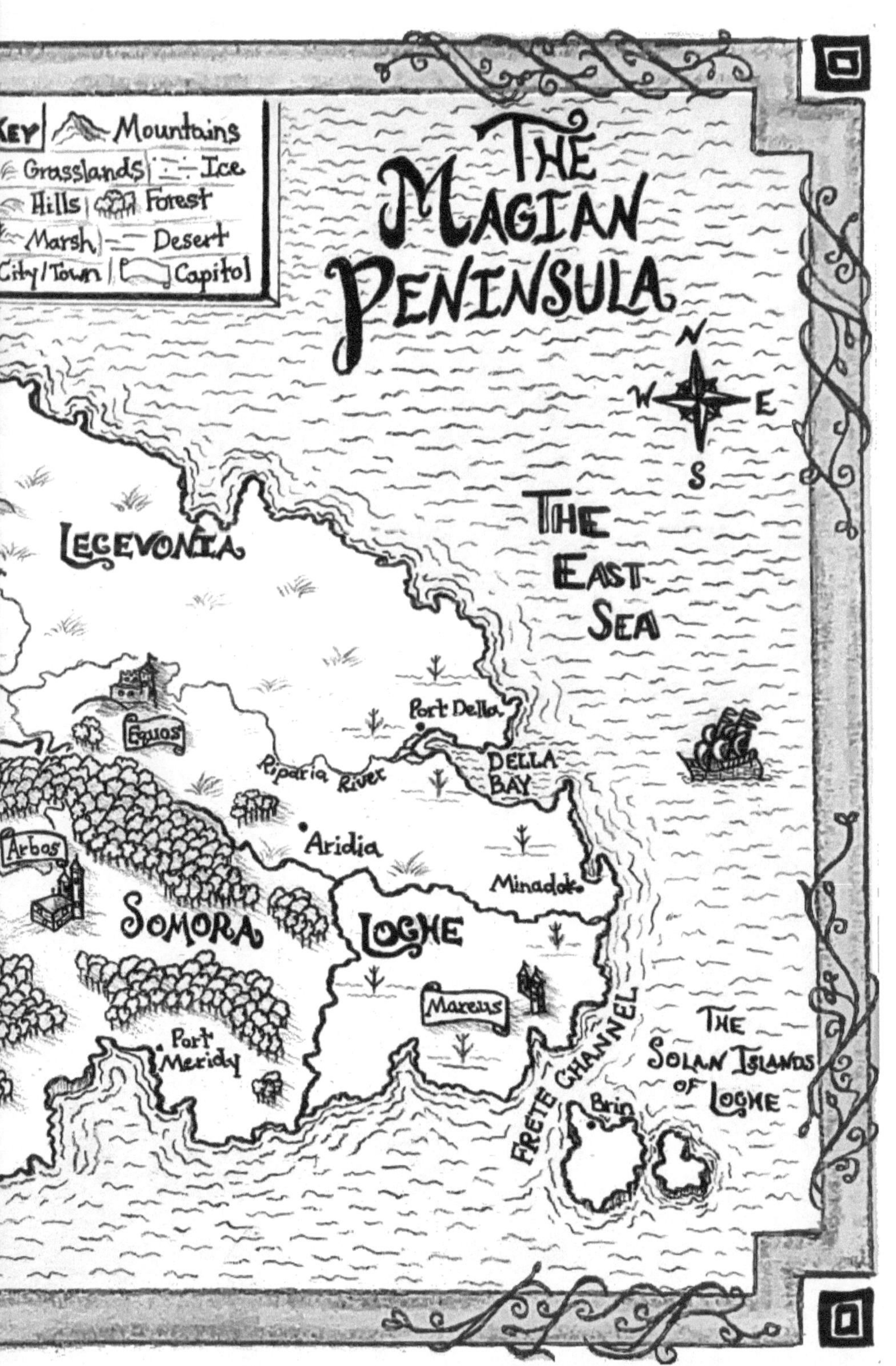

KEY
Mountains
Grasslands
Ice
Hills
Forest
Marsh
Desert
City/Town
Capitol
THE MAGIAN PENINSULA
N
W
E
S
THE EAST SEA
LEGEVONIA
Equos
Port Della
Riparia River
DELLA BAY
Arbos
Aridia
Minadok
SOMORA
LOGHE
Mareus
Port Meridy
FRETE CHANNEL
THE SOLAN ISLANDS OF LOGHE
Brin

# TABLE OF CONTENTS

Part One



Part Two

FOR MY TWO BOYS—MY LOVE FOR YOU
HAS ALTERED MY ENTIRE BEING

# OF REIGN AND EMBERS

## BOOK THREE OF
## THE CROWNED CHRONICLES

A MAGIAN PENINSULA NOVEL

3

# Part One

# CHAPTER ONE

STILL CLINGING TO sleep in the early hours of the morning, I felt Zeke's stubble graze my cheek as he kissed me goodbye.

His soft voice was low in my ear. "No wolves this time."

"No," I murmured. "No wolves this time." As I buried my head back into my pillow, the room's door quietly latched into place.

That had become our routine in the little inn in Flecte, from the very first night I'd screamed myself awake. If I let myself fall to the edge of sleep, I only saw the wolves prowling through the woods of Tarasyn, fur white as death. Only, rather than amber, their deadly eyes were crystal blue, bursting with red flecks. Their snarling teeth glinted in the moonlight, threatening to claim me as their next meal the moment I put my bow down.

My only reprieve was when Zeke stayed with me through the night.

So, it was either wake myself up every hour of the night with wailing—along with anyone else staying on the same floor of the inn as me—or let Zeke hold me steady. After he and two other guards rushed into my room two nights in a row, we both chose the latter.

I felt so silly, letting night terrors get the best of me. I'd *survived* the wolves, hadn't I? I'd survived so much.

But the fact that I'd survived did not mean I was not haunted.

Especially by those red-flecked blue eyes.

For the past three nights, Zeke had stayed with me. Nothing more than sleep, and he always left before dawn. I knew my duties, and he knew his, but that didn't stop the disappointment that rolled in every time the door closed behind him. And I was even more disappointed that his nightly stays would have to stop when I returned to Hillstone.

I rolled over in my sheets and kept my eyes closed, ignoring the light of the rising sun pooling on the floor through my window. Too soon though, a knock on my door and a familiar voice called me to reality.

"Your Majesty?"

"I'm awake, Roger."

The door creaked, and the shadows shifted behind my eyelids. "They're readying the horses."

"Thank you. I'll be ready."

As the door closed, I peeked over at the dress draped over the bronze claw-footed mirror that had been brought in for me. Burgundy satin over gold-threaded cotton, the bodice laced with shimmering silver ties. Quite the change from my leather cloak and fur garments. After surviving a frozen week in the woods, this felt a bit extravagant.

Finally accepting that my bed was no longer an option, I got up and quickly slid the gown over my chemise. Though the innkeeper's daughter had offered her services as my chambermaid, I'd declined, for doing something with my hands had become essential for my sanity. The laces in the back of the dress were a struggle, but I managed. And I'd braided my own hair enough to be able to throw something together, a pleasantly simple little weaving of my waves gathered at the nape of my neck. In four days' time, Hazel would take charge of my hair once more. She was lucky I hadn't shorn it all off in the forest.

I looked around the room for my bag of what little belongings I'd had with me—my leather clothes and furs, the book for Isabele from Gryffin's grandmother Yetta, and the three relics. But the leather sack with the broken latch was gone.

*Find them.*

That voice again. Just as I'd heard six days ago and every day since. It filled my ears, yearning and beckoning, and then disappeared as quickly as it'd come.

Coils of panic began to creep in. The relics. I needed that bag. My breathing came faster as I looked behind the mirror, tore the bedding off the mattress. I yanked the door of my room open and came face-to-face with Roger. Well, face-to-sternum. He towered over me, but my voice was one I almost didn't recognize. Curt, demanding. Desperate. "Where's my bag?"

Roger bowed in greeting, oblivious to my panic. "Good morning, Your Majesty. I saw Sir Ezekiel carrying it down with him to the carriage early this morning."

"Oh." Relief flooded my lungs. I should've suspected that. Still, behind the relief, a nagging discomfort gnawed at me. If I only could've laid my eyes on the relics, made sure they were safe . . .

I shook my head. No matter. Zeke took care of them.

With Roger at my right side, I descended the stairs and found the innkeeper laying a breakfast down, large enough to feed three Rogers. A roast pig, poached eggs, sausage, a loaf of warm rye, fresh strawberries, and peaches. My stomach, shrunken from starvation in the woods, gave a deafening roar as I took in the bounty in front of me. When the innkeeper saw—or maybe heard--me, he rushed over and gestured to the table, sweat glistening on his brow. "Might I offer you something to eat before your travels?"

"Oh, sir!" I stared wide-eyed at the laden table. "You're too kind, preparing all this."

Ever since I'd arrived at the little inn, the innkeeper had gone above and beyond for me. "Not often we have royalty in our accommodations, Your Majesty," he'd said while frantically sweeping my room when we'd shown up at his door nearly a week ago. And as much as I'd reassured him that his inn was wonderful, especially after a frozen forest floor, he fretted over every detail. The fireplace, the warm water for a bath, the block of wood in front of the tiny mouse hole in the baseboard.

I'd moved the block every night. I've been as small as a mouse before, and everyone deserved a safe place to call home.

"Where's your family?" I asked him now, and the man's eyes widened. "Invite them down. We'll all eat together."

He stuttered his thanks and disappeared into the kitchens behind the bar top. Moments later, we were sitting there with his family, his wife feeding their young son by the spoonful and their two daughters jabbing each other in the shoulders with their forks. I passionately took in each of these details. *This* was why I'd fought so hard to return home. Their laughs, their wellbeing, their happiness. These were my Lecevonians. My people.

I ate more than my fill, each bite earning itself a sigh of appreciation. But the need to return to Hillstone pressed on my soul harder than the roast pig.

After expressing my thanks and stuffing a few spare peaches in the pockets of my dress, I followed Roger out through the back entrance of the inn. Which horse had they found for me to ride on the journey back home? Would it be that fiery chestnut I'd ridden out of Tarasyn? I ached for Midas at the thought.

But down at the stables, I stopped in my tracks. Zeke had already hooked up a wooden and iron carriage to two sturdy brown horses. Roger's horse was saddled up and ready to go, and a coachman sat on his bench at the front of the carriage, reins in hand. "Your Majesty," he said, tipping his hat to me in greeting as we approached. I smiled at him and made my way to Zeke, who was cinching up his stirrup strap on Hugo.

"What's all this for?" I asked. "I can ride like the rest of you."

But Zeke shook his head. "You're not traipsing through the woods anymore, Rose. You're our queen, and you'll travel like one."

I narrowed my eyes at him. "And what'd you do with the chestnut I'd ridden here from Pruin? Surely she can't be left here."

He patted Hugo's neck. "Gave her to the innkeeper's daughter as payment for us staying here. Quite a horsewoman, her father said, like yourself." He nudged my shoulder with a little smirk.

But there was more. I could feel tension in the air. Between the coachman straightening his vest and Roger tightening his saddlebags, something was off.

"Zeke, what's the real reason I can't ride?"

He huffed out a breath and looked out the stable doors toward the hilly horizon. "We'll be passing close to the Hiddon-Lecevonian border. A carriage is safer." He opened the door for me. "Now, will you stop arguing and get in, Your Majesty?"

The border. A chill ran down my spine at the thought. To hide my own unease, I poked him in the ribs. "Quite stiff this morning, aren't we?" Gripping the sides of the wagon, I hauled myself up and settled onto the wooden bench. I glimpsed my leather bag from my room underneath the seat, and I couldn't stop myself from sliding it out.

The emerald-hilted dagger and the golden bangle were nestled inside, and the bow, now unstrung, had been tied to the outside strap of the bag with a leather cord. I stroked a finger across the bow's intricate wooden carvings. I felt the low, reverberating hum of the bow beneath my fingertip.

*Find them.*

I quickly folded the bag shut and shoved it back under the seat with my foot.

Then to my surprise, Zeke climbed inside and settled onto the bench beside me, and the coach lurched into motion.

"Where's Hugo?" I asked as Zeke stuffed a hand into his pocket and pulled out a peach.

"Tied to the back," he said. He leaned in close to my ear, every whispered word tickling my neck. "I've been assigned to be your personal guard. I'm not meant to take my eyes off you, day or night." He lifted his hand and let his fingers play at the satin collar of my dress.

I turned toward him and quickly realized that was a mistake. His brown eyes were a mere inch away, all but burning a hole through me with their fire. My breath quickened. "Assigned by whom?"

"Your sister."

*Boars.* If only Isabele knew the torture she granted me. "I don't want a personal guard."

His eyes laughed. "Your burning cheeks say otherwise."

If I could have melted into a puddle of embarrassment, I would have. "I don't *need* a personal guard."

He leaned back, and I could breathe again. A smile pulled at one end of his lips before he took a bite of his peach. "Sure you don't," he said through his chewing. "You've never needed one. Not when you were almost killed by an archer in the woods all those months ago. Not when you were stolen right from under us by a deceitful prince." His smile turned tight. "Not when wolves were after you for food."

The flash of teeth and white fur made me cringe into the seatback behind me.

"And not when you fell into a river," he continued. "No. Surely not even then."

The memory of the freezing current, so strong as it had whipped around my body, sent sharp icicles through my veins. I found myself leaning toward him for warmth. "I got myself out every time."

"Except the river."

"Yes," I allowed. "Except the river."

I expected him to look smug at my admission. But in his eyes I found something darker. Something like . . . grief. He'd lost his smile, and his hand resting on the seat between us was clenched into a fist.

I wanted nothing more than to make that smile I loved return to his face. I was here, wasn't I? The river hadn't taken me. It hadn't taken me from *him*. My own hand inched closer to his.

Then I heard the buzz of a crowd, and the moment was ripped in two. My hand retreated into my lap, and I straightened as the first throngs of people appeared outside my carriage window.

My people cheered and waved as we rode through the streets of my kingdom's beautiful river city, with sturdy buildings and stained-glass windows, light cobblestone roads and dark mortar. Some people had even made colorful banners and waved them through the air. I heard a few voices through the crowd shout, "Welcome home!" "Safe travels!" Their joy brought a beaming smile to my face as I leaned out the window and waved back, and my smile lingered long after the heavy doors to the city rumbled shut behind us.

Good mood restored, albeit fragile, I patted Zeke's knee. "I still don't need one, but I suppose having a personal guard won't be so bad."

He caught my hand in his and squeezed it. "That's what I thought." A roguish grin tugged at his lips. Still too tight to say whatever emotion he'd felt moments ago had dissipated, but at least the playful glint in his eyes had returned.

"It's a far cry from 'scout' though," I said. "Won't you miss it? Sneaking your way through the woods and into cities, being the first to know all the tantalizing news?"

He was quiet for a moment and looked out the window to the Riparia River running past us, spinning the peach pit in his free hand. Then, he tossed the pit through the window and turned back to me, eyes earnest. "My ultimate goal is to keep you safe."

His words sent a satisfying river of warmth through me.

Until he opened his mouth again. "And seeing as you can't do that yourself, well . . ."

I punched him in the shoulder.

Bouncing along in the carriage, one day carried into the next. When we'd stopped for camp, I'd slept on the carriage floor. At some point, Zeke had switched off with Roger to get some rest of his own. In the morning, the coachman—Gibson, his name was—cooked us a breakfast better than anything I'd ever eaten while on the road, eggs and salted pork and the most delicious spice buns from his wife. And then as quickly as I scarfed down the food, we were moving again. Roger and Gibson made light conversation through the morning, comparing horses and such.

But as afternoon came, the tension among the group returned. Gibson pushed the horses a little faster. Roger rode closely. Zeke stared out the window, eyes tight.

He called out. "See anything, Gibson?"

"No, sir."

But outside the window, I caught my first glimpse of the war fought by my countryside militiamen.

My chest ached as our carriage bumped and rolled over splintered wood trailing from the small collection of buildings that had been razed to the earth, charred edges on what was left of the thatched roof that laid some yards away from the stone foundations. A house, a stable, a few sheds. Not a village, but a small piece of what was once working family land, with a family now nowhere in sight. Tears stung my eyes.

War was a revolting thing.

The desolation only worsened as we continued along the road, and with each destroyed home or workshop, my anger grew.

*Gryffin* let his military do this.

*Gryffin* caused this destruction to my kingdom, my people and their land.

I would never let this happen again.

"We're approaching Cliva," Zeke said quietly. "It serves as the base of militia operations."

His words hurt my soul. The border village of Cliva had become a militia base, and I hadn't been there for them. I'd been locked away in an entirely different kingdom.

We rode into Cliva as evening set. I had visited when I was younger, and it'd been a bright village bustling with shops and inns, giving travelers between Lecevonia and Hiddon a place to rest and restock. Now, it was a ragged base of operations, alight with lanterns outside tattered tents, the shops transformed into kitchens or stables, the inns into refugee housing or healing quarters. No one even glanced at the carriage as we passed, either too preoccupied or too tired to care about who was inside.

As soon as Gibson parked the carriage on the outskirts of town, I stood to exit the carriage.

But Zeke threw his arm out, blocking my way.

"It's best no one knows you're here," Zeke said, ignoring my protest. "Being so close to Hiddon, well, word might spread to their king." He spit the last word.

My eyes darkened. "He's not their king." Gryffin was a murderer and liar, but king of Hiddon, the land forcefully overtaken by his equally murderous brother? No. But I took my seat once more on the bench. I'd wait and fight this decision later.

"Gibson sent Roger to get us some food." Zeke stretched out his legs and crossed his arms behind his head. "Just two more days, Rose, and you'll be home."

Two more days. Then I'd see Isa and Lisette and Clara, and Hazel and my advisors. I even missed Lord Castor. The hotheaded advisor always kept me on my toes.

After night had fallen, sending the inside of the carriage into shadow, Roger knocked on the door and slid in two bowls. Zeke lit a lantern and hung it on a hook above our heads.

I picked up my bowl and stirred it around with a moan of happiness. "Mmm. Dumplings."

Zeke chuckled. "You've never said *my* name with so much pleasure. You're going to make me jealous of soup."

"I don't take food for granted anymore," I said, spooning one of the meat-filled dough balls into my mouth. The creamy broth they sat in was just a bonus. And I savored every last drop of it. Almost dying of hunger will do that to a woman.

When I looked up from my bowl, I caught Zeke staring at me with a frown on his face. "What?"

"I never should have left Hillstone that day."

It took me a moment to realize that he meant the day of Tarasyn's attack. The day I was taken.

Did he blame *himself* for my misfortune? Surely he didn't. He wasn't the one who had carried me off to Snowmont. He wasn't the one who had driven me to be so desperate to escape that I'd rather have faced the snow than marriage. How could he blame himself for everything that was Gryffin's doing?

Still, the look on his face made me wish I could take back my hunger comment.

After dinner, Zeke extinguished the lantern, and I curled up on the floor with my blankets. "Good night, Zeke."

I felt his hand gingerly smooth my hair away from my face. "Good night, my Rose."

I lay there with my eyes closed for what felt like hours. Then, I heard Zeke's soft snore. He fell asleep? I peeked an eye open, and through the dark I saw him sitting on the bench, head back against the wood, mouth slightly open and face lax.

My opportunity was right there in front of me, and the only one I would get. As quietly as I could, I felt around for my bags underneath the seat and reached inside, groping until my hand closed around my leather cloak. After fastening it around my neck, I opened the carriage door, shrinking back as it squeaked on its hinges. I stole a glance at Zeke, but his head still lolled against the back of the carriage.

I slid out through the door, and my feet landed on the dewy grass with a soft thud. Around me, Gibson snoozed on his perch, and our horses lazed at the nearby water trough. Roger's horse was with them, and Roger had taken up his sleeping post against a tree.

I carefully closed the door behind me, hinges squeaking again, and padded away across the road.

Ha! "Personal guard" my boot.

My little escape success made me light on my feet. No eyes tracking down my every move, no matter how delectably brown they were. I survived on my own for weeks. I had no doubt I could handle myself for a few hours out here.

Hugging my cloak tightly around me despite the heat of the night, I began heading down the road back to town. The promise of freedom and a sense of duty grew with every step. I needed to see Cliva. I needed to see my people.

A calloused hand clamped down on my arm.

"Where are you going?" Zeke growled. His disheveled hair made a halo around his head in the moonlight.

"Zeke." I kept my voice quiet. The last thing I wanted to do was wake up Roger. "I have to see what these people are dealing with."

"It's too dangerous for you to be out here." He began pulling me back toward the carriage.

But I yanked on my arm, and he let me go. "No, Zeke. *That* is where I'm needed." I pointed toward the firelit tents. "That camp holds what I need to know."

He knew I was right, though he could never fully understand. No one except a ruler could understand. Part of being a ruler was knowing in what kind of state your people were living, what their struggles were, what their needs were. And I needed to return to that role.

He stood there, fuming, eyes dark. "Why don't you ever just *listen* to me?"

"I wouldn't be the same Rose if I did that." I winked at him in the dark, but his scowl didn't let up. Well, fine. If he played tough, so would I. "I'm going."

"No, your duty is to return to Hillstone in one piece."

"Talk of duty. I'm not the one who fell asleep at my post."

He glared at me. Once again, I was right.

"I can't let you go off on your own."

"Then come with me." I began walking again without waiting for his reply, and soon, his swearing and his footsteps followed behind me.

"If you breathe down my neck one more time, I promise to Haggard, I'm going to demote you."

But my threat only made Zeke inch closer, so close I could feel the heat from his body radiating along my back. Avoiding the urge to turn around and face him, to whatever that may lead, I slinked along in the shadows of the first tent.

Men and women were gathered in the light of the swinging lanterns, arguing over steins of cider.

"The village simply can't take in any more refugees!"

"Oh come now, they're living out here in tents—"

"We can't *feed* all these people!"

"It's only temporary, Briana! Just until they get on their way to Equos—"

"We're struggling to feed our *own!*"

I suddenly felt very guilty for the dumplings I'd eaten earlier.

Then a new voice. "Wouldn't you want the same if this had happened to our kingdom?" she asked. "The basic possibility of survival?"

Nodding to Zeke, we continued down the row of tents, keeping to the dark. Most tents had extinguished their lanterns or closed their tent flaps at this hour of night, but still others allowed me a glimpse of life for the Hiddon refugees. Through one tent's open flap, a mother hummed to her three little children dozing in her lap. Another, an elderly man clung to what looked like a woman's hairbrush, knuckles white and shoulders shaking. He sobbed quietly, and my heart hurt for him and whomever he'd lost. In another, two men pored over maps splayed out in front of them on the grass. One of the man's cheeks was glistening in the low light. Still another, a father showed his little girl how to nock an arrow with a tiny bow. All of them gaunt, cheeks sunken. All of them with tired rings under their eyes.

"We saw our first wave of Hiddon refugees in Equos three weeks ago." Zeke murmured.

"And Isabele and my advisors have been handling it?" I stole a glance at the little girl, tongue sticking out in concentration as she held her bow steady.

Zeke grunted. "They're handling it as best as they could. Once Lord Brock was thinking clearly enough to take charge, they set up some sort of system. Then Roger, Terrin, and I left for Tarasyn."

"Thinking clearly?"

"Gryffin."

"*Oh.*" They'd fought through his Talent then. Relief flooded through me. "What was their system?"

He shrugged. "They let them set up their tents outside the city. Lord Brock started a sort of food distribution for them."

"Well that's good—"

"Shh!" He pushed me into a space between two dark tents and wrapped his arms around me.

"Zeke, what—"

His lips against mine stopped any further words.

I didn't know why or to what end, but I let myself fall into his kiss, melting into his arms like wax. The tension between us snapped, and suddenly one of my hands found his hair, and the other gripped his arm, pulling him closer. He responded with a groan and pushed us farther into the shadows, almost tripping over the stakes in the ground holding the tents. His breath was like chicory and fire.

Then I heard the voices walking past our hiding spot, hushed as night and indecipherable until someone chuckled and muttered something about wild love.

As the voices moved farther away, Zeke's kiss softened from urgent to tender, lips soft and sweet.

When he pulled away, I was gasping.

"There," he said, his voice barely a whisper. I saw his half-smile through the dark. "Safe."

Part of me wanted to ask if that had really been necessary, but another, larger part of me didn't care. Necessary or not, I loved it. I loved *him*. Here with him in the dark, his arms holding me to him and brown eyes shining mischievously, I could almost forget who I was. *What* I was. I hadn't wanted to stop. Quite the opposite, actually.

But I couldn't completely forget.

"Thank you for your service to the Crown, oh good and faithful sir," I whispered. But my teasing fell flat, for everything in my body wanted to stay this close to him. He grumbled something as I slid past him out of the dark space and back into the row of tents.

It had grown darker than before, more lanterns extinguished for the night.

"Have you seen what you needed to?" he asked, following me back through the darkness.

"Yes. We can go."

Zeke took the lead this time back toward the main road. But as we passed that first tent, I glanced inside. Only one person remained seated in the lantern's glow. Her disheveled blonde hair had fallen out of its bun bit by bit as she nursed her cider and shuffled between the papers in front of her, shaking her head and sighing. I recognized the look. Stressed, frustrated, hopeless.

I peeked back at Zeke, who already knew what I was thinking and was shaking his head profusely. "Let's go," he mouthed.

But I offered him only a grimace of apology before turning back toward the tent and walking through the open flap.

The woman jolted upright, hand resting on the hilt of a dagger at her waist. Now that I could see her better, I noticed she wore a set of leather armor.

I held out my hands. "I'm weaponless. At ease, miss. Please."

When the flash of recognition crossed her eyes, her hand left her weapon immediately. "Your Majesty," she said, head bowing. "I-I didn't realize you were passing through Cliva. I'll go get the others—"

"No, no, please don't," I said. "The less people that know I'm here, the better." Though I disagreed, I gave Zeke the benefit of the doubt on that. I straightened my shoulders. "I've heard the concerns of your colleagues. Is food the main issue?"

"And space," she answered firmly. "There are just so *many* people in need."

My mind returned to Lord and Lady DeGrey at Snowmont's banquet and the state they'd said Hiddon had been in. The smoldering city of Vena, villages ransacked, forests destroyed. Given the destruction from which people were fleeing, it was no wonder my kingdom's border city was overwhelmed.

"I give you my word that I'll send aid. Once I return to Hillstone, I'll see what I can do. But I will do *something* for Cliva." After eyeing her armor, I asked, "Were you a part of the militia at the time of Roderich's attack?"

She sat up a bit straighter and smiled. "Led a party alongside my cousin, Your Majesty."

"Thank you, sincerely, for protecting our border. And our neighbors." I bowed my head to her. "What's your name?"

"Briana Gardstone."

I held out my hand to her, and after a second of hesitation, she took hold of it. "Briana, you have my promise. Relief will be sent to your village."

"Thank you, Your Majesty."

Outside the tent, I found Zeke standing with crossed arms and a fuming expression.

"Again. Why don't you ever just listen to me?"

*I listen when you're right,* I wanted to shoot back at him. But under his angry stare, I cowered and bit my tongue.

He stalked off, throwing his hands in the air. But as he sauntered down the dark road, with me following quietly behind him, he cooled off little by little. Finally, he turned back to me.

"How did it feel? Acting as queen again?"

How did it feel? It felt so good. So *right.* It felt like I'd returned to where I belonged, to what I was born to do.

My face must have given him enough of an answer, for he smiled and turned forward again. "I'm glad, Rose."

And for a wonderful moment, our walk through the moonlight felt content.

Until we saw the orange blaze rising from Gibson's carriage.

# CHAPTER TWO

THE SHRILL CRIES of our horses pierced the air, and while Zeke sprinted toward the fire, I ran around the carriage to the water trough. I found the horses tethered too tightly for an escape, flames licking at their rumps as they kicked and bucked in failed attempts to dodge the pain. I tried loosing their ropes, but they'd pulled them so tightly it was no use. With no other option, I rid them of their bridles and let them bolt down the road.

After the horses were safe, I skirted the flaming carriage and found Roger grappling with a stranger. The man was in a dangerous headlock, his face barely visible behind Roger's thick arm. Just behind them, Zeke was in an all-out brawl with a second man, arms and fists flying as they rolled through the dust. The man's fist landed a hit on Zeke's jaw, sending his head shooting back into the ground. He hit Zeke repeatedly until Zeke blocked one punch and began returning the favor.

Helpless, I swung around, looking for anything that might help.

But then, a voice sent an earsplitting scream through my head.

*FIND THEM!*

The scream sent me crumbling to the ground, holding my ears as I stifled a cry.

The relics. Inside the burning carriage!

I had no control over my body as it climbed toward the burning steps and unlatched the boiling door. There was a muffled pain that radiated through my palm, but I didn't pay it any mind. I *had* to get the relics. I had to.

Through the flames, I saw my leather bag underneath the bench. Thank Haggard leather didn't burn easily.

But my dress did. I was running out of time. I reached my arm through the fire—

But the heat was too great. Soon, the pain became more unbearable than the screaming voice.

As quick as a blink, I was in control of myself once more, and I threw myself off the steps of the carriage. I fell to the road and immediately began dusting out the flames burning through my dress.

*Stupid, Rose.* What had I been thinking?

That was the thing though. I *hadn't* been thinking.

Boars, that hurt. I looked down at the tattered ruins of my dress, to the bright pink skin of my legs, arm, and hand. Would they blister? Air hissed through my teeth as I stretched out my tender palm.

Cursing my senselessness again, I shook my head clear. My pain had to wait. As I looked around, it was as if no time had passed. Roger still held his man, and Zeke still fought with the other.

Where was Gibson?

Dress no longer on fire, I rounded the back of the carriage and found my answer.

"Oh no . . . Gibson . . ."

Poor Gibson lay on his stomach in the grass, blood pouring from a head wound and arm bent at a horrific angle. He appeared to have fallen—or been pushed—from his seat atop the carriage and then dragged around back to be dealt with later. His body heaved in shallow breaths.

I crouched next to him in the grass and ripped off the hem of my skirt, easy since it was already in ribbons from the flames, and pressed it against his head. The more I studied him, the more twisted his body seemed to be. I laid a hand against his face. "Gibson? Gibson, can you move at all?"

The old man moaned in response and muttered in garbled words. "My legs. They ache."

Oh thank goodness, at least he could feel his legs. "I'm going to flip you over, okay? We need to get you propped up for your head. Don't use your arm."

I leveraged myself under his shoulder, and mustering all my strength, I heaved the man over onto his back. A cry seeped through his lips as his arm flopped onto the ground.

"I'm so sorry, Gibson . . ." Hooking my arms underneath his shoulders and again summoning every ounce of strength I could, I dragged him to the nearest tree trunk and let him lie there, head and shoulders supported by the tree's giant roots.

I was huffing by the end of it, and my burns stung. But as I watched him settle, his breathing became more relaxed, deeper inhales and stronger exhales.

"Rose."

I turned around and found Zeke standing behind me, silhouetted by the firelight. The carriage still crackled and burned.

"These are the crites who did this." He gestured with a bloody hand to the two men lying motionless in the grass with their arms and legs now bound. Roger stood over them, a hulking shadow in the night.

"Are they dead?"

"Not yet."

Relief and disappointment battled against one another at that answer. I walked over to the men. In the glow of the fire, I saw their tattered uniforms, emblazoned with a crest that was all too familiar. A red sun rising over mountains.

"Not all Gryffin's soldiers obeyed his orders to back off the border." Perhaps his hold on his kingdom wasn't as strong as he thought.

Zeke spit at the ground and crossed his arms over his chest. "What do you want us to do with them?"

Looking at the men lying unconscious, anger swelled within me. These Tarasynians who had gone rogue, who thought arson, thievery and murder were acceptable, shouldn't walk away. They should perish like Gibson's carriage.

"Bring them to Cliva's jailhouse under the charge of arson," I said. "I'll send a wagon to escort them to Hillstone's prison, and I'll tell their king of their transgressions." The thought of even penning Gryffin's name sent a chill through me as though I were back at Snowmont standing in the cold. "Let him deal with them."

Without a word, Roger hiked the men up, one on each shoulder like sacks of potatoes.

"Could you also send a healer for Gibson?" I asked as Roger passed. I hated to ask, seeing how stretched thin the town already was, but Gibson couldn't wait. I might have spent enough time down in the healing wing of Hillstone to handle first aid, but Gibson needed more than that.

"Yes, Your Majesty." He began down the road toward town, disappearing in the dark.

I looked at Zeke's face in the light of the fire and winced. His golden hair was dark with dust and blood. His bottom lip had been split, and where his cheeks weren't bruised, they were bleeding. "Oh, Zeke . . ."

He wiped a sleeve across his lip and smiled. "I've had worse."

"It doesn't hurt?"

"Oh, it hurts everywhere. Like a horse just kicked me into a tree. But hey, I still have all my teeth." He smiled even wider as if to prove it to me, a red grin from blood and firelight.

I longed to touch his face, but I kept my hand tightly at my side. "We'll get you to a healer too."

I, a coward, hid my burns from him.

Instead, I looked at the carriage behind us. "What do we do?"

Zeke eyed the flames licking the night sky. "Nothing else we can do without water. It's unsalvageable anyway. Let it burn."

Let it burn. The words knocked the wind out of me and left a lump bobbing in my throat.

The relics were gone. How could I have let this happen? They were my only leverage against Gryffin and whatever power he'd hoped to gain from possessing them.

But if they were truly gone, then why was there still a tug on my entire being, pulling me toward the flames?

By morning, only the wheels and charred skeleton of the carriage remained.

The horses, including the small roan gelding Roger had brought from town for me to continue our journey, snorted while Zeke and I picked through the debris.

*Find them.*

That voice still echoed through my head. Was it real, or mere wishful thinking?

Zeke walked back to me with what he could salvage—a bag of flint, a jar of now very roasted nuts, a glass canister that had once held water. But no bags. I turned to return to the wreckage, but Zeke stopped me with a hand on my forearm. "Rose. You've been looking all morning. You're covered in soot." I hadn't even noticed the black soot coating up to my elbows and caking what was left of my dress. "Give it up. Please."

I ignored his plea and continued my search. "And Gibson is taken care of?" I asked, anxiously glancing over my shoulder.

Roger nodded. "The healer said he'd do what he can."

After the Tarasynian men had been dropped in the jailhouse, Roger had returned with a healer, who'd taken one look and said that Gibson would have to stay in town. He and two apprentices had carried him off on a board of wood. Gibson's horses had returned during the night, so they'd be staying in town with him as well.

I stood from the remains of the carriage and put my hands on my knees, hopelessness weighing down my heart. Perhaps Zeke was right. I should give up.

*Find them.*

That nagging . . . Something in me pulled my eyes to a long, charred wooden board. The seat inside the carriage, I realized. Could it be possible? I lifted the board, which simply turned to dust in my hands, and there underneath it were our leather bags. They'd had been cracked and curled by the heat.

I squealed, surprising even myself, and yanked my bag out of the ash. Vena's wooden bow remained secured to the strap of my bag, no mark of charring apparent. Inside my bag, Equos's dagger and Viridi's bangle remained nestled and unblemished.

Relief ran through my entire body. The relics were in my hands again. Haggard's power had given them yet another life.

I spun around to show Zeke, who looked less than pleased. He muttered "don't know how" when he touched the bow's polished finish, and he kept grumbling incoherently as he attached his own weathered bag to his saddle.

"Come on," he said, a new gruffness to his tone. "We should get moving. You see now that the border isn't safe." His eyes studied me, from my toes to my head, slower than necessary in my opinion. "You need new clothes too. I can't let you ride into Equos in scorched rags."

After acquiring a new dress for me in town, we rode on.

The forested hills turned into plains as the day dipped into the afternoon. We covered more ground than we would have in the carriage, and by the time we stopped for the night, Zeke said that we should make it to Equos by midday tomorrow.

We had no tent, so we settled right off the road and laid out beneath the night sky. We killed the fire after cooking, for the night in early June was too hot to keep it ablaze. So different than the frozen forests of Tarasyn I'd survived just a week ago.

Zeke took the first watch. While Roger was asleep, I sat down next to him and tucked my knees into my chest.

"If I hadn't left last night, we would've been there to help Roger and Gibson."

Zeke was quiet for such a long moment that I thought he wasn't going to answer me. But eventually, he let out a long sigh and said, "Or we would've been burned alive inside the carriage."

I looked down at my feet, dirty and soot stained. That might have been true. Still, had we been there, maybe Gibson wouldn't have been hurt. Maybe we would have heard them approach.

"You aren't the only one who feels guilty," Zeke said. "I'm the one who left my post." He cursed and kicked the ground with his boot. "I left them there without a set of eyes."

"But you wouldn't have been able to let me go on my own," I said in his defense. "I'm also your job."

He scoffed. "Job. You're my life, Rose."

*You're my life, Rose.* My heart tightened with his words. Oh, that ache . . . I met his intense brown eyes in the dark. I wanted to lean in until his eyes were all I could see.

Then, I found myself foolishly saying, "I suppose we'll never know what we should've done, will we?"

Zeke blinked a few times, then turned away with a mirthless laugh. "Only Haggard knows."

I immediately regretted my words. But before I could try to salvage that moment, he picked up a pebble at his feet and threw it into the tall grass. "Why don't you get some sleep, Rose? Big day tomorrow."

I didn't want to sleep. I knew what my eyes would see when I closed them. But I knew a dismissal when I heard one, so I nodded softly. "All right. Good night, Zeke." I left him there and retreated to my leather cloak that served as my sleeping mat.

But I refused to fall asleep. Those red-flecked eyes would find me too easily. I heard when Zeke and Roger switched watches, and I heard Zeke's soft snoring farther away than I could find comfort in.

Why had I dismissed him so quickly? Every time he laid out his heart to me—

No. Why was I entertaining the notion of being with him? We'd only both be disappointed in the end.

But . . .

There was always a "but." No matter which way I looked at it.

Frustrated with my own revolving thoughts, I laid there in

unbearable silence until dawn.

I was a swaying ghost atop my horse all through the morning, but when the tallest turret of Hillstone peaked over a hill in the distance, even my sleepless night couldn't staunch my excitement.

Zeke brought his horse to my side, a smile stretching from ear to ear. The bruises on his face had spread and darkened, and I had no idea how he kept so cheerful. Nonetheless, any ill feelings about last night were nowhere to be seen.

"Almost home, Rose."

"Wonderful." Boars. That sounded much more curt than I meant it to.

His smile wavered. "No sleep last night?"

I only shrugged in response. How could I admit that I needed him after brushing him off the way I had?

Unfazed, he ducked his head and spoke low. "I can fix that tonight, if you'll have me."

Tonight. In the castle. Was he crazy?

His moods—and mine—were making my head spin. Yet I still found myself nodding, and his answering smirk of satisfaction made my heart flutter as he took the lead of our party once more.

The larger Equos grew, the more excited I found myself. I soon forgot how tired I was and focused only on the giant gates getting ever closer. Then, we were upon the great wall surrounding the city. There were broken bits of the stone wall lying at its feet from Tarasyn's attack against Equos, but the wall stood strong. More rows of tents of Hiddon refugees lined the road leading into the city.

For a split second, I was conscious of the soot that still smeared my face, the shadows under my eyes, the knot of hair hanging haphazardly at my neck. The lack of a crown upon my head.

But I didn't need a crown.

I sat taller in my saddle as the gates of my capitol city swung open before me.

The great cheer that erupted as the gates of Equos swung open startled my horse and swelled my heart with pride and gratitude. Pride that my people still stood strong. Gratitude that they still stood strong *with me.*

The citizens that lined the streets and hung out of windows called out to me, welcoming me home. The city still stood, though it appeared several shops had been ransacked, ill-fitting doors and shutters holding the place of what had once been, and a handful had their thatched roofs replaced due to fires. Had Gryffin not called off the attack when he did, the damage might have been worse. But I refused to ever feel grateful to him.

I waved and smiled my way through the crowd, eyes locked on Hillstone's strong walls ahead. And finally, riding into the courtyard, I could no longer hold back. I pushed my horse to a gallop, hair flying out of my bun as I approached the little gathering of people near the oaken doors of the castle's main entrance.

Isabele's voice carried through the wind. "Rose!"

I jumped off the horse's back before he'd come to a complete stop, and I ran into Isabele's open arms. "Oh, Isa, thank Haggard you're all right!"

"Me?" She laughed through the tears already streaming down her face. "You! Thank Haggard *you're* all right!"

Then I saw her eyes, and I had to stop myself from backing out of her embrace.

In her brown irises, the smallest of red flecks had bloomed. Visible even through her tears. Suddenly, Gryffin's eyes were there instead, blue and crimson, and I had to fight off the rising wave of panic.

Determined to keep my smile on my face, I pushed the blue eyes away as forcefully as I could and tried to slow my heart.

Then I felt Clara's little arms wrap around my legs, and I reached out and grabbed Lisette by the hand and reeled her in. I let the feeling of their presence tether me here.

Tears pricked my eyes to have my sisters in my arms again. Little Clara had had a growth spurt while I'd been gone—her light brown curls had grown further past her shoulders, and she no longer stood at my hip but at my waist. It'd only been three months! Lisette and Isabele had more lines of worry around their lips than before, cheeks more sunken than I was used to seeing.

When we parted, Lisette said, "You seem different."

I certainly felt different. I'd fought for my life in more ways than one.

"Fending off wolves will do that," Zeke said as he dismounted his horse.

Isabele's eyes went wide in fear. "Wolves?"

On the other side of that thought, Clara gasped and shouted, "That's amazing!"

Behind Isabele stood my advisors. Lord Brock stepped forward, cleared his throat, and bowed deeply. "Your Majesty." Then, as he straightened, a huge smile broke across his face. "Welcome home."

Without any hesitation, I threw my arms around him. I quickly followed suit with Lords Clark, Castor, and Quince. "Thank you all so much. And you too, Isa." I reached my hand out to her. "I'm home, thanks to you."

Zeke grumbled from behind. "Would have been home sooner if I could've just had my way."

Despite Zeke's acidity, Isabele touched his shoulder. "Thank you for bringing Rose home. And my thanks to you as well, Roger," she added, bowing her head to my ever-faithful guard who'd just ridden up behind us.

Lisette lifted her chin toward Zeke and crossed her arms. "What happened to your face?"

Zeke poked her in the shoulder. "Torch-wielding bandits."

The large double doors of Hillstone opened, and a figure so close to my heart came running down the steps. "My queen!"

"Oh, Hazel!" I ran to her, meeting her halfway and falling into her arms.

The old woman blubbered into my shoulder. "You look horrendous!"

I couldn't help but smile. "I'm here for you to fix me up again."

She released me with a quivering smile, graying strands of hair falling out of place. "Let me get you cleaned up before I have an episode. What have you done to your hair?"

As she dragged me away still chiding, I turned back to Zeke and yelled, "Go to the healing wing!"

He muttered something sarcastic along the lines of, "As you wish, *Your Majesty.*"

Your Majesty. Did he mean for that to sting my heart the way it did?

My room smelled of roses that night. I'd had the most luxurious bath of my life, finally able to scrub every bit of grit and grime from my skin with Hazel's special soap. My burns were so soothed by the oils that they healed into only a few small darkened traces, shadows of the flames on my skin. Hazel had practically cried the entire time she washed and combed my hair, which now rested in a loose damp braid over my shoulder, and when I'd asked to be excused for the night, she'd hugged me so tightly I'd needed to catch my breath long after she'd left the room.

Now I waited, candles still lit. Pacing about my room didn't make Zeke appear any quicker, so I tried reading. Then humming. Then straightening up the things in my armoire. I'd been gone for so long I had to remind myself of what was in there.

Eventually I had no choice but to turn my attention to that nagging voice in my head.

*Find them.*

That same phrase, a constant echo. I was still no closer to finding out what it meant. Find who?

With nothing to distract me, the voice rose to a volume as though it were here in the room with me.

Though, perhaps, maybe it *was.* A tug—not as strong as the one that pulled me into the carriage fire, but a tug nonetheless—carried my feet to the edge of my desk, where I'd deposited the three relics earlier that day. As I ran a hand over the hilt of the dagger, I thought about the other two relics that must have existed. The chisel of Arbos, and the pearl brooch of Mareus. Where were they? Were they what I was meant to find?

The quiet knock on my door nearly made me slice my finger on the dagger's blade.

In a hurry, I gathered the relics off my desk and tucked them toward the back of my armoire.

I padded over as quietly as I could and unlocked my door. Zeke slipped through like a shadow, wearing his clever little half-smile that made my chest swell. His eyes immediately seemed to drink me in in a way that made my skin flush, from my bare feet to my damp hair. He reached out and tucked away a strand that had escaped my braid.

"No wolves tonight," he promised.

I walked into his embrace, feeling his chest rise and fall deeply. No wolves. But something almost as terrifying begged to be discussed.

"Should we talk about what happened in Cliva?"

"Which part?" he asked. "You blatantly disregarding my instruction?"

I rolled my eyes into his chest. "First, I'm the queen and I do as I see fit. Second, no. Our kiss."

"Oh, that?" His chest stilled. "A service to the Crown, like you said."

Like I'd said, but hadn't meant. "That was not all it was. You and I both know it."

I felt his arms around me falter. "Did it upset you?"

"No! I . . ."

I wanted to know that it meant the same thing it had meant in the woods in Tarasyn. Even though we were back home, I wanted it to be more than a "service to the Crown," more than how he'd kissed other women in the past.

But how did I ask such a thing?

He slid a finger under my chin and lifted my eyes to meet his. "Rose, I won't do it again if you don't want me to."

That most definitely was not what I wanted. I'd spent all afternoon yearning for this moment with him, and I had a colossal yet unthinkable proposition in mind. But I needed to know his feelings were the same here as they were when responsibility and duty weren't hanging over our heads.

Zeke looked at me sadly and released me. But he kept his finger under my chin. "I see the war in your eyes."

Under his gaze, my voice came as a whisper. "I can't have you."

"You already have me, Rose."

If my heart could collapse out of my chest, it would have. "I can't marry you."

He broke his eyes away from me, looking instead toward the dark fireplace at the far end of the room, jaw set. "I know that."

I measured my next words carefully. "What if I could?"

What if I could? What if I could marry Zeke?

Silence surrounded us. The only movement was the flickering of the candles.

His eyes finally found mine again. "What are you saying?"

"I'm saying . . . that I'm the queen, and I can do as I see fit." I deliberately repeated the words I'd used just a moment earlier. I needed to believe them myself. "If you could marry me, would you? Not right now, but . . . if it were one day possible—"

"Rose." His eyes were impossibly dark. "If you're asking if I love you enough to marry you, then I would be able to say those vows every day for the rest of my life."

His answer was enough for me. Of course, it was more complicated than simply declaring our love for one another. It required going against the perceived promise of strengthening my kingdom and a centuries-old ideal in one shot. But after, against all odds, leaving Tarasyn with my life, I was done sacrificing my love for strength. Lecevonia was only as strong as its ruler, and I was strongest without a royal match.

The next council meeting was going to be an interesting one.

# CHAPTER THREE

THE DAMAGE DONE to Hillstone was heartbreaking.

The castle still stood strong, yes, but as I ventured through the halls with my advisors over the next three days, I saw just how thoroughly the interior had been ransacked by the late King Roderich's soldiers last March. And the three months since the attack hadn't been nearly enough time to put everything back together.

My soldiers had been able to hold against the Tarasynian force when it came to the Great Hall, where the citizens of Equos had been sheltered, but everywhere else was chaos. In the hallways, tables had been flipped and carpets ripped from hundreds of thundering boots. The bedrooms had been torn apart, linens and curtains in ribbons, vanity mirrors smashed. The chapel, my safe space, had been upturned. Of all the chairs that had been lined neatly in rows, only three remained intact. The wooden tabernacle, which I now wondered had once held the dagger of Equos within, had been thrown out the window and down into the courtyard three stories below. It'd splintered upon impact. And the window . . . The stained glass of the nerys lily. Shattered.

The worst was the library. Poor Isa hadn't even known where to start in restoring the room between the soot and the debris. The bookshelves were blackened, some burned through, and only a handful of books and scrolls survived. Isabele had found those and put them aside. The fumes of smoke still lingered, rising from the ash, even after all this time.

The Tarasynian army may have long ago reduced my books to ash, but my hatred for its king blazed to new heights. It seemed I would never run out of fodder to fuel that flame.

I'd wanted to scream. But it would have felt too senseless screaming through ash and haze. Instead, I'd fought to keep my voice level as I spoke to Lord Clark that day. "We need to get a cleaning party in here as soon as possible. And those shutters need to stay open. The entire room is desperate for fresh air."

I'd gone to see Amos down in the healing wing as well. He was recovering well, though his newly formed drinking habits had slowed his progress. That was being addressed before he could return to duty, if he wished. The moment we'd laid eyes on each other, we'd both shed tears for Thomas. My faithful guard who'd stood by me to his end in the woods that day all those months ago.

"You only got a glimpse of how faithful a man he was, Your Majesty," he'd told me, holding my hands tightly.

Grief poisoned people in so many different ways.

And though I'd ridden Midas every day since being home, I refused to go down the path I'd met Gryffin on. What was once my favorite path was now an invitation for nightmares. And more, I felt Celeste's absence in the stables. I ached to see my friend again.

Zeke tried with all his might to make up for it. He took his new role as personal guard very seriously. Now that I was back, I supposed I could have relieved him of his role. But I had a suspicion that he wouldn't have given it up even if I did give him the freedom to do so.

After that first night back at Hillstone and every night since, he'd stayed with me and kept the wolves with red-flecked crystal blue eyes at bay. He always left early in the morning as he had in Flecte, an hour or so before Hazel came in and began her morning routine. And still always only sleep. My advisors and Hazel would certainly not approve if they found out, but for now, it was our secret. It had been less than a week, but I couldn't deny that I hoped his nightly visits would continue.

Oddly enough, the talk of marriage hadn't resurfaced. I certainly didn't bring it up—I was still gathering the courage to tell my advisors of my decision. That opportunity would be at the council meeting that afternoon. I felt that Zeke could sense my nerves, and maybe that was why he refrained from talking about it.

Since he was with me so much these days, silence often found us. Not that I minded. My brain was busy enough already. It was one thing to find someone you could talk to all day about anything. It was an entirely different thing to find someone with whom you could be in comfortable silence.

That silence followed us all the way through the craftsman's village to our blacksmith Jacobin's shop. The smoke stung my eyes as we opened the door to find Jacobin's sons and oldest daughter all at work one way or another, either straightening blades or sharpening axes or wiping the soot off worktables. Jacobin himself was hammering away at a new spearhead. He glanced up when one of his sons nudged his shoulder.

"Yer Majesty!" He stood from his seat and took my hands in his own, big and gloved. "Welcome! Welcome! I'd heard yeh were back!"

I smiled. "Just a few days ago."

"Good, good, my queen. No doubt with this lad's help?" He elbowed Zeke in the ribs. "I don' normally pay mind to gossip, bu' I hear this one went off to collect ya from Prince Gryffin, and now yeh two are insep'rable."

I couldn't stifle my blush, but at least I could blame it on the heat of the forge. But wait—

"Collect me from Prince Gryffin?"

Jacobin's brows furrowed together. "Aye. That yeh were goin' to marry the prince but go' cold feet an' decided to come home."

Well, that was a record I would have to set straight. Quickly.

My advisors knew the truth, and Isabele knew the truth. But my people, the citizens of Equos . . .

Are they still trapped under Gryffin's Talent?

That was the only explanation. No one had told them yet the truth of Gryffin's deceit while he'd been here at Hillstone, and so they believed he was still *good.*

How sorely wrong they were.

But for now, all I said was, "That's not what happened." I realized my fists had clenched, so I worked to loosen my fingers. My nails left crescent moons across my palm.

"I actually came by to ask you a favor. The castle is in serious need of repairs. Well, complete replacements, really . . . I know your specialty is weaponry, but if there is any way, could you work with Hillstone's carpenter on getting furniture made? Hinges, nails, door handles and locks . . . So much has been destroyed."

Jacobin bowed his head. "O' course, Yer Majesty. Send wha'ever request ya have to Duro across the way, and we'll get yer replacements made."

Beside me, Zeke whistled. "That list would be pretty long. With the number of repairs needed, it would probably be easier for you and

Duro to do a walkthrough of the castle, see what needs to be done yourselves."

Jacobin sat up a bit straighter. "Well, alrigh', if tha's best. With yer approval, my queen." He set his big eyes on me.

"Yes, of course! It's a great idea. I'll arrange it with my advisors. Thank you, Zeke," I said, my tone catching in surprise. That suggestion was . . . stately of him.

I nodded my thanks to Jacobin, and as I turned to leave, the man clapped his gloved hands. "Oh! Yer Majesty, before ya go, I do have somethin' for ya."

He shuffled into his office in the back of the shop and emerged with a scabbard in one hand and leather bag in the other.

I was already reaching for the scabbard. "Oh, Jacobin . . ."

He smiled and handed it over. "I go' it finished for ya, Yer Majesty."

I pulled the sword from its sheath and held it in front of me. It was the most balanced weapon I'd ever held. It felt like an extension of my own arms, natural and whole, like it belonged there. It felt like a lifetime ago that I'd requested this sword.

I turned to Zeke, feigning a move to the right. "You'll have to refresh my memory."

"Oh no," Zeke said, holding up his hands. "That'll be Amos's job."

"Good," Jacobin said as he wiped sweat off his brow, leaving a trail of black across his forehead. "He needs somethin' to do other than si' in the infirm'ry. He's had i' tough." He looked down at his anvil. "I can' even help him, and I'm his brother."

Well then. I planned to remedy that as soon as I could.

Jacobin put down the big leather bag. "An' these are also for yeh. Made 'em wit' yer measurements."

I peeked inside the bag and found the most beautiful set of armor

I'd ever seen. A mix of leather and metal plating, the Lecevonian crest etched into the breastplate amidst designs of swirls and rosebuds.

Jacobin swelled with pride. "My daugh'er did the engravin'."

I ran my finger along the elaborate silver leaves. "Thank you. It's breathtaking." Truly. My words nearly caught in my throat. If anyone in this shop had a Talent just waiting to manifest, it would be his daughter.

Zeke looked at Jacobin with wide eyes. "A sword *and* armor? That's very generous."

Now all I needed was my own bow. I shouldn't use Vena's forever. *Find them.*

The voice, as sudden as a gust of wind, held me in a vise like a hand squeezing my throat, so tangible that I found myself gasping for air.

"I'm sorry," I wheezed. "The smoke is making it hard to breathe." I fumbled with the leather strings of the scabbard as I tied it onto my belt. Nodding my thanks again to Jacobin and then waving to his daughter in the far corner of the shop, I all but stumbled over my own feet in my haste to feel fresh air on my face again.

The fingers around my neck disappeared, leaving me in a coughing fit that I fought hard to stifle.

Out on the dirt road, Zeke hurried to plant himself and the bag of armor in front of me, making me freeze in my retreat. "What was that?"

"Nothing." I looked past him, toward the castle. The rasp in my voice betrayed me. "Just the smoke. Like I said."

"That's a load of crite."

I stepped around him and quickened my steps. "I said it was nothing. I'm going to be late for the council meeting." He followed a few paces behind, but I could feel his eyes on me.

"Let me understand this correctly," Lord Brock said slowly. "King Gryffin is Talented. And he intends to make the rest of the Peninsula Talented as well."

"Only those who already have this magic in their blood will be Talented," I responded. "But yes."

"And he is going to stage some sort of ritual to make it happen?" Lord Clark asked. "With these three objects?" He gestured to the bow, the dagger, and the bangle on the table. He eyed them carefully, almost as if he expected them to start levitating or something of the sort.

I nodded. "On Solstice Day. He called it an Awakening. He's been collecting the relics with the help of the Rebels of the Red Sun."

Lord Castor scoffed. "Rebels of the Red Sun." He stood from his seat and began making his lap around the council room. "They've never been good for anything."

"I believe they're stronger than we once thought they were," I said. "King Gryffin spoke of them as a force, independent from the kingdoms."

"To be a part of some fundamental plan involving magic that no longer exists? It's absurd!"

"The magic does exist! See for yourself in Tarasyn!"

Lord Castor looked away dismissively. "It's all some notion proposed by an unhinged king."

Gryffin's red-flecked eyes darted across my vision, making me wince. They were methodical, certain, thinking out every detail. "King Gryffin is many things, but 'unhinged' is not the word I'd use to describe him. His every action is grounded in reason." I turned to Lord Castor. "I've told you of the abilities of those in Tarasyn. People holding fire in their hands, playing instruments and making things better than I've ever seen done before. Others making objects move without laying a finger on them. It was nothing short of fantastical, but it was all *real.*"

Still, Lord Castor shook his head. "Absurd."

Isabele stood from her place next to me, her slight fists shaking at her sides. "Does my sister seem absurd to you? Does what happened here in Equos seem absurd?"

I silently thanked Isa for stepping in. She'd been acting in my stead while I was away, so it was only right that she was here in this council meeting. But little did I expect her to speak out against one of the royal advisors.

Lord Brock addressed the hot-headed Lord Castor. "Did you not feel the shift in your mind when you were told of King Gryffin's lies? Did you not feel as though you could think clearly again?"

Lord Castor stopped walking and ground his teeth together. Finally, after a moment of heated tension rippled through the air, he took his seat next to Lord Quince once again.

Lord Clark folded his hands in front of him. "So, the matter at hand now is that King Gryffin and the Rebels of the Red Sun are scouring kingdoms for the . . . relics. Of which there are three here, with us."

"I hadn't even known about any relic belonging to Equos," Lord Brock murmured.

I hadn't either. How could something so powerful be completely forgotten?

"And they want these relics so they can bring about a so-called Awakening?" Lord Clark's voice hitched in doubt. "Do we even know if an Awakening is possible?"

"Tarasynian kings had been trying to piece it all together for the past three centuries," I said. "They certainly believed it was possible."

"And all five are needed, yes? Is King Gryffin close to gathering the other two?"

"I don't know," I admitted. "But he's in a hurry. He needs to have them all by Solstice Day."

"Solstice Day is mere weeks away," Lord Brock said. "It's not possible. At least not this year. Does King Gryffin even have an idea where they are?"

"One is believed to be in Somora and the other in Loche." The illustrations in Gryffin's book came to mind. "A wood chisel and a pearl brooch."

Lord Castor shook his head. "Well, no matter of the other two. Having these three here is not safe. They make our kingdom a target."

"I agree," said Lord Quince, wringing his hands. It looked as though he wanted to disappear into the cushions of his chair. "We need to get rid of them."

*Find them.*

The thought of the relics out of my sight was too painful. It took all of my strength to refrain from springing across the table and gathering the ancient objects in my arms. Struggling to keep my voice even, I said, "We can't get rid of them. Two of them belong to King Gryffin. I won't just give him what he wants."

"Then throw them in the Riparia River, for all it matters."

I looked at Lord Quince incredulously. "And stop any chance at all of an Awakening?"

Lord Clark held up his hands. "Do we *want* to Awaken the Talented?"

"I . . ." I looked at Isabele, at her red-flecked eyes. Not all Talented were like Gryffin. I couldn't answer his question aloud, but now I maybe knew what these relics wanted me to do. "I'll keep them in my rooms. They'll be safe there."

"And make *your rooms* the target?" Lord Brock argued. "I think not."

"I'm not getting rid of them."

Isabele reached for my hand. "Rose—"

"I'm not getting rid of them!"

My four advisors and my sister went silent, looking at me with wide eyes. Slowly, I registered my wide eyes, the sharpness in my voice, the snarl on my lips. I cleared my throat and sat back down, for I hadn't realized I'd sprung out of my seat.

"Of course, Your Majesty," Lord Brock said slowly, nodding his head once. Lords Clark, Castor, and Quince followed suit.

After a tense silence, I said, "I'd like to visit with King Merek of Somora and King Jarin of Loche. I know I've just returned, but I must tell them what's happened as soon as possible, if the Rebels are as strong as King Gryffin insinuates. And, well, to tell them that Talented still exist . . . It may be better received across a table than across a piece of parchment."

Lord Brock shared a glance with my other advisors. Then, he nodded slowly. "That can be arranged. Write letters requesting an audience, and we'll ensure they're delivered quickly."

Lord Quince sat up in his seat tentatively. "Perhaps, on your visits, you can reconnect with one of the princes in Somora and Loche as well."

Did I hear him correctly? Surely there was cotton in my ears that made me mishear. But as I looked around the table at my advisors, I saw wheels turning. "You all still believe I should marry?" I just escaped with my life from one prince, and now they wanted me to pursue another?

Isabele held up her hands. "I play no part in this."

"No. I won't marry. Not right now." I paused. Now was my chance to say something. To stand up for what I've built with Zeke. "But when I do—"

Lord Quince interrupted me. "It would guarantee an alliance against King Gryffin."

Lord Brock's gaze never left the mahogany table, wheels turning in his mind. "He's right. It would."

"Not to mention the rumors," Lord Castor grumbled.

Rumors?

Lord Quince threw his hands into the air. "We were not *going* to mention them, Lord Castor."

"That's right," Lord Clark said pointedly. "It's all nonsense anyway."

But Lord Castor didn't relent. "Our queen should know so that she can she defend herself against the accusations."

"We defend her."

"Well, there's been enough talk that it's a concern—"

"Nonsense!"

"Please, everyone!" My voice carried over the table, rippling through their squabble until there was silence. "What rumors?"

Isabele was the one brave enough to answer me. "There's been talk, well, of our lineage."

Oh Haggard.

"Sometime after Sterling Carfale's funeral . . . There have been accusations. By some purist groups, surely. But they are saying that our mother was not a legitimate princess when she married Papa, therefore making us . . . unfit for the Crown."

"As I stated," Lord Clark said, crossing his arms over his chest. "All nonsense."

How had people even speculated about my mother's parentage? Had someone overheard our conversation at Sterling's funeral?

Or . . . had Gryffin told someone?

No matter how the rumor started, people—*my* people, who were cheering for my return just days ago—were questioning my claim to the throne. "How . . ." My words fell off a cliff.

"You've been gone a long time, Rose." Isabele's voice was quiet. "To our people, you seemed to disappear right when you were needed most. Some didn't take it well. Some are calling for Uncle Merek or his sons to rule. We've been working to set it all straight again, obviously. But there it is. Now you know."

Lord Brock cleared his throat. "A timely royal marriage, especially to a Somoran prince, would solidify your tie to the throne."

Prince Hirum and Prince Berinon were my cousins, and at least fifteen years my senior. I refused to stoop to that.

But how could I marry anyone other than a prince now? Lecevonia was only as strong as its leader, and I'd thought I was strong enough to rule on my own. Instead, my very sovereignty was at stake. The more I tried to reason, the more my heart fractured, its jagged edges stabbing the illusion of security I'd had and deflating it to nothing. The crown on my head suddenly felt like a costume.

My eyes narrowed. I wouldn't stand for that. I would do whatever I needed to ensure my people knew without doubt who their queen was.

But I wouldn't marry my soul away. Not yet anyway.

"Let's keep our attention on Gryffin and the Rebels of the Red Sun," I said firmly. If anyone around the table saw how broken I was on the inside, they didn't show it. "They are the most imminent threat. Now, one last matter." I planted my hands flat on the table, wishing I was as strong as the sturdy mahogany beneath my palms. "How are we going to bring home the Lecevonians in Tarasyn?"

I still hated that I'd had to leave them there. Who knew what consequences Gryffin had for them due to my running away? And Celeste . . . Shame riddled my bones. I prayed she was safe, as Gryffin's sister Kathryn had promised.

And underneath my own shame was anger.

How could no one notice twenty-six castle workers were missing? For three months!

From the way they all avoided my eyes, I was not the only one who felt shame.

Finally, Lord Brock spoke. "I suggest writing to the king. Possibly use the relics as leverage for releasing our people."

"And if that doesn't work?"

"Then the other advisors and I will make it our personal duty to get them out, however we need to. I swear it."

I gave one final nod and pushed myself out of my seat. Isabele followed. "Thank you. All of you. I know our kingdom has never seen anything like this, and I'm so grateful to have you all by my side." The men bowed their heads to me, and taking the relics with me, I left the council room with a heavy soul.

I found Zeke standing outside the great doors, arms crossed over his chest. "That took a while. You look tired."

"That was one of the most dreadful council meetings I have ever held." The sun was sending the low glow of evening through the window in the hall. "All I want to do is return to my rooms."

Zeke uncrossed his arms and pushed off the wall, and in two easy steps, he was towering over me with his half-smile on his lips. He took the relics out of my hands one by one, and my protest was silenced by his roguish gaze. He slid a hand slowly from my shoulder down to my wrist. "Let me take you there."

His fingers left a flame in their wake, spreading like wildfire across my arm and into my chest. Was it as stifling in here as I felt it was?

Before I could catch my breath, Zeke looped my arm through his, and I numbly followed.

This didn't mean my work for the day was done. Hazel would undoubtedly be waiting for me in my rooms, with a steaming cup of tiliarose already on my desk next to a colossal stack of parchment. But I had Zeke by my side, and that in itself made everything else feel small.

In my rooms, Zeke laid out upon my bed while I wrote out letters to my Uncle Merek and King Jarin, the first step in arranging a visit to their kingdoms. And, after a moment's thought, I also wrote one to Lady DeGrey. I didn't know if I could chance a visit to Hiddon, but if I could, she was who I wanted to see.

I attempted a letter to Gryffin about his rogue soldiers who had attacked Gibson's carriage, but my hand froze after I wrote the first letters of his name. I gave up and pushed that particular piece of parchment aside.

After I handed my letters off to my handmaiden Thea to deliver to my advisors, Zeke sat up and looked at me. "You have enough to worry about here, Rose. We have three of the five relics here. Why are you so concerned if that crite is after the other two?"

"Language, Ezekiel," Hazel called from her seat near the fireplace.

Zeke looked ready to say something snarky in response, but, with Hazel being Hazel, he decided against it. He never dared talk back to the old woman, and for good reason.

"I'm simply saying that he can't carry out any sort of ritual without all five relics," he said instead. "Three of them are here, and he's not getting his hands on them. Why make the other kingdoms worry?"

"I'd want to be told if my kingdom were in the crosshairs of an attack," I said. "And . . . I have the feeling that what's coming is bigger than Lecevonia. I think it'll involve all of us."

My response to him had been honest. But really, deep in my bones, I still felt the presence of the three relics tucked away in my armoire.

And something more.

A pull toward the south and the east. I wanted to visit Somora and Loche because it felt as though I *needed* to. That whatever this pull was would never be satisfied until I saw . . .

*Find them.*

I shook the voice away and turned to Hazel. "I'm all right for the rest of the night, Hazel. I'll turn in early, I think."

Hazel looked up from her embroidery and eyed me first, then Zeke, then me again. "As you wish, my queen," she finally said carefully. Gathering her sewing needles, she stood, walked over to me, and gave me a tight squeeze around the shoulders. Then she turned to Zeke and pointed a finger at him with a stern glare. "Mind yourself."

He winked at her. "I always do, Hazel."

With a final harumph, Hazel disappeared behind the maid's door. And as the door closed behind her, Zeke let out the longest breath I'd ever heard.

I laughed and took a seat next to Zeke on my mattress. "Not much has changed between you two."

Zeke scratched the back of his head. "I think she trusts me even less now."

"She trusts you," I said, knocking his shoulder with mine. "She wouldn't leave me alone in here with you if she didn't."

But he shook his head. "She knows I love you, and I think she's scared I'll make you feel the same."

I looked down at my hands in my lap, and slowly, I reached out and stroked his knee with a gentle finger. "It's much too late for that."

Zeke chuckled and caught my hand with his. "I think she knows that too. Probably has for a while now."

He had a point. Hazel was no dote. She has probably known longer than I have that Zeke had a hold on my heart. And now that I knew, it must have been obvious to her now more than ever. Nothing got past Hazel.

Zeke squeezed my hand and smiled. "I miss our nights in Flecte."

I did too. My nights since being back in Hillstone have felt uneasy, much more than they had at the little inn. Here, I felt as though we were going to get caught at any moment. But I couldn't sleep with the wolves prowling around the edges of my eyelids, waiting for me to fall into a dream.

But if someone caught Zeke spending the night in my rooms, rumors would fly as fast as a falcon.

And I couldn't afford those rumors now.

"Zeke . . ." I looked down at our hands. Mine had gone clammy. "I . . . I don't know how we can continue on like this."

He narrowed his eyes. "Meaning?"

"Someone somehow found out about Sterling and my grandmother, and people are saying I shouldn't be on the throne. And people are already talking about us! That's what Jacobin said!" I withdrew my hand from his and hid my face. I didn't want to see his reaction. "I can't afford another weakness."

There was a second of silence.

Then Zeke huffed. "Weakness. That's what you think of our love? As a weakness?"

"No! I—" My hands fell from my face helplessly. How could I dig myself out of the mess I just created? I grappled with my swirling thoughts. "I can't challenge tradition now. There will be more talk of my legitimacy if I try."

He stood from the bed and stalked away from me. Paced up and down the room. Finally, he stopped in front of the hearth that was pulsing out heat in this already too-hot room.

I didn't want to say what I had to say next, even if it was true. That didn't lessen the blow as this realization hit us both. "I am to marry someone who makes my right to reign unquestionable."

Zeke turned toward the fireplace, glaring into the flames.

"That is why I hesitate," I said. Heat began to leave my body, sucked out with any hope I had for us left. "Because if we continue this—this *teasing*—we'll only both get hurt when we have to stop."

He spun around to face me, his silhouette burning in the light. "I can take a little pain."

His words were so resolute that I couldn't help but let out one humorless laugh.

I was utterly ripped in two. One part of me screamed, *yes, he is yours.* But another part whispered, *selfish, you cannot claim him.*

"I don't want you to have to take any pain." I stood and walked over to him, the heat from the hearth warming my insides that had frozen over. He towered over me, the fire flickering in his eyes. More softly, I said, "I don't know if *I* can take that pain."

The certainty on his face faltered just slightly. A twitch of his lips, a downward slip of his brow.

Finally, he nodded. "I understand." He turned, and the step he took away from me sent a shooting pain through my ribs.

I grabbed his hand before he could get out of my reach. "No, Zeke. You don't."

"Then help me," he said. "I love you, and you say you love me too. And you're standing there in the firelight, more beautiful than ever with this strength about you that's growing every day you've been back home. Even with this hesitation in your green eyes, they make me want to fall to my knees. But I have no hesitation. It's you or no one for me. It always has been, no matter where else I have tried to look. So, yes, like I said, I can take a little pain if it means I get to be with you, however short of a time it may be. But you can't." A tinge of hurt in his eyes disappeared as quickly as it revealed itself, replaced by irritation. "That's what I understand, Rose."

I shook my head, anger rising. "What you don't understand is that I'm not hesitating out of lack of love. I know that now. When I see you, my heart no longer knows how to slow itself. Every single one of your smirks makes my insides melt, and just a touch of your finger makes me forget what I'm doing. I got through every kiss, every touch from Gryffin by imagining you in his place."

At that, he turned toward me with widened eyes, but I wasn't finished yet.

"The difference is, between you and I, I'll be ruined in the end. Yes, I'll go about my duties, because I'll still have a kingdom looking to me for guidance. I'll be showing my husband whatever I have left of me. Respect, gratitude, companionship. But there won't be any love, because I will have given it all to you. And you're asking me to make this impossible choice, between loving you for a little while and hating my duty to Lecevonia forever for forcing me to leave you, or leaving some untarnished bit of myself to perform my duties happily."

My chest was heaving, and I realized I was squeezing his hand so tightly my muscles were aching. I released his hand and took a step back. "So, yes," I said breathlessly, my gaze falling to the fire. "I don't know if I can take the pain."

Zeke didn't respond immediately. The pressure in the room threatened to flatten me into oblivion. I almost welcomed it. At least in oblivion, I'd no longer feel the pull of Zeke or Lecevonia or the relics or my own wishes. I'd no longer feel caged by my own choices.

Then I heard Zeke's boots click as he took a step after me.

"Rose, look at me."

I didn't want to. I knew what he would say. He'd say, *I don't want to force you to make these impossible decisions.* And then he'd walk away, making the choice for me. And I'd never feel his lips on mine again.

A necessary end to something that had had hardly gotten started, yet had nevertheless already gone too far.

Steeling myself for heartache, I turned to him.

He looked at me with my favorite half-smile, and the sad resolve I'd expected was nowhere to be seen. The light from the fire flickered in his brown eyes that glowed with amusement.

Amusement?

He took my hands in his and, shaking his head, let a deep laugh rumble in his throat. "Sometimes I know you better than you know yourself."

Despite the little flare of indignation at his words, it was true. Sometimes. "Enlighten me then."

Lifting my chin with his fingers again so I had no choice but to look at him, he said, "Nothing on Haggard's green earth can make you hate your duties to Lecevonia. Not even me, no matter how much I could test it.

"Even if I could make you love me more than anything in this world, there is a part of you that is locked away. A part of you that I could never touch. And that part of you is your love for your people." He tucked a loose strand of hair behind my ear. "As much as I wish to compete with that, I know that I can't. And it's one of the innumerable reasons why I love you. That fierce loyalty forever burning in those emeralds of yours." He kissed my eyelids, one after the other. When I opened my eyes again, his gaze seared through me.

I wished him to be right, so badly, but he was wrong. He didn't know the hold he had on me. I felt the danger. The dark temptation to shirk on my duty to the kingdom was already there, as it had been since my advisors' meetings with suitors had failed one after the other. Even as strong a love for Lecevonia as I felt now, even after my determination to return for my people pushed me through every obstacle in Tarasyn, standing here with Zeke made me want to abandon it all.

And that wasn't something I could risk coming to fruition. I wasn't as strong as Zeke thought I was.

Seeing Zeke here with his hair glowing golden in the firelight, brown eyes glued to me, I gravitated toward him unlike anything I'd ever felt before, even stronger than the relics. It wasn't until my lips touched his jaw that I realized I'd lifted onto my toes and leaned into him.

He took a deep inhale, chest rising against mine, and my resolve started to fall. His arms circled around my waist, and he drew me in. I wrapped my arms around his neck and let him wash away my thoughts.

He kissed me sweetly, tenderly, hands pressed into my back to pull me even closer. And when he released me, he looked me in the eyes and said, "There. That's better, yes?"

On the surface, yes. His kisses and embraces always felt like home.

But under that comfort, I felt the turmoil of my love for him fighting its way to the top, threatening to tear me in two.

# CHAPTER FOUR

THE NEXT MORNING, Zeke was out of my rooms before I opened my eyes. His side of the bed was cold, and I tried to ignore the disappointment that riddled through me. I had a feeling this disappointment would be something I needed to get used to.

I couldn't spare a moment for my sorry heart anyway. I had too much to do, one particular thing pressing on me that brought me to Isabele's door.

I let myself in, not waiting to be announced. Isabele was sitting at her vanity, the feather of her quill flying wildly across a piece of parchment. When she turned and saw me, her cheeks turned a deep crimson, and she tried to hide the note she'd been writing under a hand mirror.

"Oh don't mind me. Finish your letter." I giggled under my breath as I hugged the book in my hands to my chest, wondering if the same boy who I'd seen her eating breakfast with once upon a time ago was the one turning her cheeks red.

Isabele rolled her eyes, but she quickly scribbled out a sign-off, folded the parchment tightly, and handed it to her chambermaid Diane. "Thank you," she said quietly.

After Diane disappeared through the maid's door, Isabele turned to look at me. This time, I was prepared for her red-flecked eyes. "You know, you may rule the kingdom, but you could still wait for me to allow you in."

"I'm your sister, and that tops any need for pleasantries." I winked at her, then took one of her hands in mine and led us to the edge of her bed. "Who was the letter to?" I asked, sitting on the corner of the mattress.

Isabele sat next to me and crossed her arms over her chest. "Are you asking as my queen or my sister?"

"Always as your sister."

Isa sighed, and finally, a slight smile spread across her face. "Henry."

Henry. The only Henry I knew worked in the kitchens. A baker.

I took her hands in mine and grinned. "Well, any man who makes you smile like that deserves a chance in my eyes."

Isabele bit her lip and looked down at her lap.

The tradition of royalty—aside from the heir—being married off to nobles throughout the kingdom had been broken by my great-aunt, who had married a carpenter from Aridia. A princess and a commoner, living quaintly in the countryside. My dream, if I ever allowed myself to dream such things.

So, Henry may have had a chance with Isabele after all.

Taking a deep breath, I asked, "Have you noticed . . . your eyes?"

"Oh." One of her hands shot to her face, cheeks reddening again. "Yes, I know they're different. I woke up one morning while in Port Della to them like this." She sighed. "The healer said not to worry, since my eyesight hasn't changed."

Despite the red flecks, her eyes still showed every emotion as they usually did, including the hint of embarrassment present now. I took her hand and squeezed it. "Your eyes are still just as beautiful as ever, Isa." I untucked the book I'd brought with me from under my arm. "And . . . you aren't the only one. I have something for you."

It was the book from Yetta. It had survived the carriage fire in one of the bags the Tarasynians had thrown off and rummaged through before Roger had put a stop to it.

Isa took the book from me and squinted at the spine. "*Of the Sighted.*"

"A woman in Tarasyn gave this to me to give to you."

"What does it mean?" she asked, briefly flipping through the pages.

I thought about coming forth, bursting with everything I'd learned. That she was Talented, with a revered Talent at that. That Gryffin had seen her potential. That she needed to learn how to hone her Talent, or else succumb to it.

But I could tell her of these things later. One bewildering truth at a time.

I squeezed her hand. "There are legends in our world that are still true. I think some things in this book may feel . . . familiar to you. Read it, and tell me what you think."

With a kiss on her forehead, I stood from the bed. But before I made it to the door, Isabele caught my wrist and wrapped her arms around me.

"I'm so happy you're home. Everything feels as it should."

I smiled, even though I couldn't truly return her sentiment. There was still so much to do. So many wrongs to right.

But for now, in this moment, yes. I supposed things did feel as they should.

I let myself just for a second imagine what a world of people like

Isabele would be like. People who were Talented with abilities that could make this a better place.

Could an Awakening possibly right those wrongs?

As I walked out of her chambers, Zeke kicked off the far wall and met me at the door.

"Where did you go this morning?" My attempt to sound nonchalant was a miserable failure.

"Hazel just about scared my trousers off," Zeke muttered. "She came in before dawn to put another log in the fireplace. Not that it needed it. I got out without being seen of course, but it sure as the freckin' Solstice wasn't easy."

I got the sinking feeling that she'd come in to check on me. Or rather, to check on my rooms in case I'd had a particular golden-haired visitor.

Anxiety prickled my skin. Nothing got past that woman.

Perhaps I should learn to fend off the nightly snarling wolves on my own.

Before I could think any further, Lord Quince rounded the corner huffing and puffing, which was quite uncharacteristic of him. I wasn't sure if I'd *ever* seen Lord Quince rushing anywhere.

"There's a carriage in the stable, Your Majesty."

"All right," I said slowly. "This is news?" There were several carriages in the Royal Stable, coming and going every day.

"It's a Tarasynian carriage."

My veins froze over. "What?"

"A Tarasynian carriage."

"I think she heard you," Zeke whispered loudly from beside me. I shot a glance at Zeke, then back at my advisor. "Thank you, Lord Quince. I'll be down there in a moment. I-I need to get my boots."

Back in my rooms, I rumbled around in my armoire for the

forsaken things. As I did so, I caught a glimpse of the gleaming emerald of Equos's dagger.

*Find them.*

Didn't the voice know I had more pressing things to worry about right now? Still, I couldn't hold back stroking Vena's bow before shutting the armoire doors.

"What do you think that's about?" Zeke asked. He handed one of my boots to me, which I had apparently left by my bed.

"Not the slightest idea," I said quietly. Only one person came to mind who would make the journey, and I desperately hoped it was not him.

I laced up my boots before I could turn cowardly. With my skirts flying behind me, I ran down the stairs of the castle, not caring who looked concerned or who jumped out of my way, with Zeke right on my heels.

The summer day was hot as fire, and it didn't take long for sweat to start beading down my back as I hurried through the courtyard and down the path to the Royal Stable.

"Your Majesty—" someone tried to greet me at the stable entrance, but I simply nodded and pushed through, following the hum of voices.

In the north-facing corridor, a covered wagon pulled by four great white horses stood surrounded by a throng of people. The Tarasynian crest, the sun rising over a mountain, had been intricately carved and painted into the front of the wooden wagon.

"Who . . ." But my question faltered as I saw the crowd of people hugging and crying, children running to their parents, spouses holding on to each other tightly. Then it hit me.

The captured Lecevonians.

"Oh thank Haggard," I whispered. Had Zeke not stepped forward and steadied me at my waist, I would've toppled over in relief.

My eyes scoured the crowd, looking for Celeste's familiar blonde hair and hazel eyes.

"Your Majesty!" A stranger's voice called.

I turned my focus back to the people standing before me, and I found so many pairs of eyes staring at me, having just noticed me, hugging heavy leather cloaks to their chests as if the cold of Tarasyn still resided in their bones. They all bowed or curtsied, and I wished them all to never worry about etiquette again after what they'd been through.

But there weren't twenty-six of them.

The one who had called out to me came forward. "A letter for you, Your Majesty."

I took the letter from his winter-torn hands. Gryffin's seal of red wax got under my skin like goosebumps. Trying to shake away my unease, I glanced up at the man again. "Thank you."

Then, I addressed them all. "Welcome home. Please, take however long you need to yourselves, steady your homes and your families. Three months away from home is plenty long enough."

A grateful murmur passed through the crowd. Before the man could step away, I touched his shoulder. "How many of you traveled back?"

He looked down at me somberly. "Fourteen, my queen."

Only fourteen.

"Thank you," I said again, and I turned back to Zeke. "Only half of those taken are back. Why?"

Zeke nodded at the seal on the letter and scowled. "I'm sure the crite's reasoning is in that letter."

As I turned out of the stables, I tore at the wax seal, releasing the parchment from its bonds.

His familiar handwriting burned off the page, scorching my blood.

I was crushing the parchment in my fist before I even registered my actions.

Bribing me with the freedom of my people. My friend.

How low would he sink to get what he wants?

Truly, I was left with no choice, and he knew it.

I looked at Zeke, my expression dark. "It seems I finally have to waste good ink and parchment on this man."

"Is he here? Already?"

"Yes, Your Majesty. He arrived just ten minutes ago."

Hazel quickly pinned the remainder of my hair into the bun at my neck and brushed off my shoulders. "There."

I grabbed my crown out of its wooden box on my desk, checked my dress in the mirror one final time, and half-ran out my door with Zeke and Lord Brock close by. A strange tug I felt in my chest careened me toward the Great Hall.

When Uncle Merek had written back that he'd come here instead,

I'd felt the prickle of nervousness run down my back. He hadn't been here since my coronation, and what was more, Hillstone still needed repairs done. What would he think when he saw the scorched library, the upturned hallways? We'd only just replaced the bedding in the guest wing two days ago.

Would he think I've failed my kingdom? Like Isabele said, I'd disappeared just when I was needed most.

And Sterling . . . If Uncle Merek had an inkling that the kind old groundskeeper had been my mother's father, would he think Lecevonia would be better in the hands of someone else?

Someone like his own sons. I still wasn't sure if I forgave him for sending them to my court.

The anxiety ate at my insides. But after sitting with it for a few more days, the excitement of seeing my uncle had creeped in. Any time his booming laugh and colossal hugs came to mind, I smiled. He may have sometimes had a hidden agenda, but his heart was good.

Lisette and Clara bouncing off the walls in anticipation to see him helped too. It was easy to share in my sisters' excitement.

I rushed into the Great Hall, straightening my crown. "Hurry, hurry!" I coaxed the waiting guards to line up properly. Then I haphazardly took my seat, and just as my bottom touched the throne, the Great Hall doors burst open.

Uncle Merek strode into the Hall, his traveling cape flowing behind him. "Niece!" Despite his age, Uncle Merek was as boisterous as ever. I stood as he walked through the line of guards with his own entourage following behind him. "Why'd you wait so long to request a visit?"

He ascended the short stairs to the throne, arms opened wide. He hobbled a bit, his knees giving him problems for as long as I could remember, and the tufts of once-red hair above his ears were silver. His freckled face beamed with sincere delight.

"Why'd you wait so long to make the trip? You know you're always welcome here." I stepped into his arms and hugged him around his thick waist. I didn't realize it until now, but I had truly missed my uncle.

He stood back and smiled, and my mother's eyes shined through his. He and Mama may not have looked very much alike, but they did share the same green eyes of my grandmother. The same ones I shared with them.

Uncle Merek appraised Zeke, nodding his head. "Who is this young man? Another suitor?"

Zeke smirked and bowed as he was addressed. "If only I could be, Your Majesty."

My heart dropped to the stone floor. What was he thinking!

"This is Sir Ezekiel," I answered, giving him a shushing side-eye. "My personal guard. And friend of many years."

Uncle Merek's eyes went wide, recognition raising his brows. "Ah, Ezekiel! The scout's son." I thanked Haggard that he seemed none the wiser to my mortification.

Then a voice called from the Great Hall's doorway. "Uncle!"

Clara came bounding up the steps and launched herself into Uncle Merek's outstretched arms.

"Oof! Little Clara has grown!" Uncle Merek groaned as he lowered Clara back to the ground. Isabele and Lisette weren't far behind her, striding between the lines of guards and curtsying before the throne. Uncle Merek preened as a peacock. "My dear nieces."

I stepped forward. "Uncle, there is something important that I wish to discuss—"

"Oh Rosemary, not today. I've only just arrived. Now, where is the feast?"

I had in fact arranged a welcome feast for my uncle, but it wouldn't be ready until dinner. I mentally slapped myself on the wrist for not planning that a bit better.

Zeke stepped forward. "I assure you, King Merek, Her Majesty has been busy preparing for your stay. While things are coming together, why don't you both walk the courtyard? Catch up. Maybe have some wine while you're at it."

Uncle Merek nudged my shoulder. "This one isn't so bad. Shame."

I pursed my lips to hide just how much I agreed with him. When Zeke met my gaze, he gave a nonchalant smile, but it didn't meet his eyes. Oh, what I wouldn't do to make that smile real . . .

Yes, shame indeed.

So, we did exactly as he suggested, with my sisters following in our steps and Zeke lingering further behind. The days were sweltering their way into mid-June now, and the sky above was too blue. Not a cloud in sight to give reprieve from the sun. Uncle Merek's forehead started beading with sweat, and with the once-shady forsythia trees just barely budding through their burn scars, we opted to sit on a group of benches in the shadows of the castle instead.

Arranging my blue skirts around me, I glanced up at Uncle Merek. "How are the princes?" Hirum and Berinon came to mind much too easily again, and their request for my hand still made my skin crawl.

"My eldest is waiting for me to die." Uncle Merek winked at me. "He already has heirs of his own, all growing into fine young men. Hirum is still whimpering over your refusal, and Berinon found himself a wife just last month."

I took a much-needed sip of my wine.

My uncle's eyes lifted to the gaping hole where the chapel's window had once been. "We'd heard no word in Somora from you for months. I'd had no idea what had happened here." He looked back at me sadly. "Why didn't you send for aid, Rosemary?"

"I don't have the answer to that," I said around the rim of my glass.

"Isabele's been queen regent for the past three months."

Isabele blushed, and Uncle Merek looked back and forth between the two of us. "Why?"

Zeke shoved himself off the nearby tree he'd been leaning against. "Because your niece here has been held up in Tarasyn until just two weeks ago."

Uncle Merek's face, already red from the heat, turned a new crimson. "You would do well to avoid eavesdropping, boy."

*Boy?* The heat in my blood climbed. Zeke narrowed his eyes and shot his gaze over to me, then gave a deep bow. "Your Majesty." With that, he backed away.

I shook my head and frowned at Uncle Merek. "You shouldn't speak to him like that. He is a noble in service to the Crown. And as a scout, eavesdropping is precisely what he does."

Uncle Merek waved away my words and took a sip of his wine.

In a move that surprised everyone as well as myself, I took the wine from his hands, a few drops sloshing over the rim. "You *will* respect him, as he respects you."

That at least got his attention.

Reaching for the return of his glass, Uncle Merek glanced back and forth between Zeke and me. "Do you defend all your guards like this? 'Service to the Crown,' you say." He harumphed and brushed at the red spots on his vest.

Excuse me? What exactly was he insinuating? What kind of freedom did he think I had? Indignation made my fists clench. If he only *knew* just how hard it was to resist what I felt for Zeke—

Isabele stepped in then, my saving grace. "Rose, let's go back inside. This heat is too much."

"Wonderful idea," I muttered. Anything to stop Uncle Merek's interrogations.

But I was positive he didn't miss the way Zeke's hand lingered on my waist as he helped me to my feet.

Uncle Merek's roaring laugh filled the council room as we sat there with my advisors the next morning. It took him a few seconds to catch his breath, but each of those seconds made me angrier.

"Talents?" He sat back in his seat, still struggling to stifle a chuckle. "That's ridiculous. You men believe this?" He looked at each of my advisors.

"They are not who's in charge here," I said. My heart thumped against my ribs. "And rest assured, they've talked through every bit of this with me and stand behind me in solidarity."

Zeke had warned me of this. This disbelief, this unforgiving scrutiny. But what else was I to do? Let Gryffin continue on his way through the Peninsula, using his Talent to subdue the kingdoms village by village?

I took a deep, steadying breath and started again, resting my hands flat on the table. "Uncle. I know it seems unthinkable. Believe me, I did too. But remember that I have *been* in Tarasyn for the past three months. I've seen it. The magic. The plans. Please, you have to trust me."

He frowned, brow tightly furrowed. The humor from his eyes was gone, and a beat of silence stretched on before he spoke again. "And you say King Gryffin of Tarasyn is planning something with the Rebels of the Red Sun. The Rebels have been an annoyance in Somora, certainly—but a danger to the Peninsula? Nonsense."

I sighed. Given what I knew of the Rebels, I didn't see what strength they had, either. But Gryffin was confident in them, and I had no doubt he'd made sure they would lead to his victory.

"And what's this about a wood chisel?" Uncle Merek opened his hands wide in confusion. "A relic of Arbos? I've never heard of such a thing."

Hopes that I hadn't even known I'd been holding onto were dashed, like a blade piercing my ribs. Did the chisel even exist? Or was it another one of Gryffin's lies?

*Find them.*

Hush, voice. Not now. The incessant tug on my body I'd felt since Uncle Merek's arrival was hard enough to ignore already.

"You say if King Gryffin gets this chisel, an . . . 'awakening' of Talents will happen?"

"He'll be one step closer." I sat back in my seat. "I know this all sounds absurd. But please, for the sake of Somora, think of the possibility of Gryffin or the Rebels setting their sights on Arbos. The chisel makes you a target. You truly have no idea about it?"

Uncle Merek shrugged his shoulders with pursed lips.

Another stab to the chest.

There was no sound but that of my uncle grinding his teeth back and forth. Even the voice in my head was quiet for a change. Finally, Uncle Merek blew out a heavy breath, nodding his head as though he'd just made some monumental decision. "I will consider what you've told me." Then he smiled and banged his hands on the table, making all of us jump. "Now! I'm much too old to be sitting in meetings for so long. How about we go out to the archery range and have some target practice?"

I sighed and stifled a roll of my eyes. "I suppose our council meeting is dismissed. Thank you, gentlemen." I nodded to my advisors as I stood and followed Uncle Merek through the doors.

It'd be good to practice my newfound archery skills anyway.

But as soon as the doors swung shut behind me, Uncle Merek surprised me by gripping my arm.

"Come. This way."

He made a beeline for the main doors of the castle and led me out into the bright light of morning.

"Uncle Merek—"

"Just come with me." He released my arm and didn't turn around to see if I was following him.

I saw Zeke catching the heavy door after us, but I held up my hand, urging him to stay. At first I didn't think he would listen, but after a very displeased grimace, he took a step back and held his ground.

Uncle Merek continued down the path through the courtyard, and despite the hobbling of his knee, I had to jog to keep up. The invisible tug on my body grew stronger, only deepening my confusion as I followed wordlessly.

He led me all the way down to the Royal Stable. Through the doors he went, and he continued down to the south wing where his carriage was held.

His Somoran carriage was truly brilliant, with thick polished wood and intricate designs expertly crafted throughout the entire body.

"Quickly," he said to two stablehands. "Fetch my horses and ready them."

As the stablehands hurried off, I crossed my arms over my chest. "Going somewhere, are you?"

He stepped into his carriage and rummaged through the leftover luggage, producing a travel cloak. He held it out to me. "You're coming with me."

The stablehands returned with two bay horses, already tacked up and ready.

Silently taking the cloak from him, I stepped up into the carriage after him as the stablehands hooked the horses up to the front of the carriage.

*Find them.*

The voice swirled through the carriage and left through the open window. I nearly turned my head to follow. How was it even possible that no one else heard it?

We settled into the thick wooden bench lining the walls of the carriage, and Uncle Merek stiffly straightened out his leg, hissing through his teeth. A coachman appeared from I hadn't a clue where and climbed up into his seat. The carriage lurched forward, and we were off, bouncing down the dirt road headed south.

The interior of the carriage was an even greater work of art than the outside. Ancient forests were depicted around us in the wood, so intricately done that the natural whorls of the wood of the carriage were incorporated into the design. Towering treetops, with leaves so detailed I could even see the holes where wooden bugs and caterpillars had munched through them, carved across the ceiling.

As we jostled down the road, Uncle Merek's gaze drifted out the arched window. His eyebrows were firm in their furrow as some thought seemed to torture his mind.

"Uncle Merek." I leaned forward and softly touched his hand. "What are we doing out here?" We were still going south, the forests outside the window growing deeper.

His eyes flitted to me then back out the window. Finally, he let out a sigh so arduous it was as if he'd been holding the entire weight of the Peninsula on his shoulders.

"Young Rosemary, there are ancient traditions that we still adhere to in Somora. This is one of them."

He stood and hobbled to the back of the carriage. On the back wall, he pressed his hand into a section of the engraved forest, just below a great swooping branch. He pressed inward until the wood clicked, and out popped a wooden knob to the right of the branch, displacing a bird's nest that had been chiseled in twig by twig.

I watched, mesmerized as the square of wood opened like a cabinet as Uncle Merek turned the knob. I'd never seen such mechanisms before.

Inside the cabinet was a wooden box. Uncle Merek slid the box out and laid it in his lap.

*Find them!*

My body nearly seized with the sudden energy running through me. I sat on my hands to keep them still and bit my lip.

"This stays between you and me, Rosemary." He gave me a look of warning.

I hardly heard him over the buzz in my ears. "Of course."

With another heavy sigh, he opened the box. His crown lay inside, gold glinting.

"Very few people know that this is how Somoran rulers travel. We cannot trust this box to be left in the castle while we are gone."

I looked at him, unable to make sense of it all. Why go through so much trouble to protect the crown? Certainly, it was an important symbol, but if anything did happen, couldn't a goldsmith forge a new one?

Then, he laid the crown haphazardly on the bench next to him. We hit a bump, and it clattered to his feet upon the wooden floor.

There was a small mechanical click as Uncle Merek unlatched a hook inside the box, and the back side of the box fell open to reveal a tiny compartment carved out of the wood.

The voice this time was a whisper on the wind.

*Find them.*

I was at Uncle Merek's side before I realized that I'd moved from my seat.

Uncle Merek reached inside the compartment and drew out a wood chisel.

He'd been lying. He'd known about the chisel all along.

And suddenly, I needed it. I couldn't explain it, but I needed that chisel in my possession. Both of my hands leapt forward before I could think otherwise.

Uncle Merek let me take it from him. "Good. Get it out of my hands."

"I-I'm sorry. I don't know what—" My words stumbled and failed as I gripped the chisel's handle. So ordinary, small.

But it hummed just like the other relics.

The voice was silent, but I felt its satisfaction in every facet of my mind.

Uncle Merek scratched at his chin, grabbing my attention once more. "That chisel has been passed from king to king. A word had been thrown around, 'awakening,' as you mentioned. I never knew what it meant. I don't think any Somoran ruler over the last two hundred years knew." He wrapped his hand around mine, closing my fingers more tightly around the chisel. "I don't want any part of it."

"Truly?" I asked. But I didn't know if I could have given it back if he'd wanted it.

"I'm getting old, Rosemary. The last thing I want is war, and if that thing makes Somora some sort of target, then the farther away it is from me, the better."

I couldn't tear my eyes away from the chisel.

Four relics I had now.

I needed the fifth.

Uncle Merek removed his hand from mine and snapped his

fingers. "Rosemary. Back here."

"I am here," I countered.

"I don't like that faraway look."

"I am here," I said again, more sincerely this time. I looked him in the eye, green to green.

He shook his head slowly. "I do hope you know what you're doing."

No. I hadn't the slightest idea. But I stuffed the chisel into the pockets of my dress, where it continued to hum. Uncle Merek showed no sign of hearing it.

He beat his fist against the ceiling of the carriage twice, and the moment the road was wide enough, the coachman turned the carriage around, back toward Hillstone.

# CHAPTER FIVE

WHEN WE RETURNED to the Royal Stable, Zeke was waiting for me with rage in his eyes. He offered a hand to help me from the carriage, but I refused, eyeing Uncle Merek hobbling out behind me.

He snatched his hand back to his side, fist clenched. "You cannot just disappear like that."

"Everything is fine," I said lightly. "Uncle Merek and I just needed to . . . to escape the castle walls for a moment."

Uncle Merek grunted as he stepped foot on solid ground again, giving his knee a stretch. "Haggard knows we sovereigns grow tired of stone on every side of us."

Zeke narrowed his eyes and turned on his heel, grumbling all the while.

"Who put horse crite in his boots?" Uncle Merek muttered, nudging my shoulder with his.

I took a few steps after Zeke. "Thank you again, Uncle Merek," I said over my shoulder. "I'll see you for lunch."

I lifted the skirts of my dress and ran after Zeke, finally catching up to him in the courtyard. "What was that about?"

He kept storming on without glancing at me. "You could've been snatched from under us again. Or killed."

I rolled my eyes. "It's only Uncle Merek, Zeke."

But Zeke stopped in his tracks and wheeled around to face me. I collided into his chest. His brown eyes held furious flames. "And what if he was under Gryffin's Talent? Leading you off somewhere to put you back in Gryffin's hands?"

Well. I hadn't thought of that. But how likely would it have been that Gryffin had gotten to Uncle Merek before me? I put a hand on Zeke's forearm, and his fist clenched tighter. "Zeke."

"I could have lost you again." The anger in his voice had an undercurrent of pain.

My hand begged to reach up and touch his cheek. "I'm still here."

"I can't protect you if you disappear."

"You can't protect me from everything." He was so close to me I felt as though I could hear his heartbeat. Could he hear mine thundering like a storm?

The flames in his eyes were smoldering. "You underestimate me."

Despite better judgement, I let a playful smile tug at my lips. "How bold. It'll be your undoing."

His fist slowly unclenched, and the fire left his eyes. As smooth as silk, he slid his arm around my waist. "You are already my undoing, Rose."

My breath caught as he pulled me closer, and he knew as well as I did that he was my undoing too.

The sudden snickering behind the bushes had me wriggling out of his grip.

It was too late though. I saw Clara's and Lucinda's bouncing curls retreating across the cobblestones of the courtyard.

I quickly looked around, and a few other eyes had spotted us too, wide and intrigued as they found a new piece of gossip to pass along behind raised palms.

Cheeks burning, I turned away from Zeke and took hurried steps back down the path toward Hillstone's doors. Zeke, whispering foul words behind me, hurried to keep in step a distance away.

At lunch, Uncle Merek announced he would be leaving tomorrow afternoon to prepare for anything Gryffin might have planned for Somora.

He smiled at me in a way that reminded me of Mama across the long table. "Despite your circumstances, you're handling your affairs well. I'm glad to see it."

His unexpected praise felt good. It was what I was so worried about before he arrived, wasn't it?

The chisel still burned in my pocket.

As a send-off, our supper was nearly as grand as his welcome feast with roasted pheasant and smoked ham, creamed potatoes and carrots in a sweet and savory glaze.

So much tastier than the pine bark I'd resorted to in the Tarasynian woods.

But even the blueberry pastries served last weren't able to distract me from the sideways glances of the kitchen workers. My stomach went uneasy. Zeke must've felt the scrutiny too, for he kept his distance, standing behind the table silent as a stone.

He didn't follow me as I opened the doors to my rooms, and I didn't ask him to.

However, late in the night, long after Hazel had left, there was a quiet knock on my door.

For a moment, I considered not answering. What would people think if Zeke was missing from my door at this hour?

But we needed to talk. About more than just what had happened in the courtyard. So I slid on one of my night cloaks, though I'd never cared if he saw me in just my chemise before, and padded over to the door.

With a pull of the handle, I let in a sliver of the light from the corridor, which was quickly blocked by Zeke as he stepped into the darkness of my rooms.

Before I could say a word, his lips found mine. Immediately, a fire lit in the pit of my stomach, and I threw my arms around his neck. His fingers trailed down my back through my cloak and came to rest on my waist, and he pulled me in.

I didn't know how I could ever do without it, this feeling of home he gave me. Every kiss, every touch, every stolen glance felt as though I was where I was meant to be. As if I belonged perfectly in that moment.

Too soon, Zeke pulled away. I wondered if it tortured him as much as it tortured me.

The forlorn glimmer in his eyes told me *yes.* Maybe even more.

His whisper against my cheek dropped heavily in my heart. "I just had to do that, since I figured I might not be able to for a while."

I lowered my head, and he rested his chin against my forehead. "People are talking," I said.

Zeke chuckled into my hair. "They always talk."

True. Celeste had told me so. Word around the castle always traveled quickly, heavy with speculation. And part of me wanted to simply say, *Let them talk.*

But the scandal of their queen romancing with someone she cannot marry was too dangerous. There were already too many rumors spreading that were, in the eyes of my people, deteriorating my claim to the throne.

"I'm still not happy about your going off with King Merek," Zeke said.

I raised my head and squinted my eyes at him. "Everything was fine."

"Still. You never know."

"You're right, you never know." I backed out of his arms as I felt a flame of indignance rising in my chest. "What I *do* know however is that I can take care of myself. I fought off a pack of wolves. I stayed undetected in the mountains for days. I'm capable." I poked him in the chest. "As I said, you can't protect me from everything."

But Zeke waved away my words. "I can if I never let you out of my sight. What was the real reason you two left the castle? I know it wasn't just for fresh air. I'm not a fool."

Biting my lip against my ire, I glanced toward my armoire where I stashed the chisel alongside the other three relics. The tug I felt to go to them rivaled Zeke's pull on my body. "I . . ." I didn't want to tell him. Zeke wouldn't approve.

Still, I never hid anything serious from him. I wasn't about to start now.

I took out my bundled up cloak and the bow leaning against the back of the armoire and returned them to my bed. I slowly lit a candle near my headboard as I tried my best to stave off the forceful whispering in my head. Inside the cloak lay the bangle, dagger, and now the chisel.

*Find it.*

It.

That subtle change in the voice's words. Find that last relic.

As Zeke's eyes zeroed in on the chisel, his expression hardened. "How did you get it?"

I crossed my arms over my chest uncomfortably. "Uncle Merek gave it to me. He said he didn't want to be a part in any of this."

Zeke ran a hand through his hair. "Rose . . ."

"I know."

He threw out his arms in front of him. Zeke's voice rose, almost panicked. But Zeke never resorted to panic. Instead, he began shouting.

"This isn't *safe*, Rose! Four of them are here in this castle now. It's like you're throwing out some freckin' beacon for trouble!"

"You think I don't realize the risk?" I shot back.

"And now what? You have them here! They can't be returned to their rulers—the rulers don't even want them!"

"Shh, Zeke, be quiet! Someone will hear you!"

Zeke grunted and whirled away from me, hands in his hair again. He paced back and forth, his boots clacking angrily against the stone floor.

Once he seemed to gain control of himself, he slowly returned to my side. Looking at the relics instead of me, he said, "Well, I suppose there's only one option left then."

"One option?

"Do you want me to get rid of them so you don't have to?"

Not this again. "I'm not getting rid of them."

He finally turned his eyes to me, accusation strong in them. "What are you going to do with them? There's no reason to keep them here."

His words echoed in my head. *What was I going to do with them?*

I thought of Isabele. She'd just found her Talent, hidden away her entire life. She had so much to learn of what she was capable of. She was on the brink of finding answers to questions she might've had for such a long time.

And I thought of Yetta. That old woman who has seen more than possibly anyone else alive on the Peninsula today. Her power, such a strong part of her. I remembered her words.

I'd been thinking about them a lot, actually.

She'd said that awakening the Talented could very well be a good thing.

The tangible voice had increased to such a pitch that it was impossible to push away.

"I'm not getting rid of them," I said again.

"Rose." Zeke put his hands on my shoulders. "Why not?"

"I want an Awakening to happen."

My words were firm, resolute.

Zeke let go of my shoulders and leaned against my bedpost, fingers pinching the bridge of his nose. "Boars, Rose."

"And I want to be the one to do it." I set myself between Zeke and the relics on my bed. "I want it to happen correctly. Without bloodshed." If I could do this—if I could bring back *magic*—no one would want me off the throne.

His voice sank into desperation. "I've seen the bad that can come of the Talented, Rose. *You've* seen the bad!"

"I've seen the good too. Isabele. Yetta. August. Sir Hilderic, the seamster in Tarasyn who made the most beautiful gowns I'd ever seen. Our world could be filled with that beauty in so many different ways. Think of what the Magian Peninsula could be like."

Instead of considering it, like I'd asked him to, irritation gripped his face. "That is possibly the dumbest thing I have ever heard come out of your mouth."

I took a step back from him. "Excuse me?"

"How in any Haggard-forsaken world would you want the same thing Gryffin wants?" Then his eyes shifted. Did he look . . . frightened? "He's brainwashed you. You aren't in your right mind, Rose."

"What? No—I am completely in control of my own head."

But he didn't hear me. He took hold of my hands tightly. "We can break his Influence. Somehow, I can help you, Rose."

"Zeke!" I yanked my hands away from him. "I am not Gryffin's!"

Right . . . ? Yes. Of course I wasn't under his Influence.

But what of the voice? Was it *him*?

No. I didn't feel that fog anymore.

Zeke's wide eyes narrowed, fear still there, but more and more morphing into something I'd never seen in his eyes before when he looked at me.

Distrust.

"I can help you, Rose," he said again, carefully. "But only if you let me."

His suspicion led to a rise of wariness in the pit of my own stomach. I felt as though I was walking on ice. "I don't need your help."

His face was hard as stone. "I don't believe you."

I fell through the ice. The shock overtook me, freezing my veins. I was once again in the frozen river, tumbling, no longer clinging to the trust I thought was steadfast between us.

I narrowed my eyes. "Leave my rooms."

Now it was his turn to be shocked. "Why?"

I felt the familiar castle walls constructing themselves in my mind, the very same fortress I'd used to block Gryffin's Influence over me. This was still self-preservation, but now it was against the disbelief of the man I loved. "If you can't trust me, then I can't trust you." I bundled the relics up into their cloak and held them to my chest.

At that, he drew his shoulders back. My heart ached to see the fear once again flash across his face. "Rose—"

"Get out. Please."

He stood there for a moment, one hand outstretched toward me. Then, eyes hardened, he let his hand fall with an irritated sigh and spun on his heels. "Fine."

As the door closed shut behind him, the wood burning in my fireplace sputtered out, and I felt as though the very best thing in my life had taken all the light with him.

# CHAPTER SIX

I WAITED BY the large window facing the northwest. The ostentatious Tarasynian carriage would surely be rumbling down the road any moment, despite the dark clouds of June's afternoons hanging overhead. It wasn't until I tasted a bit of blood that I realized I'd bitten the inside of my lip too hard.

I was not ready to see him.

I'd waited similarly at our west-facing window, nearly four months ago now, for him to appear over the hilltop before with his brother Roderich. But the fear I'd felt last time was nothing compared to what I felt today.

My entire being felt though it was being wound up by a crank, on the verge of being torn in half.

When I'd received Gryffin's letter the morning after Uncle Merek had left saying that he'd be arriving in a week's time, I wanted to run off into the woods never to be seen again. But my stubborn sense of duty—and a bit of pride—had kept me rooted.

I still didn't want to see his crystal blue, red-flecked eyes.

I didn't want to relive every memory.

I didn't want to think of conservatories or lavish halls or gaudy queen's quarters. Of snow-covered mountains or dense evergreen trees. Of wolves or hunger or mind games.

The silence between Zeke and me did nothing to help.

He was strictly my personal guard. Nothing more. Whatever we'd had before that night of the farewell feast had dissipated into thin air. All week, not a word aside from cordialities had been spoken by either of us. The wolves had returned and stolen any chance of sleep, but I didn't dare ask him to stay the night with me. The distrust still loomed in his brown eyes, a dagger to the heart each time he looked at me.

I was sure my own eyes mirrored his.

If he didn't think I was in control of my mind, how could I speak to him of anything about the relics? About my anxiety of seeing Gryffin again? He would have thought it was all fabricated by Gryffin himself to purposely drive a wedge between us.

Well, Gryffin's Influence or not, that wedge was well in place.

The rumors of us had also stopped as quickly as they started. With the coldness between us, there was nothing more to gossip about.

But the coldness hurt.

I still loved him. I still wanted him to be the one I talked to about everything. I still wanted his words to lighten my day and bring a smile to my face.

I stole a glance at Zeke, who was leaning against a pillar behind me, arms crossed over his chest and a brooding scowl on his face.

When he caught me looking, he didn't immediately turn away. His frown might've even softened. Just a little. His lips might've parted as if to say something—

Then the carriage appeared over the hill, out of the corner of my eye.

I turned back to the window quickly. It started as just a pinprick on the horizon, then slowly grew into a deep black carriage with golden wheels glinting even with no sun. Behind it, a wagon. Both pulled by white horses.

I turned to a guard in the hallway. "Quick. Find my advisors and tell them he's arrived. And pass a word along for Celeste Shillrene to visit me when she is able."

As he scurried off, I began down the corridor. As much as I wanted to go down and greet Celeste myself, I'd agreed with my advisors that the Great Hall was the best place to receive Gryffin. Fewer entrances than the Royal Stable, and more soldiers could fit in the grand room.

I'd let Hazel dress me in one of her beloved gowns, green as my eyes and the hills outside the window, with golden buttons and silver threading. I tugged at my long sleeves and adjusted the crown on my head before gripping the handles of the double doors.

Then a hand was on top of mine, and I nearly jumped out of my skin.

"Rose," Zeke murmured from behind me. He placed his other hand on my shoulder and urged me to turn to him. My hand was shaking under his, and that was when I realized my entire body was trembling. Even my teeth were clattering. Suddenly, tears pricked the backs of my eyes. I slowly turned on my heel.

"I thought I wasn't afraid," I whispered. "That he held no fear over me anymore. But I was wrong." I glanced up at him, focusing on the tiny scar under his eyes that he'd had since we were children. "Zeke, I'm terrified to see him."

His eyes searched mine, and for the first time all week, I saw something other than distrust. They were pleading, as if he wished he could pass strength over to me. Zeke gave a minute shake of his head and said, "Don't let him hold *anything* over you. You are stronger than him."

With a deep breath, I nodded, and Zeke's hand nudged mine off the door handle.

"You'll need a proper entrance, Your Majesty," he said, a smirk still stained with a hint of suspicion in his voice.

I rolled my eyes, but thanks to him, I felt a bit more like myself. I took a step back and let Zeke open the double doors for me.

Inside the Great Hall, they'd already set everything up for Gryffin's arrival. Guards at the entrance and rows two men thick lining the path to the throne. Swords already drawn and at the ready.

"You can put your weapons away," I said. "He's only one man, and though he's an excellent swordman, that is not his Talent." What was more, I didn't want Gryffin to know how much he'd rattled my people.

I strode down the path, my soldiers bowing their heads to me as I passed. Near the steps, my advisors all stood in a row, and at the base of the throne, my sisters. I took the steps one by one up to the grand mahogany chair that my father had once occupied.

*Lecevonia was only as strong as its leader.*

Zeke was right. I was strong. Stronger than ever.

I should have sat in my seat, as was customary when receiving visitors, but I couldn't make myself sit down. My every nerve was on fire.

Then, before anyone appeared around the open doors, I felt it. That pressure on the inside of my skull, trying to nudge its way into my mind.

The feeling brought me back to the guest chambers of Snowmont, and my heart raced. What I wouldn't do to have a Talent that would somehow banish this panic for good.

But I kept my mind tightly closed to Gryffin, my castle walls already erecting stone by stone.

No one else reacted as if they'd felt anything. Just stony faces and steely eyes turned toward the door. Zeke stood closer now than he had this entire week on the step below me, almost shielding me. I sidestepped just a little, and I saw his feet shuffle, wanting to follow.

Then a man in a Lecevonian uniform appeared around the doors. "King Gryffin Danicio of Tarasyn, and Princess Kathryn."

Kathryn's name gave me a jolt of surprise, followed by excitement, but I refused to show it.

Gryffin appeared first, his crown glinting silver despite the lack of sun streaming through the windows. His black vest and trousers matched his dark curls, and his eyes gleamed. His face had been hardset and serious when he first entered, but upon meeting my eyes, his expression softened into the barest smile, just for a moment that passed so quickly I would have missed had my own eyes not been cemented to his.

Those eyes.

I felt my chest tighten, my breath coming too fast. The panic. The need to flee.

But it was Zeke's reaction I hadn't expected.

He drew his sword and charged down the steps. He didn't stop until he was face-to-face with Gryffin, whose expression had hardened once more, though this time to one of hatred.

Gryffin made no move toward his sword. Zeke could have skewered him then and there.

"Come to kill me so quickly, did you?"

"Why shouldn't I?" Zeke shot back. "You loathsome crite."

Gryffin peered around Zeke, once again fixing his eyes on me. "Rosemary, would you mind calling off your guard dog? He's drooling over his own insults."

I saw Zeke's hands around his sword's hilt shake, aching so badly to take the swing. The soldiers around them were also stirring, unsure of how to react.

Their encounter was just the distraction I needed. Looking into Gryffin's red-flecked eyes again, I pushed the panic down into my belly. I was the one in control here.

"Both of you need to check what's more in charge," I said as I descended the steps. "Your head or your vanity." As I passed the soldiers down the aisle, they snapped back into their positions.

I stopped just short of the two men, behind Zeke. "Zeke," I said quietly, placing a hand on his shoulder. "Put your sword away. He has no power here."

Zeke's jaw worked as he decided whether or not to trust my words.

I didn't have time for his doubt. I turned to Gryffin. "Sir Ezekiel has every right to be angry, as does everyone here in this Hall." I felt my own flare of anger lighting in my chest. "You were going to kill me."

A volatile murmur rumbled through the rows of soldiers.

Gryffin's eyes swept over the men that surrounded him, and after a bare moment of thought, he raised his hands slowly, signaling peace. "I mean no harm. I never wanted to harm you, or anyone."

"Tell that to Xal's father," Zeke said through his teeth. But he finally sheathed his sword and took a step back.

Gryffin's eyes narrowed. "Loss is never a happy thing."

Then a throat cleared from behind Gryffin. "Now that the two of you men are through comparing egos, may I please say hello to my friend?"

Gryffin turned to the side and revealed Kathryn, in a glorious yellow travel dress and a fur-lined cloak. Her cheeks were already flushed from the heat.

And close beside her stood Celeste, in a green dress of her own and her hair done in a braided updo. I smiled. I'd never seen Celeste with her hair done before, and from the uncomfortable grimace on her face, I had a good guess that she hated it.

Leaving Gryffin and Zeke, I took Kathryn and Celeste into my arms. "Welcome to Hillstone," I told Kathryn, squeezing her hands. Then I turned to Celeste, and the prick of tears returned. "And welcome *home*."

"What I wouldn't do to return to the stables now," Celeste responded with a lift of her chin, pulling roughly at the hem of her sleeves.

I smiled. "I wasn't expecting you to come to the Great Hall. I'd sent someone to find you and ask you to come see me later." Poor man, I hoped he wasn't hopelessly wandering around.

"Kathryn wouldn't allow me to be stuffed in the wagon with the others." Celeste nudged Kathryn's elbow, and Kathryn rolled her eyes.

"And you've all returned?" I asked. "The other Lecevonians who were taken?"

It was Gryffin who answered from behind me. "Every last one."

I turned and found him standing right at my shoulder, almost touching me. Zeke glared over his shoulder.

Up close, his eyes were eerier than before. There was almost no blue left.

Then a glimmer of metal brought my attention to his chest, and I noticed around his neck hung a silver chain with a gold ring. An emerald sat in the middle, surrounded by tiny diamonds.

I'd have recognized that ring anywhere. I'd worn it on my finger for weeks.

But why was he wearing it?

His lips turned upward into a daring smile. "I *am* happy to see you alive, Rosemary."

But I shook my head, anger flaring again. "You are the reason why

I almost didn't make it home." He was the reason for many things. My capitol in disarray, my castle in shambles, the border of my kingdom made weak. Hiddon's refugees camped outside Equos's walls. I hoped he'd seen them on his way in and felt some sense of remorse. "What was it you wanted to discuss?"

He shifted his weight from one foot to the other. "Can we talk somewhere a bit more private?"

"No."

He frowned before his face turned stony again. "All right, then." He took a step back and folded his hands behind him. "Yetta is gone. Amicka took her and is holding her captive."

My heart suddenly dropped like a stone into my stomach. "That can't be right."

Gryffin looked down to the floor. "I—I know." His show of grief surprised me.

*Yetta is gone. Yetta is gone.*

I took step back. "How? Who's . . . who is Amicka?"

"Amicka is the leader of the Rebels of the Red Sun. And she's why I'm here."

The Hall was quiet as a bone-dry riverbed. I certainly imagined my advisors were ready to burst with questions. I hadn't told them about Yetta.

"We'll move this to the council room," I finally said.

I turned to Kathryn and hugged her again. "We'll have a guest room set up for you. Please stay?"

She smirked. "My brother couldn't make me leave if he tried."

Her answer made me smile. She was finally getting to experience someplace other than Tarasyn. And truly, I missed her.

But the news of Kathryn's stay didn't staunch the growing unease within me.

In the council room, Gryffin claimed a seat next to me, much to Lord Brock's dismay. Zeke stood behind me, still glaring as we all settled into our seats. "His eyes are unnerving," he whispered in my ear.

The chill of apprehension that creeped across my skin did enough to convey my agreement.

Then I addressed Gryffin.

"Start with this," I said. "Who is Amicka?"

"As I said, she is the leader of the Rebels of the Red Sun."

"I still don't understand their part in all of this."

Gryffin nodded slowly. "I figured as much. The Rebels, like I told you, want an Awakening to happen as much as I do, if not more."

"Why?"

"Why not?" He shrugged. "They live to see the magic of the Magian Peninsula thrive again. That is their entire reason for organizing. They want the relics too."

"Is that why they burn down villages?" I asked. "Looking for the relics?"

Gryffin sighed. "A waste, isn't it?"

Having him here was so . . . perturbing. The last time Gryffin had been in this room was to protect me from his brother Roderich, and the time before that, to tell my advisors he wished to marry me.

All part of his game.

"How do I know you are telling the truth?" I asked. "You've lied about so much."

"I'm not trying to fool anyone anymore, Rosemary. I can't, actually, seeing as though you all are aware of my Talent now." He sounded less than enthused by that fact.

I turned my head and side-eyed Zeke. *See?* I wanted to shout at him. I was completely in control.

Zeke cleared his throat. "Go on, you crite."

Gryffin's eyes narrowed. "Again with the insults."

I didn't acknowledge their little battle. "How do you know they've taken Yetta? Do you know where?"

Gryffin shook his head. "No. But I know they took her because her husband flew into Snowmont screeching up a storm. Corvus nearly took his eye out in midair."

Corvus, that dreaded crow. If he'd have hurt August, Yetta would surely have her revenge when she returned.

"What did August say happened?"

"He said Amicka found Yetta in the woods while out hunting. Yetta of course would have known Amicka was there, and she would have known of her intentions. I don't know why she didn't run . . ." He shook his head, perplexed as I was.

Yes, why wouldn't she run? Why wouldn't she hide?

It was obvious why Amicka took Yetta. Yetta knew so much—possibly more than anyone else on the entire Peninsula.

"Aren't you and Amicka partners in all of this?" I asked. "Why would she take Yetta and not come to you first?"

Gryffin looked away, out the high window where rain now poured down. "Amicka . . . wants things done a certain way. I suppose I have told her no too many times."

"Are you no longer allies?"

He drummed his fingers on the table, unable to meet my gaze. "It seems that way."

A heavy silence blanketed the room.

Then he looked up at me again. "That's why I've come here. To tell you that I have no clue what the Rebels are planning now. To stage an Awakening, surely. But if you have three of the relics here . . . I fear you are their next target."

Three. He didn't know I now had four.

He leaned forward. "They *need* those relics. Nothing can happen without them. There will never be peace—the Rebels will always be against you. Against Lecevonia. They've been using Lecevonia as a base for years. This land is no stranger to them."

Those words. I was suddenly on the riding path in the woods outside Hillstone, on the day Gryffin had killed Thomas and exposed his true nature. He'd told me this months ago, but I'd been too blindsided by everything else to realize what he'd meant.

The fires. The complaints. Was that why? Because the Rebels had been using my kingdom as a base? I looked at my advisors, and they looked as shocked as I felt.

To my dismay, Gryffin noticed. "Turning a blind eye to them was a mistake," he murmured with a shake of his head. Then, after measuring our silence, he said, "I propose we stage an Awakening before they can. We have more relics than they can possibly get. And you have ties to Somora and Loche. Maybe—"

It was Zeke who interrupted him. "Absolutely not."

My advisors felt that was an invitation to chime in as well.

"*We* are not allies!"

"Tarasyn has done nothing but hurt this kingdom!"

"The gall you have to even suggest—"

I held up my hand, silencing the room. "Without even considering an Awakening, what do we have to fear of the Rebels? Was Tarasyn not their army?"

"They have a large enough following to be a danger."

"Even against Lecevonia's forces? I find that hard to believe."

"Rosemary." His red-flecked eyes pleaded with me. "They have Yetta."

"You care?" I didn't think he gave his grandmother a second thought.

"Of course I care," he shot back. "And so do you."

Yes, I did care. The old woman had given me so much more than just the know-how to survive in the Tarasynian woods. She'd made me believe I *could* survive.

But what was more, his answer surprised me. Perhaps Yetta had had a point when she'd said Gryffin did not enjoy the demise of others. That he just saw it as a necessary evil.

"How do you suggest we get her back?" I hedged.

By the gleam in his eyes, Gryffin hadn't missed the *we*.

"An Awakening is all they want," he said. "If it happens, they will have no more use for her and they'll let her go."

I'd already decided I was going to do so, but I didn't want Gryffin to know that yet. I must have been quiet for too long, for Gryffin shook his head and leaned forward.

"If you won't do anything, then give the relics to me. Take the target off yourself. Please." There was actual worry in his voice. He was begging me.

Did he truly care what happened to me?

No. Of course he didn't. He only cared that I'd been able to give him a kingdom, once upon a time.

But strangely, there was no pressure of his Talent prodding my mind. No trickery today.

"Solstice Day is in two weeks' time," he said, an edge in his deep voice. "It's now or never."

Two weeks. That was all the time I had.

Then, tentatively, he reached forward to touch my hand.

I slid mine back quickly as though his hand was a viper. I could feel Zeke's shadow looming over me.

"I'm keeping the relics here," I finally said. "I will do with them as I wish."

If my advisors thought anything of that, they didn't show it. The only one in this room who knew I had four of the five relics was Zeke, and I already knew his stance.

Gryffin, however, did nothing to hide his displeasure. His mouth set into a stony frown, his eyes cold. "Then I have nothing more to request of you. But take this as your warning—Amicka is no game, and she isn't known for her patience. The end of her spear has been the last sight of too many people to count."

He pushed himself up from the table and turned toward the door.

"What about Yetta?" My words made him pause mid-step. "What will you do?"

He was quiet for a beat, then looked back over his shoulder. "I don't know."

Without another word, he left the council room.

Gryffin left that same day, leaving the carriage for Kathryn and taking the wagon back to Tarasyn, which was surprisingly considerate of him. He said he had no further reason to stay and would rather go back to Tarasyn before "any more damage was done." I hadn't a clue what he'd meant by that. But it was a weight lifted from my shoulders to see him go. I could breathe again.

Having Kathryn here and seeing the excitement in her eyes was a reward in itself. This was the first time she'd ever felt the heat of summer in all her life, and since all of her dresses were fur-lined, we had to have a few made for her by the castle's seamstress. Hazel loved having a royal around to dress in bold colors and daring necklines, and Kathryn turned the heads of many around Hillstone.

But no one claimed her attention as much as Celeste. And because of that, Kathryn spent most of her time in the Royal Stable.

I, on the other hand, only had time to go down to the stables once a day to ride Midas, an hour in the early morning that was becoming sacred to me. I would be leaving for Hiddon tomorrow, and so much of these past three days since Gryffin's visit were spent in council meetings, most often about the remaining repairs needed to be done to Hillstone and Equos. Not to mention the Hiddon refugees to provide for outside our city walls. There were also preparations to be made for Solstice Day, a most treasured holiday across the Peninsula. At least that was a more joyful event to focus on, even if I still had one more relic to find before then.

But for now, in this hour, I only focused on Midas's hooves pounding on the ground beneath us. The rain from the night before had just barely softened the earth, and the forest glistened with lingering raindrops, the cleansing smell of rain welcoming the dawn of day.

I glanced behind me, and Zeke followed as he normally did, a few lengths back on Hugo. Hugo seemed much happier in the heat than he had in the snow.

Since Gryffin's departure, we still hadn't spoken to each other any more deeply than "hello" and "good night." I wasn't sure who was holding out on who anymore, to be honest. Gryffin himself had said he had no control over the minds of anyone in that council room. The lack of trust Zeke used to wear plainly wasn't there anymore when he looked at me, for the most part anyway. We'd just fallen into this new routine, and neither of us fought to change it.

I didn't want that to be the case anymore, though. Perhaps it was from my lack of sleep, courtesy of the wolves still prowling through my dreams, but the silence between us had become unbearable.

Conjuring up my courage, I wheeled Midas around and brought him side by side with Hugo.

Zeke smiled the warmest smile I'd received since our argument before he seemed to catch himself, settling his face back into a scowl.

"Hello," I said quietly.

Zeke looked at me with careful eyes. "Your Majesty."

I nudged him with my stirrup. "Can we stop this? Please?"

"Stop what?"

"The formalities. The distance."

Zeke's eyes held a daring flicker. "You told me to get out. I'm doing so to the best of my ability."

"Zeke," I said, sighing. "I did not mean get out of every aspect of my life. You know that."

"I know. But maybe it's what is best."

I reined Midas to a stop and crossed my arms over my chest. "Why do you get to decide what's best?"

Zeke's eyes steeled over, challenging. "Why haven't you unassigned me as your personal guard yet?" He shot back.

This question surprised me and sent a bolt of sadness through me. "Do . . . do you want me to?"

"No," he said softly. "But that doesn't answer the question." He led Hugo in a circle. "If you can so undoubtedly take care of yourself, then why am I still here, by your side every moment of every day?"

Why hadn't I unassigned him yet? Did I truly need his constant eye on me?

No. But I had other reasons. I dismounted from Midas and tied his reins to a low branch, avoiding Zeke's eyes. "Because I *do* want you around. Because your presence is comforting. Because . . ."

Because having him here meant he was safe. Because if he was with me, even if he didn't completely trust that I was myself, I didn't have to worry about scout assignments or captures or whatever other trouble he might have gotten himself into.

Because he still felt like *home.*

Because I loved him.

I heard his feet land on the ground, and the crunching of soft dirt under his feet grew louder as he approached me. A strong hesitation sat in the dewy air.

"Rose," he finally said. "I can't protect you if you keep putting yourself in risky situations."

I felt his hand on my shoulder, and I turned to face him.

"I don't need protection from everything, Zeke."

But Zeke shook his head. "I don't like the sound of this 'Amicka' woman. And yet you insist on keeping the relics here?" He scoffed. "I wish we'd just destroy the things."

"Why don't you trust my judgement?"

He threw his hands into the air, then let them fall to his sides with a thud. "Because I don't understand it, Rose. I see now that it's you who wants this, not some hold that Gryffin has over you, but I don't understand, and I usually don't trust things I don't understand."

I felt my anger rising again, but I tempered it. The direction of this conversation wasn't going to solve the silence. "I don't want to talk about the relics. But I need you to know that I don't keep you assigned as my personal guard because I want protection."

He narrowed his eyes. "Why, then?"

"Because you're the one I want to do everything with. From the smallest parts of my day to the most stress-inducing council meetings.

I can't explain it. I just want it to be you."

Finally, Zeke's expression softened, and he chuckled. He placed his hands on my waist, eyes now glinting mischievously. "I can explain it."

I rolled my eyes, but the fire in his touch was impossible to ignore. "Of course you can."

"It's because you love me."

"You know that already," I said, feeling the scorch rising to my cheeks.

"It's still nice to hear. And, well, after how I acted that night in your rooms, the things I said, I wasn't sure . . ."

How odd for him to sound unsure of himself. Zeke, who always walked around with the confidence of a peacock.

"Well, to be honest, I also wasn't sure what was left between us," I said. "You didn't trust me. What room did that leave for love?"

Guilt pulled one corner of his mouth up into an apologetic smirk. "I'll admit I jumped to conclusions based on my own feelings about the freckin' relics. I can tell they aren't good for you. I never stopped loving you though."

*Why aren't the relics good for me?* I wanted to ask. But his hands were already tightening around me, pulling me in, and I wasn't about to interrupt that.

"I'm sorry for failing to take you seriously," Zeke said quietly. "I should have believed that you were stronger than anything that crite could've done to you."

"Thank you." My voice was breathless as he began trailing his finger across my back.

"In fact, you're the strongest woman I know."

I'd have believed anything this man said while he was kissing my hair like he was now.

"And . . ." His fingers lifted my chin, and his eyes peered into mine hungrily. "There is no one to spread gossip out here on the trail."

He coaxed me backward until my back hit the trunk of a tree. He wrapped his arms tightly around me, protecting me from the rough bark.

I couldn't take it anymore.

I grabbed the front of his vest and pulled him into me, and as his eyes widened in surprise, I crushed my lips to his.

He was right, after all. There was no one here. No need to be careful. It was as if we were in the Tarasynian woods again, utterly alone, with nothing to fear but the cold that would encroach between us if we moved one inch apart from each other. Here, the cold may not have been a problem, but my responsibilities would bring about their own kind of cold if he and I stepped away from each other.

Letting this continue would only lead to misery.

But he'd said he could take the pain, and here in this moment, so could I.

His breath mingled with mine and his fingers curled into my hair. When he felt the metal of the small golden tiara I'd opted to wear this morning, he lifted it out of my hair and hooked it onto a nearby branch, out of the way and out of mind.

My breathing hitched as he moved his lips to my jaw, my neck, my collarbone. I clung to him as if I'd float from the earth if I let go, my fingers in his hair and my body aligning with his, every curve and edge touching.

When his lips found mine again, the tip of his tongue trailed my lower lip. I shuddered. "You've had too much practice."

His breathy chuckle against my lips felt like feathers. "Any practice has been worth it if I can use it on you." His hand smoothed its way down the side of my body, caressing the curve of my waist, the swell of my hip. He grabbed a handful of my skirts, and slowly, he began to inch the fabric up. I felt air swirl around my calf muscles. His hand found the back of my knee, and he tugged my body impossibly closer to his.

The quietest moan escaped both of us when we kissed each other just once more, as deep a kiss as we dared. Then I pulled away, biting my lower lip.

Zeke rested his forehead against mine, his heavy breath sending cool air across my flushed face. "So soon?"

I nodded. As I glanced toward the tiara hanging from the branch, Zeke groaned and pushed us off the tree, steadying me with his arm around my waist.

"I think," I said, reaching for the tiara, "it's best if we keep up the formalities in public, as we always have."

That garnered a tight brown-eyed stare. "Do you now?"

I hedged despite the disappointment I felt in my words. "People have stopped talking, and, well . . . that's how it needs to stay."

He scoffed, but he knew it was true. He'd said so right after our last kiss, when he'd suspected that would be our last for a while due to the rumors that were spreading like fire. Still, that didn't stop him from sneering now as he said, "Of course, *Your Majesty.*"

But I looked at him with a smile and put my tiara in Midas's saddlebag. "We aren't in public yet."

That mischievous glint in Zeke's eyes returned, and he pulled me close again. "In a perfect world we could stay out here forever."

"Have a little cottage built right over there." I pointed to a patch of sun shining through where the trees thinned.

He smiled and kissed my forehead. "With a couple of blonde-haired, green-eyed children playing hide and seek in the bushes."

His dream mirrored mine in a painstakingly beautiful way.

We stayed there in the woods for a moment longer, standing in our embrace, both of us too stubborn to let it end just yet. Our reverie. Our beautiful, impossible future.

# CHAPTER SEVEN

THE CART HIT a giant rock in the road, sending me flying out of my seat—and my nap. Disoriented, I whipped my head around until I remembered where I was.

Rocky hills claimed the landscape on the other side of the cart's canvas. Not covered in green grass waving in the wind like in Lecevonia, but instead topped with giant boulders, layers of light and dark rivulets running through them. In this part of Hiddon, trees were scarce, but the landscape was dotted with clusters of green brush.

The Silver Mountains surely weren't far off, and at their base before Ferox Pass, Vespost. That was where we were headed. My entire body was being pulled in the opposite direction though, toward the seaside cliffs of Loche, and the voice was a constant disgruntled presence in my head. It didn't say anything, but I felt the weight of its displeasure. Hiddon wasn't where the last relic was, and the Solstice drawing ever nearer pressed on all my nerves.

But I needed the DeGreys to be on my side of what was to come.

In Lady DeGrey's replying letter, she seemed leery of visitors.

However, by the end of her correspondence, she'd given me her acceptance as long as I'd promised to arrive as discreetly as possible. We were in the heart of Tarasynian territory, after all.

The thought made my stomach turn in both anger and fear.

We'd opted to take the most inconspicuous carriage, a simple covered wagon, pulled by two gray horses that could ride swift enough if needed. I'd even left my crown back in Hillstone. Only Zeke and Roger were riding along in the back of the wagon with me.

I peeked through the canvas flap to Amos up on the coachman's bench. Seeing his healing progress, I had readily let him come back to duty just as readily as he accepted the invitation. "How much longer, do you think?"

"Just another day, my queen. We'll get there by tomorrow's twilight." He turned to me and winked. "Then there won't be any more sleeping on that wooden floor."

I retreated back into the canvas. I'd been increasingly tired lately, and my guards had noticed. Any time I sat still for longer than half an hour, I was struggling to keep my head up and eyes open. Zeke grumbled about it on occasion, and he said it'd started when I'd begun to wear Equos's dagger at my waist since we left Equos three days ago.

I tried to pay no mind to his complaints. I felt better having it with me, especially here in unfamiliar terrain. Less cumbersome than a sword, and at least some sort of protection.

And I couldn't lie that having it close quieted the voice down too.

The other three relics were beneath my seat. The thought of leaving them behind at Hillstone had been too horrible to endure.

We bounced along until the evening rays of sun blasted directly into the wagon. I heard Amos mumble, "Utterly blinded." Then a louder, more confused, "What's this?"

Then, the wheels of the wagon shook beneath us.

Zeke and I leapt to our feet, and Roger had already drawn his sword even as we struggled to stay upright amidst the shaking.

What on Haggard's green earth was happening?

Amos's shout from outside ended with a thud, followed by curses. The horses squealed. A horrendous creaking filled my ears as the wagon began to rise into the air.

My body lurched, my shoulder slamming into the side of the wagon and sending a shot of pain down my arm and back. Zeke caught me before I could fall to the floor, which pitched so violently Roger fell to his knees.

Amidst curses and grunts, we worked our way to the back of the wagon and glanced over the gate.

We had to be over ten feet off the ground. But Zeke yanked me forward by the wrist. "We have to jump!"

Jump?!

The ground danced in my vision. But I took a steeling breath, set my gaze on the road beneath us, and forced my feet to leave the wooden floor.

I felt like a rag doll plummeting to the earth. Then, before I could smack face-first into the dirt, a strange force like water rippling over my skin enveloped me and slowed my motion.

My feet slowly sank to the ground, and suddenly, arms were around my waist and neck.

A woman's harsh voice spoke near my ear. "You're not going anywhere."

Only one thought came to mind as I registered the woman's words. Amicka. This must have been Amicka. Fear ripped through me, and a scream bubbled up in my throat, but the woman's arm around my neck was too tight for it to be heard.

The sight around me was so unreal I never would've believed it possible.

The wagon was high above our heads, Roger ready to jump and Zeke already in mid-air. But he was floating just like the wagon. The horses too, though utterly wide-eyed and frightened, were supported by some unseen force. Amos had his feet solidly on the ground, grappling with a man clad in a brown smock, gold earrings glinting at his lobes. As the man spun away from Amos, he drew his sword.

And from the bushes, a young girl no older than ten, only a year or two older than Clara, had her hands lifted, eyes jumping between the wagon, the horses, and Zeke.

I wriggled an arm free and fumbled for the dagger at my side. But the woman kneed me from behind and knocked the breath out of me. I frantically stole a glance at her through my periphery. She was dressed similarly to the man, even the earrings, but her amber eyes held a fierceness that brought me back to the face of the female wolf in the Tarasynian woods. I didn't see the spear Gryffin had mentioned.

Zeke landed on the ground with a growl and drew his sword, already making for my captor. But before he could think about taking a swing, the sword flew out of his hand and hurled itself into the brush.

I saw the woman's eyes swiftly follow the sword, and in a burst of courage, I took the chance to jab my elbow behind me. She loosened her grip just enough that I was able to find the dagger's hilt and whip it out from its makeshift scabbard. Her arms immediately left my body, and through my gasping and coughing as glorious air raced to fill my lungs, I spun around to face her, dagger out in front of me.

"No!"

The scream came from the girl in the bushes, and just like that, the wagon fell to the ground. The wheels splintered, and the axles crunched and broke under the sudden pressure. At least she was gentler with the horses, who were placed gingerly back on their feet.

They tried to bolt, but the cart dragging across the dirt was too much for them.

The girl sprinted to place herself between the woman and me.

Lowering my dagger just slightly, still catching my breath, my eyes traveled between the woman and the girl. They looked so much alike that they must have been mother and daughter. They shared the same beautiful brown skin, and hair in wild ringlets as black as a raven. They had the same amber eyes, but the girl's—and I wasn't sure if this surprised me or not—were flecked with red.

Of course. Only a Talented could pull off something like that.

But something about this pair didn't scream "Amicka" to me. From their plain clothes and defensive glares, they seemed more like survivors than conquerors.

I heard a sword fall to the earth behind us, and I turned and found the man among their party contemptuously staring down the tip of Amos's blade.

Zeke sent out a string of expletives behind me before turning to the man at Amos's mercy. "What the boars is going on here?"

There was a shuffling of feet. When I looked back over my shoulder, the girl had rushed into her mother's arms. Roger then stepped, or stumbled more like, out of the wagon, sword still clutched in his hand. Despite his clumsy exit, the woman's eyes widened at his size.

A thick tension hung suspended over the craggy road as we all stood our ground. The only sound was that of the horses anxiously snorting and scraping the earth with their hooves.

The girl peeked from her mother's smock, and I saw terror deep in her amber eyes. In a flash, I was back at Hillstone, Clara terrified in my arms as Sterling lay bleeding in front of us.

No, these people weren't the enemies I had initially taken them to be.

Shaken, I took a deep, raspy breath and slipped my dagger back into its scabbard. "Let's not do any harm to each other, yes?" I eyed the girl again. "No lifting us into the air?"

The girl slowly nodded, and I let my shoulders relax, though my heart still drummed in my chest. Amos took a last up-and-down glance of the man in front of him before sheathing his sword. But he snatched up the man's weapon before the other had a chance to bend over to retrieve it.

"All right," I said casually, trying my best to poke holes in the tension. "What are the three of you doing here lifting up carts by their wheels?"

The woman crossed her arms over her chest. "You wouldn't have to ask if you'd had everything taken from you," she responded harshly.

"And using your daughter's Talent like that?" Zeke said, narrowing his eyes. "Quite the lesson you're teaching her."

As if Zeke knew anything about raising children. But I supposed he did have a point.

The woman pursed her lips and shielded the girl from our line of view.

"Well," I said. "Our wagon is broken beyond repair here. But we aren't, and the horses aren't, so I thank you for that." I smiled at the girl peeking from behind her mother's shoulder, and her eyes crinkled.

"I've been getting better," she answered quietly, before her mother could shush her.

The man stepped up next to the woman. "Thank you for letting us keep our hands and heads."

Amos silently came to stand at my side as an uneasy truce formed.

"I'm Jerime," the man said. "This is my wife, Renera, and our daughter, Clementine."

With a glare at her husband, Renera turned and walked away, taking her daughter with her. The sun was setting quickly now, almost completely obscured behind the rocky hills.

"I'm—Rosin," I said, catching myself. We didn't even know these people, and here I was about to tell them exactly who I was. For all we knew, they could be Tarasynian. "And my friends." I cast a glance to Roger, Amos, and Zeke, my eyes begging for help. I wasn't any good at coming up with fake names.

"Hamish," Amos said, extending his hand to the man.

"Rochester," Roger said from behind us, deep voice filling the air. He nodded to the family. "Ro for short."

Finally, Zeke sighed and stepped forward. "And I'm Zee." He slung an arm over my shoulder. "Rosin here is my wife." He winked at me, and my insides fluttered. I hoped to Haggard that my face wasn't too easy to see in the low light of dusk.

Amos and Roger both chuckled, smashing those hopes to smithereens.

"We have food," I said quickly. "We can't go anywhere for the night anyway. Might as well share. Right, boys?" Less for us to carry in the morning, too.

Zeke narrowed his eyes at me just for a moment before flashing the strangers a convincing smile. "Right."

While the men unpacked what they could, I made sure to grab the bag of relics, bow included, before anyone else could.

Renera and the girl, Clementine, sat off by themselves on a cluster of smaller boulders off the road. The light of the fire that the men had built just barely lit my way as I walked over to them.

When I sat, Renera glared.

But Clementine perked up. "How did you know I was Talented?"

Before her mother could shush her again, I smiled and said, "Well, besides the wagon levitating off the ground?" That garnered a little giggle from her, and I pointed at my eyes. "I see your red flecks."

The girl's hand shot up to her cheek, just below her eye, and looked down at the ground. "Momma told me they weren't very noticeable."

"They're beautiful," Renera said softly, running a hand over the girl's hair. She shot a glare in my direction. "Don't let anyone tell you otherwise."

I nodded once slowly. I could not help it that, given my harrowing experiences under the scrutiny of Gryffin's eyes, red flecks still made my skin crawl. But perhaps, between this girl and Isa, I could see beauty in them. "They are very unique," I said, offering a smile to the girl. "Don't hide them. Be proud of what you can do."

After all, wasn't there a time I wished I'd been Talented? Maybe I still did. I would be a queen with *real* power, no longer made to feel inferior. A queen that wasn't questioned.

I looked at Renera. "What happened to your family? Why do you have to steal?"

Her amber eyes glowed angrily in the dim firelight. "Wouldn't you? If your house was burned to the ground, for no reason other than an army passing through, and you were left with nothing but the singed clothes on your backs, wouldn't you try to provide for your family in some way?"

I knew I couldn't truly understand what she'd been through. Hillstone had been damaged, but we all still had provisions.

"I'm sorry," she quickly added. "I mean no disrespect to the king."

"Your disrespect doesn't bother me any," I muttered under my breath. Renera looked at me strangely. Probably trying to figure out who we were, who we stood with. Just as we were doing to them. From what I gathered, these were people of Hiddon, and terribly upset with the hand that had been dealt to them by Roderich, and now Gryffin.

It seemed Tarasyn had more enemies than allies.

"Why haven't you traveled to Lecevonia?" I asked. "I heard there are places for refugees of Hiddon to go."

"And be another mouth to feed?" She scoffed. "We can handle ourselves. We always have."

A shadow passed over us, and Jerime sat, followed by Zeke, Amos, and Roger. In Amos' hand was a roasted leg of a wood grouse, which he handed to me.

"Jerime here is quite good with a bow," he said, sounding impressed. "Food surely isn't their problem."

"Then what did you want?" I asked, turning back to Renera.

She nodded toward the wagon. "That canvas looked pretty nice. Would make a nice tent, or decent trade. And money's always a welcome find."

"Does lifting a carriage off the ground normally work for you?" Zeke asked. His brows were pinched together, mouth set in a dissatisfied frown. If it were up to him, we would probably be traveling through the night.

This time, it was Clementine who answered. "Normally the people inside are scared off. Since they don't stick around, we take what we want."

I leaned forward. "How long have you known you were Talented?"

"Since I lifted my baby brother out of his crib without moving a muscle," she said, laughing. "Gave Momma and Daddy a fright. I never did it again, even though it made him happy."

Though the group laughed gently, none of us missed the glaring tragedy. There was no baby traveling with this family. Renera looked toward the fire, her face etched in stone.

So much fire, so much loss.

Was Gryffin even aware of how much he and his family had taken from these people?

Jerime scratched the back of his head. "We don't have to worry about you reporting us to the king, yeah?"

It was Zeke who answered. "If your lips are sealed, ours are as well."

Jerime responded with a slow nod. "What brings you out this way? Headed to Vespost?"

My mind turned. If they were people of Hiddon and hated Gryffin as much as we did, then maybe—just maybe—they could help us.

"We're on our way to visit a noble there." I glanced between Jerime and Renera. I felt Zeke's hard stare boring into the side of my head.

If they had any question of our alliance before, it was clear now.

Even Clementine seemed to understand. She looked up at her mother.

"They don't accept visitors," Jerime said carefully after a moment.

Amos shrugged nonchalantly. "We've got an invitation."

"Well," Renera said, sneering. "Tell them their people are dying out here. Tell them our people should not have to find shelter in another kingdom. Tell them the cruel people that claim the throne have no right. That the rightful ruler is sitting in that manor, and he is doing *nothing*." She stood abruptly then and disappeared into the dark.

"The royals' absence has been a hard deal," Jerime said quietly. "They've lost family, true. But we've lost our families too, *and* our leaders." He sighed. "Now the entire kingdom is grieving, and we have nowhere to turn without facing the promise of death ourselves."

"I'm sure this isn't what the DeGreys want either," I said quietly. But my excuse for them felt flat in the tense air. After all, weren't we all just trying to survive?

"I best go find her," Jerime said, standing. "We'll take our leave now. It isn't often we run into folks like your lot. It's been . . . nice." He nodded to us and turned to his daughter. "Come, Clementine."

Clementine stood, offered me a smile, and took hold of her father's hand. Together, they went off into the night, following Renera.

Alone once more, our group looked at each other.

Amos whistled through his teeth. "The people of Hiddon are a tough bunch, aren't they?"

I nodded. Every single person I'd met from Hiddon thus far was strong. Yetta, Lady DeGrey. Even Lord DeGrey, still standing underneath the numbing grief that had overtaken him.

Zeke kicked the dirt. "They certainly have strong feelings about Lord and Lady DeGrey staying tucked away in Vespost. I would too, if it were Lecevonia."

But I shook my head, still feeling loyalty to Lady DeGrey. The fierceness in her eyes when I'd met her did not give off any sentiment of giving up. "You're making a lot of assumptions. We don't even know what type of forces Hiddon has to fight back. It might be a death sentence to try."

"Well, we'll see tomorrow," Amos said as he got to his feet. "Or the next day, since half of us are walking now."

That pained me to hear. The Solstice was too close for me to have these setbacks. But what was I to do besides sulk?

After a restless night, we packed up what we could on the horses and on our backs. Our food, water, clothes. A few pieces of splintered wood off the wagon for firewood that night, if we needed it. I held on to the relics on my horse, bow and bag strapped to the saddle. Zeke and I would switch off on horseback, though he did not know it yet. But if he thought I'd make him walk the entire way to Vespost, he was sorely mistaken.

And with that, we left our broken wagon behind us on the trail.

# CHAPTER EIGHT

THE MIRRORED PEAKS of Ferox Pass towered above Vespost like two watchmen. The pass was easily visible, high up in the southern Silver Mountains, a clear cut in the valley between the two peaks. The mountains were capped with snow, but here in the south, that snow went no further, leaving the slopes a mosaic of lush green and rock.

Looking closely, a path down from the pass could be seen snaking through the mountains. But just from a glance, I wouldn't be tempted enough to make the journey. It would take a lot for me to brave the steep drop-offs and rickety bridges, and that's not even considering the Haren Desert waiting just on the other side in the West Lands.

It had indeed taken us that first day of walking and well into the next to reach the city. It still bustled with activity despite the recent change of rule.

But that change of rule meant most of the people we encountered were clad in a Tarasynian uniform.

Vespost had become a base camp for Tarasyn's forces.

I quivered with unease as we walked down the streets, hair mussed and clothes wrinkled after a day and a half on foot. Not to mention a woman traveling with three men. Soldiers turned their heads, eyes glued to our backs as we passed. Thankfully, Roger's hulking form kept them all at bay.

Spires peering over the tops of buildings led us to the manor. A steel gate hidden underneath a blanket of ivy closed everything in and everyone out. A guard stood in the watch house high above our heads, and when we approached, he gruffly called out, "You are not welcome here. Go on."

I cleared my throat and recited the line Lady DeGrey had told me to say in her note. "There shall be no wine until the vine comes forth."

The man looked at us through the barred window again, pursed his bearded lips, and finally grumbled something indecipherable and disappeared. The next time we saw him, he was on the other side of the gate.

With a massive ring of keys jingling in his hand, he found the correct key and unlocked the gate, which was so rusted it hardly opened enough for us and our horses to fit through. And once we were through, the guard locked it tightly behind us.

The manor house loomed over us as we walked through the courtyard, dark spires piercing the blue sky. More vines climbed their way up the stone walls, but beneath the vines, something had been sculpted into the layered rock. When I looked closer, hunters and huntresses chased their quarry through a thick forest, bows out in front of them.

"Why does everything feel as though it hasn't been touched in fifty years?" Zeke muttered.

A voice spoke from behind us. "Because it hasn't."

Skirts and cloaks swirled as we all turned, and we found Lady DeGrey standing there in the middle of the courtyard. Her graying hair was gathered into a tight bun at the nape of her neck, and her dark green skirts and black blouse blended in with the shadows of the twining vines along the wall behind her.

I stepped forward, and in a surprising move, she enveloped me in her arms. "I'm glad to see you made it out of there alive, girl."

"Me too," I said over her shoulder. Unlike in Tarasyn, I didn't mind that she called me *girl*. It felt more endearing here. "I had three days to spare before he would've killed me."

Her voice darkened in disgust. "That man doesn't know what he's doing." She released me from her embrace, then looked at the men behind me. "Welcome to Bowsrock. You all look like you've seen better days." She let out a sigh, shook her head, and looked at Amos. "Well, you can bring the horses to the back stables. It's modest, but our stablehands will find a place for them. Come, I'll show the rest of you inside."

Waving her hand, she led us through the manor house's oaken double doors.

The inside of the manor seemed just as forgotten as the outside. The walls were dark with dust, the carpets lining the halls musty and discolored. There were portraits hung along the wall, but moisture in the air had made them bubble and warp.

"Why hasn't this place been touched for fifty years?" I asked, remembering her words. "You and Lord DeGrey hadn't been living here?"

Lady DeGrey snorted. "For Haggard's sake, no. We lived in Vena, in Arrowshield with King Theon and Queen Alys." She let her fingers graze over an old wooden buffet. "No one has lived here since my husband's uncle. We moved out here with plans of renovating, but that was just one month before Tarasyn's attack on Vena. Since then, we've kept to ourselves here."

"If I can say so, Lady," Zeke said. "Some of your people wish it were otherwise."

Lady DeGrey shot him a glare. "Who said you can say so? We have bigger ambitions than bombarding Vena unprepared. The capitol has more Tarasynian soldiers watching the streets than we do here in Vespost."

Zeke bowed his head and said no more.

"Bigger ambitions?" I asked.

She looked at me out of the corner of her eye and smirked. "You'll see, when the time is right."

We walked through a stone doorway, where a long table draped with magenta cloth embroidered with green leaves would have dominated the room had it not been for the enormous elk's head mounted above the fireplace.

"But first," Lady DeGrey said, taking a seat and waving her arm for us to do the same. "Tell me why you want to speak to us."

I sat in the faded velvet chair to her left. "Will Lord DeGrey be joining us?"

Lady DeGrey's eyes held an angry fire, her lips set in a hard line. But behind that fire, the sadness was impossible to ignore. Finally, she said, "No. Perhaps later."

I nodded softly, not wanting to pry. He must not have been much better here than he'd been at Snowmont.

As Amos walked into the dining hall and took a seat, I folded my hands in front of me. "Gryffin came to Lecevonia to talk to me."

"And you didn't have him killed on the spot?" She threw her head back and snorted. "I'm surprised."

I bristled a little. "He had my Lecevonians. I gave him my word that he could speak to me for their return."

Her eyes steeled over. "Words are only that in times of war."

I didn't believe that. If honor were dead in this world, what kind of people were any of us? But I decided to leave it there for now. "He asked me to join him against the Rebels of the Red Sun. I declined."

"Against the Rebels of the Red Sun?" Confusion narrowed her eyes. "We haven't had any issues with them in ages. Not since King Roderich took everything from us. They'd been an annoyance before, surely, but they have no real power."

"Not according to Gryffin," I said, shaking my head. "Both the Rebels and Gryffin want something to happen. An Awakening of the Talented. And it can't be done without these."

I hoisted the bow and bag of relics on the table and untied the dagger from around my waist.

*Find it.* The voice finally decided to speak up. I tried to shake off the goosebumps that had risen on my arms.

Lady DeGrey stared at the bow, some dark emotion in her eyes. "That was hung in the king's quarters."

I looked down at my hands. "I know."

"Vena's bow. Or so we were told." She looked up at me. "An Awakening of the Talented?"

I nodded. "All five relics are needed. We have four of them here."

She was silent as she stared at the relics laid out on the table. I looked up at Zeke, who would have had steam rolling out of his ears if that were possible, and Amos and Roger, who both sat there stoically. This was probably the first time they'd heard any of this too.

I turned my attention back to Lady DeGrey. Now, out of earshot of Gryffin, we could speak freely. "How did you feel about the Talented in Tarasyn?"

"Unnerving," she said immediately. "Bizarre. A bit frightening." Then, a smile spread across her thin lips. "Yet awe-inspiring. I had no idea abilities like that existed. Extraordinary people."

I smiled. "I thought so too. And I know others who are Talented. An Awakening could be a good thing. Let these people find themselves again."

She narrowed her eyes. "What are you asking of me?"

I realized then that I was hoping for the same thing Gryffin had asked of me. "An alliance. To stand with Lecevonia against Tarasyn and the Rebels."

Lady DeGrey sighed, drumming her fingers on the table in thought. Finally, she said, "Hiddon is in shambles. Hiddon does not even belong to *Hiddon* anymore." She stopped her drumming and shook her head. "We're in no place to promise aid to anyone."

"All right, then simply your word," I said. "I still believe in the strength of promises. I ask for your word that should Gryffin come to you, you'll refuse his offers."

She leaned forward, fierce. "And if he offers the return of our kingdom?"

I shook my head vehemently. "You cannot trust anything he says. His Talent—it skews the mind, distorts the truth."

If the news of his Talent of Persuasion was any surprise, she did not show it. Her eyes only narrowed again as she leaned back in her chair.

"I never trusted him anyway," she said. "His eyes unsettled me from the beginning. But I cannot promise anything to you. Hiddon has always done what was best for us. Should any opportunity arise to better the kingdom, we take it."

"What of the budding alliance my mother and father established with King Theon and Queen Alys?" I unfolded my hands and leaned forward. "Surely that should be honored."

She sat a bit taller. "And where exactly did that get the late king and queen?"

"Lecevonia has taken in hundreds of Hiddon refugees!" I countered. "Does *that* count for nothing?"

"Your kingdom did that of its own accord," she responded sharply, never looking away. "I thank you for it. But we did not ask you to do so."

Well, that was rather cold.

Zeke stood. "Are you truly doing what is best for your people if they are fleeing and living in fear?"

Lady DeGrey's voice rose. "Who are you to question our actions? You have no idea what we are doing for the sake of Hiddon." She then turned her seething eyes on me. "We've risked everything by allowing you and your party to visit! I suggest you prepare your horses and leave just as discreetly as you've come!"

Just then, a voice spoke from the doorway. "Tell them why we live in secret, Aunt Sophine."

I turned, and in the doorway stood a young woman. She seemed to be about my age, maybe a year or two younger, with golden hair hanging to her elbows and a dress of white muslin with a leather vest laced up over the bodice.

She stepped into the room. "Tell them why we've been holed up in this place for the past *year*, ever since King Roderich's attack on Hiddon. Tell them why we haven't responded to our people's cries for help."

In the young woman's brown eyes, the resemblance to Queen Alys—from what I remembered years ago, anyway—was unmistakable.

Shock waves coursed through my blood.

This was her. The princess I had no idea existed until Lady DeGrey mentioned her during the engagement festivities in Tarasyn.

She bowed in my direction. "Hello, Queen Rosemary. It's wonderful to finally meet you."

I stood and slowly walked around the table to meet her. "And you, Princess Lilyana." Staring at her wide-eyed, I took her hands in mine.

I'd only known her name from revisiting the Hiddon family tree upon my return to Hillstone. How could I not have known her, the only other princess on the Peninsula near my own age?

I assumed she'd been murdered with the rest of her family. Seeing her standing here was like seeing a phantom.

Zeke, Amos, and Roger all turned to look at us. Zeke's eyes scrunched together in confusion. "Princess?"

Behind me, I heard Lady DeGrey rise, wooden legs of her chair scratching against the floor. "I told you to stay in your quarters when they arrived." There was an odd quiver in her voice.

But I only looked at the princess. "How . . . how are you here?"

Her eyes never wavered. "I was here in Bowsrock with my aunt and uncle when the Tarasynians attacked. King Roderich would have killed me with my family had he been able to find me."

Princess Lilyana was the true heir to the Hiddon throne. An heir that the people of Hiddon might have actually rallied behind, if they knew she was still alive. And she was Lady DeGrey's secret. "Bigger" ambitions, as she'd said.

I squeezed her hands gently. "I'm so sorry about your family."

She blinked quickly, but otherwise kept her strength on her face. "We've all lost something. I've been fortunate compared to some."

Lady DeGrey was suddenly there, squeezing herself between us. "You've met now. Now go." She eyed me and the men sitting at the table. "You all need to leave."

Before she could usher the princess off into the hall, I said, "Promise me this in the very least. You and your husband won't give up on your kingdom. Hiddon still has people willing to stand with you, if you show them that *you* stand with *them*."

Lady DeGrey gestured to her niece. "Does it look like we've given up?"

With that, she and Princess Lilyana disappeared around the corner.

We worked to ready the horses in the stable. We were still in our traveling clothes from the journey here, and being ushered away so quickly surely wasn't something any of us expected.

"Think we can brave stopping somewhere in Vespost for the night?" Amos asked. But, remembering how many Tarasynian soldiers prowled the streets, we all knew that answer was no.

I patted the horse I held by the reins on his neck, feeling guilty. We couldn't ride them all night without wearing them down to nothing.

"Wait!"

We turned, and Princess Lilyana was running through the door. She stopped just short of Zeke, breathing heavily.

"I apologize for my aunt," she said. "I know things are dire, and that I must be kept safe until I can claim the Hiddon crown, but I can't let you all leave without at least knowing your names. I haven't met anyone new since living out here."

I smiled. "Well, you've met me. This is Zeke, Amos, and Roger."

"A pleasure to meet you, Princess," Amos said, bowing.

"Likewise," she answered with a breathless smile.

She turned to me again. "Will you . . . will you tell the people of Hiddon that we haven't given up on them? I know nothing of rule—I was never supposed to take the throne—but . . . but I do feel like this is something they should know."

I nodded. "Of course, Your Grace."

"And if—if among the refugees there is a Rafael Turnbulle, can you give this to him?" From the pockets of her dress, she pulled out a letter. Wrapped around the letter and secured under the hastily done wax seal was a thin golden chain, with a tiny charm of a lily hanging from it.

I tucked it safely into the bag with the relics. Then I took her hands in mine and squeezed them. "Stay safe, for your people."

She nodded once. Then, backing away, she said, "I certainly hope this isn't the last time we see each other."

"Me too," I answered.

Amos piped up from behind me. "Do you know of any safe place to stay in the city, by chance?"

She shook her head. "No, I'm sorry. I haven't been outside these gates in ages."

Something in her tone told me that wasn't entirely true.

"But if I were to guess," she continued. "I would say that every inn in this city is overrun by people up to no good." She did poorly to hide a mischievous little smile spreading across her face.

Oh yes, she had definitely been outside those gates.

"I should return to my rooms before my aunt realizes I've left." She turned away from us. "I wish you safe travels. Don't take any backroads. There are bandits and thieves these days, I've been told." And with that, she disappeared around the doorway of the stable.

# CHAPTER NINE

THE SIGN BEARING the name *Hog's Head Inn* swung in the wind, creaking on its old hooks. I looked back at Zeke, and he shrugged. "We'll let Amos do the talking," he said. He leaned back against the inn's railing and patted the spot next to him.

I felt filthy after the days of travel we'd had, but I'd been filthier. We wanted to get out of Vespost as quickly as we could before the sun set, but we'd only made it as far as the next town over. The horses truly needed to rest, and if we wanted to make it across the entirety of Hiddon and back into Lecevonia *before* the Solstice, we needed more than a couple of tired horses.

As I leaned on the railing next to Zeke, he swung an arm over my shoulders and kissed the side of my head. Oh, how nice it felt to lean into him. There was no one out here to spread rumors—aside from Amos and Roger, but I was certain that they already knew our secret.

"Was Lady DeGrey that dismissive in Tarasyn?"

I almost defended her, but after I thought for a moment, I chuckled without humor. "Actually, yes she was." I frowned as I lowered my voice. "I can't believe she'd consider trusting Gryffin to give her what she wanted." What her kingdom *needed*. He would never do something like that without another, self-serving motive. "I was not expecting to see the late Princess Lilyana today."

Zeke spoke so low under his breath that I had to lean in to hear. "Nor I. It's very bold, hiding the princess away. No wonder the DeGreys keep to themselves." He pulled his arm back and stretched both of them over his head, yawning as he did so. "But the people of Hiddon need help."

"We're helping them," I said, eyes flashing to him. "And that's what they have for now." Lady DeGrey may not have seen Lecevonia's aid as an alliance, but I did.

The inn's door opened behind us then, and Amos appeared.

"Any luck?" Roger asked, looking up from where he'd been tending the horses.

Amos nodded. "Aye. We'll be able to stay here tonight, and the innkeeper's nephew wants to buy our horses. Seeing as they're such beauts, he's willing to pay very fair. We can use that money to buy a wagon and two horses tomorrow."

I was sad to see the horses go. They were of Lecevonian stock, so no wonder the man was willing to pay us well. Still, I liked them.

Yet that was exactly what we did. We found a wooden wagon from a carpenter in town, two simple yet sturdy brown horses from a stable, and just after dawn the next morning, we were off to Hillstone.

Traveling by wagon again was an appreciated change. We didn't run into any more bandits, and within two days, the gates of Equos welcomed us home.

My advisors waited by the doors of the castle, no doubt eager to hear how my visit with Lord and Lady DeGrey had gone. But Clara bounded up to the wagon as soon as we stopped in the stable. She grabbed my hand and practically pulled me off the back.

"Rose, you have to see something!"

Leading me away from the wagon, bag of relics clutched to my side and bow slung over my shoulder, she took me through the doors and up the main staircase, all the way to an inner room near the library.

Isabele and Lisette were inside, along with a family whose mother I recognized from the kitchen. Isabele was staring intently at the mother, holding her hands.

Isabele's eyes had more red flecks than ever. I could see that even from my distance.

"What is she doing?" I whispered to Clara. But Clara shushed me and nodded toward Isabele.

After another moment's silence, Isabele shook her head, eyes full of remorse. "No, I'm sorry. I don't see anything."

The woman sighed and nodded, then took hold of the boys' hands who had come with her. "Well, it's a blessing to have two in the family," she said, smiling at the boys. They bowed to me and skirted past Zeke, who had followed and come to stand in the doorway behind me.

"Two in the family?" I looked back at Isabele. "Isa, what's going on?"

"Oh, Rose!" She rushed to me and took my hands in hers excitedly. "Thank you!"

"Of course, but for what exactly?"

Lisette cleared her throat from behind Isabele and held up a book. She shook it at me, giving me an odd look. "Isabele's been exploring her *Talent*, Rose."

The words *Of the Sighted* gleamed from the book's spine. I looked at Lisette wide-eyed, then to Clara, then back to Isabele. "Truly? The book's been helpful, then?"

The red flecks in her eyes burned brightly, embraced by her brown irises like rubies nestled into a soft forest floor. "Rose, I've never felt more like myself!" She spun in a circle, skirts flying around her. It was hard to believe this was the same timid Isabele who'd run the kingdom in my absence. "While you were gone, I spent every day confused by my own thoughts. I constantly fought with the advisors who couldn't see what I saw, that haze around Gryffin. Being doubted when I tried to explain it. And now, thanks to you, I have answers! I feel like a part of me had been fighting to come to the surface but couldn't get past some barrier. And now, somehow, that barrier is gone, and it's the most amazing feeling!"

She took my hands again and stared, eyes boring into every crevice of my face. She was concentrating so intently I almost expected a vein to pop on her forehead.

How dare a sliver of hope return to me. How dare a piece of me still long for an ability, when I'd already proven I was capable of so much without a Talent. But I did hope, as she looked at me, seeing through me. I hoped so dearly that there was something that made me stronger. Something that could give Lecevonia the strongest leader it had ever had. My heart swelled at the idea—

But her eyes soon turned downcast, and she frowned at me. "I'm sorry, Rose."

Clara hugged me around the waist.

The same disappointment I'd felt months ago, back in Snowmont on the archery field, reared onto its hind legs like a beast and charged through my heart. I chided myself for even hoping. I'd already *known* what she would say. I'd already known I wasn't Talented.

No matter. After I brought Talents back to the Peninsula, no one would question my ability to rule, even without a Talent.

In the end, I smiled and shook my head. "I don't need one."

She pursed her lips sadly, then glanced behind me and gasped. "But Zeke, you have one!"

I whipped my head around to look at him.

Zeke jerked back at her words. But he corrected himself and leaned against the doorway, returning to a picture of indifference, his arms crossed over his chest. "Surely not."

Isabele stepped closer to him, squinting her eyes. "You do. Your aura is so bright I almost can't look at you now that I've seen it."

Zeke rolled his eyes. "Oh? What color is it? A beautiful lavender with forsythia petals floating around my skull?"

Isabele pinched her nose. "Chartreuse, as sour as you are."

Clara giggled beside me.

I couldn't help a sting of jealousy that pierced my resolve like a needle. Of *course* Zeke had a Talent. And I didn't.

"Wait," I said, massaging my temple. "I thought Sighted could only see another's Talent as they were actively using it?" I looked back at Zeke's eyes. They remained a clear, warm brown.

Isabele shook her head. "*Some* Sighted can only see active Talents. Others can see Talents before they've even manifested."

"Yes, with practice . . ." I did remember reading that in the book in Tarasyn's library now. But the book had said it took *years* of practice to have that ability.

And that rushing it would drive a Sighted to madness.

"Isa," I said slowly, taking her hands in mine. "Maybe it's best to take it slow. This is all so new."

She shook her head, arms stiff in indignation. "But it comes so naturally."

"Has the book mentioned what happens if you push yourself too far too early?"

She looked away and yanked her hands out of mine. "Yes, but—I haven't done anything that's felt too challenging." She frowned, disappointment creasing her forehead. "I can't tell *what* one's Talent is, only that it's there."

I looked at Lisette, who only shrugged. "I'm not Talented either, Rose."

Isabele turned on her. "I said there *might* be something there. But it's faint." Then, she groaned and threw her hands up in the air. "I need to practice. Lisette, come with me."

Isabele pushed her way past us and stomped through the doorway, Lisette in her wake wearing an apologetic grimace. Clara left with them, clearly infatuated with Isabele's new abilities.

Zeke whistled. "Well, Isabele's found her confidence."

"And that's amazing—I *want* her to be confident." I closed my eyes and let my head fall into my hands. "I just want her to be careful too." I thought of August and Yetta. Yetta had a constant urge to use her Talent despite the dangers it posed. August had to rein her in multiple times during my time with them.

That train of thought led me to thinking more about Yetta. What had Amicka done to take her away from her storybook cottage in the snowy woods? Had she done something to August in order to get to Yetta?

I wasn't sure I wanted to know. But not knowing if either of them was still alive was killing me.

I had to set this Awakening into motion before Amicka could do any more damage.

I felt Zeke's hand on my shoulder. "She seems fine, Rose."

It took me a moment to realize he was talking about Isabele.

"Yes," I said through a heavy sigh. "I'm sure she is."

Then I punched him in the arm, making him wince. "That's for being Talented without me." I walked out of the room, passing by the library that had finally been cleared of all the soot and ash. Zeke followed, rubbing his arm.

"We don't even know if it's true or not." He nudged me with his shoulder and flashed me his little half-smile. "I don't want one. And like you said, you don't *need* one."

I rolled my eyes and stopped in my tracks, blocking his way. "Zeke. Seeing Talents is *exactly* what Isabele's Talent is. And she just told you that you were Talented!" I poked his ribs. "How do you feel?"

Zeke shook his head and laughed. "No different, Rose." He leaned in, his chest an inch from mine, his eyes mischievous as they glanced down at my lips. "No different at all."

My breath quickened. All it would take was a lift of my chin—

We heard footsteps from behind, and we jumped back from one another. Zeke cleared his throat and put his hands behind his back.

A man carrying stacks of rolled parchment rounded the corner, heading for the newly restored library.

Zeke bowed to me and said, "Your advisors will want to know how your trip proceeded, Your Majesty."

"Indeed." I turned back in the direction of the staircase. "Thank you, Sir Ezekiel."

The man with the scrolls bowed quickly as he passed in the hallway. "My queen," he said, catching a scroll that had been jostled out of place by his movement. "Welcome back." Then, he disappeared into the library.

The moment the man was out of sight, Zeke stroked a slow finger down my back.

I slapped his hand away, but every one of my nerves in the wake of his touch was on fire.

The council meeting left my advisors flustered and disappointed that Lady DeGrey hadn't accepted an alliance. Lord Castor had even threatened to stop sending aid to the refugees camped outside our walls, as well as to those taking refuge in Cliva. I'd shot him down quickly.

And I kept the bit about Prince Lilyana to myself, as did Zeke, Amos, and Roger.

After the meeting, I sent Zeke off with Princess Lilyana's letter to Raphael. If anyone could find him in the sea of Hiddon refugees, it was Zeke. Furthermore, there was something I wanted to talk to Isabele about, and I didn't need him glaring over my shoulder when I did.

That evening, I knocked on my sister's door softly. I didn't barge in this time per Isabele's wishes. It took a moment, but finally, one of her chambermaids answered. She curtsied and let me pass.

"Isa?"

Isabele was curled on her bed, sheets pulled over her head. Her other chambermaids were by the fireplace readying tiliarose, with the addition of peppermint by the smell of it.

Seeing Isabele as she was now in a pained heap on her bed, I was glad I'd come alone.

I sat next to her and gently reached a hand under the hem of her bedsheets, stroking her hair and tucking an auburn strand behind her ear. "Isa? What's wrong?"

She moaned from underneath her sheets. "This splitting headache that even the smallest bit of light aggravates. That's what's wrong."

I pursed my lips. "I told you that you should take it slow."

"Ah yes, the older sister always knows best." Isabele pulled the sheets back from her face, which wore the biggest pout I'd ever seen.

I motioned for the tiliarose from her chambermaids, and I held the steaming cup while Isabele righted herself, whimpering the entire time. She gingerly took the cup from me and took a slow sip, her frown melting away as she swallowed.

"Is that why you've come?" she asked. "To gloat?"

"No, of course not." I settled myself onto the pillows next to her. "I wanted to ask how you're feeling now that you've been working with your Talent. Aside from your headache," I quickly added. "Are you feeling . . . different?"

She seemed like she was about to nod, then grimaced as she thought better of jostling her head like that. "Yes," she said. "Extremely different."

"How?"

She was silent for a moment. Then, after another thoughtful sip, Isabele turned to look at me. "Before my Talent made itself known, I went as far so as to think I was mad. Seeing too deeply into everyone's situation, everyone's word, everyone's emotion. I thought I was constantly making something bigger out of what was actually there. I'd talk myself out of believing certain things, convince myself that this intuition was nothing but an imaginative mess on my part.

"But since I've learned what I can do, I . . . I have more faith in what I think and feel. More confidence in myself. I can *see* right there in front of me that I'm not mad."

"Oh Isa." I laid my other hand on top of hers. "I had no idea you felt the way you did. I could've helped you."

She waved away my remark. "Of course I wasn't ever going to share with you that I thought I might've been mad. You had so much to be responsible for already. There was no way I was going to add 'sister in the asylum' to that list."

Still, I shook my head. "I never once thought that you were mad. I wouldn't have let them throw you into the asylum." Though, when she had mentioned seeing a fog around Gryffin, I *did* dismiss it as some type of response to trauma. I kept that shameful bit to myself.

"My point being," Isabele continued. "I'm so grateful to know *why* now."

I felt my shoulders relax, thankful to have the reassurance I didn't even know I needed. If I could make others feel as Isa did when her Talent manifested, I would have done well by my people by bringing about the Awakening. That feeling was something I would never experience myself.

"Rose," Isabele said, leaning her head on my shoulder. "I do love you dearly. But can I please curl up into a ball of misery?"

I laughed and nuzzled the top of her hair. "Of course. But hopefully you won't be miserable for too long." I kissed her forehead and pushed myself off her bed. "Please, for me, take your Talent slowly, all right?"

Isabele sighed and nodded. "If it'll stop these headaches."

Her chambermaids were ready with another cup of tiliarose as I was closing Isabele's door behind me.

Kathryn left to return to Snowmont the next morning.

I hugged her tightly to me as stablehands readied her carriage. "I'm so sorry that I've been away for most of your visit."

She huffed in sympathy. "Being queen doesn't leave you much time to yourself, does it?"

"The next time you come to Lecevonia, I promise that I will take some time to spend with you." I held onto her hands. "Please come back?"

"Oh, don't worry, I will." She winked at me. "I think summer suits me."

I looked around for Celeste, but there was no sign of her. "Where is—?"

"We already said our goodbyes," Kathryn said quickly, giving me a sad smile. "I have a feeling that I'll be back sooner than you think."

"I'll take that as a promise."

The coachman cleared his throat behind us. "Excuse me. Your carriage is ready, Your Grace."

Kathryn sighed and leaned into me for one final hug. She spoke in a whisper only for me to hear. "Give Ezekiel a goodbye kiss for me, yes?" When she backed away, she wore the most devious grin. The heat I felt in my cheeks was a dead giveaway that her suspicions were right.

For Haggard's sake. Had Celeste told her *everything*?

Kathryn accepted the help of a stablehand as she climbed the steps into the black carriage. She leaned out the open window as the door was closed behind her, and when the coachman snapped the white horses into motion, she gave one final wave goodbye. I watched the carriage until it disappeared around a curve in the road, not realizing until I sniffled that I'd begun to cry. I swiped a sleeve across my face and turned back toward the castle.

The courtyard was a bustle of energy as preparations were being made for Solstice Day, which was now only six days away. Banners hung, flags erected, tables set up for the vendors that came out every year to sell their creations as Solstice Day gifts to commemorate Haggard giving his gifts of magic to his children.

I was sad to miss it this year.

Our setback in Hiddon had taken away two precious days that would've ensured I was back home in time for the holiday. Now, I needed to leave tomorrow for Loche to arrive just in time for Solstice Day and to, somehow, collect the fifth relic.

The voice purred in delight.

*Find it.*

The dagger I still wore at my waist hummed just a hair louder.

My own chill of anticipation ran up my arms.

In the busyness of my days, I did at least make the time to buy Solstice Day gifts for my sisters.

I sat with them that night after supper had been cleared from the table and took out my gifts for them. Clara was the most upset to learn that I wouldn't be home for Solstice Day, so I gave her her gift first. She stroked her new dress in her hands, the silver embroidery shimmering in the candlelight. When I'd found a dress with peonies on it, I'd known I just had to get it for her. Peonies always brought Sterling to mind even to this day. The smile on Clara's face now told me I was on my way to forgiveness.

I gave a leatherbound journal, falcon feather quills, and bottles of ink to Lisette for her writing. And to Isa, a set of golden hair clips with rubies on the ends.

"To bring out your eyes," I told her with a wink. She gave me a grateful smile and, in a manner that was true Isabele, started to cry.

Looking at my sisters, I thought of the world I was about to bring to them. This would be my first Solstice Day away from them, but it would be worth it. I *knew* it would be. They were going to see it too. When I saw them again, I would have awakened the magic that was desperately begging to be seen again. To be used again. The world would be different.

I would be different.

*Find it.*

Lecevonia was only as strong as its leader, and when I returned, I would be a stronger queen than ever.

# CHAPTER TEN

"COULDN'T WE STAY home for just *one* week?"

I rolled my eyes. Zeke has been grumbling since we left Hillstone, and I wasn't sure how much more I could take. "The Solstice is just days away," I said. "So no, we couldn't stay. Aren't you used to hopping from one place to the next, anyhow?"

"It's different traveling with you." He looked out the window of the carriage, arms crossed. "I feel like someone is always watching. Like there's something I have to be ready for." Then he looked back at me and smirked. "On my own, I can simply throw caution to the wind, because I know *I* won't get caught."

"Well, I'm so sorry to inconvenience you then."

He gave me this funny look, narrowed eyes and a smile, before scooting across the bench seat and landing right next to me. He grabbed my chin and held my gaze to his, playful and daring.

"I live to be inconvenienced by you, my Rose."

Then he planted a quick kiss on my lips and pushed himself away back to his original seat just as Amos rode up to the window of the carriage.

If Amos saw the flush in my cheeks, he pretended not to. "Almost to Mareus, my queen."

"Thank Haggard," I said, brushing off my skirts. "Between Zeke's muttering and these marshy roads, I could do without either of them for a while."

Zeke scoffed. "You can't get rid of me that easily."

I was certainly aware.

The golden spires of King Jarin and Queen Seraphine's castle, Gildshoal, could be seen glimmering in the sunlight above the salt marsh we were traveling through. The swaying of the cordgrass rustled all around us, and mosquitos and locusts had taken up residence inside the carriage. But I took solace in the fact that with each length, we grew closer to the coastline where the insects would give way to shore wind and sea waves.

The spires growing taller and taller weren't the only things telling me we were getting closer.

*Find it.*

*Find it!*

The voice was growing more and more excited in my ear. The bag of relics between my feet, with Equos's dagger returned to it, buzzed with an energy unlike anything I'd ever felt before. I had to fight the urge to jump out of this carriage and run the rest of the way, as foolish as that was.

Finally, the sea of cordgrass met the gates of Mareus. Past the gates, the seaside city sprawled out in front of us, all pale mortar and terracotta roofs rising above cobblestone streets. Reaching out to the horizon, the East Sea glistened in the last shards of light as the sun dipped beneath the salt marshes behind us.

"Come, Your Majesty," Amos said, surging ahead. "We're late."

Indeed, men were up on rickety ladders lighting lanterns at the tops of lampposts along the street.

It was dark by the time I stepped out of the carriage in the refuge of Gildshoal's stable. A footman bowed and cleared his throat. "Good evening, Your Majesty. Welcome to Gildshoal."

"Good evening." I looked around the stable, lit by lanterns. Seashells adorned the posts above each stable door, and it was quiet, only broken by horses snorting and shuffling as they settled in for the night.

"If you please," he said, waving me forward.

"Our bags—"

"They'll be brought to your guest rooms." Another footman was already unloading the carriage. I saw him grip the leather handle of the bag of relics, barely noting Vena's bow laid across the top.

I lurched toward him. "Careful!"

I'd made my entire party jump. Zeke's hand rested on my shoulder. "I'm sure he can handle bringing everything to your rooms securely." He eyed me warily.

"Y-yes," I said, shaking my head to clear it. "Of course."

As the second footman carried our bags through a doorway, it felt as though a part of my soul was being ripped away.

The tug on my body, which had grown more persistent as we approached Loche, split in two, baffling my nerves. One way toward my bag of relics, the other toward the interior of the castle.

I heard whispering again, but for the first time, it sounded like multiple voices. And they all had the same thing to say with glaring clarity.

*Find it . . .*

What was coming over me?

I tried my best to turn my attention back to the first footman. I followed as he led us through a pair of doors into a marble-floored foyer. It was all I could do to hold in my gasp.

I'd heard of Gildshoal's beauty, but I'd never seen it firsthand. The only palace more ostentatious was Snowmont, but not by much. The entire place glowed warm with lanternlight glinting off marble pillars, golden accents spiraling their way up each one. The stained glass, though subdued by night, pictured all sorts of vibrantly colored creatures of the sea, and alabaster statues of people clothed in fishing nets interwoven with seashells stood like dazzling sentinels along the walls.

My eyes drifted to the gold-plated rafters as the footman continued forward. "His Majesty and the Queen are awaiting your arrival."

"I'm sorry to have kept them waiting."

"It's of no consequence," the man responded, stopping in front of a grand marble door. "They've had enough company to keep them entertained." He unlatched the golden handles and ushered us through, and the tug on my body almost pulled me off my feet.

A room full of people in the throes of a party filled my vision.

I suddenly felt like I'd intruded, and that distracted me from the tug just enough to reel it in to a bearable degree.

Men in gold-studded coats and women in ruffled dresses fell silent, and a lively melody of string music came to an abrupt stop as heads turned toward us.

The footman stepped in behind us and cleared his throat again. "Queen Rosemary Avelia of Lecevonia, and company."

The crowd shuffled to either side of the room, leaving a path for us straight to the king and queen sitting upon their thrones.

I felt severely underdressed in my traveling clothes, skirts rumpled and sweat clinging to my skin, and I was pretty sure I had a mosquito bite on my cheek becoming redder by the second.

King Jarin's voice boomed as he stood. "Ah, Rosemary! Little cousin. Welcome." He strode forward with a grin that gleamed so brightly I was sure it could have been seen back in Hillstone. He wore a brightly colored cloak, woven through with silver threads and embroidered seashells along the edges. The silver threads matched the handsome streaks in his beard so well, I wondered if it was intentional.

"I hope I'm not interrupting," I said as he came forward and kissed my hand.

"Nonsense," he said, his golden earrings catching the candlelight. "You can't interrupt your own welcome party."

Queen Seraphine sidled up beside her husband. Her dark skin glowed, her golden bangles on her wrist jingling as she lifted her hand and put it on his shoulder. "Sweet dear, we haven't seen you since your birth." She leaned toward the king. "She looks a bit like her grandmother had at that age, doesn't she?"

"I see her eyes, yes."

I smiled and eyed the crowd around me. "I hadn't expected such a gathering."

"We'll take any excuse for a party," Seraphine replied with a wink. "Come now," she shouted through the room, clapping her hands. "Start the music again and dance! No need to stop now—the sun has a long journey before it rises!"

I noticed Amos and Roger slink off to the pastry table as Seraphine took my hand. "You're as beautiful as Helena was when she left for Hiddon. Married King Toman, she did. Your mother looked so much like her, though absolutely nothing like Toman, didn't she, Jarin?"

"You knew my grandmother Helena?" I asked.

"Of course! I was her lady-in-waiting when she was just a princess. Got to know her brother." Seraphine nudged King Jarin's shoulder with her own.

"Quite the scandal back then," Jarin said with a chuckle.

"And you married anyway, despite the scandal." My eyes traveled to Zeke, who stood silently a few paces away.

"The more scandal the better, I always thought," King Jarin answered, smiling and nuzzling Seraphine's hair.

I felt Zeke's hand in the small of my back, and I turned. "This is Ezekiel, my . . ." Best friend? Forbidden love? Biggest nuisance in my kingdom? "Personal guard."

"Personal guard?" Seraphine raised her eyebrows. She leaned in close to my ear. "Not with those devoted eyes of his." Then the music drifted into a new song, and she straightened and grabbed Zeke's hand. "Come, Ezekiel. Sweep an old lady off her feet!" And with that, she whisked him off to the dance circle.

That left me alone with King Jarin.

"There is a reason for my visit," I said quietly.

"I'm certain I know what it is." Jarin raised his eyebrows. "You aren't my only visitor, you see." His eyes settled into the corner of the room, and I followed his gaze.

Gryffin stared back at us. He raised his glass in greeting.

My veins iced over, and my eyes darted around the room to find the nearest escape. The castle in my mind began constructing itself.

What on *Haggard's green earth* was he doing here?

He began making his way toward us through the embellished crowd.

Zeke's hand was on my shoulder in an instant.

Gryffin stopped in front of us. If the fury in my eyes could burn a hole through Gryffin's head, it would have scorched the marble wall behind him. But what was more, he knocked uncertainty back into my resolve. How could he have known we would be here? Surely it was not simple coincidence. *Don't let him hold anything over you.* Zeke's words came to mind, and I held onto them as hard as I could.

Our tension must have been palpable, for a few partygoers glanced at us nervously before continuing out of harm's way.

King Jarin looked between me and Gryffin, eyebrows pinched. "I was unaware of any ill tidings between you lot."

"It's quite all right, Your Majesty," Gryffin said with a smile. "Just a bit of history."

At his words, King Jarin relaxed and raised his glass. "Then all is well." He took Queen Seraphine's hand, who had come up beside him, and led her to the dance floor.

I scoffed and glared at Gryffin. "Using your Talent wherever you can, aren't you? Unbelievable. Why are you here?"

"I take it that we are both after the same thing."

"What use is it to you?"

"I only want to have it before Amicka can get her hands on it. What use is it to *you,* Rosemary?" The glint in his red-flecked eyes frightened me.

He knew. He knew I was after an Awakening.

I lowered my brows into a scowl. "You should be ashamed for using your Talent on these people. They've done nothing. They have stayed out of it all and have never once quarreled with the other kingdoms."

"I use my tools as I need, Rosemary. Not that it has amounted to anything yet." He nodded toward the dancing couples. "See the queen's pin."

As the king and queen twirled and laughed, I noticed it then, catching the lanternlight. The brooch of pearls pinned to the bodice of Seraphine's dress.

*Get it.*

My body moved as if I were a puppet on string.

My sight zeroed in on that brooch.

I had to get it.

I vaguely heard Gryffin's confused remark as I turned away from him. Suddenly, I was walking through the crowd of whispers and laughter, pushing my way between throngs of people. Each step made the voices in my head happier, louder, more insistent.

I had to get it.

I felt a hand on my arm, and a snarl ripped through my throat. To my own ears, I sounded like a starved animal, like the wolves in the Tarasynian woods. I wheeled around, ready to claw the eyes out of whoever was stopping me from getting what I needed.

Zeke's eyes bored into mine. "Rose."

It was all I could do to focus on his brown eyes. And it was then that I came back to myself.

"Zeke. I . . ." My words turned to cotton in my mouth. I had nothing to say. I'd turned into a mindless beast in the middle of a crowd of nobility of a foreign kingdom, as a visiting sovereign, and I had no explanation for it.

"You're not making a very good look for yourself here, Rosemary," Gryffin murmured.

I looked around me, and a few people eyed me with caution, whispering to their companions.

What were these relics doing to me? Was I losing my mind to them, no better than I had to Gryffin? Did Zeke's fears have merit?

Zeke placed himself squarely in front of me. "Rose. Talk to me. What do you need?"

*You need the brooch.*

I shook my head. "I need to retire, I think."

As Zeke called over the king and queen, I met Gryffin's eyes.

Something in them . . . As if he *knew* what I was feeling. The pressure of the voices. He opened his mouth to say something, then snapped it shut again. But the sympathy in his eyes was impossible to miss, even through the red flecks.

I realized then that the castle my mind had begun to build was not against Gryffin, but against the *voices.*

King Jarin walked over to us, Queen Seraphine on his arm. The proximity of the brooch, now that I was aware of it, made the voices almost unbearable. "Our man Hostings here can show you to your quarters," he said, gesturing to the footman that had led us to the Great Hall. "I'm sure it's been a long journey for you. I believe your other two men have already turned in for the night as well. The marshes are not an easy trek. I'm glad you all could cross before the tides come in." He took my hands in his. "It's so good to see you, dear cousin." His warm smile did little to calm my mind, but I returned it all the same.

"Likewise. Thank you for the kind welcome. I wish I could stay to enjoy the party a bit longer."

"We take any reason to have a little fun," Seraphine said with a wink. "And with Solstice Day in just two days, we'll be celebrating to no end."

I did not need to be reminded one bit when Solstice Day was. I was losing precious time by not just reaching forward and taking the brooch off her dress.

*Rose,* I chided myself harshly. My mental castle added the next layer of bricks.

"Indeed, one of the biggest celebrations of the year," I said with a smile. I hoped it didn't look as fake as it felt.

"And be glad you're here in Mareus for it. There is nothing like a Solstice Day by the sea."

The pearls embedded in the walls of the Great Hall almost seemed to mock me with their shimmer as Jarin shook his head firmly.

It was early the following morning, but I must have been awake long enough already today to have had this conversation five times over. I certainly had done so in my head.

Solstice Day was tomorrow. The dwindling time I had left gnawed away at my stubborn hope. Desperate, I pled my case again.

"Amicka and the Rebels of the Red Sun are after Mareus's brooch. There is a target on your kingdom. Please, let me take it away from here, for the safety of your people."

"Rosemary, I will tell you just as we've told King Gryffin. We've protected it for centuries. It's quite safe here."

"Surely there's something I can do in exchange for it."

"And take away my wife's most beloved accessory?" Jarin let out a hearty laugh. "Any husband knows better than to do that."

I knew he was simply jesting, but something about reducing a priceless relic to costume jewelry made me bristle. Or maybe it was the voices growing louder and louder in my ear, jeering at me through the bricks of my castle.

*GET IT!*

"Jarin, please—"

"Whatever the Rebels are capable of, we can handle it. I refuse, Rosemary, and that's that. Enough of this now." He raised his hand up to the sun streaming through the high window and smiled. "As hard as it may be for you to do, try to relax and enjoy your stay while the weather holds."

Without waiting for a response, he clasped his hands behind his back and turned his attention to another man nearby, who was gesturing wildly with his hands now that he had the king's eye.

When I found Zeke toward the back of the Great Hall, his smile was smug. "Not so easy, was it?"

"Hush, you."

"Come now, Rose. Think about something else, will you? You can't drag me all the way to Mareus and refuse me even a glimpse at the East Sea."

I admittedly did feel a longing at his words. The urge to feel the ocean's breeze was almost as strong as the voices.

Actually, no. Not even close. Everything in my body told me to march back to King Jarin and demand that the brooch be handed over to me.

But the pleading in his brown eyes held me in a vise even the voices couldn't loosen.

I rolled my eyes. "All right, then."

He beamed such a bright smile that my stomach fluttered. "Think we can sneak out from under the noses of Amos and Roger?"

I peeked through the corner of my eye. Roger was speaking with the Crown Princess—was that an admiring sparkle in his eyes?—and Amos seemed to be telling a joke to a group of men near the breakfast table.

Then, a most unwelcome feeling I knew all too well. The stabbing stare of red-flecked blue eyes.

Gryffin sat at a long table, a woman of court at his side. From the way she was fanning herself and sighing loudly, she wasn't getting the attention she'd hoped for from him. Gryffin's own frustrations were clear on his face across the room. Apparently, his Talent couldn't solve everything.

As I met his eyes, there was the shortest moment of shared emotion between us. Disappointment. He must have seen my failed attempts to persuade King Jarin.

I quickly turned my gaze back to Zeke. Try to relax. Right.

"We'd better be quick. Amos's joke is almost over," I said, letting Zeke take my arm. "Knowing you, you've already picked your way down to the beach."

"And when would I have done that? I haven't left your side in Haggard knows how long."

I nudged him with my shoulder, smiling. "No need to sound so disappointed about it."

The salty air met us as soon as we made it through the castle doors. A path had already been laid out from the courtyard, winding through the bit of sea grasses and dunes, to the golden sand lining the coast. As the breeze dared my hair to escape its careful updo, the whoosh of the waves against the shore filled my ears, replacing the voices just for a moment. There were certain charms about a castle by the sea. I envied King Jarin and Queen Seraphine, just a little.

I looked around briefly, and finding no one too near, I kicked off my shoes.

I'd never felt sand against my feet. The shores of Port Della were covered with rocks, so Papa had always made us wear shoes. Here, the soft grains scraping my soles were almost painful, but I liked it all the same.

"Rose."

I turned, and Zeke was standing a few paces back, with this curious look on his face. I couldn't place it.

"What are you staring at me for, Zeke? Am I embarrassing you?" I asked, wiggling my toes deeper into the sand.

He flashed my favorite half-smile. "On the contrary." He rocked back on his heels. "Marry me."

My toes stopped wiggling. Haggard, my heart stopped beating. "What?"

"I'm asking you to marry me."

His words echoed through my skull, through my bones. They made my blood simmer, in a good way. Like a bolt of lightning through my veins. "Marry you?"

Zeke chuckled and took my hands in his. "That's what I said."

Our future surged forward in my mind again—a cottage in the woods, a golden-haired, green-eyed child running through the trees. My belly round with another. Zeke's warm arms encircling us all.

But where was Hillstone? Where was the leader of my people?

"I . . ."

I pulled my hands away from his. Hillstone was my future. Equos, Lecevonia was my future. Not a cottage in the woods, as badly as I may have wanted it to be.

My people were my future.

"I can't, Zeke. You know that."

He groaned and took my hands in his again. "Is there no sympathy for a man who has promised his life to you many times over? Look at Jarin and Seraphine, Rose. That was a scandal, too."

"Jarin was a prince who had his parents for his security. And he was just that! A prince. Not a king. He wasn't already under the scrutiny of his people, left to make alliances and strengthen bonds."

"I bet he would tell you otherwise."

"He didn't have people questioning his lineage."

"Let them question."

"And he undoubtedly didn't have a war chasing his heels!"

At that, Zeke laughed. "All the more reason. We shall die happy."

But I shook my head and kept my eyes glued to my feet, still buried in the sand.

"Rosemary." His hand was under my chin, lifting my eyes to meet his. They held such tenderness. "I'm going to ask you again. Will you marry me?"

My eyes were swimming in shocked tears. Haggard knew I wanted to say yes. That I might have said yes anyway, under different circumstances.

Could he actually be happy with the life I had to offer him?

"You would be king-consort," I said slowly. "You would be locked away in Hillstone like I am. Day in and day out. No longer a scout, no longer free to go and do as you wish. Is that the life you want?"

At that, his gaze faltered and fell.

There it was. That one thing that made it all too good to be true after all. I'd known it all along, in my heart. Even being married to me was not enough to keep him satisfied, tethered to court for the rest of his life.

I held his hands tightly. "Your future and mine are not one in the same, Zeke. You want something different."

His eyes snapped back to mine. The sea wind grazed through his golden waves, and the pain that shot through me at the realization that I was, after all these years, actually *not* enough for him felt like ice. Or flame. Sometimes, it was hard to tell the difference between that searing sting.

Zeke opened his mouth to say something. *Please, say anything.* I would've taken any denial. Maybe, if he'd said I was wrong, I would have said yes to his marriage proposal then and there. *Ask me again.*

But no denial came.

As I slowly let go of his hands, a billow of thick, black smoke rose to the sky behind him.

# CHAPTER ELEVEN

ZEKE TURNED, FOLLOWING my horrified stare. His eyes went wide. "What is happening?"

A window high in Gildshoal's turret exploded, and glass rained down onto the sand around us. Zeke was over me in an instant, veiling me from the shards. Screams erupted from somewhere too close by.

Zeke grabbed my arm. "We need to get somewhere safe!"

"The relics!" I tugged my arm out of his grasp and raced toward the castle. Tiny pieces of glass pierced my feet before I hurriedly put my shoes back on at the stone path.

"Leave them!" Zeke yelled from behind me.

But I was already bounding up the path to the courtyard, where the sea breeze was replaced by smoke and ash.

"Rose!" Zeke called from behind. But I didn't slow. I couldn't. The quicker I could get up to my guest rooms, the quicker I could grab what I needed. *Then* I could get to safety.

The voices screamed in my head in agony behind the walls of my castle. Agony of being so close to their fifth and final piece. Agony of being . . . aflame.

Oh no.

Gildshoal's halls were shrouded in smoke. I couldn't even tell what was on fire—everything was just black, thickening, suffocating. People coughed and pushed past me, desperate to get to clean air.

Thankfully, the guest chambers were only on the second floor. My eyes burned as I pushed through the doors and scoured the room for my leather bag. Fire licked the thick curtains and jumped to the rug on the floor. I could hear the faint hum of the relics. I followed it, and finally, I found my bag under the bed, Vena's bow lying over the top of it. I grabbed the bag by its handles and the bow by its leather grip. Haggard, my skull wanted to split with the screaming. I wheeled toward the door.

Through a haze, a figure stood in the open doorway.

"Rosemary!"

A chill so intense ran up my spine. Though I couldn't see, I'd have known that voice anywhere.

"Stay away from me." I reached into the bag and closed my hand around the hilt of Equos's dagger. "Or I'll cut you to shreds, Gryffin."

He coughed and reached for my arm. "You might get your chance later, but right now we'd do best to get out of here!"

I pulled my arm away, but I still found myself following him through the smoke. My lungs were burning in my chest. What on earth was causing so much smoke?

We ran down the stairs taking two at a time.

Then, others were moving past us, wearing red tunics and dark cloaks down to the floor and cloths over their noses, carrying what seemed like balls of embers in their gloved hands. Smoke billowed from their palms as the embers glowed.

Before I could ask who they were, Gryffin cursed under his breath and pulled me into a small hallway off the main corridor. Here, the smoke wasn't quite as thick.

"Rebels," he said quietly, trying to stifle his cough. "We're lucky they didn't recognize you, or what you're carrying."

"Rebels? Here?" Dread washed over me. "Jarin and Seraphine—"

"They don't matter now. You need to get to safety, Rosemary." His eyes traveled to the bag in my hand. "You and the relics."

I sneered at him and held the bag and bow closer to my chest. "Of course that's what you care about."

His blue eyes glinted in the low light, red flecks sharpening. "Don't you?"

Point taken. "Where do we go now?"

He pointed behind me, down the dark hallway. "I think there's a way out that leads to the city streets."

We began down the hall, but voices made us stop before a doorway. It was one of the many drawing rooms in the castle. The relics in my leather bag were humming louder than ever.

"Please, don't do this." Queen Seraphine's voice. Shaking, wheezing.

The female voice of a stranger answered her. "I'll do as I shall, Your *Majesty.*" The way she said "*majesty*" felt like a stab in the chest.

Gryffin took a strong inhale from behind me. He put his hand on my shoulder very gently, as if he were scared I'd make any sudden movement. I looked at him, and his eyes were wide. He mouthed one word. "Amicka."

"Amicka?" I whispered. "As in the leader of the Rebels?"

He put a finger over his lips and pulled me back toward the main corridor. I'd never seen him so . . . afraid.

But Rebels still flooded the corridor, immune to the smoke emulating from the balls of embers in their hands. Gryffin cursed. "I'll talk to Amicka and distract her so that you can get through to the streets."

I felt my eyes steel over. "I don't trust you."

"Then you may as well hand the relics over to her. And I have a feeling that Amicka having all the relics won't be a good thing."

I didn't understand any of this. But the voices in my head were a thundering storm as though my castle walls weren't even there, the humming of my leather bag a whirlwind. I could hardly think straight.

Gryffin shook my shoulder. "Rosemary. We need to move. I think there may be a chance she won't see you with all this smoke."

"All right. Fine." I shook my head, trying to clear it. I needed to get out of this castle.

Gryffin nodded, then straightened his shoulders and walked around the doorway and into the drawing room. "Amicka," he said.

"Gryffin?" The squelch of something sliding out of something sticky reached my ears. Then there was a heavy thud. "What a treat to see you here." Her tone made it sound like it was more of an annoyance than a treat.

"Likewise." Gryffin went farther into the room. "I see you've gotten what you came for."

With any luck, they were both looking at whatever Gryffin was referring to. Now was my chance. I crept as quietly and quickly as I could past the doorway.

From what Gryffin told me of Amicka, I already expected to see turmoil in the briefest glimpse as I passed. But I didn't expect the carnage, and a whimper rose in my throat when I saw Queen Seraphine lying on the floor, her lifeless eyes staring straight ahead. Blood coated the tip of Amicka's spear, which she held tightly in one hand, and the pearl brooch in her other.

I didn't spend too much time looking at Amicka herself, only catching her wild dark curls and a headpiece made of branches.

I slinked to the other side of the doorway, and once there, I took a gulp of air and had to stifle the choking of grief and smoke.

"I did," replied Amicka. "Though I'd hoped I'd have better luck with the remaining four."

"Solstice Day is tomorrow. Between the two of us, we only have that one relic. What do you plan to do?"

"Thanks to your failing with the young queen, I'm having to start from scratch. Your grandmother has been quite the asset, though." I felt the wicked smile in her voice.

"Where is she?"

"Closer than you would believe."

"And she's been helping you? I find that hard to believe."

"She doesn't make it easy. She holds certain people close to her and is reluctant to talk about them. Like your queen. But we coaxed enough out of her to know that she heard Rosemary's mind here in the city—*with* the relics you've lost us." There was a wicked smile in her voice. "And I think she is closer than you want me to think."

Hands caught my arms.

In a knee-jerk reaction, I rammed my foot backward into my captor. It hit his knee, and it was just enough to make his leg buckle. The moment I felt freedom, I wheeled around and ran down the hallway.

Someone touched my shoulder, and I heard Gryffin shout.

"Keep going!"

Finally, a door with light seeping through the cracks lit the hallway just enough for me to see the handle. I pushed through with all my might, Gryffin following behind me.

The door emptied us into Gildshoal's rear courtyard. The sunlight was choked out by black smoke, and alabaster statues of fish and dolphins were smeared with soot from the burning trees around them.

The relics screamed as I ran further and further away from the castle, away from the pearl brooch that was now in Amicka's hands.

"Your Majesty!"

In the corner of the courtyard, Amos had his sword drawn and was fending off a Rebel wielding a club in one hand and a dagger in the other.

"Protect yourself, Amos!" I yelled back. The last thing I wanted to do was distract him from saving his own life.

Then, Amicka burst through the door behind us with one of her Rebels.

Her spear was even more formidable out in the open. It was easily taller than me, completely wrapped in leather for better grip. The spearhead was a shining red metal, glinting in the sun. Blood coated the leather near the tip. Queen Seraphine's blood, and according to Gryffin, who knew how many others.

I heard Amos growl, and when I tore my eyes away from Amicka, I saw him bring his sword down onto the forearm of his opponent, making him drop his club. The Rebel tried to jab Amos in the side with his dagger, but Amos disarmed him easily.

Then, it happened so quickly. Amicka merely lifted her hand, and Amos was flung into the courtyard wall. Even from my end of the courtyard, I heard his skull crack. She threw her spear, and the red tip sank deep into Amos's chest.

A strangled scream ripped through the air. It took me a moment to realize it was coming from me.

*Amos.*

Gryffin spoke low beside me. "Rosemary, you need to go."

Though my feet were heavy as lead, I managed to put one foot in front of the other until Amos's slumping body disappeared from my view.

We crossed the marble streets to the nearest building that looked somewhat safe, an inn. Smoke trickled up from the roof and the outer walls were charred black, but it appeared its flames had died a while ago. Inside, the air was still stifling and hot, soot coating every surface, the wooden rafters crumbled on the floor, but thankfully, since the foundation was stone, the building itself was still sturdy. There were only two floors to the inn, and a quick sweep told us that it was empty.

While Gryffin went on a hunt for water and food, I found a guest room that was still mostly intact. There, I slumped against the wall, my breath raking in my chest from the smoke I'd inhaled. I set the leather bag of relics and Vena's bow down next to me, and it felt as though I'd released a bag of rocks that left my arms aching. The voices were quiet for once.

In this brief moment of safety, my tears fell for Amos. I wiped them away, big, hot, heavy tears, and my hand came back wet and sooty.

Despair crept in. Where was Zeke in all of this? And Roger? Haggard, after seeing what Amos had been subjected to with just a swipe of Amicka's hand . . . None of us were safe.

Gryffin appeared in the doorway, carrying ceramic jars. He handed one to me. "Water," he said, his voice raspy like mine. He must have felt just as suffocated as I did.

I carefully took the jar from him and removed the wooden lid, almost in disbelief that it actually did contain water. I took big gulps, the water washing the sting of smoke from my throat before settling in my aching stomach.

Gryffin settled across from me, leaning against the bed. Resting his elbows on his knees, he let his head hang, breathing heavily. I couldn't help but notice the emerald ring still swinging on the chain around his neck.

I sat as still as I could across from him. As I eyed him, I tried to place what I was feeling. Did I still hate him? Undoubtedly. Was I still scared of him? Well, my heart wasn't pounding at the sight of him. His red flecks didn't send my thoughts running for cover.

Back in Gildshoal, amidst the chaos, he'd gone back for the relics and found me instead. And he hadn't killed me on the spot. He'd actually *helped* me get to safety. And now that I knew what Amicka could do, that was a greater danger than I'd known. But he had known, and he took the risk anyway.

Maybe I didn't understand him as well as I'd thought I did. But the tension in my body told me at least some of my fear was still there.

No more thinking. The smoke and adrenaline had muddled my brain enough. No need to add in complex emotions at the moment. What I knew for certain was that I needed to bide my time until I could somehow get to Zeke and Roger.

"Amicka is Talented," I said, breaking the silence with a shaky voice. "That's clear enough. With what? The power to move things without touching them?" The little girl on the road in Hiddon, Clementine, came to mind.

Gryffin lifted his head and rested it back against the mattress, keeping his eyes closed. "Actually, no," he said, shaking his head slightly. "She isn't Talented."

As if I believed that. I narrowed my eyes at him. "Not past lying, are you?"

"I'm not lying to you, Rosemary."

"She threw Amos against the wall." My voice had found some of its strength again, saying Amos's name.

He opened his eyes and found me. "It's the spear."

"What does her spear have to do with it?" Aside from finishing the job . . .

"It belonged to Adria," Gryffin said. "Haggard's older sister. She lived and died centuries ago, in the arctic plains."

Another relic. Wonderful. Just what the Peninsula needed.

Great Haggard, I was starting to sound like Zeke.

*Keep him talking, Rose.* "How does it give her that magnitude of power?"

Gryffin straightened his legs, groaning as he did so. "Like the other relics, it has the power of the magi embedded in it. But it's only one object. Its magic isn't as great as the five relics, at least once they are brought together."

"None of the relics ever gave us power like that." I could have used it, as Talentless as I was.

"Well, I can't be certain—it's just a theory." Gryffin rubbed his chin with a sooty hand, eyes downcast. "But I believe that's because the relics of the Five Talented are Haggard's power purposefully split five ways, given as gifts to his children. The spear is simply the residual magic of Adria, concentrated into one object."

"But right now, it's stronger than any one relic on its own," I said, beginning to understand his thought.

"Yes."

"It's as good a theory as any, I suppose." Gryffin and his theories. I would never hear the end of them. "It doesn't matter how it works anyway. What matters is she has that power, and she's willing to use it against anyone in her way."

"Especially you." He looked at me pointedly. "She won't hesitate to kill you."

Were my tense shoulders from his stare or the threat of death? Probably both.

"You're her next target, Rosemary. You need to stay as far away from her as possible." He shook his head. "I should have never mentioned any of this to you. Nothing about the relics, nothing about an Awakening. The city around us burns, and it's all for nothing. Amicka is as wasteful as Roderich."

The name still made my blood boil. But more pressing was the target I felt on my back. How long would it be until the Rebels searched this inn? My heart quickened at the thought of being found by them. How much time did I have?

Very little.

"I shouldn't stay here," I said, my gaze flickering to the door.

"You're right. You shouldn't." Gryffin extended his hands to me, pleading. "Give the relics to me, Rosemary, so you can be done with all of this."

My hand instinctively went to the bag at my side. "Not a chance."

He dropped his hands. "What do you plan to do, then?"

I didn't need the voices to tell me what I needed to do. Especially after seeing Amicka's power today, I still planned to do what would bring the most strength to both me and my people. The injustice of it all infuriated me. How did someone as evil as her, as Roderich, as *Gryffin,* gain such power? What sacrifices had they made to be good and strong? It had been used against me, my parents, my kingdom, countless others . . . It was time to tip the scales. "I'm going to stage an Awakening."

Gryffin narrowed his eyes. "Are you, now?" But there was no surprise in his voice as I expected there to be. "You'll never get the fifth relic from Amicka."

He was right. I would be mad to face her alone.

But maybe I didn't have to be alone.

Did I trust him? Not one bit. But he still wanted an Awakening to happen. Something told me that was enough to ensnare his aid. "You're going to help me."

"Am I?" Now there was the surprise I'd expected.

"Yes. Help me, and an Awakening will happen. Just as you want."

If Gryffin could try to use others for his endeavors, I could do the same to him. He was still Talented, and he knew Amicka better than I did. That felt valuable.

He studied me for a moment. Then, his lips slowly drew up into a smile of amusement. "All right. Same team then, I suppose," he said, resting his head back against the mattress again.

Though the thought made me uneasy, I suppose we were.

Though my mind wanted me to surge forward, my body was too tired to move. We stayed at the inn in separate rooms through the afternoon to recover from our escape. I didn't trust Gryffin enough to sleep in the same room as him, nor to leave the relics unattended. I had no doubt in my mind that Gryffin would take the relics and run off to meet Amicka if he could.

I had to wonder. Why hadn't he killed me yet? What use was I to him? Was wanting the same thing as him truly enough to place my life in his hands? I certainly didn't think so. He always had some reason that served himself.

Whatever his reason was, I would be ready to fight against it.

As I rested, the voices seemed to be biding their time. They whispered and roiled inside my mind, a hum of energy waiting to explode through its boundaries.

I ate what was left of the food Gryffin had brought me from the inn's kitchens. Half an apple, a bit of a loaf of bread, some dried meat that reminded me too much of my cuisine in the Tarasynian woods.

Smoke still rose from the castle, casting the city in an orange hue as the setting sun fought to shine through the haze. It should have been impossible for the sun to shine so brightly after a kingdom had lost its king and queen. Did the sun shine just as much when Roderich slaughtered the king and queen of Hiddon? It certainly had on the day Gryffin slayed his brother.

Three of the Five Kingdoms had changed reign just in the past six months. This was our reality.

Haggard. Where were Zeke and Roger? My chest tightened, aching to know if they were safe.

There was a quick knock on my door. Defiantly, I made him wait. Then, I took a deep breath, stood, and walked over to remove the latch. The moment the door swung open, Gryffin strode in and began pacing across the room. His angst was tangible, and it was another moment longer before he spoke.

"King Jarius and Queen Seraphine are dead."

I looked down at the dust-covered floor. "I was just thinking about that. It all happened so quickly."

He sighed and stopped in his steps. "Rosemary."

I eyed him carefully. "Yes?"

"Are you—what—" He stumbled over his own words before taking a breath and a careful step toward me. "How are you?"

"As well as I can be, given the circumstances," I answered shortly. Really, I was scared, sorrowful, heartbroken, confused. But I couldn't allow myself to sort through those feelings yet. Not when I was in the room with a liar, in a foreign city with a spear-wielding killer and a myriad of her accomplices.

Gryffin chuckled mirthlessly. "The circumstances are rather dour, aren't they?" He sighed and started to take another step toward me, then seemed to think better of it and shuffled back to his spot.

"Despite everything that has happened, I'm glad that we are here together. I know that you are safe."

"Ah, yes." I crossed my arms over my chest. "Because surely you care about my safety."

His eyebrows pinched together. "I do care about your safety, Rosemary."

I felt my skin prickle with angry heat. "You have no right to worry about me. You were going to kill me. Yetta told me as much."

He held up his hands and took a step back. "I'm sorry."

I scoffed. "Yes, 'sorry' makes it all fine now."

"I know it doesn't." He began walking across the room again as though it helped him find his words. "Rosemary, I was doing what I thought I had to do. The Peninsula needs an Awakening. Its magic is dying with each generation. Yetta said so herself."

Yetta. The mention of her made my heart ache.

"I visited her at her cottage before she went missing," Gryffin said. "And she told me that an Awakening would put things *right*. That it would make the earth hum, that the feeling of freedom would affect every living thing on the Peninsula. And I thought you were going to try to stop it." He stopped his pacing then, but his eyes stayed glued to the floor. "But truthfully, I don't know if I could have gone through with killing you." His voice broke on those last two dreadful words.

Another trick of his. I was sure of it. "You killed Cassia and Xal. You locked me away in my rooms!"

He looked up at me then, making me freeze. His red-flecked eyes were stone and glass. "Cassia committed treason. My mind is stretched thin as I have my entire kingdom believing something that I desperately wish I didn't have to hide! I didn't know what else to do!" His fingers weaved into his hair, then fell heavily to his sides. "Do you think that I don't wish my father and brother were better men? Do you think I enjoy manipulating and lying to my own people?" He took a shaky breath and turned away from me, staring at the wall. "I know it's sick, as hard as I tried to believe otherwise. It seemed innocent enough at first. Father deserved what my brother did to him. But as Roderich did things just as heinous as Father . . . He needed to be stopped before he took Tarasyn down with him. But if I lift my Influence now, everything will have been for nothing." His shoulders fell. "I'm too far into this, Rosemary."

I didn't want to believe him. But no veil of deceit could hide the torture of this man. He was exhausted of holding everything in his power together by a fraying thread.

"Gryffin." I couldn't believe my own two feet were carrying me closer to him. My own hand lifting and touching his shoulder.

He jumped at my touch, and a deeply rooted sense of survival wanted me to yank myself away from him. But I held fast, even as he tentatively laid his hand over mine.

He turned to look at me over his shoulder. "You'd still kill me, wouldn't you?"

I thought back to all those months ago, when he'd first arrived in Lecevonia. I'd been seeing a different man, a man that Gryffin had wanted me to see. But with his remorse and weakness worn on his sleeve, he just showed me that that man wasn't a complete falsehood.

It did not redeem him. But no, I wouldn't kill him. Not just to be rid of him. I wouldn't stoop to his diabolic solutions to ridding himself of things that displease him.

"Rosemary, I can see the hate you have for me on your face." He released my hand. "Once all of this is over, I *will* have your forgiveness, somehow."

I didn't know why my forgiveness mattered to him. Though, from the ring he wore around his neck and the way his hand had felt on mine, I had an inkling. But whatever feelings he thought he had for me were skewed. None of it mattered anymore, anyway. What was happening with Amicka and the Awakening was bigger than Gryffin. Bigger than whatever had transpired between us.

Then, the door kicked in, breaking off one of its hinges and hanging to the side.

Zeke stood in the doorway, Roger's hulking figure behind him.

My heart leapt at the sight of them in a mix of relief and disbelief. How did they—?

It took Zeke all of one second to cross the room and ram his fist into Gryffin's jaw.

# CHAPTER TWELVE

"QUIT WORRYING OVER that crite, Rose. I barely hit him."

I rolled my eyes and held the cool wet cloth against Gryffin's jaw. "Tell that to your red knuckles and his purple face."

Not that I didn't enjoy seeing Gryffin get a bit of what he deserved.

I handed the cloth to Gryffin and went over to Zeke.

He stood with his hands on his hips. "How was I supposed to know he hadn't been in this inn holding you captive? Again?" He shot daggers in Gryffin's direction. "I should punch him again."

Gryffin simply grunted and moved his jaw back and forth with his hand.

Quietly, I stepped forward and wrapped my arms around Zeke's waist. "I still can't believe you found me."

I felt his arms tighten around me, his lips in my hair. "I wouldn't have stopped searching the city until I had you in my arms again."

Haggard, this man.

I heard Gryffin suck in a breath behind us, and I left Zeke and went back over to the bed where Gryffin was sitting. "Is the cloth helping at all?"

He moved his jaw again and winced. "Ice would be better."

"Well, we aren't in Tarasyn anymore, and it's the dead of summer everywhere else. Ice is hard to come by."

"I've taken harder hits," Zeke muttered behind us. "Look, we need to move. So I'd start sucking it up if I were you."

After Zeke's assault on Gryffin's face, they'd told us that on their search for me, they'd spotted the base camp of the Rebels. There, Amicka was stationed, planning her next move. They'd only overheard a planned raid of the buildings surrounding the castle looking for me, and the relics, before they'd almost been spotted and had to disappear.

Well, Zeke had overheard. He was the stealthy one. Roger had stood guard from a distance, ready to barrel in if Zeke needed him.

Solstice Day was tomorrow, so Amicka and the Rebels would be moving quickly. We were still so close to the castle. And with the brooch now in Amicka's possession, if it even gave her the slightest pull toward the other four relics, we would be found within the hour.

"We have to find her first, then," I said. "I have four relics. They can lead me to the brooch." Now that I'd rested, the tug on my body was returning, and the voices were growing louder behind my battered castle walls. I could already feel the pull toward the brooch narrowing. "Someone is going to need to scope out the streets to make sure we don't run into anyone unprepared."

We all looked at Zeke leaning against the wall, and with the biggest scowl I'd ever seen on his face, he shrugged. "Fine."

"We'll need someone to ensure we have a way out of here too." Of course, that was assuming Amicka didn't kill us first.

"I will find everything we need," Roger said. "I'm going to get you back home to Equos safely once again, Your Majesty."

It didn't escape us that we were already one soul down.

Remembering Amos's death felt like I'd taken a sword hilt to the chest.

"That leaves—"

"Me and you," Gryffin said, smiling as much as his injured jaw would let him.

Boars.

But however I looked at it, it made the most sense. He would know how to speak to Amicka more than I would.

"Don't worry, Rose," Zeke said quietly. "I'm not letting you go anywhere alone with that crite."

Roger left the room to look around the inn for anything that we could take with us that might be of help on our journey back home.

Zeke took my hand and gently tugged. "Come with me?"

I let Zeke lead me out of the room, very aware of the bag of relics sitting in the corner of the room, now alone with Gryffin. The farther I got from them, the angrier the voices grew.

Zeke snapped his fingers in front of my face. "Rose? Are you there?"

I nodded. "Yes, sorry. Had you said something?"

He placed a hand on my cheek. "Where did you go?"

I considered telling him of the voices, *why* I needed the fifth relic so badly. There was this drive that seemed to leave me with no other option than to do what the voices said. *Find it.* But he wouldn't understand. I hardly understood it myself. He would just reiterate why I never should've gotten involved with the relics in the first place.

Once the Awakening happened, I would be rid of the voices. I was sure of it.

"I'm here," I answered indignantly. "No where else. I'm here, in this hallway with you. I promise."

Zeke quirked a tiny smile. "Good. There's something I want to talk to you about." He shuffled on his feet, suddenly uneasy. "I couldn't leave our conversation on the beach like that."

A fresh ache surged through my heart. "We don't have to talk about that right now."

But he continued anyway. "I know that things would be . . . complicated. I had never wanted to be king-consort, that's true. But I wouldn't have to be. I could remain a scout, working for the Crown. Working for *you*, for the good of Lecevonia. We could somehow still make it work."

The pain of considering an actual life with him was too great. For the good of Lecevonia? No. If he was ever captured on an assignment, they would have my *husband*. He would make me vulnerable, and I could not allow vulnerability. My weakness was my people's weakness.

Desperately trying to turn my heart to stone, all I said was, "That's not how things would work, Zeke." I shook my head and turned back toward the stairs.

"Rose."

I looked back at him, and his brown eyes were serious, unyielding. "Don't give up on this yet."

Could I ever truly give up on the idea of a world where Zeke and I could be together?

I heard Roger's footsteps coming up the stairs, and I took the opportunity to turn away from him and follow the voices pulling me back toward the relics.

A split second of panic made my breathing hitch.

What if they weren't there? What if Gryffin had taken them? Surely, we would have seen him escape down the hall. But what about the window?

I turned the corner almost in a frenzy, and I found the bag of relics still there, untouched, Vena's bow lying across the top. Gryffin lay on the bed flat on his back, eyes closed, wet cloth still pressed to his jaw.

I grabbed the bag, slung the bow over my shoulder, and cleared my throat. Gryffin peaked an eye open. "We need to move."

He nodded and pushed himself up, dropping the cloth beside him on the bed. "I'm ready when you are, Rosemary."

An Awakening was so close. All this turmoil and grief caused by the single idea of awakening the magic of the Magian Peninsula—Hiddon's demise, Lecevonia's attack, my imprisonment in Tarasyn, all of those who had lost their lives . . . It would all finally be worth something.

Roger appeared in the room, and Zeke sauntered in after him. Roger appeared empty-handed. "I found nothing, Your Majesty."

"We have the most important things right there," Gryffin said, pointing to the leather bag in my hands. "After the Awakening, one of you may be able to bring us all home on the wind, or who knows what else." He flashed a smile, hurt jaw and all. And I had to admit it, the prospect of magic all around us kept me hopeful too.

Following the pull of the last relic, I guided Zeke through the city as he scoped out our path before us. Gryffin trailed behind me, and Roger took up the rear. It was dusk, the moon just a sliver in the sky above the orange horizon. Most of the smoke had cleared now, but the thick smell still filled my nose as we walked down the silent streets.

Silent except for the humming in my ears that was growing louder with each step.

Only once did we hear the footsteps of others. We didn't linger to see whose they were, but I took it as a sign that the Rebels were already on the move. Did that mean Amicka was too? Zeke led us to safety, and after that we moved more quickly, hustling around corners and running as quietly as we could.

Zeke started down another street, but the voices in my mind whined. There were so many cracks in my mental castle that they weren't hard to hear. I tapped his shoulder and pointed in the other direction. By now, it was night.

The next street corner was on the crest of a small hill, and what we saw stopped us in our tracks.

Lanternlight poured from the windows all down the street. But no. The more I looked, the farther the lanternlight continued, until it reached the wall of the city.

There had to be at least fifty buildings that housed the Rebels now.

Their forces were larger than I'd ever anticipated.

How had I let this go on for so long? They'd been using Lecevonia as their base for years now, according to Gryffin! Had I acted a year ago when I'd first taken the throne, they would never have grown to these numbers.

Then I reminded myself—they had been growing for far longer than my reign. They might have even been forming before Atroxis swept through.

"This feels impossible," I whispered. "There are so many of them."

Roger lifted his head. "Do you hear that?"

"The humming?" Zeke asked. "Yeah, me too."

I caught Gryffin's eye. They heard it, too? Then I looked down at my bag. Inside, the relics were glowing the faintest blue hue.

"There," Roger said, pointing down the hill. Just a few streets over, a stable with a thatch-covered roof peeked from behind the corner of a house, and next to its gate sat a produce wagon. "That's our way out. I have no problem stealing from the Rebels unless you object, Your Majesty."

"Not at all," I answered. We were only stealing back what was already stolen.

Roger nodded to each of us and sauntered out into the dark.

As we rounded another corner, the pull on my body tightened like a rope. The voices surged. "She's close," I said breathlessly. But it didn't make sense. If she was searching for me, why would she be farther into their base camp?

Without waiting for Zeke, I felt my feet take one step toward a row of shops down the street. Then another.

I heard Zeke's voice behind me. "Rose?"

But the voices behind the crumbling wall in my head were louder than him.

*Find it.*

"What are you doing? Stop!"

Stop? How could I stop? The last relic was right here. I felt it in my bones.

*Get it.*

I felt a hand on my shoulder. Gryffin.

"Rosemary," he said. "Think about what you're doing."

Then he was pushed away. "Don't touch her, you crite!"

The wall of my castle fell.

What was I doing? I was finally going to end all of this. I was going to bring the power of magic to my people. *I* was going to do it.

Without Gryffin's hand to hold me back, I ran, clutching my leather bag of relics to my chest.

The voices, now unfettered, screamed at me. I was down the street, ignoring the curses spewing behind me. Something quiet in my brain told me that this was foolish, that I was going to get myself killed. But my legs wouldn't listen to my brain. I didn't want them to listen.

I *needed* that brooch. I needed the five pieces of this intricate puzzle to fit together and pour all of their magic into the earth beneath my feet.

I followed the pull of that last relic to the doors of a blacksmith's workshop. I was ready. I burst in, and a wall of heat and smoke hit me.

"My, my, Rosemary. I hoped that we would meet sooner than this."

The voices fell silent.

Amicka sat in a throne-like chair in front of the lit forge, one of those strange balls of smoke and embers in one of her hands. In the other was her spear.

This was the first chance I had to truly take in her appearance. Her dark hair was as wild as her eyes, which were violet and dangerously cunning. Her headpiece was a crown of sorts, not of branches as I'd originally thought, but of antlers. Upon seeing her more closely, I caught wisps of grey in her curls. She would have been very pretty, had her face not been drawn into a murderous snarl. She was wearing leather pants and boots, and a vest of tawny fur that clasped together at her chest over her tunic. There it was—the pearl brooch. Right there pinned to her vest. The voices goaded me to lunge at her, but now here in front of Amicka, I hesitated.

Smoke billowed from the ball in her hand. The walls of the smithy were already black from years of soot and backbreaking work. The smoke only further darkened the room.

I straightened my shoulders. "Amicka."

She hadn't come after me. Instead, she'd waited for *me* to come to *her.*

"Do you like this kingdom I've built?" Amicka said. "A kingdom of rejects, castoffs, the excommunicated. Many of them mourn and seek vengeance thanks to your father."

My father? "What does he have to do with you?"

"You didn't know he'd burned out a company of Rebels seven years ago in Aridia? Simply because we had different ideals than most.

Because we *cared* about a priceless magic about to be lost forever." Under her crown, she seethed. "His actions were fuel to the fire in our hearts."

Though this was the first time I truly met her, I felt as though I'd known her for years. This kind of anger that radiated from her, so rooted in hatred, demanded recognition.

I myself had felt it before when I had found out Roderich had created Atroxis, killing my parents.

I felt Zeke's presence behind me. Then, Gryffin appeared to my right. He gave me a quick glance, and his eyes were almost entirely red. Then he turned back to our adversary. "Amicka."

"Hello again, Gryffin." She nodded to me. "Why don't you grab that bag from your lost queen and give it to me?"

He held his hands out in front of him. "Please, consider what's most important here."

She smiled. "Your Talent can't persuade me. Stop trying so hard. You'll make your eyes bleed."

Gryffin cursed.

*The greedy will bleed while the righteous will heed.* Was it not just an old saying after all? How horrific.

I found my voice. "Give me the brooch, so this can all be done."

"Absurd," she answered with a sneer. "Give me the other relics."

"No."

I felt a pinprick in my left eye. Then another in my right. I looked at Zeke, and when his eyes met mine, he took a sharp breath. "Rose, your eyes . . ."

I felt something warm and thick sliding down my cheek, and when I wiped it away, my fingers were smeared with blood.

*I* was the greedy one?

Then, Amicka dropped the ball of embers, and it extinguished upon hitting the ground, erupting in smoke.

Through the haze, I saw Amicka lift her hand high.

Zeke's feet left the earth. His body slammed into the wall of the smithy, and his shout of pain ripped at my heart. She'd slammed him into a mace mounted above a worktable. When Amicka released his body, he fell in a heap onto the worktable and then rolled to the ground. Blood coated every surface.

I ran to his side, but his body left my grasp as Amicka dragged him to her feet near the forge. Now, she no longer needed to use her power. She raised her spear with both hands and rammed it into Zeke's torso.

A scream ripped through my throat.

It felt like I had been stabbed too.

I couldn't draw breath. I took a step to run to him, but a force kept me in my place.

Amicka had her hands raised once more, this time against me, holding me back from Zeke. "Take one more step without handing the relics over to me, and he'll die. All it takes is one twist toward his lungs." She turned the handle of her spear just slightly, and Zeke cried. There was so much blood.

The voices in my head were agony. *I* had four of them, not Amicka. Grab the last one, they told me. I just needed one more. I was close enough, wasn't I?

*Enough.*

But that wasn't the voices of the relics.

It was my own.

I held the bag out to Amicka. "Here. Take them. Please, just—don't hurt him anymore."

Amicka flashed a wicked smile. "Gryffin. Bring them to me."

Gryffin looked at me uncertainly. "Are you sure?"

I took the bow off my shoulder. "Yes." No, that was a lie. I wouldn't be the one bringing power to my people. I wasn't strong enough to do what needed to be done. My failure enveloped me, and I wanted to sink to the floor under the weight of it.

But Zeke was bleeding to death in front of me.

I just couldn't let him be hurt anymore.

Gryffin took the bow and leather bag from my hands. Slowly, he walked them over to Amicka.

With the relics out of my possession, the voices in my head stopped too. Nothing but a ringing in my ears, and a haze thicker than the smoke in the smithy, thicker even than what I'd felt under Gryffin's Talent.

Amicka lowered her hand, and I felt the force holding me in my place disappear. The moment the pressure lifted, I fell forward to the blackened floor. I didn't realize I'd been resisting it so intensely. I caught myself with my hands and immediately began crawling my way over to Zeke. Bloody tears stung in my eyes.

Amicka yanked her spear out of Zeke, leaving him sputtering on the ground. When I reached him, I balled up the hem of my dress and pressed it to his midsection. I didn't even try to hold back my sobs.

"Zeke, w-w—we'll get you out of here. I promise." I touched his cheek with my free hand, wiped the blood from the corner of his mouth.

"Rosemary." Gryffin touched my shoulder. His voice was grave. "It's happening."

It must have been after midnight then.

It was Solstice Day.

But there were no presents or celebrations, no giving of thanks with candles or feasts of pheasant and venison. Instead, there was only Zeke lying there in front of me, threatening to leave me alone in this world.

It was astonishing to realize how much I'd been controlled by the relics rather than my own mind. My castle walls had done *nothing*. It'd been worse than Gryffin's Influence. My want for an Awakening to occur had been true, and all my reasons still glared at me through my failure, but my need was not nearly as intense now that the relics were out of my possession. It was as if a force had been taken off my chest, but now it'd been replaced by the fragility of Zeke's survival. If I hadn't run in here utterly convinced that I could get that last relic from Amicka, the man that I loved would not be dying before my eyes.

But it didn't matter now. The ground was already shaking beneath me.

# CHAPTER THIRTEEN

I LIFTED MY EYES away from Zeke just briefly enough to see that Amicka had arranged the relics, all five of them—Equos's dagger, Viridi's bangle, Vena's bow, Arbos's chisel, and Mareus's brooch—in a star-like pattern on the ground, all radiating from the tip of the bow. She kept one of her hands centered over them, touching one relic with each of her fingers.

The ground continued to shake. The blackened alabaster walls around us began to crack.

"Gryffin," I said shakily. "What's happening?"

"I . . . I don't know." He shook his head. "This isn't what Yetta said it would be like."

Amicka laughed, a dark throaty sound that caressed the smoke in the room. "Yet it is happening just as I anticipated."

Cracking stone filled my ears. The mace on the wall fell to the ground.

Then, a great wind gusted through the open door. It whipped around the room, ripping my hair out of its bun, though really it felt like it was being ripped from my scalp. It cleared the smoke out of the room and lifted Amicka's hair into a hurricane around her head, her wicked smile outlined in shadows. She still kept one hand on the relics, and the other wrapped tightly around the shaft of her spear.

"Yes, I can feel it," she shouted into the wind. "I feel the power growing within me!"

Then, Roger barged into the smithy. A quick stab of relief lanced cleanly through my panic. Had he been close enough to see—or *feel*—that something wasn't going right with our plan?

Haggard, it'd *all* gone wrong.

Eyeing the room in horror, Roger picked up the mace that had fallen onto the ground. Amicka narrowed her eyes at him but didn't move.

An Awakening. It was something that had only been a theory all these years, and we were seeing it happen now. Only, it wasn't what any of us expected.

The cracking walls began to crumble.

I looked up at Gryffin. "We need to get Zeke out of here!"

Gryffin, mesmerized by what was happening to Amicka, tore his eyes away and looked at me. Nodding quickly, he lifted Zeke by the shoulders and hiked him onto his back. Zeke cried out, making my blood run cold. As fresh tears, no longer bloody, sprang to my eyes, I took Zeke's hand and squeezed it. What else could I do? I was useless. The Awakening hadn't given me a Talent. Of course it hadn't. I knew it wouldn't. Still, I felt a spark of betrayal. *Foolish, Rose.* Another trickle of blood seeped from the corner of Zeke's mouth. The spark died in my chest, replaced by anguish. I had to look away from his face, turning instead to the chaos of the smithy.

Roger swung the mace in his hands at Amicka's skull. She blocked it with her spear, but the mace's chain wrapped around its center, ripping the spear out of her hand. Its shaft snapped in two as the chain swung around and smacked the blood red metal spearhead against the wall. It ricocheted across the floor, gleaming red in the light of the forge. The centuries-old relic of Adria, broken.

Amicka snarled. But then, the pressure in the air shifted, and her smile returned.

Suddenly, Gryffin fell to the ground, gasping. Zeke landed on top of him.

I pulled at Zeke's arm with every ounce of strength I had and pulled him off Gryffin. "Roger! Help!"

Roger took one last look at Amicka, then stuck the handle of the mace into his belt. He picked up Zeke as if he weighed no more than a sack of flour. As he rushed toward the door, I touched Gryffin's shoulder. "Are you all right?"

Gryffin shook his head, grimacing through pain. "I feel like I've been ripped apart."

When he opened his eyes, I inhaled sharply.

They were nothing but blue. Deep ocean blue as when I'd first met him.

"Gryffin, your—your eyes . . ."

Then, the wind stopped. The shaking stopped.

*Everything* stopped. The silence surrounding us was louder than I'd ever heard it. Not knowing what else to do, I lunged forward and grabbed the spearhead, then scooted back to Gryffin's side.

Slowly, we both looked back at Amicka. Lifting her hand from the relics, she rose from the ground with her eyes closed. When she opened them, her violet eyes had been overtaken by red, as deep and full as the pools of Zeke's blood on the ground.

She laughed deeply. "It's all mine! My bones feel alive with the magic coursing through my very marrow."

On the floor, the relics glowed a bright blue, now a star in its own right. They seemed inseparable.

Amicka lifted her hand, and the relics all lifted together, never breaking their star. She rotated them in midair with a twist of her wrist before setting them down again gingerly.

She hadn't needed the spear's power to do it.

Gryffin groaned and rolled to a crouch. "Amicka, what . . . what in Haggard's name happened?" He was panting, and when he tried to stand, he lost his balance. I offered an arm to steady him. He closed his eyes again and put a hand to his forehead. "My head is splitting."

Amicka smiled. "Feeling powerless, Gryffin?"

At that, his eyes sprung open. "What did you do?"

"I did what others were too weak to do. I did what was needed to ensure the power of this Peninsula is revered rather than forgotten." Her red eyes flashed. "I did what will keep those of us who never faltered in the belief of the magi safe from ridicule and harassment for the rest of our existence!"

My breath hiked. "She absorbed all power."

Gryffin looked back at me. "She *what?*"

"She didn't summon an Awakening. She did the opposite." The crimson gleam of her eyes told me I was right. "She absorbed all power from the Peninsula."

"And powerful I do feel," Amicka said, stretching a smile across her lips. She twisted her wrist, and the walls began to rumble.

I glanced down at the spearhead in my hand. Could I be quick enough?

"No, you would not be," she said. She smirked at my quiet gasp.

She could read minds too. Yetta's Talent.

She twitched a finger, and the fire in the forge flared. "I'd take your chance and leave now if I were you, while I have more important things to do than kill you. Your dear Zeke is bleeding out through his stomach."

I only questioned for a second how she knew Zeke's name, but it didn't matter. We were no match for her.

"Gryffin," I said quietly. "We need to go."

Still holding his head, Gryffin finally responded to my pulling on his arm and followed me toward the door.

A Rebel walked in through a door in the back of the smithy, and Amicka nodded to her. "Get this decree printed and distributed immediately. No longer are there kingdoms, or powerless kings and queens." She shot a glance in our direction, and though she wasn't speaking to us, I could tell she meant for us to hear every vile word. "I claim the Magian Peninsula as my own, and all will answer to me." Her smile deadened my bones. "Who can stop me?"

I refused to hear anymore. Mustering up the courage, I turned away from her, and we ran out of the smithy.

Roger had already loaded Zeke onto the flat wooden bed of the produce wagon he'd found, a stray mule hitched to the harness. Gryffin and I scrambled into the back of the wagon, and I sat myself next to Zeke, cradling his head in my lap. He was barely awake, lids shuttering his eyes halfway, and he had the nerve to smile at me through his grimace of pain. "Rose, I feel like crite."

I scoffed, tears welling in my eyes. "I bet you feel worse than that."

"I might, yeah."

The streets were dark as Roger drove us away from the Rebel base camp and through the city, no fires or lanternlight. My eyes scanned each house, each shop, each stable, but there was no life in any of the buildings. It appeared the entire city had fled.

Even the healers.

"Where is the nearest city?" I asked Roger.

"Minadok I believe, Your Majesty."

"Oh, I'll be all right," Zeke tried to say evenly. But that proved too much for him, making him cough and groan.

"Roger, take us to Minadok. As quickly as possible." I looked down at Zeke and stroked his clammy forehead with my fingertips. "And you. Don't talk anymore. Put all of your energy into staying alive for me, okay?"

"His color is horrible," Gryffin said quietly. He'd been distant ever since we left the smithy, staring out into the city, eyes unfocused. Now, as we exited Mareus and ventured into the salt marshes, he looked over his shoulder at us, brow creased.

He wasn't wrong. Zeke's skin was so pallid in the moonlight, almost green. That, as well as the blood still seeping from his wound, made ice run through my veins. Every bump we hit on the marsh road made him suck in a breath of pain. Before we even reached the border of Lecevonia, he was slipping in and out of consciousness.

I allowed this to happen. *Me.* I should have given Gryffin the relics like he'd asked and been done with it all. If Zeke died, my world would lose its light.

That kind of grief was too great for tears.

Gryffin sat silently facing out of the back of the wagon. A tendril of smoke could still be seen in the distance rising from Mareus, a dark smear through the stars.

"How's your head?" I asked him.

"Half there. As if a piece of my mind has been torn away, leaving a jagged edge that still throbs." He turned toward me just slightly, blue eyes glinting. "I feel no trace of my Talent."

*That's not such a bad thing.* "I'm sorry."

"I don't understand how this happened." He turned away from me and looked down at his hands. "I did everything King Malus had said. The relics, Solstice Day . . ."

My question was this: how did Amicka know that this would happen instead of an Awakening?

The wagon jostled over loose gravel, and Zeke moaned quietly. He was getting worse as each minute passed.

I let my head fall into my hands. "This is my fault."

After a moment of painful silence, Gryffin said, "The relics have a powerful hold over whoever possesses them. I know. I've felt it. And you had *four* of them." He shook his head. "The voices must have been driving you mad."

He knew about the voices. Experienced them even. I didn't feel quite as alone.

"The relics convince you to do things you would never have considered before," he continued, his voice quiet. "Don't feel guilty."

I'd taught myself so resolutely to never believe a thing he said. But in this moment, I wanted to believe him. And if it was true, if he was truly Talentless, I had no reason to dismiss his words of comfort.

But simply hearing someone say I wasn't guilty did not take the guilt away. Zeke was still dying, and Amicka was still the most powerful person on the Peninsula.

I turned my gaze again to Gryffin. "Who is Amicka to say we no longer rule our kingdoms?"

His expression darkened as a cloud drifted over the moon. "She is a mage, Rosemary. She can say what she wants and make it true. And I assure you, we don't want to see the consequences of disobedience." The next time he turned to look at me, his eyes held so much hopelessness. As if the absence of the red flecks had left room only for misery. Gryffin, the most determined man I'd ever met, even when that determination stemmed from questionable reasons, had lost that fire. "What are we going to do?"

I didn't miss the "we" he used, and I didn't miss the acceptance in my heart when he used it. We suffered the same consequences of this mess. We were both dethroned sovereigns, made weak by Amicka and our own desires for strength.

What would I do without Lecevonia? What purpose would I have, if not to rule and provide? I looked up at the stars. "I don't know."

I did know, however, that I wasn't going to let Amicka hurt a single Lecevonian. I'd failed. I hadn't been the strong leader my kingdom needed, and I'd given my mind away to the relics. But no matter Amicka's power, if I was still standing, so would my people. For in my mind, they were still mine to protect. I would prove to them that I could still be the ruler they deserved.

I felt a soft touch on my hand, and when I looked down, Zeke's eyes were open, staring straight at me. They held an emotion I'd never seen in his eyes before. Fear. Fear of dying, fear of losing. "Rose." His voice was raspy and weak.

I smoothed the hair away from his forehead. "Stay alive," I said softly. "Like you told me to do in Tarasyn. Now it's your turn."

I wasn't losing anything else today.

# Part Two

# CHAPTER FOURTEEN



*~TWO MONTHS LATER~*

"WHY ARE THERE only ninety-two bushels of wheat?"

I crossed my arms over my chest. "Ninety-two is what we could harvest in time before your pickup."

"You're eight bushels short." The man looked up from his parchment and shook his head, his brow beading with sweat. "The Sorceress won't be happy." His gaze was almost sympathetic. Shocking for a Rebel.

"I will handle her if she's that troubled," I told him.

He nodded once, probably just happy to be out of the line of fire of "the Sorceress", and hopped onto the back of the wagon, carrying away to Loche what would have made a feast of pandemain for my people.

The moment the wagon disappeared behind the bend in the road, I huffed out a sigh and relaxed my arms, letting them fall to my sides. I turned to face Lord Brock. "Well, that went as well as we could have hoped."

He nodded, but then he looked across the bare fields. He'd rolled his sleeves up in this heat, the last heat wave of the summer. "I'm not sure how much more of this the kingdom can take."

My former advisor was right. The past two months had been brutal, to say the least. Amicka had been making extreme demands from the beginning, wiping out not just Lecevonia's supply of goods, but Somora's and Hiddon's as well. She and her clan of Rebels in Loche were not above gluttony. Thankfully, Equos had been able to keep up thus far. We certainly didn't want the same fate as the village in Hiddon who'd felt Amicka's wrath through lightning bolts.

I hadn't heard from Gryffin since he'd left Minadok to see how Tarasyn was doing, but I imagined they weren't faring the best, either.

"At least we've survived another pickup," I said, tying my small sack of grain around my waist. I saved a little from each bushel, my small act of defiance. I wasn't going to let them take *everything*. I had a kingdom to feed, even if that kingdom was no longer recognized by Amicka and the Rebels of the Red Sun. The next pickup would be in two weeks. We would find some way to survive that one, too. I patted the sack of grain at my side. "I'm going to go deliver this to the kitchens. Take the rest of the day for you and your family, Lord Brock. It's too hot to be out here in the fields."

He bowed his head. "Yes, Your Majesty."

I had given up on reminding him that I wasn't technically "His Majesty" anymore.

The kitchens of Hillstone looked different these days. The fires still burned in the ovens, and the kitchen workers were still a blur of motion. Only, Clara was helping Lucinda knead loaves of bread dough, and Isabele was holding a metal pan for her Henry as he doused roasted slices of meat with salt for storing. Lisette was probably down in the stables, mucking stalls or learning how to repair a wagon wheel. We all worked now. We all shared what provisions were available. No one was paid. We all simply survived.

Isabele looked well enough physically, but the excitement she'd adopted had gone out like a candle flame. She no longer smiled as much. She had that same glassy, unfocused look in her eyes as Gryffin had. The red flecks had disappeared, leaving her eyes the warm brown I had grown up seeing. But the sadness, that was new. And I didn't like it in her eyes.

I emptied out my sack into a grain barrel and, after securing the lid tightly and making sure the makeshift curtains hiding them from view of any inspecting Rebels were back in place, made my way down the hall to the infirmary.

The moment I opened the door, Zeke asked, "How'd the pickup go?"

I walked over to him and sat on the edge of his cot. "We live another day," I answered with a smirk.

The sight of him still here, on this earth with me, made my throat tight each time I opened that infirmary door. The healers in Minadok had said we'd gotten there with no time to spare. The spear wound to the stomach had hit his intestines, and he'd begun to go what they called "septic." I was certain that one of the healers there had been Talented before the Silencing, as we now called what had happened in Mareus—for a ring in the air we hadn't realized was there had stopped, leaving things much quieter than we were used to. The healer's skill with caring for Zeke had still been phenomenal. He'd known exactly what would stop the sepsis, a type of mold of all things, and that bought Zeke enough time to mend before continuing on our way to the healers at Hillstone. I hoped to recruit him to the castle if this mess of an existence ever improved.

After a series of infections with his sutures and a bout of pneumonia, Zeke was still sequestered to the infirmary for now, two months later.

I cradled his cheek with my hand. "How are you feeling?"

"Right as rain."

He said that every time I asked. But I could tell something was different. He seemed weaker. Not only physically, which made sense from all the bed rest, but mentally as well. His smiles were not as bright, smirks not as teasing. It was as if he were half there.

I remembered what Isabele had said about Zeke's strong Talent that had yet to manifest, and I couldn't help but wonder if he was feeling the effects of the Silencing too.

I gave him a soft kiss on his forehead. When I started to pull away, he caught the side of my face with his hand and brought my lips to his.

At least that part of him, his love for me, was just as fervent as ever.

When we parted, I couldn't help but smile ear to ear.

One of the castle's healers, Merieda, walked in then, arms full of linens and tincture bottles clasped between her fingers. I rushed over to help her, taking the linens out of her arms so she could focus on the tinctures. "Has he been behaving himself?"

"Not even a little, Your Majesty," she said, shooting a teasing glare in Zeke's direction as she set the tinctures down on the wooden counter. "As always. The day this patient is out of my infirmary will be a day for celebration."

"I'm not that bad of a patient!" Zeke protested.

Merieda only answered with a roll of her eyes.

"You don't have to call me 'Your Majesty' now, Merieda," I said quietly. "I'm not your queen anymore."

Merieda studied me briefly before shaking her head. "It'd be too strange. Besides, you will always be my queen." She turned away and began folding the linens, as if her statement hadn't meant everything to me.

"Speaking of getting out of this infirmary . . ." Zeke pouted his lip. "May I go?"

I spun around to look at Merieda. "Is today the day?"

Merieda turned her pursed lips into a smile. "Today is the day. If"—she pointed a stern finger at Zeke—"you come down here once a day for a while so that I can still keep an eye on you. I don't like that lingering cough."

"My word is yours, my lady," he said solemnly, bowing his head. Then, smiling at me, he swung his legs off the bed.

Merieda immediately scolded him. "Careful!"

He sighed and stood slowly. He wrapped me in his arms and buried his nose into my hair. I closed my eyes and breathed him in. Despite his extended stay in the infirmary, his smell of sage and leather remained.

We didn't have to hide our feelings for one another anymore. There was no title to protect, no duty to uphold. This was another, larger act of defiance against Amicka. *See?* I wanted to shout at her across the Peninsula. *You can't take away all of my happiness.*

When he released me, he smiled and took my hand. "Where to, Rose?"

I turned back to Merieda, who had returned to organizing her bottles of tinctures. "Is horseback riding still out of the question?"

"Most definitely."

Zeke sighed. "Shame. Hugo probably feels abandoned like some common mule."

"Hugo has been well taken care of," I said, patting his hand. We'd had to claim both Hugo and Midas as essential to our crew of workhorses, though truly they spent most of their time out to pasture.

It was the only way we'd kept the Rebels from taking them when Amicka sent her sycophants trooping into our stables. "We can still go see him, though."

He smiled. "Perfect."

We took our time making our way down to the stables. It was still before lunch, so the kitchens didn't need any extra hands. The craftsmen's village in the distance was quiet. A midmorning lull, everyone recovering from another two weeks of backbreaking work, harvesting and preparing for a pickup.

We found Celeste and Lisette working together in the tack room, cleaning the plowing harnesses. I peeked in through the slightly ajar door, and they both looked up. "I brought a visitor with me today." Zeke poked his head in above mine.

Lisette smiled ear to ear and put down the harness she'd been scrubbing. "Zeke! You're out of bed!"

Celeste stood and punched Zeke—very softly—in the shoulder. "The healers finally released you, did they?" She smiled. "Now you can do your fair share of work like the rest of us."

"Do you need help in here?" I asked.

"No need. We're almost done. Go enjoy Zeke's first day of freedom." Celeste winked at me. "I know there are things you need to do."

I immediately regretted telling Celeste of my plan. Though excitement coursed through me, my chest was gripped with nervousness. It was that very tightness that had kept me from asking him for so long . . . Though surely I had no reason to be anxious. Right?

"Okay, then." I hoped to Haggard that the tremor in my voice wasn't noticeable.

Hugo and Midas were indeed still out to pasture, in the eastern fields. It was sweet when Hugo recognized Zeke. He came trotting right up to him at the fence line, nuzzling his hands, no doubt looking for a treat of some sort to explain why Zeke had been away for so long.

"I know. I'm sorry, my friend," Zeke said, patting Hugo's dappled neck. "I've missed you too."

"I've been riding him in the meantime," I said, absentmindedly picking loose grass out of Midas's mane. "When Midas wasn't feeling too jealous, that is." I ran my hand over Midas's flank as he sauntered off, Hugo soon following behind.

"Ridden by the best rider in the kingdom?" Zeke laughed. "I'm sure Hugo was thrilled."

We followed the horses a ways, but Zeke's labored breathing didn't escape my notice. I imagined the hills weren't an easy trek for him, particularly in this late summer heat. Then when he started to cough, I took his hand, leading him back to the fence line, and sat down in the browning grass. He leaned against a fencepost, trying to control his breath.

"Boars." He angrily uprooted clumps of grass at his feet. "I can't even manage a simple walk anymore."

"Give yourself time," I said gently. "You're still healing."

"That's all I've been doing for two months now."

"You haven't had a choice." I laid my head on his shoulder. "Besides, I enjoy getting to take a break with you." As much as I felt like I needed to get back to some task, I got to sit here in this meadow with Zeke, and *only* him. Gratitude swelled within me for the opportunity. "When was the last time we were truly alone?" I asked.

He chuckled and kissed my hair. "Much too long ago. Before we'd left for Hiddon all those months ago, I believe."

I remembered that day very well. Our morning in the woods, dreaming of cottages while our hands and lips ventured to places they'd never gone before. My pulse quickened.

It was much too hot out here to be thinking of such things.

Zeke took my hand in his and rested it in his lap. "Just think, no healers will be traipsing in on us out here."

"And no former royal advisors coming to find me for some reason or another," I added wistfully.

"You know they still respect you as their queen, don't you? That does not simply go away because some almighty mage said otherwise."

"I know," I said, looking down at my feet. And I was glad for it. But until circumstances changed, I was not going to endanger my people and challenge Amicka's words. No one wanted to feel the wrath of the Sorceress. It was always too high a price. Uncle Merek had found that out the hard way. All it took was a scoff against her and a Somoran ship sailing without her permission, and she took his sons and grandchildren away from him, whisking them off to Loche for us to only hope they were still alive . . . Yes, that was much too high a price.

Zeke played with my fingers in his hand, bringing me back to this moment. Here and now. I should ask him, I told myself. If not now, when? I focused in on the feeling of his fingertips leaving trails of warmth all the way down to my wrist.

"Do you want to tell me why you're so nervous?"

I gasped, and my face burned from more than just the sun. "You weren't supposed to notice."

"What? The shaking in your voice or your clammy palms?" He let out a deep laugh and tucked my loose hair behind my ear. "Observation is part of what I do. And it's you, Rose." He smiled my favorite half-smile. "I've been studying you my whole life, and I'll gladly continue to do so, any chance I get."

His words knocked the air from my lungs. Why was he so much better at this than me?

"You can tell me what you need to tell me," he said softly. He put his thumb under my chin and lifted my gaze to his. "It's just me."

I struggled to look directly at him. I knew my face was red as raspberries. "Well, it's really more of a question."

His brown eyes glinted. "Ask away, then."

I'd been thinking about this for some time. Ever since Mareus, and especially ever since I'd been given hope in Minadok that Zeke would live. If I was certain of anything in my life, I was certain that I wanted this. I wanted this so badly. I just hoped Zeke still wanted the same.

"Marry me?"

It took Zeke a moment to register my words. When he did, his eyes widened, and I felt his hand on my face stiffen. "You—you're asking me to marry you?"

"Well, I'm not formally the queen anymore." That had been the problem, hadn't it? My duties as the Crowned to marry for advantage of the kingdom. Now that was no longer a concern, and Zeke wouldn't have to be the king-consort. Two victories.

His silence sent my insides in turmoil. For just a split second, I doubted my confidence in his desires. But—no. I knew he wanted this too. Right? Why wasn't he answering me?

"Zeke." My voice was only a whisper. "I need you to say something."

"You're asking *me* to marry *you*," he said, slowly letting his hand fall from my face. Then, he reached inside his vest pocket. "For the record," he said. "You asked me first this time." When he extracted his hand, it held a piece of white linen cloth. He began to unfold it, but I was already smiling.

Inside the cloth was a gold band, fitted with a cluster of rubies in the center and small golden leaves carved along the sides. A rose.

"I had Celeste run a few errands for me while I was stuck in the infirmary," he said with a wink. "Turns out the goldsmith was happy to have something to work on other than Amicka's demands." He took my hand in his and slid the ring onto my finger. "Of course I'll marry you." Then he slid his hand into my hair at the base of my neck, and he kissed me.

My heart stopped its nervous patter and melted at his touch. I would never grow tired of this sense of home Zeke brought to me. This sense of familiarity. Of everything suddenly fitting together. Nothing was perfect in this world, but being with Zeke felt as close to perfect as it could be.

Like a dam bursting, my heart was flooded with that special kind of ache reserved only for immense joy.

He kissed me again, this time falling into something deeper. He pulled me into his lap and held me there, his hands squeezing my hips. I let my lips part, and I breathed him in, his love for me, his everlasting devotion. I hoped he knew that he had the same from me. I wrapped my arms around his neck and melded myself to him, breaking our kiss only to breathe.

As he trailed small kisses along my jaw, I said, "I'm keeping the ring, even though I asked first."

I felt his warm breath against the skin of my neck as he laughed. He lifted my hand, watching the ring shine in the sunlight. "I beg you, keep it. Never take it off."

I watched it too, glinting back and forth.

Another ring came to my mind. An emerald. A ring that had felt like a shackle. A ring now worn around the giver's neck, for reasons I did not fully understand.

This ring felt so different. Already a part of me, though it'd only been on my finger for mere minutes. This ring felt like a reminder of home. Of warm fires and spice wine, sage and leather. I laid my head on Zeke's chest, grateful for the gentle rise and fall of his breaths. This was real. "I'll never take it off."

He rested his cheek on the top of my head. "Rose, I don't . . . I don't think you realize how long I have yearned for this moment. For a time when I was certain that you would spend the rest of your life with me." His short laugh sounded incredulous. "Years, Rose. Years of thinking this would be impossible. Years of knowing, *knowing*, that it was not my place to love you. Yet I did anyway. I couldn't help it." He lifted my hand and kissed it softly. "I tried not to love you. I tried to look elsewhere, to find what I felt for you in another woman or in my assignments. But each and every time I saw you again, your smile and that brilliance in your green eyes . . . I realized I hadn't replaced any feeling. Only stifled it, for a little while. When you were troubled, I only wanted to erase your pout and the creases of worry from your face."

I poked him in the chest. "You put them there more often than not." But through my teasing remark, my heart was fluttering.

He lowered his head and murmured into my ear. "Like I've said before, I'm honored that you worry about me so much." Goosebumps ran down my arms at his words.

"I did worry," I said. "I worried so much, and I thought it was simply because you were my friend. But you've always been so much more than that." I turned my face up to look at him. "Zeke, I didn't know why my heart skipped when you'd flash that little smirk at me, or why I felt such relief every time you returned home after an assignment. I had built a barrier so carefully around any complicated feelings I might have had for you." I stroked his hand softly. "But you were always my safe place. My light. The moment you made me realize my feelings for you with that first kiss . . . I have been permanently changed."

He drank in my words as if they were the finest wine throughout the Peninsula.

I lifted my eyes to him again, feeling bold. "And now we have this freedom we've never had before. This possibility of being just Rose and Zeke. Not Queen Rosemary Avelia and Ezekiel Celar, King-Consort." I shot a smug glance in the direction of Loche. Take that, Amicka.

He crinkled his nose. "I think 'Rose and Zeke' works just fine."

I smiled at him, but a part of me still felt a sting at his words. Would Zeke have agreed if I'd still been queen? Why did that part of me have to change?

But Zeke's lips coaxing my mind elsewhere made me forget why I felt disappointed at all.

We returned to the stables hand in hand. Celeste was of course the first to find us, and she reached for my hand with a smile. "Is it a perfect fit?"

I looked at her with narrowed eyes. "I can't believe you were able to keep this from me. You, who couldn't keep your lips sealed when I'd told you I had spilled ink all over Isabele's favorite dress, or when I'd lost that goose feather pen Zeke had given me."

"You know, I still don't know if I've forgiven you for that," Zeke said, pursing his lips. "My poor goose Harold deserved better. I plucked that feather and gave it to you as a heartfelt gift."

"I didn't tell Ezekiel of your plans, either," Celeste said to me matter-of-factly.

I was in too good of a mood to argue otherwise. With Zeke's hand in mine, everything around me seemed to be coated in the soft tint of a rose.

Someone called from the stable door. "Your Majesty!" It was a young soldier, jogging toward us with a folded parchment in his hand.

"You don't have to call me 'Your Majesty' anymore," I reminded him. But I took the letter from him, and he bowed before taking his leave.

The Tarasynian seal emblazoned in the wax made me pause. My name was written in Gryffin's familiar perfect script.

Seeing my name in his pen still caused a chill to race through me. But rather than a chill of fear, it was of anticipation, which was the last thing I expected. Maybe it was curiosity, or maybe it was concern for Kathryn. I couldn't place it.

Shaking my head, I released Zeke's hand and tore open the letter. After reading the first few lines, my heart fell to my feet.

"Send word for a council gathering," I told Zeke quietly. "Tarasyn needs aid."

# CHAPTER FIFTEEN

WE FORMED THE council when I'd returned from Loche. Without a definitive ruler, there still needed to be some structure in place to delegate aid and workload throughout Lecevonia. It consisted of my former royal advisors, Isabele, Lisette, Jacobin, myself, and now Zeke. I was considered the head of the council. If that made me somewhat of a queen, well, I wasn't going to argue otherwise.

We met in Hillstone's council room. Sometimes it seemed as though things were the same as they'd always been, though in reality, nothing was the same. I was no longer queen, my sisters no longer princesses, advisors no longer lords. Lecevonia's borders were mere lines on an old map, and its land was bare of our agriculture, the rolling hills brown from lack of rain.

Nothing was the same.

I placed Gryffin's letter on the table for the others to read. "He says the people of Tarasyn are cold and starving. Without Dothymus's Talent of controlling the weather, or Viridi's power coursing through the forests, the entire kingdom is starting to freeze over. Their greenhouses can't keep up. Some villages have already seen sweeping deaths."

My words hung heavily in the room. Which was less harrowing? Death by fire, or death by ice?

Lord Castor put down the letter and crossed his arms over his chest. "I see no reason to do anything. He's done despicable things. I struggle to understand what he even thought he'd achieve by asking us for help."

Lord Quince nodded along. "He's got some nerve, that man."

"He thought he'd achieve giving his people a chance at survival," I answered Lord Castor. When your people were dying, you needed to have nerve.

"Even if he is a monster, he probably feels like you are the only one that he can turn to for help," Isabele said thoughtfully.

Zeke scoffed. "With no right. He can send his people into Hiddon. They have food prancing around in the forests."

"Oh yes, decimate the wildlife with an influx of thousands of people," Lisette said with a roll of her eyes. "That is precisely what we should be doing at a time like this. Especially during this heat wave."

"Not to mention the strain of the people of Hiddon on Lord and Lady DeGrey," I said. Since the Silencing, the DeGreys had been playing a larger role in providing for their people. Since Gryffin was no longer a king, or Talented, they could dare to do more.

Though, as far as I could tell, Princess Lilyana was still kept under lock and key. Just in case Gryffin felt threatened, I presumed. Or worse, if Amicka did.

"Let Gryffin worry about Hiddon," Zeke said as he leaned forward. "They were supposed to be his subjects anyway."

"Where would they go in Hiddon?" I asked the table. "So many are still recovering from Roderich's rampage. Villages leveled, charred to nothing but cinders. We still have so many of Hiddon's own at our border and outside the gates of Equos. They haven't been able to return because there is nothing left of their villages to return to." Even Jerime, Renera, and Clementine, the family we'd been lifted into the air by in Hiddon, had joined the other refugees outside our city gates.

Zeke touched the back of my hand. "Rose, you can't take care of everybody."

I sighed. "I know."

"Gryffin and his brother are the reason why Hiddon is in shambles." He retracted his hand and leaned back in his chair. "If Gryffin can't find space for his Tarasynians there and provide for them, then it's on him."

Him. Us versus him. That was how it had felt ever since he'd taken me from my kingdom. But truly, there was no separation anymore. Gryffin wasn't a king. He was a powerless man who felt responsibility for people who had once been under his rule, people who had once relied on him and still did, despite everything that had happened. I felt the same for the people of Lecevonia. And he cared enough to reach out for assistance.

I slowly rose to my feet. "Lecevonia was once the strongest kingdom on the Peninsula. We still are." I looked at the group seated around the table. "I am not your queen anymore, so I cannot make any of you do anything. But I ask you this. Are we going to let innocent people starve and freeze to death? These people that have been tortured and lied to by their rulers for the past near-century?" I shook my head. "I don't think I could have that on my conscience."

"Nor I," said Isabele quietly. She stood with me at my left shoulder. "The people of Tarasyn are not the guilty ones."

Lisette stood as well. "I agree with my sisters."

Jacobin cleared his throat. "What of food an' work, Yer Majesty?

Takin' in another kingdom when we've already go' one under our wing won' be an easy thing."

Jacobin was still managing his shop and his family well, but he'd also taken in his nephew after Amos's death. *Murder,* I thought angrily. I needed to call it out for what it was. From what I gathered, Amos's son didn't have the skill for blacksmithing. Finding his place in all of this had been a challenge. Especially after losing his father . . . My heart ached for him.

"We can make an agreement that they will have to work too," I said. "More hands to help in the fields, more hands planting and tending and harvesting. Building things too, of course, to share your load as well as the other craftsmen's." Gryffin would certainly go for that. He was all about using every resource possible, no waste.

As for food, well, I hadn't been stowing away all that grain for nothing.

The men around the table stared at me. Then, Lord Brock pushed himself up. "I stand with you. We will find a way to support others, as we always have."

Lord Clark nodded. "Yes, we will." That prompted Lord Quince's agreement as well.

"Aye," Jacobin said. "More hands around here coul' be a help."

But Zeke gave me a stony-eyed stare. "This could be a mistake, Rose."

I looked back at him evenly. "Anything we do could be a mistake. Who are we to stop taking chances for the good of others just for fear of making a mistake?" I touched his hand softly. "I would not bring harm to my people. Surely you know that by now."

He pursed his lips, but eventually, he nodded in agreement. Lord Castor did as well.

"It's settled, then. I'll write to Gryffin to tell him his people may make encampments in our land, given they will work their fair load."

As we stood, Lisette cleared her throat. "Don't you have something to tell everyone?"

I saw Lord Brock's eyes immediately fall to my hand, where my ring from Zeke sat glistening in the low light. He smiled as he looked up at me. "Congratulations, my queen. It was only a matter of time, given the circumstances we are in now." Slowly, the rest of the men caught on, and smiled their congratulations. Jacobin clapped Zeke on the back.

Lord Brock's congratulations meant the most to me. He was the one who pushed the hardest to find a husband for me. And seeing how happy he was for me with this news made me consider that maybe he was after more than just Lecevonia's security.

As everyone left the council room, Zeke pulled me aside by the shoulder. "Rose. I know I've been absent from all of this, holed up in the infirmary, but—to have that crite back here?" He shuffled from foot to foot. "I don't like it."

"Gryffin has no power. He cannot harm me nor my people." I at least knew *this* with certainty.

Zeke grumbled. "I'll believe that when I see it." Then, he narrowed his eyes. "You noticed that ring he wore on a chain around his neck, didn't you? What's that about?"

I twisted my ring around my finger. "It was an engagement ring. I left it in my rooms when I left Snowmont. I don't know why he wears it."

"I think you do, Rose."

Of course I had thought about it. Who wouldn't? But Gryffin's actions did not exactly align with those of a swooning heart. Maybe he wore it as a reminder of what once was? An echo of feelings he thought he had?

"I'll believe it when I see it," I said, copying Zeke's tone as best I could, which garnered a serious eyeroll from Zeke.

He wrapped his arm around my waist and hugged me tightly to his side. "You know, Rose, I can't help it if I get a little jealous." He ducked his head and lowered his voice to a whisper in my ear. "Since I actually have grounds for jealousy now."

I pulled back just slightly, a grin playing at my lips. "Oh? What grounds are those?"

His arm tightened. "I can't have some tall dark brooding man mooning over my soon-to-be wife."

"You think he has a chance?" It was all I could do to keep my breath even. "Where is your usual confidence, Ezekiel?"

At that, Zeke sighed. "Lying at your feet, my Rose." He loosened his arm just enough to look at me squarely. His brown eyes sang of uncertainty. "Does he? Have a chance?"

I softened my gaze and brought my hand to his cheek, and I let my gentle kiss suffice as his answer.

Tarasynians began finding their way to Equos a mere week after I'd sent back our response. Many of my Lecevonians took pity on the frostbitten people and welcomed them into their homes. Though this heat wave bothered us, to the Tarasynians it seemed to be a blessing. I felt pride for my people, for their kind hearts. Mama and Papa would have been proud, too.

Kathryn was among the first to arrive, leading her people to safer conditions. I hadn't seen her since she'd left for Snowmont, before we had gone to Loche, and happiness swelled in my heart at the sight of her.

"Gryffin will be staying until the last Tarasynian willing to leave is ready to do so," she told me one night over a modest dinner of rolls and roasted hen. I sat to her right, and Celeste to her left, who was the happiest I'd seen her in a while. Kathryn's eyes turned uncertain, a look that seemed misplaced in her usual confident nature. "My brother isn't the same man, Rosemary. It's rather unnerving."

"What do you mean?" I asked.

"He's . . ." But she hesitated, wringing her hands. "Well, you'll see for yourself."

I took hold of her hands, gently stilling them. "To be honest, you don't seem quite like yourself either, Kathryn." Her blue eyes still shined, but there was a tiredness there. A lack of her normal exuberance. Much like Isabele.

She sighed and looked down. "I feel different. Incomplete, somehow. Ever since the world around me has been silenced." Then she nudged Celeste with her shoulder and smiled. "But I'm feeling a bit better, now that I'm here."

I couldn't help but wonder if she had an unmanifested Talent too, if Isabele would have seen an aura around her as brightly as she'd seen Zeke's.

The twin Danicio brothers, Michael and Laris, arrived with their families and another large group of Tarasynians just two days later. Equos's inns were bursting at the seams, and the gathering of tents outside of our gates stretched over the hills.

It was another week until Gryffin arrived in my courtyard with the last of the Tarasynians. He rode in on his white horse Lucy, the poor horse's saddlebags bulging, with a little girl sitting in front of him and accompanied by two wagons full of people. Some of them had blackened spots on their cheeks and noses. Even Gryffin himself looked sickly as he dismounted and landed on the ground unsteadily. Sallow cheeks, slumped shoulders. Skin paler than I was used to seeing. He grabbed hold of the little girl riding in his saddle and placed her gently onto the ground, and she ran to her mother, who gathered her into her arms.

"Quick, summon a healer," I said to Isabele. As she rushed away to the infirmary, Gryffin's eyes met mine, and my old wounds bristled as he made his way over to me through the courtyard. But his eyes, no longer flecked with red, looked at me earnestly. Openly. For a moment—just the briefest of an instant—I was brought back to his time here in Hillstone before all of this started. When I still believed Talents were only a legend. When I believed Gryffin had wanted me, not my kingdom.

"Rosemary," he said.

Then, in a surprising gesture that shook my core, he descended to one knee in front of me, head bowed. "Thank you for aiding Tarasyn. My people would have died if you hadn't answered."

Funny, how just a few months ago, I was ready to go to war against him and his kingdom. Now, I sheltered them.

I grasped his elbow. "Please, stand. I'm simply helping people in need."

He rose to his feet, and as he did I saw the emerald ring on its chain quickly flash before disappearing beneath his tunic again. Heat rushed to my cheeks. Turning away from him, I gestured toward the wagons. "This is the last of them?"

"Yes. From Borea. Needless to say, they have been traveling for far too long."

"All the way from Borea?" I asked, eyes wide.

He nodded. "The pass froze before anyone could even consider escaping into the West Lands. Traveling south was their only option for survival."

"Well, our healers will tend to them and give them the care they need," I said, my promise strong in my voice.

"They certainly fixed me up, didn't they, Rose?"

I turned, and Zeke was there. He'd regained some of his strength in the past two weeks, and here, compared to Gryffin, Zeke looked like he could run miles around him.

Zeke threw his arm over my shoulder and glared at Gryffin. "Crite."

Gryffin's mouth settled into a hard line, eyes narrowed. "Guard dog."

Gryffin reached his hand up to my forehead, and I felt Zeke stiffen. "Your scar is fading."

I hadn't thought about my scar in a while, in all honesty. But Zeke's next words were acidic. "You mean the one *you* put there?"

Gryffin retracted his hand and held them up in surrender. "I apologized for that."

Zeke snarled and dropped his arm. "I could smack you again just as I did in the inn in Mareus. Let me tell you, it was truly satisfying."

"I won't take two hits from you," Gryffin said, his voice thick with warning.

"Why don't we demonstrate our sword fights again? We'd give Rose a real show now, wouldn't we?"

I stepped between the two men. Facing Zeke, I eyed him pointedly. *Play nice.* There was no need having these two testing whose sword was sharper.

Gryffin's eyes flashed before turning away from us and walking back to the wagons. "You'll be taken care of here," I heard him say. "Healers will tend to your frostbite and you will be given food and shelter, in exchange for working hands."

A mumble flowed through the people, and as they all disembarked, a man spit at Gryffin's feet.

I expected Gryffin to do something. Say something, exude some show of authority over the man.

Instead, he turned his gaze toward the ground. He murmured something to the wagon driver, then stepped back as the wagon slowly rolled away.

What was that about? I'd never seen him take that sort of treatment. Not that he didn't deserve it, but . . .

He scratched the back of his head, then, taking hold of Lucy's reins, turned back to me. "Is there a stall open for old Lucy here?"

"Yes, of course. You can take her down to the Royal Stables."

He patted the bursting saddlebags. "Most of this will be going to your library."

"Oh," I said. "Zeke can take—"

"No that's quite all right," Gryffin said, holding a hand up. "I'll take it there myself. I spent enough time there to remember." His gaze met mine. "Will you meet me there when you have a chance?"

"*We* will," Zeke answered over my shoulder.

I shot daggers at him. Since when did he speak for me? I turned back to Gryffin and said, "Yes, I'll meet you there."

With a final nod and tight smile, Gryffin turned away and led his horse down the path leading to the stables.

I turned my wrath onto Zeke. "What are you doing?"

He gave me an innocent simper. "What?"

"You were being exceedingly rude."

"Doesn't he deserve it?"

I sighed and turned my attention to the Tarasynian people filing into Hillstone. They'd been through enough. We all had.

Later, while Zeke took a shift in the fields, I took the moment to talk to Gryffin on my own. Before opening the door of the library, I took a steadying breath. He's just a man, I reminded myself. He'd had his chance to kill me in Mareus, and he hadn't taken it. I was among my own people.

And I had my sword strapped to my waist.

I pushed open the door.

Gryffin was already there, arranging scrolls and stacks of books onto one of the new cedar tables built by the castle's carpenters, one of the many pieces of furniture needed after the fire. The cedar's fragrance combated the lingering smell of smoke that seemed to have decided to forever embed itself in the stone walls and the few surviving books. Gryffin looked up at me as I entered.

"Rosemary." He slowly walked toward me, palms facing upward toward the ceiling. He stopped a few feet away, but close enough for me to see that his sapphire eyes bled remorse. "I'm so sorry that my brother did this." So, he'd taken in everything. The ashes that were impossible to clean from the corners of the room, the blackened edges of what few books and scrolls were spared. "I wish I'd been able to stop him before he inflicted so much irreparable damage."

"Yes, well, I wish that we could have stopped him, too. I wish that we would have stopped many things." I rested my hand on one of the bookshelves. The cedar and smoke together smelled of autumn. "But we're rebuilding, and I think that this is just a small taste of what Lecevonia is capable of."

"That is because they have you as their queen."

"They had my mother and father first."

"But they have you now."

I was rattled by his words. I didn't know what to think. He spoke so sincerely, yet . . . I'd conditioned myself to not believe a word he said. But he couldn't trick me now. Not without his Talent. *Was* he being sincere now? "Thank you," I finally said. "I care for my people more than you could know."

He gave me a gentle smile. Taking a seat at the table, he smoothed his hands over a book. "I care for my people too, I hope you know that. That was why I asked for your help. You have my utmost gratitude, Rosemary." He looked up at me, gaze burning. "Truly."

With his sapphire eyes no longer flecked with red, it was easy to fall back into a strangely familiar feeling I'd had with him before all of this. An open-ended curiosity. I took a seat opposite him. "It's a great thing you did, staying behind for the last of your people." It was something I would have done. "I was surprised when Kathryn told me you'd done so."

"Surprised?"

"You've never seemed like the 'put yourself in danger for the lesser' type."

He winced. "Ouch."

I admittedly took a bit of joy in the sting he felt, but I still explained myself further. "What I mean is, you felt the very last of your people was worth risking your own life to hunger and frost. You, who sees no value in wasting."

"Perhaps I feel like my life isn't worth much anymore."

Without thought, I reached for his hand. "Gryffin."

In that moment, I was glad that Zeke was not here. He without a doubt would have said or done something very unhelpful.

"My people hate me, Rosemary." He shook his head. "Without my Talent, they see how much I covered up for my brother. They see how much I lied to them. Any respect they had for me, as a king or as a man, has been obliterated. For good reason. I hardly have respect for *myself* after what I've done." His hand twitched under mine. "All for what? Unrequited care for my brother? A botched Awakening?"

The flame of a candle flickered off the ring hanging from his neck, making my chest tighten. I retracted my hand. "You led your people to safety. You reached out for help. You didn't let pride stop you. That is worth so much."

He let out a humorless chuckle. "It was never about pride." Then, he leaned back in his chair and looked out the open shutters at the fading light. "The people of Tarasyn only followed my instruction to come here because it was either this or die in a kingdom I can no longer protect. The very land back home is claiming that life is impossible. Had that not been the case, they would have stayed. For Haggard's sake, they would have killed me if I hadn't given them a way to live. They may just kill me yet." His voice had reduced to such a low volume I found myself leaning forward.

More than I cared to, I felt his words deeply. I often felt as though I couldn't protect Lecevonia anymore either, despite all my efforts. In fact, Gryffin was the only one here who could truly understand how that made me feel. Sovereign to sovereign, we shared a sense of duty that hadn't died just because the title was taken away.

But at least my people didn't hate my guts. That made his sense of duty even more stubborn than mine.

He gestured toward the books and scrolls in front of him. "I hope to make up for my wrongdoings, in what way I can."

I came around the table to stand behind his chair, and I felt his eyes following me as I did. Looking at the feast of information laid out, I saw familiar drawings—the relics, and I wanted to curl in on myself. Either in fear or shame, I did not know. Maybe both. These objects had brought nothing but devastation. "Why are you still looking at all this?"

"Something Yetta had said . . ." I couldn't be sure, but I thought his voice cracked at the mention of his grandmother. "Remember when I told you I'd gone to visit her at her cottage? It was right after you left

Tarasyn. I hadn't known if I'd wanted to kill her or thank her for helping you." He let out a single dark, saddened laugh. "Shameful. Anyhow, she told me she wouldn't trust Amicka. That people like her always knew more than they let on. Amicka's father, for example."

"Yetta knew Amicka's father?" I didn't even try to hide my shock.

Gryffin nodded. "He'd worked with my grandfather, then my father for a short time, before Atroxis took him in his old age. Yetta told me his mind was angry, like Roderich's, but calculating, like mine. I wasn't sure if that was a compliment or not," he added with a tight smile. "She told me he would always say one thing, then think another. And that if his daughter was anything like him, I should tread carefully."

"Your grandfather, and your father . . . The Rebels have been involved that long?"

"Longer." He picked up a scroll and pointed to the date inscribed at the top. "See? This was written by King Malus. This is the oldest document I have that speaks of the relics, and he mentioned in here that he had aid given to him by 'the Red Sun.' He had to have meant the Rebels, yes? Though their numbers would have been far fewer at that time. Maybe even only one, the one called the Red Sun himself." Gryffin quieted, deep in thought.

I hadn't even known the "Red Sun" was a person. Once again, Gryffin made me feel naïve. Quick with a desire to fix that feeling, I pushed on. "So you're studying these books to see if anyone had laid out specifics of what they expected to happen during the Awakening."

He nodded, his eyes scanning over all the books in front of him. "I *know* something went wrong. What happened with Amicka, absorbing all the power . . . That wasn't supposed to happen. It may have been what all those before me who had written these books were after, but that's not what I had planned." He shook his head, as if willing away the wickedness that was trying to pry its way into the space around us.

"I just need to figure out what made that happen, and then we can go from there."

"Go from there?" I looked at him in surprise. "You mean . . . this might be fixable?"

He pursed his lips. "Maybe. I hope so."

Oh Haggard, I did too. It felt almost unbelievable, yet I found myself tentatively asking, "And how do you suppose we do that?"

Gryffin let out a deep exhale and folded his hands in front of him. "Well, King Malus had figured that bringing them together would harness enough power for an Awakening. He didn't know what would *happen* during the Awakening, exactly. I'm still looking for any insight from the notes of others in the past who studied this. But." He held up a finger and gestured between me and him. " *We* now know all that power had the tendency to collect inward, rather than spread outward. If we could theorize a way to make the latter happen instead . . ."

"We would reverse the effects of Amicka!" Did I dare to feel this optimistic? "Gryffin, whatever it takes. We have to try anything."

"I agree, but we only get one chance," he said darkly. "Amicka is the single strongest being on the entire Peninsula. Whatever we try, we have to be as certain as we can be that it will work. She will kill us before we can try a second time." He scoffed. "If we even get that far."

I crossed my arms over my chest. "You aren't supposed to be the negative one. That's Zeke's job."

At Zeke's name, Gryffin's eyes tightened. "Are we going to talk about your guard dog, or are we going to get to work?"

I heard it, then. The jealousy in his voice.

I hadn't noticed how close we'd grown during our conversation, a gravitational pull that neither of us had resisted. I leaned over him slightly, and he looked back at me with utter verity in his eyes. As I drew away just a hair, I noticed the nagging familiarity I felt with him.

Back here in Hillstone, no longer afraid of him, I could not forget how I'd first felt around him. Important. Seen for my strength that I had struggled to feel at the time. Understood even now, willing to do anything for our people. Our sense of duty had tied us together back then, and it still did, as I was realizing in this moment.

But thanks to Amicka, it had become my personal mission to kick that sense of duty into a ditch when it came to whom I could love.

Though Gryffin's sapphire eyes threatened to set me ablaze as they once had, I craved the gentle warmth of my browns instead.

"My *guard dog* should be finishing his harvesting shift soon," I said, tossing my hair over my shoulder as I turned away from him. "I'm going to tell him what's going on."

At that, Gryffin grumbled his disapproval and turned back to the papers in front of him. "As you wish."

"Your shift starts tomorrow," I called out. "No one stays here for free these days."

I felt his eyes trailing me as I walked through the library doors.

# CHAPTER SIXTEEN

I WENT DOWN to Zeke's rooms, in a hurry to get out of Gryffin's breadth. The impact he had on me made me uncomfortable, like I had cotton in my brain. Was it some residual effect from his Talent, even though he no longer possessed it?

I rapped my knuckles against Zeke's door, head still foggy, and he opened it just as I began to knock a second time. He was wearing a soft cotton tunic and leather trousers, feet bare, hair damp from his recent bath.

The sight of him stole my breath from my lungs.

Before I even fully thought about what I was doing, I flung my arms around him and crushed my lips to his.

He made a little noise of surprise, but he quickly recovered and gathered me into his arms. He kicked his door closed with his foot and carried me further into his rooms. I almost protested, as he was still healing, but I refused to let this moment escape.

We dropped into a chair near the dark fireplace. My hands curled into his hair while his roved over my dress, sliding down my waist and settling into a grip on my hips so hungry my breath hitched. I held him close to me as his lips left a trail of fire along the side of my neck. Over my collarbone. Slowly back upward to my jaw. Fresh from his bath, he smelled like sage and summer rain.

"You are my Rose," he murmured into my ear.

I nodded breathlessly and brought his mouth to mine again, holding his face in my hands. He'd shaved off his stubble, leaving his skin smooth beneath my touch. I felt his fingers on my hips twitch as they fought the urge to slide lower.

The heat between us was building dangerously, beautifully, and I knew one of us had to decide where our boundary lay.

That turned out to be Zeke. Ever the gentleman, I thought ruefully, as he loosened his grip on my hips. But as disappointed as I was, I silently thanked him. I couldn't handle any more fire without completely melting.

Our kiss sank into a deeper, calmer rhythm. Zeke slowly wound his arms around my waist, and I softened my grip on his face, my palm settling into a gentle caress on his strong jaw.

When we parted, I felt Zeke's grin against my cheek. "I wouldn't be opposed to you greeting me like that every time we see one another. In fact, it'd be most welcome." He nibbled my ear lobe, which did nothing to help calm the hammering of my heart in my chest.

I laughed softly, still fighting to gain my breath, and repositioned myself into a more comfortable seat in his lap, my back against his chest. "I'll consider it if you behave yourself."

His warm brown eyes danced as he leaned forward and whispered into my ear. "You know I can't promise that."

His skin was cool against mine, a much-needed contrast to the heat that had bloomed deep in my abdomen.

Why had I rushed down here in the first place?

Oh. Right.

I sighed and straightened up, responsibility sneaking its way back into place. "I have something to tell you. Gryffin has been doing more research."

Zeke immediately stiffened at Gryffin's name, and his arms tightened around me. "Is he now." Spoken as a statement. A very irritated statement. "You met with him, then?"

"I did," I said, pretending I didn't hear the annoyance in his voice. I rotated around to face him. "He's trying to figure out why the Awakening happened the way that it did, and if there is any way to undo it."

The angry crease in Zeke's brow disappeared, and his eyes widened. "Undo it? That might be possible?"

"Maybe. I hope so." My fingers, which had been playing with the strings at the neck of his tunic, froze as I realized that same phrase had come out of Gryffin's mouth just moments ago in the library.

Thankfully, Zeke didn't seem to notice my unease. "Great Haggard, me too," he said, staring into the empty fireplace. It hadn't been lit all summer. Even now, deep into August when autumn would normally first stretch out its fingers with crisp air, this unrelenting heat wave kept any hint of relief stifled. "I have to give it to the crite. If anyone could figure out how to beat Amicka, it'd be him." Then Zeke sneered. "Of course he would want it reversed. He'd get his Talent back and can continue bending people's minds to his satisfaction."

I gave Zeke a small kiss on his cheek and disentangled myself from him, setting my feet on the floor. "Believe it or not, he's too remorseful to act out of selfishness. I'm going to help him."

Zeke scoffed. "No, I don't believe it, and yes, of course you're going to help him." He pushed himself to his feet and stood beside me. "I am too."

We spent days poring over the books that Gryffin had brought with him, between working shifts in the fields and kitchens. Gryffin surprised me with the work he was willing to put in—he'd taken off his ornate velvet vest, rolled up the sleeves of his tunic, and loaded sheaves of wheat onto the waiting wagons as if he'd done it all his life. With the extra hands provided by him and his Tarasynians, we'd been able to meet our quota for Amicka and the Rebels that week.

I didn't like the prowling Rebels she'd sent along with the pickup this time, but as far as she knew, we had nothing to hide. Still, I'd promptly told them to shove off.

Our wheat fields across Lecevonia were almost through. When the harvest was over, what would she ask for then?

I didn't want to give her the chance.

"My eyes are crossing from staring at these words," Zeke grumbled. He pushed the book away and rubbed his eyes.

Gryffin smirked from his corner of the table. "Didn't read much as a child?"

"Of course I read as a child," Zeke shot back, crossing his arms over his chest. "Just not for hours on end."

Gryffin said, "Pity," just as I said, "That's a shame."

Gryffin flashed a smile my way, but I kept my head lowered, heat rising to my cheeks. I felt Zeke's stare boring into me.

But something else caught my attention then.

A certain word kept appearing. I wasn't sure I even recognized it as a word. *Aequi. Aequi.* Here, in this scroll that dissected Vena's bow and its carvings. And earlier, in a section of a book detailing the events of a Talented who could manipulate vines harnessing the power of

Viridi's bangle. And yet another time yesterday, in an account of a ray of light that seemed to come from the emerald in the hilt of Equos's dagger when in the sun on a certain day of the year.

"Have either of you seen this word?" I asked. "*Aequi?*"

"*Aequi?*" Gryffin asked. "As in 'equal'?"

"I have seen it a few times, now that you point it out," Zeke said, leaning forward in his chair. "*Aequi* and *solstit*. Pretty often actually."

"I always assumed *solstit* referred to Solstice Day," Gryffin said. "It was undoubtedly the word I saw most often in these old books. But *aequi* did appear from time to time as well."

"Well if *solstit* refers to Solstice Day," I said, "then maybe *aequi* means the Equinox?"

Equinox.

A far-off dream found itself in my head. Or rather, the dream of a memory.

*Solstice or Equinox.*


*My father twirled my mother around in the Great Hall on the night of Solstice Day, long after my sisters and I were supposed to be in bed. Isa and I watched them from around the edge of the great doorway, snickering and shushing one another.*

*But we weren't very sneaky. Papa spun Mama all the way to the door, where she popped her head around the door and said, "Boo!"*

*We squealed in laughter as Papa caught us both in his big arms. "Today was the longest day of the year," he said through a big grin. "Yet it wasn't long enough for you two?"*

*Giggling, I fought and squirmed out of his embrace. "Why can't we stay up with you?"*

*"Yeah, why can't we stay up?" Isabele echoed, still wrapped up in Papa's arms. "When we go to bed, it's like you aren't there anymore."*

*Mama and Papa looked at each other, then back at us. Papa kept Isabele locked in his arms, and Mama put her hands on my shoulders. "Whether it be the Solstice or Equinox," Mama said, smoothing my unruly hair, "we are always here, even after the sun sets."*

*It would be another six weeks before Atroxis claimed them, and they were no longer with us, no matter when the sun rose or set.*


I had to blink away sudden tears. My mother's familiar voice said those words, and I repeated them in a whisper. "Solstice or Equinox."

Gryffin and Zeke both looked up at me. Each of their expressions turned to ones of concern at my sadness, but I didn't give them—or myself—time to think further about it. We had the Peninsula depending on us, though no one knew it yet.

"What if." My voice broke, thick with the memory, but I cleared it and started again. "What if . . . the relics could have been brought together on another day? The Equinox?"

The relics were brought together on Solstice Day, when the most sunlight was channeled into one day—the longest day of the year. The power of the relics was channeled into one person. Amicka.

But on the Equinox . . .

"What if the power of the relics would have been distributed across the Peninsula had they been brought together not on Solstice Day, but rather on the Equinox?" I looked at Gryffin, who sat there deeply considering my words. "When day and night are equal. *Aequi.*"

In an instant, Gryffin's eyes brightened. "Rosemary, you brilliant woman!" He stood with the book in his hand, head buried in the pages. "If we can somehow break the bond between the relics and reunite them on the Equinox, then maybe a true Awakening will take place!"

Zeke quickly leaned forward in his chair. "Yes, that's all wonderful, and you'd get your Talent back." He nodded his head toward Gryffin with harsh eyes. "That's what you're really after, isn't it?"

Gryffin's excitement faltered, and he looked at Zeke with no light in his eyes. "I'm the last one that I care about."

His candor stunned Zeke into silence. Me too, for a moment. Gryffin thought himself so unimportant, when really, all of this was possible because of him. The very idea of fixing what had been done was his, and his alone. It was his hope in a solution that made me believe at all, and for that, I couldn't help but admire his determination. The determination I thought he had abandoned on the road out of Loche.

I rapped my fingernails on the table, calling back their attention. "Enough, you two. Now, how do we break the bond between the relics?" I asked. "Do we even know if they *can* be broken apart?"

Gryffin sighed heavily and put the book in his hands down on the table. "I don't know. But as much time as we've spent over these books, I feel we would have found anything written about it."

"Then we need to figure it out on our own," Zeke said. "But I know sure as the Solstice that there isn't much time to spend thinking about it."

"Then we'll act quickly." I pushed my chair away from the table and stood, unable to sit any longer like a spring too tightly coiled. "We'll go to Loche. Find where Amicka is keeping the relics. Somehow not get killed in the process. We'll rip the relics apart with our bare hands if we have to."

"I'm almost certain that it will be harder than that," Gryffin said with warning in his voice. "The relics are drawn to each other with every ounce of Haggard's magic. Simple manpower won't be able to break them apart."

"Then we'll wedge Amicka herself between them!" I exaggerated my words with a wave of my arms. "What matters is doing whatever we can to make this work."

"The Equinox is in less than two weeks," Gryffin said. "I agree with you that we need to act quickly, but we should figure some sort of plan before we go striding in there and find out we're unable to break apart the relics at all."

Zeke groaned and stood from his seat next to me. "I hate to say it, but I agree. We'll get killed if we go blindly." He took my hand in his and brought it to his lips, a kiss so soft and full of love it made goosebumps run up my arms. He lifted his gaze to mine and smiled his charming half-smile. "And I've got a lot to live for."

I thought my heart would beat right out of my chest.

He stepped forward, and it was as if it were just Zeke and me in the library. He wrapped his arms around me, and he brought his lips close to my ear. "We have a cottage to build. A family to raise. Nights and days to spend together."

Gryffin slammed his book shut.

"Yes, quite a lot to come home to," he said. His deep voice was laced with sarcasm. "I'll just leave you to it, then." He pushed his chair in, wood screeching against stone, and gathered up a few scrolls under his arm. Then before I could blink, he was storming through the library doors, boots clacking thunderously in his wake.

I looked back at Zeke, who wore the smuggest look I've ever seen.

"That did him in, didn't it?" he said with a smile.

"'Did him in'? Is that what you were trying to do?" I backed out of his arms, ignoring his protest. "Think about what you said, Zeke. His home is frozen. He has no kingdom. He has no people. His younger brothers stay as far away from him as possible, thanks to their father. Not even his sister Kathryn relies on him. He has nothing to come home to." And that thought alone made my chest ache in sympathy for Gryffin. I shook my head and bookmarked the book I'd been focused on. "I'm going after him."

Zeke grabbed my hand. "Rose, let him go. We've made headway, haven't we? We can figure the rest out on our own."

"No, we can't. Gryffin understands all of this more than you or me. We need him." I pulled my hand away, but he spun me around by the shoulder.

"Rose, he's in love with you! Can't you see that?" Zeke looked at me incredulously. "He wears that ring on a chain around his neck. His eyes linger on you. He'd steal you right from under me if he could. I can't stand here and let that happen."

That was when I whirled on him. "And what of us?" I asked, my voice echoing through the library. "Do you really think so little of us that you feel threatened by him?"

Zeke's eyes widened. "Well, no, I—"

I didn't give him a chance to finish. "Have some faith, Zeke. Have some faith in me."

I turned away before he could see the hurt prickling the backs of my eyes.

# CHAPTER SEVENTEEN

I WAS STILL wiping away tears when I turned the corner of Hillstone's guest wing. The only sounds were my sniffles, my footsteps, and my skirts sweeping the floor behind me. No other footfalls, boots, or voices. Zeke hadn't followed me. Fine. I was on my own.

I stopped in front of Gryffin's door and took a deep breath before knocking. I waited, but there was no answer. I rapped my knuckles on the door a second time, but again, no one responded. There was no sound from inside to even indicate that someone was in there. Hesitantly, I lifted the handle, and the click of the latch releasing resounded through the hall.

"Gryffin?"

I peeked my head around the door. The smell of a candle having recently been blown out reached my nose, and I saw the sheets of his bed thrown around the room, lying there in heaps of linen. His chest of belongings was wide open, cloaks and boots and parchment strewn across the floor as though it'd been ransacked by a bear. There was no sign of Gryffin. Only his anger.

I closed the door and looked around the hallway, searching for any telltale thing that would lead me in the right direction. Where would he have gone so fast?

Before I could think any longer on it, my feet led me through the castle and out into the courtyard. I saw Clara with her friend Lucinda sorting through a batch of apples that had recently been harvested from Hillstone's orchard. "Clara!" I waved my hand overhead and ran to them.

Lucinda curtsied quickly. "Your Majesty."

The last thing I felt like right now was a queen.

"Have either of you seen King Gryffin?" The title, said out of habit and for the first time without malice, felt funny on my lips.

Clara scrunched her little nose and nodded. "He stormed through the gate there." She pointed at the creaking wrought-iron gates that stood on the path to the stables. "Didn't even take the time to close it behind him, in a mad dash as he was."

Maybe he'd gone for a ride to clear his head. That was what I would have done.

"Thank you," I said quickly to them both. Then I turned and hurried down the rough cobblestones.

When I walked through the doors of the stables, no one even noticed. I looked too much like everyone else now—work dress, hair quickly done up in a bun, tired eyes and hunched shoulders. I'd been neglecting to wear even a tiara, to Hazel's dismay. I was grateful for the lack of pomp and circumstance as I scanned the stalls.

The door to Lucy's stall was open wide, with Lucy nowhere to be seen.

I heard Midas's shrill whinny and knew he'd caught sight of me. Even if no one else noticed me, there was no fooling him. I couldn't help but smile as I made my way to his stall and patted his sleek black neck. "Hey there, big guy. I know it's been a while. I'm sorry." I didn't even worry about tacking him up as I opened his stall door. I stepped up onto the crossbeam of the stable wall and hoisted myself up onto his back.

I had no way to know for certain which way Gryffin might have gone, but I had an idea. All it took was a nudge from my heel for Midas to spring into action. I held onto his coarse mane and guided him down the path I'd taken several months ago, the rocky one with the stream and the twists and turns. The one on which I'd been in the crosshairs of an assassin, an arrow trained on my chest. The one that used to be my favorite but now held dark, unforgiving memories.

But it was the trail Gryffin would be most familiar with. He'd kidnapped me on it, after all.

Midas and I careened through the trees just as we usually did, the new lack of magic in Midas's blood no hindrance whatsoever. He cleared the stream with a powerful leap and tore down the path, hoofbeats pounding.

Finally, in the distance, a white speck could be seen. Gryffin's mare, Lucy.

I coaxed Midas to a trot, then a walk. His tail flicked behind us and he threw his head back with a snort, but he begrudgingly obliged. We approached them slowly, until I could make out Gryffin's form standing near Lucy's rump facing the forest, his back to the path. He had his head in his hand, the other resting on his saddle as if ready to mount and bolt down the path.

I slowed to a halt and slid down from Midas's back. The drop was bigger than I was used to, but I landed on my feet with a thud. I smoothed out Midas's mane, biding time, before turning to the tormented man. "Gryffin."

"This was where it all began," he said, raising his eyes to an ancient oak tree near the edge of the path. I recognized it—the oak tree the archer had perched in and aimed his arrow at me. "All of this mess. I should have never come to Lecevonia to court you. Then you wouldn't be involved in any of this."

"I'd probably be involved by now anyway." I shrugged, feeling as helpless as any attempt to avoid the path my life had taken since Gryffin had entered it would have been. "Amicka would have probably killed more people to get what she wanted. She would have killed my Uncle Merek to get the chisel had he not given it to me already." Instead, I'd had four of the five relics together. Might as well have tied them together as a gift for her.

"Rosemary." I heard it in his voice then when he said my name. Beneath the tones of pain and regret, there was a caress. A gentleness reserved only for those you deeply care about. He turned and looked at me, blue eyes shining. "I didn't want any of this to happen. I didn't want the Peninsula to be sucked dry of magic. I didn't want people to suffer. I didn't want you to be in danger. And I most certainly didn't want you to end up loving *him*." He scoffed and turned away from me.

I didn't end up loving Zeke. I'd always loved him. It had always been there in my very soul, and I'd just refused to acknowledge it, for fear of its impossibility. But I didn't say any of that. He was in enough pain, and I didn't want to cause more.

"What *did* you want?" I asked instead. "What has been your motivation in this from the beginning?"

"I wanted our home to thrive. For everyone to see the worth of the Talented. To see this magic strengthen and live on for generations. I was willing to do anything for that to happen."

I hated that I understood his desires for the good of his people.

"Then, I met you," he said, pacing in the dirt. "In person. Not the naïve princess-turned-queen-too-young that my brother made you out to be. Even in the face of that archer, Haggard-forsaken idea as that was, you stood so brave, so sure, calculating your next move."

I scoffed. "I was terrified."

"You would have gotten out of there on your own," he said, waving off my remark. "You might not have felt it then, but you would have done it. You didn't need me." He stopped in his tracks, his bright gaze finding me. "But the moment I saw the strength in your bright green eyes, I wanted more than just the Talented to be seen. I wanted you to need me. I wanted my future, magic and all, to be spent with you."

He spoke of strength, even when I hadn't been strong enough to stop the Silencing when I had had all the power to do it. I saw weakness. But he saw strength.

He'd walked toward me while he'd been talking. He only stood a foot away. Not so tall that he towered over me as Zeke tended to do, but tall enough that I had to lift my face to meet his eyes. Eyes that no longer looked frightening, or controlling, or hungry for success. These eyes reflected only *me* back out into the forest.

"Before I met you, I was so sure about what I wanted and how I needed to make that happen. I've done terrible things, Rosemary. I know I have. I'm a murderer, a liar, and a captor. I have blood on my hands, and I have put you in danger. I don't deserve you. But if I don't try, I cannot forgive myself."

He took my hand in his, warm in the summer's afternoon. He took a step forward, his chest inches from mine, his blue eyes piercing. I couldn't breathe. He lowered his head, our noses touching, and I felt his fingers graze my chin. I tore my eyes away from his, but they found his lips, suddenly so close to my own. The next time he spoke, they brushed against mine.

"May I kiss you?"

Gryffin's words, hardly a whisper, sent electricity through my chest. I would be lying if I'd told him I wanted him to back away, and for a split second, confusion rattled me.

The Gryffin standing here in front of me felt so much like the Gryffin I'd first met. The Gryffin for whom I'd felt a blooming of love in my heart. The Gryffin who'd made me blush at a picnic by the stream's bank not far from here. Who had politely opened the door for me and my sisters at Clara's birthday party, giving her a proper grand entrance. Who had taught me how to use a sword. The Gryffin who'd sworn his fidelity to me. The Gryffin who'd defended me against his brother.

That was when I realized that it hadn't all been a lie.

He had no Talent to try and persuade me this time, and my heart foolishly raced inside my chest at his proximity.

But as I felt myself leaning forward on my toes, I couldn't forget the other things Gryffin had done. Awful things that he'd wrongly convinced himself needed to happen. I could accept his apologies, but forgetting would take some time, if I ever could.

I had felt something for him once. And maybe a part of me still longed for that devoted, stronghearted Gryffin. Even since he'd been here at Hillstone, there had been moments I'd felt drawn to him. He *knew* me in a way like no one else could. He understood what it was like to be a ruler with nothing to rule, yet so many people to feel responsible for. To feel the need to be strong at all costs. Perhaps our strength together would be enough. In the static between us now, I could tell he felt the same.

But whatever this was, it couldn't hold a candle to what I felt for Zeke. He was the man who'd always had my best interest in mind. That was love. There was no comparing what Zeke and I had to anything else in this world.

I put a hand on Gryffin's chest, putting another inch of distance between us. I needed to breathe.

Gryffin at first stood firm against the pressure, denying our reality. But eventually, he relented, boots crunching in the dirt as he took a step backward. Wind rushed through the space between us.

"I've wronged you too much." His voice was small, impossible to hear if we hadn't been standing so close. "I understand, Rosemary."

"It isn't only that." I lifted my eyes to meet his. "My heart belongs to someone else, and it has for a long time. I am strengthened, supported, and loved by him, and he is who I want for the rest of my life." I leaned away from him, stretching the static between us. "Not even Haggard could change my mind."

At each of my words, Gryffin's eyes lost a little bit of hope. He rocked on his heels, and in the silence that followed, I could see gears turning in his mind to somehow fix this.

But there was nothing to fix. He saw that too.

Eventually, he gave a small smile, blue eyes a mix of acceptance and sadness. "You deserve all of that and more," he said.

"Come back to the castle," I insisted. "The Peninsula needs you now more than ever."

He studied my face, and he nodded. "I will. But not yet. I need a moment out here."

I pursed my lips and took a step back. Then another. The charged air between us crackled away. Something in Gryffin's eyes snapped and he turned away quickly, but not before I caught the moisture welling in them.

He strode back to Lucy and I to Midas, and the sudden, silent tears falling down my cheeks caused my heart to falter. I climbed up onto Midas's back and turned him back down the way which we'd come.

I was sure of Zeke. He'd been my past and he was my present, and

I was certain that he would be my future. Gryffin needed to know where my heart lay. This was a good thing.

But I hadn't expected the pain in my heart as I put more distance between us.

I stayed in my rooms for the rest of the day, unable to talk myself into doing anything else. I wasn't sleepy, exactly, but fatigued. Over the course of the evening, Hazel had made me two steaming cups of tiliarose, drawn me a warm bath, and turned away Lord Brock who'd come to discuss some issue of numbers of wheat bushels. It could wait until tomorrow. The workday was almost done anyway.

It was selfish of me to stay holed up in my rooms while everyone else pulled their weight. I should have been out there, trying to be everywhere at once as I usually did, or poring over books in the library looking for anything that might help us against Amicka. Haggard knew this wasn't the time to be wasting precious daylight, not when the Rebels made demands so high it was impossible to deliver. Not when the Equinox crept ever closer, after we'd just made a huge breakthrough in setting everything right. But I just couldn't.

I'd cried the entire way back to the stable, alarming Celeste who'd come to meet me. She'd offered to take care of cleaning up Midas for me, but I'd refused, putting all my energy into brushing the dust from Midas's coat and scrubbing his legs free of mud, until I hadn't been able to see through my tears anymore and Celeste had gently nudged me out of the way. Then I'd looked for Zeke, but I hadn't found him in the library or in his rooms.

It was probably for the best. I'd needed time to recover from my surprising heartbreak, for that was exactly what it was. My heart broke for the man whom I'd loved once upon a time, but hadn't loved enough to forget the things he'd done. How could I? He'd betrayed my trust, used me and my people and made us vulnerable, killed people I cared about. Why did my heart hurt so much for him?

I sipped on my tiliarose. Something Yetta said had been burning in my mind. *He thinks and acts as if he has no other choice. That does not mean he wants to do what he does.*

I pitied him. This man who had thought conquering and dominating were his only options to restore magic to the Five Kingdoms. Who seemed utterly remorseful, torn apart by his past choices now that his Talent was no longer a factor. Could his wrongdoings be forgotten?

The small, aching part of my heart wanted to.

I put my cup down beside my bed and curled into a ball beneath my sheets. My chest felt so tight. My entire *being* felt so tight. I wanted to beat my fist on my sternum, as if that would dislodge the pain settled there. Instead, I squeezed my eyes shut and curled into myself even tighter.

There was a quiet knock on my door, and I heard Hazel murmuring hushed words with whoever was on the other side.

After a moment, she shut the door, I heard her feet patter across the floor, over to me. She laid a hand on my shoulder through the sheets.

"It's Ezekiel, my queen."

I was nobody's queen, but I had no energy to correct her. "He can come in."

I heard Hazel's footsteps travel back to the door, and the hinges creaking as she opened it wide. Heavier footsteps followed. Zeke was silent for a moment. Then he sighed, and the bed shifted as he sat down somewhere behind me. Metal clinked as he unbuckled his boots, and then he was there, lining my body with his through the sheets. I felt his soft kiss on the top of my head, and new tears sprung to my eyes.

His fingers traced light circles on my shoulders, and when he spoke, his voice was soft. "I know it must be bad if you've been here all afternoon and evening rather than working yourself to death."

"Evening?" I peeked my head out from under my sheets and saw the light outside my window was gone, nothing but darkness on the other side. The sun did start to set earlier during this time of year, but still, I was shocked. I'd truly managed to shirk off my duties for an entire half a day.

And Hazel was nowhere to be seen.

Zeke peered over the top of my shoulder, and I glanced at him. His brown eyes searched mine, trying to understand.

I rotated around under the sheets so I could face him, and I answered his questioning gaze honestly. "My talk with Gryffin took all of my energy."

The corners of his eyes tightened just slightly but otherwise seemed unbothered this time. "Did you convince him to stay?"

"Yes." I nuzzled my face into the curve under Zeke's chin. "You were right."

"I normally am."

I looked up at him just so he could see me roll my eyes. Then I sighed and laid my head back down. "I . . . cleared the air with him. Don't worry." There was a bit more acid in my words than I'd meant for there to be.

"Rose." He put a finger under my chin and coaxed me to look at him again. "I'm sorry. About what happened in the library. You were right. I was jealous, and worried. Worried that I could lose you to him.

Can you believe that?" His nervous chuckle shook us both, and he pressed his lips to my forehead. "I do have faith in you. In *us*. Haggard's sake, my faith in us is the strongest thing I believe in. I guess what I don't have is . . . faith in *me*."

I narrowed my eyes. "Why would you lack faith in yourself?"

"Because I make mistakes, too, Rose. I'm certainly no more perfect than that crite."

I poked him in the side and smirked. "You're admitting that you aren't perfect? Pinch me, this can't be real."

He all but stuck his tongue out at me. "Har har. What I mean is, I don't want to make some stupid mistake and somehow lose you. Mistakes like I made in the library, making you think I don't trust you. I do, Rose. I promise I do. And—and if you would've decided that you wanted *him* instead of me . . . well I can't say that I would not spend the rest of my life trying to change your mind."

His stammering was endearing and so unlike him. I nudged his nose with mine, and he met my eyes.

"Zeke," I said. His breath hitched as I said his name. "You are the one who I am meant to spend my life with, and nothing will ever convince me otherwise. It's you, or it's no one."

His next smile lit a fire in my chest, all but smothering the pain I'd felt earlier for Gryffin. I felt that, maybe, that pain would resurface from time to time, as memories of past loves often do, but this fire that Zeke lit within me would burn without ceasing. I could handle that tinge of pain if it meant this burning would bring warmth to my soul forever and always.

The heat in my eyes must have been evident, because a low growl escaped him as his hands found their way to me beneath my sheets. I gasped at his touch, at how easily he joined me in the warmth of the covers and trapped me in his arms. I laid a hand on his chest, right over where his heart beat.

His voice was low in my ear. "You'd soon as well reach in and take it, because it's yours." He gripped my hand tightly with his.

I wrapped an arm around his neck and wasted no time in crushing my lips to his.

"Let's have the ceremony," Zeke said suddenly, breaking away from me. "Before we leave on any Haggard-forsaken quest that might kill us."

I wrinkled my nose. "I prefer not to think of it that way. I like to give us *some* hope of succeeding."

Zeke shook his head. "I'm only being realistic. I want to be married to you, Rose, and I want to do it while I know some evil sorceress can't do anything to stop it."

True, but something still held me back. "This hardly feels like the time for a wedding."

"On the contrary. It's the perfect time. Everything is all 'doom and gloom', so we could all use something to lift our spirits."

"The Equinox is just under two weeks away!"

"Then we better ask Lord Castor to officiate as soon as possible."

"I don't know, Zeke . . ."

"Look at you worried about time." He narrowed his eyes, teasing. "You're already nineteen. If you're not married by the time you're twenty, people will call you an old maid."

I rolled my eyes. "That's the last thing I care about, and you know it."

He held his hands up and pouted his lips. "I'm just saying. You know all of Hazel's friends will be gossiping . . ."

I pinched his side. "You sound like an old maid yourself, going on about gossip. Besides, they already gossip about the amount of time we spend alone together."

He gave a devilish smile and draped an arm over my hips, pulling me flush to him. "Their gossip is warranted." He nipped at my ear, and a quick shiver ran through me.

Then he held my cheek and gazed at me, eyes somber and serious. "Please, Rose."

I bit my lip, letting hesitation quiet the air between us. With everything that was happening, everything that we still needed to do, there was no way I could spare any focus on a wedding. What of the relics? Amicka? The dire need to set everything straight before winter hit and starved half the Magian Peninsula? A wedding would just be a distraction.

But maybe a distraction was long overdue.

I wanted to marry him, didn't I?

"Hazel is going to be upset that she won't get to help me plan a grand royal wedding," I said, drawing out my words. "The balls, banquets, dresses . . ." To be honest, I'd had enough of that in Tarasyn anyway.

Zeke looked at me with careful hope. "Is that a yes?"

I nodded, letting a smile break through my reservations and obliterate them into dust.

A new light shined through Zeke's eyes as my approval sank in, and he combed a hand through my hair. He pulled me close, and when his lips found mine, they carried so much tenderness that my heart trembled. His next words were whispers across my skin.

"Our forever starts soon, my Rose."

Though, truly, our forever started ages ago. When he and I had just been children passing secret notes and jumping across rocks.

# CHAPTER EIGHTEEN

I WAITED FOR Hazel as the first rays of daylight brightened the sky outside my window. I'd gotten a little sleep, but as wound up as I was, I couldn't keep my eyes closed. Hazel was the first person I wanted to tell. She'd been the one to take care of me all these years. But what would she think? She could hardly be in the same room as Zeke without shooting him daggers.

Finally, when I heard the maids' door open and Hazel's quiet humming, I sat up in my bed and bucked up my courage. "Good morning."

"Your Majesty!" She put down her tray of teacups onto my makeshift breakfast table. "What are you doing awake? Go back to sleep!"

"I can't." I worried at my bottom lip. "I have something to tell you."

Her shoes click-clacked as she walked over to my side of the bed and smoothed out the front of her dress. "Well, go on then, if it's pestering you so much."

"Zeke and I are going to have a wedding."

Her hands stilled.

"Within the next two weeks," I clarified.

Hazel's jaw dropped, eyes wide. Her only movement was the rapid blinking of her eyelids, and just when I was about to reach over and shake her shoulder, she threw her hands into the air. "A wedding!" She fretted about the room and found my robe. She draped it over my shoulders and took my hands in hers, already breaking into tears. "Oh, Your Majesty! You will finally have your wedding day!"

That went much smoother than I expected. I looked at her uncertainly. "You approve of Zeke, then? You've never seemed to care for him before."

She sighed, patted my hand, and sat next to me on the edge of the bed. "Let me explain, dear. I wanted Ezekiel to stay at arms' length because I didn't want you to give your heart to a man that you could not spend your life with. Of course, I always saw how he felt about you. Any old woman would have noticed that boy has been lovestruck for years." She rolled her eyes and chuckled before continuing on earnestly. "What I feared was that you would fall too and be unable to live happily with a man you had to marry by duty. But, my queen." She gave my hand a squeeze and smiled warmly. "In these times, take advantage of the fact that you can marry whom you wish. Watching you two grow up together, I can tell you this—Ezekiel truly is a good one, even with his . . ." She wrinkled her nose. "Less than pristine reputation. He would do anything for you. He's utterly hopeless when it comes to you."

Utterly hopeless. The thought made me smile. I felt utterly hopeless too.

Before I could say a word, Hazel stood abruptly. "We've got to find you a dress! We'll see what Hilda has left. Maybe she's got a bolt of spare satin hiding somewhere . . ." Her voice trailed as she disappeared through the maid's door, no doubt already off to the seamstress.

I sat on the bed, looking down at my hands and smiling. Soon, the ruby ring on my left hand would have a band to go along it. I needed to ask Jacobin if he could make Zeke's. Or the goldsmith. Were men's rings gold? Haggard, I was clueless when it came to things such as this. I'd been too busy running a kingdom to keep up with marital trends.

I was just throwing on my boots when there was a knock at my door. It opened without my answering.

Kathryn rounded the corner, looking serious, followed by a smiling Celeste. Kathryn clapped her hands and threw open my wardrobe, black hair swinging over her shoulder. "There is so much to be done!" She turned and put her hands on her hips. "How can you just stand there lacing up some old work boots?"

"Well I have a shift in the fields this morning—"

"You're getting married in a matter of weeks and you're worried about your *work shift?*"

I rolled my eyes. "News does travel quickly, doesn't it?"

Celeste smirked, sitting on the edge of my bed. "Especially good news. Ezekiel was grinning from ear to ear before a word even left his mouth."

"Really?" I smiled. Zeke's excitement had my own insides fluttering. "Well since you two are already so invested, plan the wedding for me."

An impish look crossed Kathryn's face. "Be careful what you ask for, Rosemary."

"Well, help is what's expected from my bridesmaids, yes?"

Celeste laughed and stood, and taking my hands, she spun me around an excited circle. "I honestly never thought I'd see the day you *actually* get married. Miss 'I Have Too Many More Important Things To Worry About.'" She made her best attempt at mocking my voice.

I gasped. "Yes, like a kingdom!"

Celeste released my hands and held her palms out. "I'm not saying you were wrong. What I'm saying is that if there is anything that could have pulled you to the altar, it would have always either been your obligation to Lecevonia, or Ezekiel."

And now only one of them mattered. Amicka took one away, but she gave me the other in the process. The irony tasted bittersweet. I rebelliously focused on the "sweet."

I stood from the bed and fixed them each with a meaningful look. "Well, while you two fret over dresses and flowers, I'm going to get to work."

Just then, someone cleared his throat outside my rooms, and Lord Brock rounded the corner of my open door. "I'm sorry, my queen, but I'm afraid you're needed elsewhere. Please, come with me." He held out his arm and gestured me through the door, leaving Kathryn and Celeste to sift through my wardrobe again.

Despite Lord Brock's gentle smile, the air around him crackled with tension.

Apprehension crept down my spine. "What's wrong?"

"You will see," he responded grimly.

He led me down to the kitchens, to the corner where our private stores of grain were kept. The curtains were drawn back, and a mass of people had gathered. I saw my other advisors and Zeke, who looked grave, and Isabele stood there biting her nails. Even Jacobin was there. The entire council.

Oh yes. Something was very wrong.

To my surprise, Gryffin was there too, standing near the center of the group, forehead in his hand. I didn't even have time to decide whether I was ready to see him or not. The tension in the air was too great and seemed much more important than matters of the heart.

He was the first to notice our approach, and when he lowered his hand, he met my eyes with a strange emotion. Sadness. Remorse?

Then others began to turn, and Lord Clark looked up from the parchment in his hand. "There's a problem, Your Majesty."

"Our reserves," Isabele said, glancing between me and the barrels of grain. "They're—"

"Infested," Zeke said darkly.

"What?" I rushed to the storage bins. I immediately caught a sour odor, and when I looked inside the first bin, mouse droppings were scattered throughout. "That's impossible," I said, lifting another lid. It looked and smelled the same as the first. "We close the bins securely every time!" But every bin I opened had suffered the same fate.

"And that's just the wheat," Gryffin said, running his hand through his hair. "The meat cellars . . ."

One of his Tarasynians trudged forward, holding a salted cut of pork in her hands. The meat was covered in sickly green splotches. "Everything down there looks like this, ma'am," she said quietly. "The smell in the cellars is unbearable."

I looked at the pork in disbelief. This wasn't possible. We took care to preserve everything correctly! In all the time I could remember, we have never had food spoil!

But the true problem glared at me, and panic stole my breath so brutally that my voice was but a devastated whisper. "We have no food for winter."

I wanted to take a staggering step back, but I held my ground. My people were watching, and I couldn't falter now.

"How could this happen?" I asked.

Gryffin stepped forward solemnly. "This is akin to Roderich's Talent."

It was, wasn't it? Roderich's Talent was to create diseases. Spoilage and vermin were another way to create disease.

It was the dark side of magic.

"Amicka did this." I couldn't tell if my voice carried more disgust or hatred. They both contended for the forefront of my brain. "Amicka poisoned our food."

Our group stood there in a tense silence.

"But why?" Lord Brock asked, holding his hands out in confusion. "Why would she do this?"

Gryffin answered. "It must be because you took in my people." He kept his glare down at the ground, unable to meet my gaze. "She must not approve of your mercy."

So that was why he'd looked so guilty.

Lord Castor, usually dignified even if hotheaded, turned suddenly on Gryffin, eyes scorching with hostility. "We should have never let your people past the border."

I stepped into the heated space between them. "Lord Castor, stop. The Tarasynians are not at fault here."

"What of the Rebels that were poking around here during the last pickup?" Isabele interjected, stepping in beside me. "Perhaps they have something to do with this."

She was right. When the Rebels had come last week, there were too many to just be hauling off bushels of wheat. A few people had reported seeing them around the castle grounds, recognizable by their red tunics, and I'd told the unwelcome lurkers to leave. "It's possible that one of them had somehow seen that we were stockpiling food from each pickup," I said. "They reported it back to her."

Zeke let out a loud curse and kicked his boot into the floor.

Amicka had found out about my act of defiance, and this was how she'd handled it.

"We're going to starve," Lord Quince said, voice trembling. His words stirred a nervous tenor in the crowd that had gathered around us.

I held up my hands to stifle their panic. "No. We won't. We will fix it." I looked around to the rest of the council. "We—Zeke, Gryffin, and I—have been trying to figure out a way to somehow take Amicka out of power and release the magic of the magi back throughout the Peninsula."

The group was silent.

"Is that possible?" Lord Brock finally asked. He kept his expression carefully guarded.

"In theory," I answered cautiously. "And if that happens, Tarasyn can use the released magic to grow food again. Couldn't you?" I turned to Gryffin.

He nodded. "With Viridi's power back into the land, and if even just one person is Talented with plant growth or something of the sort, there would be enough to feed both our kingdoms."

Though I let out a sigh of relief, another thought sobered me.

I was putting the survival of my people into the hands of this man. There was no way we'd be able to gather that much food before winter on our own. It was either swallow my pride and trust him, or let my people starve.

With this in mind, I stared at Gryffin evenly. "You must vow that you won't abandon me. That once all of this is over, you will help me as I have helped you."

Gryffin looked at me as though I'd hurt him. "Of course, Rosemary. Without question."

"But first we need to actually *succeed* in breaking apart the relics," Zeke said sardonically. "Can't forget that bit."

"Is there a plan?" Lord Clark asked.

Gryffin, Zeke, and I all looked at each other. "Not exactly," I finally answered. "We don't know how the relics are bonded or what could break it."

"One way or another, we need to do it before the autumn equinox," Gryffin said. "We think if the relics are brought back together on that very day, the magic of the magi will be dispersed throughout the Peninsula. Which is what we are counting on if we are to get through the winter."

Jacobin grumbled. "Or we coul' steal our food back from the Rebels."

At that, Gryffin smirked. "That can be the fallback plan."

Lord Brock swayed on his heels. "I don't like this. We don't know enough. And after seeing this?" He waved toward the barrels of grain. "Over just eight bushels of wheat short? Amicka is merciless."

"We don't have a choice now." I tried to bolster as much confidence in my voice as I could. "But we are going to go to Loche, and we are going to fix all of this."

A trembling voice spoke behind me. "No."

It was Isabele. Her clear brown eyes flashed angrily.

"No?" I reached my arms toward her. "Isabele, what's wrong?"

She flinched away, hands curled tightly into fists at her sides. "You can't leave. Not again. Not when you're walking into your own death sentence."

Death sentence. Impulsively, I looked at Zeke, who I found staring right back at me. This could not be a death sentence. I had too much to lose.

Bright tears slid down Isabele's cheeks before she turned away and hurried through the doorway to the staircase leading up into the castle.

"Isa!" Avoiding everyone's stares of shock, I rushed after her.

I found her in the seamstresses' quarters, running her hand across a swath of taffeta with a small smile on her face, something only this place could do these days. Where my place of solace was Hillstone's chapel, hers was here, surrounded by the flowing bolts and textures of fabric. She and the Talented seamster Sir Hilderic would have gotten along. I was sure of it.

Just as the thought crossed my mind, I saw Sir Hilderic approach her. A jolt of surprise coursed through me, but I knew that was silly. Of course he came here with the rest of the Tarasynians. I was happy to see he'd found his place here amidst all the chaos.

He handed my sister a piece of silk and they both nodded enthusiastically over something, and once he left, I approached her. "You've met Sir Hilderic then?" I smiled. "He's undoubtedly the best seamster I've ever met in my life."

Isabele dropped her smile, but she nodded. "He is still very good, even without his Talent. He said there is no more fabric in Tarasyn. That they'd had to use it all for warmth before coming here." She glanced up at me. "He feels the same way I do now. How I've felt for months, ever since the Silencing."

"How is that?" I asked softly, laying my hand atop hers. The silk she was holding was smooth and cool.

She glanced up at me. "Lost. Incomplete. It's hard to explain, and I don't think you could understand anyway. You didn't have some inert part of yourself ripped away from you without warning." She looked away, back to the silk in her hand.

I pursed my lips. "You're right, I probably wouldn't understand. I didn't have a Talent to lose. But that doesn't mean I can't try to see it through you." It might not have been exactly the same, but I'd very nearly lost Zeke, and he was as much as part of me as any Talent could be.

"Henry has been helping me," she said, raising her eyes to mine. "He's been good to me, even though I don't feel like myself anymore."

"I'm happy to hear that," I said earnestly. "Don't ever settle for less than that. But Isabele. That's why I need to *try* to fix this. You would feel whole again if we succeed."

"If." She scoffed. "If you succeed, for if you don't succeed you die. I went through the fear of losing you once. You expect me to be okay with it happening again?"

Oh, Isa. A concern reserved only for her surfaced in my heart. My sweet sister who had shouldered so much of the weight that fell off my shoulders. She was the one left to pick up the pieces for Lisette and Clara after our parents passed while I had endless lessons on court policies. And she was the one who took care of a kingdom in shambles while I was locked away in Tarasyn. Despite all that, the loss of her Talent had shaken her more than I'd ever seen before. The thought of adding more loss to her life threatened to break my resolve. If I *didn't* return, would she be okay?

I gently took the silk from her hands and laid it aside, wrapping my fingers around hers instead. "Would you forgive me if I go?"

She was silent for a moment, and I didn't think she was going to answer. That in itself would have been answer enough. But just when I'd felt my heart begin to drop, she met my gaze again. "Only if you come back alive."

I smiled at her. "Good, because that's exactly what I plan to do." I could not promise I was going to come back, but I could promise to try. "Before we leave, I'll need your help with something."

"Yes?"

"I need you to keep Celeste and Kathryn reined in with this wedding as my maid of honor."

In Isabele fashion, fresh tears sprang to her eyes, and she made no attempt to wipe them away as she leaned in to hug me. "Of course, Rose."

I could breathe again. All was well between us again, for now. Underneath though, there was a sting of guilt. I'd asked her to be my maid of honor because of course she was who I wanted by my side, but also, the wedding would keep her mind off messier things.

"We haven't had a wedding here in ages," Isabele said with a smile, which proved truth in my line of thinking. "Hilderic!"

Before I could turn, Sir Hilderic appeared at my side.

"Hello again, Your Majesty." He smiled brightly at me, though his cheeks seemed sallower than before. His eyes were no longer flecked with red, and for him, it made it seem as though some part of his style was missing. "I hear you're in need of another wedding dress."

"Oh," I said. "I was just going to wear something from my wardrobe upstairs."

He gasped. "Surely you can't be serious." He looked back and forth between my sister and me. "No. That's nonsense. We can sew up a gown befitting a queen by the end of the week. I still remember your measurements, so don't you worry about a thing."

His kindness touched me. I may not have officially been queen anymore, but I knew in one of his dresses, I would certainly look like one.

"Simple, though," I added quickly. "I . . . I don't want to scare Zeke."

Isabele shook her head. "You think that man will be scared off by a bit of regality? Shame on him if he is. It's part of who you are. Besides, it's never dissuaded him before."

As far as she knew. But I kept my mouth shut.

"It will need to be warm though," Hilderic said, holding out an ivory length of fabric against my arm. "Dothymus said the first cold snap of the year will be here any day now."

I wanted to ask how Dothymus knew that without his Talent, but I supposed if one spent his entire life attuned to the weather, he'd simply be able to tell these things by now.

That cold snap did indeed roll in two days later, bringing thunder, wind, and torrents of rain along with it, making the parched earth muddy and satiated once more. The heat gave way to a deep chill, the shadows of summer finally relinquishing their grasp, and the trees, which had already started to turn color from lack of rain, burst into the shades of fire.

Through the next week, the spoiled grain and meat were thrown out and the bins and cellars thoroughly cleaned. But otherwise, wedding preparations dominated.

In the spare time between harvesting and winnowing, the Great Hall was transformed into a grand space primed for a banquet. People would gather here after the ceremony in the chapel and spend the day dining and dancing. The long oak tables had been brought out, and garlands of red and orange leaves hung across the fireplace mantle and adorned the tabletops. Wild sunflowers and goldenrods had been placed in big jars of water along the tables, making the room an autumn meadow.

Today, as I walked through the Great Hall taking in all these details, I saw a side of Kathryn I hadn't known existed. She proved herself to be quite the decorator. Her brothers should have given her full rein in restoring Snowmont. Perhaps this was her Talent? It had to be. The sunlight shining through the golden petals of the flowers reminded me of Zeke's hair, leaving me breathless. That couldn't have been an accident.

I looked to the back of the Hall, where the thrones would have been. They'd been removed months ago to make room for more citizens frequenting the castle who had been displaced from their homes, but now, a table set for two had been situated in their usual place. Seeing the two chairs there sent my heart into uncontrollable flutters, imagining Zeke and me sitting there as husband and wife.

*Husband and wife.*

What a bizarre thing. It truly was happening . . .

The wedding was tomorrow. I ran my fingers over the petals of the arrangement of wildflowers nearest me, trying to still my sudden nerves. I was to be someone's wife. An entirely new role, one I hadn't been sure I was going to ever willingly fill.

But it wasn't just *someone's* wife, I needed to remind myself. I was to be *Zeke's* wife. Why was I still so nervous?

Warm, familiar arms wrapped around my waist.

"Can you believe all of this is for us?" he said into my ear. "I'd always imagined my wedding would be in a tiny family barn somewhere, with sheep dung mucking up my boots."

I glanced up into Zeke's teasing smirk with one of my own. "What? You didn't see yourself marrying royalty?"

"Quite the opposite." He planted a kiss on my forehead. "I always pictured myself marrying you. It just wasn't possible, so . . . sheep dung it was." He shrugged and eyed the garlands hanging overhead. "The only way I would put up with court life is if it were next to you."

Before I could make an answering quip, Gryffin came around the corner, from the direction of the library. He'd been knee deep in scrolls and books even more than the rest of us. Though he was certain he would have seen something about breaking apart the relics before, he insisted on continuing his reading.

My advisors had joined the research party too. It was my idea to let them in on the research. Fresh eyes and whatnot. Neither Zeke nor Gryffin had protested. But with no headway, having a plan had begun to feel hopeless. The Equinox was less than a week away, and we were running out of time. The reality of facing Amicka without any clue on how to break apart the relics was hanging over our heads like the Reaper's scythe. And thinking of it now, of course there was no information on breaking them apart. The goal throughout history had only been bringing the relics together for ultimate power, and even that had never been done before. Why try to undo it?

Gryffin stopped short just a few feet from us, and I didn't miss the flash of dejection cross his face before it smoothed out again. Unnecessary guilt stabbed my chest, and I gently extricated myself from Zeke's arms.

Gryffin's voice, though spoken through a strained smile, was light with optimism. "Lord Quince may have found something."

We followed him to the library, my mind grasping onto little threads of hope the entire way. This was the first lead we'd had all week. My feet practically bounced off the stone with each step. When we entered the library, Lords Brock and Castor were standing toe to toe in, unsurprisingly, a heated argument.

"Well that's all fine and good," Lord Castor said scathingly, "but where are we supposed to find *another* one?"

Lord Brock pointed an angry finger at him. "You have some nerve smothering our last shred of hope—"

"I'm being realistic!"

"You're *giving up!*"

"Gentlemen!" My voice carried through the library and cut off their dispute. Great Haggard, how much longer could I put up with the bickering?

Lord Clark stood. "Finally." He came forward with a smile and nodded his head back to the table, where Lord Quince sat with his finger glued to a page in an old scroll. "Your Majesty, look."

I felt Gryffin buzzing with excitement beside me as I walked over to the table. "What is it?" I asked, peering over Lord Quince's shoulder.

"That word right there," Gryffin said. "*Unexsuis.*" The ancient word's pronunciation rolled off his tongue smoothly. "Roughly, it translates to 'one of their own."

"One of their own?" Zeke's voice was tinged with skepticism. "As in . . ."

"Another relic." I finished for him in a whisper.

"Yes, another relic." Lord Castor sneered. "Where are we supposed to find another relic?"

I met Gryffin's eyes. He knew, and I knew. Hope flashed between us and a slow smile spread across my face. "In my rooms. We can find another relic in my rooms."

That stopped Lord Castor's fuming in its tracks.

Zeke looked at me with narrowed eyes. "Rose. What are you talking about?"

"Amicka's spearhead." Of course he wouldn't remember. He was dying when I grabbed it from the crumbling blacksmith's shop in Loche. "I'd taken it to use as a weapon if I needed it."

The men around the table absorbed my words, and a new energy livened the library. Even Zeke, ever the cynic, had a flash of hope in his brown eyes.

"And I . . . I think we may have an advantage here," Gryffin said carefully. "If Amicka had known that spearhead could be used for this, she would never have let you take it from her."

An advantage against Amicka. Just when I'd begun to believe there was no such thing, we finally stood a chance. A real chance. One not simply fueled by our willpower, but an actual, tangible reason to believe we could succeed in making Amicka powerless.

"The Equinox is in six days," Gryffin continued. Suddenly, his tone turned into that familiar no-nonsense cadence, and he began to pace, his brain already at work. "We can't waste any more time. We should leave at once, figure out a plan once we're on the road."

His need for action was infectious. Everyone in the room had begun to squirm.

But it was an odd mix of eagerness and distress. We had an idea of what to do, and it suddenly made the journey to Loche feel closer than ever. We really were going to try this desperate, final attempt, and we really were possibly walking to our deaths. That threatened to sap out all my optimism.

Determined to push through my fear, I broke the electrified silence. "Yes. Okay. We'll leave the day after tomorrow, as we originally planned."

Gryffin stopped pacing. "Rosemary. It takes four days to get to Mareus. We need to leave tonight. Tomorrow morning at the latest."

I shook my head. "You know why we cannot leave so soon."

"The wedding?" Gryffin scoffed. "You can get married after we ensure the security of the Peninsula."

Haggard, why did he have to make so much sense? I looked at Zeke, but he kept his eyes glued to Gryffin.

Gryffin began closing books and rolling up scrolls. "We *cannot* miss this opportunity. It's the only chance we have. We won't survive through the winter to wait until the spring equinox."

I knew he was right. But I hated it.

Zeke still refused to look at me. I touched his arm softly. "Zeke—"

"Then we'll have the wedding tonight." He finally tore his eyes from Gryffin and looked at me, eyes bright. He smiled and slid an arm around my waist. "Everything is ready, and it's only a dozen hours early. Why wait?"

I looked around the room quickly, passing over each of my advisors. "Excuse me, please." I grabbed Zeke's arm probably a little too hard and walked stiffly out of the library.

As soon as the doors closed behind us, I was hyperventilating. "Why wait?" I nearly shrieked. "Because I had one more day! One more day and one more night! I'm not—I can't—" How to even put into words the sudden anxiety I felt? My entire life would change the moment I said my vows. I wanted to, of course I did, but . . . My head began to feel light, the hall spinning. I felt as though I could have fallen to the floor right then and there. Between this and the weight of our upcoming endeavor suddenly making my shoulders want to cave in on themselves, it was a miracle I didn't collapse.

"Breathe, Rose."

As always, Zeke's voice was a beacon of stillness in the noise of my mind.

He lifted my hand to his chest, and just that small touch gave me something on which to center my focus. "Zeke, I don't mean that I'm not excited to marry you or—or spend the—" Suddenly heat rose to my cheeks, and my tongue stopped working properly.

He chuckled and cupped my burning cheek in his hand. "I know, Rose. You don't have to explain yourself." I finally looked up at him. His eyes swam with warmth. "You know you can trust me when I say you have nothing to worry about, but you also know we don't have to go forward with the wedding if you aren't feeling ready."

I did know, but hearing him say it made such a difference.

Only, the difference it made wasn't quite what I'd expected. My breathing slowed to match the calm rise and fall of Zeke's chest. I let his heartbeat beneath my hand guide me to stiller waters.

My hand on his chest balled into a fist. "No," I said. His clear eyes held me steady. "We're getting married tonight." Amicka was not going to take this away from me.

A smile spread across his face, and he leaned down and pressed his lips to mine.

There was a meaningful cough behind us. Gryffin had exited the library, books and scrolls tucked under his arm. "That's all well," he said stiffly. "Just be sure you leave *some* time tonight to ready yourselves. We leave first thing in the morning, and the last thing this realm needs is two unprepared saviors." Then he turned away from us without another glance and walked down the hall, disappearing around the corner.

# CHAPTER NINETEEN

HAZEL SNIFFLED DELICATELY in my ear as she added a few more pins to my hair. In the mirror, my intricate braids twisted into a collection of pearls and white asters at the nape of my neck. Just a few strands were left free, framing my face in gentle brown waves.

"Hazel . . ." Words lost their way. This woman, who'd raised me when my mother no longer could, was readying me for an event she'd dreamed for me since I was a little girl. Yet it wasn't to a prince, and it wasn't in a grand royal wedding. I preferred it this way, but Hazel probably felt as though it was happening too quickly.

It *was* happening too quickly.

"Hazel, I . . . I know this isn't as you'd pictured it." She met my eyes in the mirror. "I know this is simpler and so much quicker than either of us had ever imagined. But I—" My voice broke. "I'm happy that it's you here with me."

"My dear." Hazel placed her hands on my shoulders. "There is nowhere else I'd rather be." She reached for a golden circlet resting on the vanity and delicately placed it atop my head. A subtle crown.

The small clusters of rose-red rubies that were fastened in the curves of metal gleamed as Hazel studied my hair one last time and smiled. "There."

With just a few short hours to work with, and the title no longer mine, Hazel managed to make me look like a queen once again.

The maid's door opened, and first Kathryn, then Celeste, and finally Isabele came into the room, with a white gown I'd yet to try on or even lay eyes upon draped over her arm. There was a thrum of excitement in my chest, and that alone almost brought tears to my eyes. It was the first true excitement I felt for this whole ordeal.

They'd all decided to wear gowns of various shades of purple. Celeste's was darkest, a deep mauve that complemented her complexion, and it beautifully draped over her frame, while Kathryn's was a rich and regal hue with lengths of taffeta that hugged her figure. Isabele's gown was the lightest, the folds of fabric like the petals of a lily swaying as she laid the wedding dress on my bed.

*My* wedding dress.

"Hilderic truly outdid himself," Kathryn said, a delicate note of envy in her tone. "I don't think he's ever made me a dress this fine, and I'm one of his favorite clients."

I touched the lace shimmering through with silver thread, mesmerized as the candlelight seemed to dance across it in iridescent rivulets. Where did he even find such fabric?

Hazel and Isabele slipped the gown over my chemise. As the weight of the dress settled onto my hips, I slid my arms through the long draping sleeves and fidgeted while Kathryn laced up the back. Hilderic certainly had my measurements down to perfection. Even the neckline framed my collarbone seamlessly, the dip in the center leaving just enough to the imagination.

Hazel's eyes sprang forth with new tears.

I turned to the mirror once more, and the woman staring back at me was a queen.

A queen with confident green eyes and proud shoulders, adorned with a golden crown and a wedding dress that was regal in its simplicity, the lace hugging her body and sleeves just barely sweeping the floor at her feet.

I felt like her.

I *was* her.

I was me.

Hazel blubbered beside me and dabbed her eyes. "My queen, you are stunning."

I felt the sting of tears behind my own eyes as I looked at this woman—at *me*—in the mirror. When Isabele, Celeste, and Kathryn joined me in my reflection, I smiled.

"Ezekiel is going to lose himself when he sees you," Celeste said with a smirk.

Kathryn nodded fervently. "I haven't known him for very long, but she's right. Any man willing to go straight into the center of enemy territory to search for the woman he loves is already hopeless."

I nudged her shoulder with mine and laughed. "It's a good thing he had you to point him in the right direction when he didn't find me there."

With a final pin added to my hair, we all admired the handiwork of Hazel and Hilderic for another bated breath.

Then, Isabele gave me a kiss on the cheek. "Let's get you two married."

My heart began to pound standing outside the doors of the chapel. I had to remind myself to breathe. I'd done much scarier things in my life. I'd faced wolves, a raging river, and I was soon to be facing an all-powerful sorceress. Why did this suddenly feel like the most nerve-wracking thing I'd ever done?

I loved Zeke. I wanted to do this. To spend the rest of my life bound to him, and him to me. It was just—it was just happening so quickly. Any other marriage proposed to me had been under pressure, or falsehood. This one was not. This one was my choice. *Mine.* Something I'd spent so long thinking would be impossible.

Then why was I shaking? Why were my palms slick?

Whose idea was it to leave me alone out here?

Great Haggard, I needed to pull myself together.

Lord Brock peeked his head through the chapel door. "Your Majesty—" He stopped. The nervousness in my eyes must have been more apparent than I'd thought. He quickly squeezed through the door and closed it behind him.

"My queen." He took my hand in his. If he noticed how clammy it was, he didn't let on. "What's wrong?"

"Nothing," I said, but my quivering voice betrayed me. "Why am I so nervous? Is there something I'm not doing right?"

To my surprise, Lord Brock chuckled. That simple, light gesture eased some of my trembling. "My queen," he said. "What you're feeling is what many people feel before facing that altar. I did, and I was thrilled beyond measure to be marrying my Giselle. That was thirty years ago. I think it'd be near impossible to find a couple who has gone into their union without an ounce of nervousness, and I don't think that will ever change." Then in the dim light, he smirked. "Sir Ezekiel is probably out there sweating in his boots."

I laughed unsteadily. "Zeke doesn't get nervous."

"Now *that* is an utterly false statement, and I say that most respectfully, my queen." He patted my hand. "Let's put the nerves of both of you to rest, hmm?"

I took one final, steadying breath, and letting the air blow out through my lips, I nodded.

Lord Brock smiled, and he gave a quiet knock on the door. The handles clanged and the door creaked on its hinges—all details I clung to as Lord Brock settled into step behind me.

Zeke's form was the first thing my eyes sought out. There he was, at the end of this short aisle, knuckles white from clenching his hands together. He wore a vest the color of cream, with Lecevonia's cobalt and carmine coat of arms embroidered upon it. His hair had been tamed back into neat golden waves over the top of his head, and I almost giggled. He'd let someone style his hair?

When our eyes met, his clenched hands slowly uncurled, and my heart stopped pounding. Suddenly, the warmth of his smile was what propelled one foot in front of the other, and it was only when I placed my hand in his that I realized I had a bright smile of my own making my cheeks ache. Not that I minded at all. He lifted my hand to his lips, and the whisper of a kiss washed across my skin as he said, "My Rose."

If my heart could have melted even more than it had already, it'd have been a puddle on the ground.

Lord Castor called everyone's attention, and he opened the same old tome from which he'd read for my coronation. He cleared his throat, and he looked back and forth between me and Zeke.

Then, with a small smile, he closed the book with a soft thud.

I had to stifle a gasp. Lord Castor was a pedant of tradition.

Without another hesitation, he began the ceremony.

"Lecevonia has for centuries relied on the love of one's neighbor," he said. "Malice was never the way for the people of this kingdom. So, when two people come before us all to proclaim that love between them, it is no small matter. It is the kingdom's very essence, manifested between two people who care so strongly for one another as they vow to uphold that love of neighbor to the highest degree—the love between husband and wife. That bond is sacred. It is unmoving. It is the choice made *every* day by each spouse, to be true to one another in selflessness and sacrifice, which is reciprocated by the other without question. And by that choice, it is the constant source of strength through every trial this life may have in store."

I peeked at Zeke through my periphery. He was my choice. The most tumultuous yet *right* choice I'd ever made. I was choosing my home in his heart. And I would choose him every day.

Lord Castor pursed his lips. "Seeing as I'm going off-script, I may soon as well also say that King Doran and Queen Ryia, their souls rest in peace, would have been thrilled to stand here today to see this union, and it goes without saying that they would be extremely proud of their daughter."

At the mention of Papa and Mama, tears welled in my eyes.

*They would be proud.*

They would have approved of my choice. I heard Lord Brock suck in a sharp breath behind me, and I looked at him. He met my eyes, pursed his lips, and nodded. *Marrying for the kingdom's strength be forever damned,* he seemed to say. But, oddly enough, I *was* marrying for the kingdom's strength. Lecevonia was only as strong as its leader. And here and now, I felt very strong.

Lord Castor then produced the black horse's hide from behind the newly built tabernacle, the very same hide used in every other important celebration, including my coronation and Gryffin's vow of loyalty to Lecevonia. Some vow that had been. He draped the hide over both our shoulders in true Lecevonian tradition.

Lord Castor cleared his throat. "Your Majesty, your vows."

Taking a deep breath, I turned to Zeke. With the events leading up to the wedding moving so quickly, we hadn't even considered rehearsing anything beforehand. I was a bit shocked to have to go first. Though I wasn't Queen by title, I supposed it maybe felt too odd to Lord Castor to act as though Zeke and I were of same rank. I held Zeke's hand in both of mine and met his steady gaze.

"I, Rosemary, take you, Ezekiel, to be my husband."

That half-smile I loved appeared on his lips.

"I promise myself to you and only you. I promise you my heart, for it is yours. I promise you my love, my faithfulness, and my alliance in every moment, both good and bad, throughout the rest of my life."

Zeke let out a happy chuckle and kissed my hand, and I recognized Hazel's sniffle from somewhere over my right shoulder.

Lord Castor smiled. "Sir Ezekiel, your vows please."

"I, Ezekiel, take you, Rosemary, to be my wife." His voice rang clearly and triumphantly through the chapel. "I promise myself to you and only you. I promise you my heart, for it has always been yours." His subtle change to the vows made Lord Castor crinkle his nose, but otherwise went unnoticed. Except by me. I'd always cherish those words. "I promise you my love, my faithfulness, and my alliance in every moment, both good and bad, throughout the rest of my life."

His vows would forever be inscribed onto my heart.

Hazel, that sweet woman, blubbered behind me.

Lord Castor nodded with approval. "The rings, then?"

Jacobin stepped forward and gently dropped two gold rings into Lord Castor's outstretched palm. I was glad we'd at least had *that* done ahead of time. The goldsmith, on a whim, had taken on Amos's son as an apprentice. As it turned out, the boy had quite the natural ability to work with fine metal. He'd made these rings, and in a way, it brought

Amos here to the chapel with us. He would undoubtedly approve of my marrying Zeke, and the thought brought a smile to my face.

Lord Castor handed one ring to me and the other to Zeke. "These rings symbolize your union. Unbreakable and unending. As you place these rings on one another's finger, you seal your vows."

Zeke slid the ring onto my finger, right next to my ring of rubies, so quickly that I laughed. As I slid the ring onto his, he let out a breath he'd seemed to be holding for a long time. His smile was so bright I could've been fooled that the sun was shining through the chapel's open window instead of the moon.

"You are now husband and wife." Lord Castor raised his chin and smiled. He slid the hide off our shoulders and folded it over his arm. "Before this moment, you've walked a path alone. Now, take your first steps together as you partake on a new path of love, union, partnership, and trust."

Hand in hand, we descended the short steps, and the chapel erupted into cheers. And when we kissed, his hand caressing the back of my head grounded me to that moment I knew I would revisit for the rest of my life. We parted, and in my husband's eyes, I saw unbridled joy and pride.

I smiled at him and leaned in close. "I'm yours, Zeke. And you are mine."

That half-smile slid back onto his features. "About time." With our hands holding fast, we nearly sprinted down the aisle to the chapel doors amidst the shouts of approval from those around us.

I expected to feel different. That my vows would make some inherent shift in me. All my nerves from before—I'd thought that warranted some huge change in myself. But truly, I felt like the same woman as the one before. Comfortable here with Zeke, his hand strong and warm in mine. This amount of love and promise was already there. Nothing had changed, and yet, officially anyway, everything had.

Perhaps that said something about marrying one's best friend.

Music from the Great Hall drifted through the doors as we walked in, and Zeke immediately dragged me to the floor space cleared for dancing. His scent of sage and leather filled my senses as he pulled me close.

We hadn't ever been allowed to dance with each other in public. By the time I was eight, my royal status had begun to matter to visiting dignitaries, and I was forced to stay by Papa's side while Zeke got to romp around the Hall and hide under the pastry table. So now, as he settled a hand on my waist in front of all these people, it felt like we were breaking all the rules.

My chest rose and fell with his as we swayed to the musicians' tune. When he elegantly twirled me in a circle, I flashed an impressed smile at him. "Since when do you know how to dance? I know they didn't teach you this for your scouts' assignments."

His breath tickled my ear when he chuckled. "I've watched you a lot, and I practiced."

My heart skipped a beat.

While we danced, others joined in around us. Lord Brock and his wife Giselle, Isabele and Henry, Jacobin and his wife. Hazel and Lord Quince even found their way to the floor.

Then the smell of food coaxed us all to the banquet tables as the kitchen workers on duty rolled out tray after tray of food. Since our preserved food had been spoiled, we had no way to store food while the storage bins and cellars were being cleaned. Thus, a feast for us tonight. Bread rolls, cheese, roasted ham and hens, smoked venison, potatoes and carrots, cinnamon buns. Mead and huge jars of spice wine were met with heavy applause, and when a tray of my favorite blueberry pastries was placed on the small table set for Zeke and me, I could have burst out in song.

As we ate, our friends stopped by our table with congratulations. Sir Terrin clapped Zeke on the back, and Roger gathered me into a bear hug. General Gambeson and Colonel Burnstead, Zeke's higher officer, bowed to me and shook Zeke's hand, as did my old guards, Sirs Hugh, Robert, and Geoffrey. I'd been thrilled to learn that they had survived Roderich's attack on Hillstone after following my orders to return to the Great Hall and protect my advisors there. Sir Hugh's wife had her baby while I'd been away in Tarasyn. A little boy, just as they'd hoped.

I felt the stark absence of Amos and Thomas. They'd spent years serving the Crown together, the best of friends, and they had both died protecting me. Guilt flattened my smile, and Zeke squeezed my hand beneath the table as if he could tell what troubled me. I touched the gold ring on Zeke's finger, and I could almost hear Amos recalling the time Thomas had put cheese in his boots.

There was another absence I noticed, and it was one for which I was grateful. Gryffin hadn't shown himself all night, aside from Celeste saying she'd spotted him taking a glass of spice wine back to the guest wing.

Good. There were enough complicated emotions circling through the Great Hall.

As the night drew closer to the end, an air of sadness shifted through the crowd. We were all finally facing the truth that tomorrow, Zeke, Gryffin, and I were leaving on a nearly impossible quest. One that we might not return from. But no one dared say goodbye. That would have made it too real.

Instead, I clung to Zeke as we danced, a stubborn smile on my lips as the cool autumn night drifted in through the windows. My fingers traced a line light as a feather from the collar of his vest up to his ear, and back down again, raising goosebumps on Zeke's skin in their wake.

His eyes blazed. They lit a fire in my chest that burned through my veins and settled low in my stomach. He ran his hand down my arm, and when his touch left the lace of my dress and grazed the bare skin of my wrist, a shiver ran through me. He took hold of my hand and leaned in close to my ear. "I need to be alone with you."

I nodded breathlessly, and we subtly left the noise of the banquet behind us. People would notice our absence soon, but in that moment, I didn't care. All that mattered was Zeke's smile and his brown eyes looking back at me through the dim candlelight of the halls. We finally reached my chambers, and the heat in the pit of my stomach grew as Zeke quietly closed the door behind us.

Just us.

The air changed a bit, the heat altering into something more hesitant.

"Rose," he said quietly, still facing the door. "I know . . . I know tomorrow we leave, and we might not come back. I can't stand the thought that we have this beginning, and that we might not see it through."

I touched his shoulder, and he turned to me. The fire in his eyes, though still alight, had died down from a blaze to smoldering embers. "Zeke." My voice was a whisper in the great expanse of these stone walls. "I'm going to say something that we both already know. Our future is in as much jeopardy now as it is if we don't go to Loche.

Amicka will starve us, belittle us, kill our loved ones—until we are no more than a husk of ourselves. And that's if we even survive this winter." My voice grew louder, and Zeke's eyes narrowed. I grabbed his hand and held steadfast. "I want to see this through too. I want to live life with you and experience new things with you and—and someday have a family with you and grow old with you. I don't want it to end because of Amicka. Because of something *I* had a hand in making possible. I—I couldn't live with myself—"

He silenced me with his lips against mine. Tender but unwavering, just as my heart felt for him, and just what I needed to step back from spiraling.

He broke away and whispered in my ear. "I never want you to blame yourself for what has become of this world."

I blamed myself every day. That was why I had to make everything right again.

But my thoughts evaded me as Zeke pressed kisses just below my jaw, on the sensitive skin of my neck.

"This world doesn't matter to me right now," he said against my skin. I felt his lips stretch into a smile, and the heat returned to my veins. "*My* world is what I care about, and my world is you." He lifted his head and looked me in the eyes.

Outside this room, another world went on, a world where we might not see next week. But here, Zeke was my world, sun, and stars.

I wrapped my arms around his neck and crushed my lips to his. With him, I was exactly where I was supposed to be. I was exactly *who* I was supposed to be. I was Rose, his wife. His home.

His fingers played with the stays at the small of my back, asking for permission, and I nodded. The dress loosened around me, and I let the sleeves fall off my shoulders and the fabric slide away until I stood in a pool of lace. I was wrapped in his arms in my chemise, which was nothing he hadn't seen before, but his eyes drank me in like he was seeing me anew. His gaze wasn't hungry, as men had looked at me before. It wasn't possessive—well, maybe a bit. I didn't mind that so much, not with Zeke. Above all else, though, his gaze was admiring. Maybe even awestruck. As if he couldn't believe his fortune in being here with *me*. And that warmed my cheeks and heated my blood more than anything.

Then he lifted his eyes to mine and smiled. He pressed a sweet kiss to my cheek. "Let's get those pins out of your hair."

I laughed breathlessly and let him lead me to my vanity. It didn't escape me how lucky I was to have a man so concerned with my comfort. But this was Zeke I was with. Of course he cared about my comfort. He always had. One by one, he fished the pins and pearls and tiny white flowers out of my hair, letting my brown waves fall around my shoulders. The release of the pressure on my scalp was like magic itself. He met my eyes in the mirror as he removed the golden circlet from the top of my head and placed it on the table of my vanity.

When he finished with my hair, I stood and turned to him, and he held out his arms to me. But I shook my head. "You should be more comfortable too," I said, reaching for the top buckle of his vest. As I slid the strap free, he placed his hands on top of mine. I'd never done anything like this before, and it was then I noticed the nervous tremor in my hands. Zeke chuckled, flashing his teeth. "We don't have to do anything, Rose."

I smacked him in the shoulder. "Stop trying to discourage me."

"Believe me, I'm not." He followed my hands down as I unfastened the next buckle. "This is a first for me too." I raised my eyebrow at him, and he shrugged. "I've always taken off my own vest. For what it's worth, I think you're doing a wonderful job."

His teasing softened the edge in me, and I felt the muscles in my shoulders relax. With the last buckle undone, he shrugged out of his vest and let it fall to the floor, his eyes never leaving mine. My heart beat faster as he slipped a finger beneath the strap of my chemise, teasing my skin with his warm touch.

Then he lowered his lips to mine again, and I found it easier to let myself feel that warmth he always brought to my mind. That sense of belonging. That sense of home.

Everything became easier after that.

I'd never been with a man before. Yet here, with my husband, my best friend and soul's complement, it felt like the most natural thing. My inexperience hadn't mattered as we fell into a rhythm as old as humanity itself. I completed his heart, and he completed mine. Everything else simply fell into place.

Afterward, lying there with him in the crook of his arm, I held onto this moment as long as I could. In a few short hours, we'd be on our way to face Amicka and all her magic. My heart ached to think that tonight might be the only night we had. That our beginning was already coming to an end.

But I didn't want to focus on the end. Instead, I focused on Zeke's fingers writing "I love you" on my shoulder, until I slipped under the draw of sleep to his humming of that familiar Lecevonian lullaby.

*Hush now, my sweet darling,*
*Oh, the pink hues of the sun creep,*
*Hush now, and just maybe,*
*On Equos's horses you will sleep.*

# CHAPTER TWENTY

WE WERE DOWN in the Royal Stable before dawn. Midas, Hugo, and Lucy were each saddled and pawing at the ground, anxious to get on the road as much as we were.

I looked over at Zeke. We'd rolled out of bed less than an hour ago, holding on to each minute together that we could before facing what lay ahead. He was tying bags of oats to each of the horses. Without knowing what the road would be like, there was no guarantee we'd be able to stop anywhere and buy food for the horses—if there was food to buy at all.

"Will it be enough?" I asked him anxiously.

He took a deep breath and shrugged. "It's going to have to be. It's all that can be spared."

"They can graze too," Gryffin said from behind Lucy. It was the first time he'd spoken to us this morning. "It's not like the frozen ground in Tarasyn. They'll be all right." Then he fell silent and went back to tightening the straps of his saddlebags.

I turned to Midas and patted his neck, like black velvet beneath my palm. This would be the longest journey he'd ever been on. Aside from being taken to Port Della, which was only a two-day trek. Spoiled palace horse, thanks to me. Worry creased my brow, even though worrying felt foolish. He was a direct descendent from Equos's line. Of course he would be fine.

And, well, maybe I was picking things to worry about instead of the task at hand.

I pulled aside my traveler's cloak and eyed Amicka's spearhead tucked into the belt of my trousers. If I listened extremely well, I could hear the faintest hum of magic still swirling within. Certainly not as strong as before the Silencing, not strong enough to speak to me as the other five relics had done. But still present nonetheless. Amicka's absorption of power hadn't drained the spearhead completely. And there was no way I was letting this off my person. This was our last hope, our futures relying on this spearhead and a hazy theory.

After one final check of our saddles, we mounted our horses and rode them out into the violet dawn.

We traveled hard, too fast for talking. The chill in the air nipped at my neck, the hood of my cloak flying uselessly behind me at the speed we were traveling. Zeke and I had let Gryffin set the pace.

He hadn't looked either of us in the eye yet today.

I, on the other hand, was very aware of Zeke's presence. And from the way he kept meeting my gaze, he must have felt the same. Last night had changed our dynamic for the rest of our lives, however long or short that may be. Becoming that intimate with him—sharing in something so special, so sacred—made it impossible to ignore his presence. As if a new thread had been woven between us, forever making each of us aware of the other. The small smiles shared between us were a new rendition, yet still the most natural in the world.

How much longer would I be able to enjoy those smiles?

The main road loosely followed the Riparia River, and I felt time slipping out of my grasp as the ground rushed beneath the horses' hooves. There was no pull toward Loche like the last time I made this journey. If anything, I felt an aversion to continuing forward, like fighting against the wind. Now that we were on the road, every fiber of me wanted to give up, turn around, and return to my bed with Zeke.

But I fought forward. Lecevonia was only as strong as its leader, and I wouldn't let weakness win. Besides, giving in to defeat wasn't something I'd ever been good at.

We careened too quickly first through the fiery trees, then through the browning grasslands. We hadn't stopped yet today, and the sun was well past noon in the autumn sky. Part of me wondered if Gryffin was in such a hurry because it meant he didn't have to speak to us. If we rode ourselves to the bone, maybe he would never have to.

Midas seemed to be handling the breakneck pace fine, but the horsewoman in me told me we needed to stop and give the horses a chance to breathe. And, surely, we could use a chance to breathe too.

Then, just as I was about to suggest so, Gryffin clucked his tongue and slowed his horse.

But he didn't slow out of concern for the horses, though they were all huffing in earnest.

There was a pungent odor in the air, as though a hen's eggs had cracked and gone bad in the coop. I lifted the neck of my cloak over my nose, and Zeke's face wrinkled in disgust.

"What the Haggard is that?" he asked.

Gryffin slowly crested the hill. He stopped there, staring at whatever lay on the other side. His horse's ears lay flat against her head, and she let out a shrill cry.

When Gryffin turned back toward us, his face was bleak. "Rosemary. You should see this."

Dread settled in the pit of my stomach. I urged Midas forward, then jerked to a stop next to Gryffin on the hillcrest. My heart pounded in my throat.

Below was unlike anything I'd seen before. A deep gouge in the earth carved straight through the center of a collection of thatched-roof buildings and small wooden homes. Or, at least, what *had* been buildings and homes. From here, it looked as though almost every structure had been reduced to cinders, the thatch and wood nothing but smears of smoldering black soot. Only a handful of homes far enough away from the gouge still stood, meek amongst the carnage. Framed by two jagged edges of charred rock, the earth inside *boiled*. Bright, thick liquified earth that churned and spit.

I'd never seen lava before. There wasn't supposed to be anything like this in my kingdom.

What could have caused such catastrophe? What could have caused the very earth to melt in its place?

Or . . . who.

My blood began to boil like the earth below me as I pieced together a theory.

I kicked my heels, propelling Midas into a gallop. He didn't protest as we bounded forward down the main road. What village was this? I wracked my brain as I rode, trying to figure out where in Lecevonia we were exactly. We hadn't reached the Port Della-Aridia fork in the main road yet, and the Riparia River's rumble could still be heard, though out of sight. So this had to have been Corin, a small village north of Aridia. Thanks to Gryffin's pace, we'd shed off an extra half-day's travel—

Gryffin suddenly materialized in front of me, sending Midas back on his hind legs with a shriek, along with a few choice words of my own.

"What do you think you're doing?" I said. "Let me through!"

"Rosemary, think!" He steadied Lucy and looked at me with steely blue eyes. "Amicka can't know we're on the road. What if she's still down there? What if Rebels are down there tying up loose ends?" I tried to rush past him, but he wheeled his horse around and blocked my path once more. "We can't be recognized, Rosemary. *You* can't be recognized!"

I glared at him, anger and the need for some sort of action still roiling inside me. The horses' snorts and the stomping of their hooves filled the silence between us. How could I stand by as my people and their livelihoods burned to the ground in front of me?

Zeke quietly rode up behind me. "He has a point, Rose."

I knew he had a point. I was too recognizable within my own kingdom's borders, and the risk of Rebels raising the alarm to Amicka was far too great. But that didn't calm me in the slightest.

I hit them both once more with a stabbing glare before throwing my hood over my head. "Fine. Let's just continue."

After a moment's silence, I heard Gryffin click his tongue and the sound of hooves clomping forward on the dusty road. Zeke stayed by my side, and I realized he wouldn't move until I did. Probably in case I tried to make a run for it. I nudged Midas forward, and just as I suspected, I heard Zeke's reins jingle as he guided Hugo into stride behind me. I kept my eyes glued to Midas's withers, refusing to look at either of the men.

We followed the main road down the hill, then cut into the grass to avoid the village and the lava-filled gash. The seedheads brushed my knees, the rustling of the grass as the horses forged ahead almost too loud.

Then, above the rustling, I heard a shout. I quickly turned my head, back toward Corin, and I saw the dark figure of a person facing us, waving their arms in the air. They shouted again, louder this time.

Gryffin growled under his breath and urged Lucy faster through the brush. "They've seen us," he said over his shoulder. "Hurry, we need to move."

"What are you saying? They're asking for help. We have to go back." I was already wheeling Midas around.

Zeke pulled up beside me, stopping me. "Rose. No. Look, we have to go."

I pulled my eyes away from the figure in the road and looked at Zeke. In his eyes I saw the need to keep going, the pressure of leaving this behind us. Worse dangers lay ahead. Why endanger ourselves here? This was nothing compared to what we would soon be facing.

But if we left my people to die, what were we even doing this for?

I set Zeke a steeled look, lips pursed. Then I pushed past him and kicked Midas into a gallop.

I would not run from my people when they needed help most.

I could just barely hear both men groaning over the rush of the grass around me as we sped toward the road. I found the person's figure again and ran straight for it. The person's shouts grew louder and louder until finally I broke through the grass and hit the packed dirt of the road.

The figure, a young woman with red hair, sooty cheeks, and flame-licked skirts bounded to my side. "Thank Haggard," she said, out of breath as I lowered my hood. "Thank you, thank you so much. We were beginning to think any hope for help was useless—Your Majesty! Oh—I—" She stammered over her own words and dipped into an awkward curtsy.

I quickly dismounted Midas and took her hands in mine. "Please. No formalities. What can I do to help?"

Without another word, she grabbed my hand and pulled me toward the scorched town. I held Midas's reins tightly in my other hand. I heard the rush of grass behind me as Zeke and Gryffin burst through the brush, but I didn't spare the time to turn and look at them.

"It's like Cliva all over again," Zeke said, just before we rushed out of earshot.

The woman and I rushed around huge black piles of soot, smoke still rising into the air above them. She didn't lead me anywhere near the boiling earth, but the heat radiating through the entire village was almost unbearable. Midas protested, pulling at his reins and grunting against the heat.

Finally, I could see where we were headed—the only three houses left standing on the edge of the village.

Clustered around the houses were a small group of people. "Survivors?" I asked the woman.

She nodded. "Fifteen of us."

Fifteen.

On the last census, Corin had reported two hundred living within the village.

The anger in my chest grew, and I blinked back red-hot tears.

The people that were gathered turned as we approached, murmuring. I could tell when they recognized me, for they stood a little straighter in surprise. But I held out my hands, silently asking for no acknowledgement.

The woman led me to the first house and hurried through the open doorway. I dropped Midas's reins and followed.

We were immediately greeted by the smell of singed flesh and a glowering man, well over six feet tall, blocking our way further into the house.

"Arin," he said, in a voice deeper than Roger's and full of warning.

The woman, Arin, laid a hand on his broad shoulder. "It's the queen. We can trust her."

He looked back at me quickly, hesitantly bowed his head, then turned back to Arin. "How will she able to help? She isn't a healer."

"Luka might not make it if we don't try *something*."

After the longest second, he stepped aside and let me through.

Arin knelt down by a bed, where a little boy lay, grimacing and semi-conscious, with a big golden dog quietly whimpering by his side against the wall. One of the boy's fists was curled tightly into the dog's fur. The boy's other fist—and entire arm and right side of his torso for that matter—was blistered and seared.

My hand flew to my mouth. "Oh great Haggard."

Arin touched the boy's forehead gently. "Luka."

The boy stirred and moaned. But he didn't open his eyes.

I stood there feeling utterly helpless. What could I do to help this boy? These people? The only thing that crossed my mind was the pack of medicines and first aid in Midas's saddlebag. I'd never treated a burn before, much less seen one so severe, but maybe something in that pack could be of help. Healing had never been a focus in my political studies, but I'd read something . . . What was it—?

"Honey," Zeke's voice behind me said.

I hadn't heard him enter the house. Clearly the man to whom Arin had spoken hadn't either. He rounded swiftly toward the doorway, fists at the ready.

Zeke held his hands up. "At ease. Honey will help his burns."

Arin looked back and forth between Zeke and me. "Honey?" She darted into another room and returned just a second later with the smallest jar I'd ever seen, full of amber-colored honey. Zeke looked at the jar with a pitiful grimace, but he took it and knelt beside the boy. The boy moaned, and the dog next to him lifted his head and growled.

"Jo, quiet," the glowering man said, and the dog settled back against the boy and closed his eyes.

As Zeke got to work, I pulled Arin aside. "This will help for a little while, but he's going to need more than that. Is there any more?"

Arin pursed her lips and nodded. "Only one more jar though. Seb's guilty pleasure is honey on his flax biscuits every morning, if we have any. These two jars were a birthday gift a few months ago."

"Seb?"

She nodded toward the glowering man. He now stood over Zeke, watching his actions carefully, mumbling questions every now and then. "Sebastyn. Family name for generations, and he doesn't like it. Everyone calls him Seb, but I'll call him Seabass when I'm teasing him." She flashed me a little smirk before her face settled back into grim lines.

We left Zeke and Seb to their work and walked outside the house, which had begun to feel cramped. I walked to where Midas stood dutifully near the house, now joined by Hugo and Lucy. Gryffin was nowhere to be seen. Grabbing the pack of medicines from my saddlebag, I handed it to Arin. "Here. I know it's not much, but something in there may be useful."

Arin hesitated before taking it from my hands. "Thank you, my queen. 'My queen.' Is that right? I've never addressed any royalty." Her giggle hitched with nerves. "Either way, thank you."

I almost corrected her, that I was no longer queen, but at the last second, I decided against it. What would have been the point? "Is Luka your son?" I asked instead.

"Oh no," Arin said. She tucked a hair behind her ear and looked down to the ground. "Seb and I haven't had any children of our own. Luka is our nephew. His parents—my sister and her husband, well, they . . ." Shaking her head, she took a deep breath and looked up at me again. "They didn't make it out of their house. Luka is lucky he was outside feeding the chickens."

I placed a hand on her arm and offered a small smile, and I felt sadness along its edges. "Luka is extremely lucky to have you and Seb. Did the Sorceress—?" A fresh burst of anger stopped my words. Of course she did this. I didn't need to ask. I caught myself grinding my teeth together. "Why did she do this to Corin?"

Arin shot a glare toward the gash in the earth. Even from this distance, the heat rising from the lava distorted and shimmered in the air. "Couldn't meet our quota for flaxseed. Ridiculous. Why would they need fifteen hundred pounds of flaxseed? It's just a small farm we have here in the village."

Ridiculous indeed. "How long ago did this happen?"

"Just yesterday," Arin said. "One moment we were harnessing up the horses for the field, and the next, the Sorceress was standing there on the main road. I'd never seen her before in my life, but it couldn't have been anyone else. She stood in this billow of smoke that was black as pitch, and she had her hands raised. The earth opened—" She struggled through a lump rising in her throat. "The earth opened, and our village was aflame."

My veins iced over. Amicka was here just yesterday. Unlike creating spoilage in our food, she hadn't been able to carve out the earth from afar. Had we left Hillstone when Gryffin wanted to, we would have been here, and we might've been killed as simple as that.

Oblivious to my dread, Arin looked out to the main road, sliced through by the gouge. "We've been waiting for someone to come along since then. Thank Haggard you three stopped for us. My queen, I . . . I don't know how much longer we can go on like this."

Taking a steeled breath, I took her hand in mine firmly and spoke with conviction. "Once Luka is healed enough to be moved, all of you pack your belongings and go to the capitol. You will be cared for there. I promise you. And when everything is set right once more, you can focus on rebuilding your village."

"Set right?" Arin looked at me, the smallest shimmer of hope welling in her eyes.

So many villages to rebuild. So many lives that had been cut short, gone forever.

Yes, this needed to be set right. Amicka needed to be brought down from her high perch and rendered powerless, before the entire Peninsula was destroyed. What was her goal with all of this anyway? To torture us until there was no one—and nothing—left for her to ruin?

I saw a silhouette walking close to the boiling gouge, as close as humanly possible with that raging heat. Gryffin, I realized. Seeing Amicka's wrath at this magnitude, uncertainty clouded any confidence I'd dared to feel. How were we going to face her and live? Gryffin's figure finally turned away from the gash and began walking back toward the surviving houses.

Zeke exited the house behind us with Seb.

I turned back quickly to Arin. "We'll be going on our way soon. Please, go to the capitol when you can. And I beg of you, keep our presence here a secret."

Arin dipped into a quick curtsy. "Of course, my queen. Who would we tell?"

I nodded my head and smiled in thanks. But I knew we weren't completely safe. Fear did strange things to people. Made them do strange things, like reporting that their former queen had arrived in their village, so far from where she should be in Equos. Any morsel of information in exchange for protection from Amicka's wrathful magic was enough of a motivation for just about anyone in these days of hardship.

Zeke came up behind me then and slid an arm around my waist, hugging me to him. His embrace still warmed me, made me want to forget all that was happening.

"Luka should be stable for a while," he told Arin. "There were bandages in one of the other two houses, and there are more in that bag there." He nodded to the medicinal pack in her hands, and then he side-eyed me. I could hear his sarcastic tone clear in my mind. *Not like we needed those, right?* "I showed Seb what to do, how to change the dressings on the burns. But . . . you will need more honey before long, and preferably proper medicine. Once Luka can manage traveling—"

"Head to the capitol." Arin looked at me and nodded. "Got it. Truly, thank you both so much." She reached out and took my hand. "Your reputation for kindness is true. Thank you, my queen. Wherever you are going, please, safe travels."

As she slid her hand from mine, the metal of my wedding ring touched her fingers. She glanced down, then back up at me, then down, and back up again. "Is that a wedding ring, my queen?"

I felt heat rise to my cheeks. Had that been only yesterday? I nodded and looked to Zeke. "Yes. My husband."

She looked at Zeke, speechless, then bobbed down into a rough bow. "Sir? *King?*"

Zeke held out his hands, shaking them profusely. "Oh, Haggard, please don't," while at the same time I said, "Definitely *not* 'king.'"

Arin's eyebrows pulled together in confusion, and I could tell she was fighting back a startled laugh. "Well, that sounds more complicated than I care to ask about. You both have our thanks and well-wishes." With a final tired smile, she turned away and headed through the door of the house, back to Luka.

Zeke crossed his arms over his chest. "When all of this is over, and if we come out of it alive, you'll be queen again."

It wasn't that the thought hadn't crossed my mind. But to hear it said aloud . . . I leaned against Midas. It felt like my legs were ready to give out. For me, it was out of relief. To have an identity again. My title had been stripped from me just as I'd begun to feel worthy of it. I'd fought wolves and starvation to get back home to my people. My father would have done the same, I thought.

No, my father would not have gotten imprisoned in Tarasyn in the first place.

But that was beside the point. If by some miracle I did survive this, I would be queen, and I would lead my people with as sure a hand as my parents before me.

It seemed, though, that this was maybe Zeke's first time realizing it. His eyes stayed pinned to the ground, mouth set in a hard line. "And that would make me—"

"Don't worry about it until we succeed," I said quickly.

After a moment, he nodded silently. He gave me a quick kiss on my cheek, sending warmth through me, and walked over to Hugo without another word.

He was upset. That much was clear. And that . . . hurt, honestly. I watched him check the straps of his saddle, and a heaviness began to set in. Did he regret marrying me now? As quickly as that? Surely not, when we were likely to die anyway . . .

I was talking myself out of the thought when someone cleared his throat behind me. Gryffin. I turned to him, willing away any thought of Zeke's regret and back to what needed to happen first, before we could even discuss titles and duties. Facing Amicka. I pursed my lips. "Did you know Amicka had this much power?"

His grave eyes answered my question.

She was stronger than we thought. Much stronger.

"Can we still do this?" My voice was as small as I felt.

He looked away, back toward the boiling earth. "If she's capable of something like this, what choice do we have but to try?"

The darkness in his tone told me he was thinking the same thing I was.

We weren't going to make it back home.

# CHAPTER TWENTY-ONE

WE MADE CAMP near Aridia, far enough from the village to avoid attracting attention. Any extra headway we'd made earlier that day by riding so quickly had been undone by our stop in Corin. I could feel the tension radiating off Gryffin's shoulders as he unsaddled Lucy and rolled out his pack on the ground.

After tonight's sleep, it was three days to Mareus. Four days until the Equinox. Just four days to fix what had been done to our world.

Only four days left with Zeke.

Zeke set his pack flush with mine. After seeing what Amicka was capable of, there was a subtle shift in the way he moved around me, and I around him. Each touch was longer, each gaze deeper. Like we were trying to fit a lifetime of contact into these next few days. In the tall grass and under the buzzing of cicadas, we almost had privacy.

As we lay there together, blankets tucked tightly against the chilly night air, I looked up at the clear sky. No moon. Countless stars. How did they still glimmer and blink so brightly when it felt as though we were on the brink of existence? A balance scale tipping toward oblivion?

When I looked back at Zeke, his dark eyes were studying me.

"You look like the world is resting on your shoulders."

"It feels like it." I took his hand in mine. "But I'm sharing the load. It isn't just on me."

He squeezed my hand, and I tucked my head closer to his. His hair was unkempt and still bright gold despite the darkness, his eyes twinkling even in the absence of the sun.

He was still my light. My light in the oblivion.

We crossed the border into Loche late the next day, and we stopped for the night before the plains gave way to marsh. None of us wanted to battle boggy earth and mosquitoes. Gryffin's pace had again shaved off time, and if the horses could continue at this speed, we could make it to Mareus before nightfall the following day. Again, Zeke and I laid our bed rolls next to one another, while Gryffin settled a bit farther away without a word.

The next morning's trek started early, but my heart fell further with each length—for the closer to Mareus we rode, the more destruction we faced. Burned towns, deserted ramshackle villages, marshes black with soot and debris. The stilts that once raised homes and shops above the wetlands appeared like cracked bones rising out of the water, broken and blackened. It was as though Amicka's wrath fanned out, with the once beautiful capitol of Loche at the epicenter.

Where were King Jarin and Queen Seraphine's children in all of this? Princess Avirine, next in line for Loche's throne, and her brothers? Had Amicka hunted them down too? Or had they disappeared into hiding well enough to survive this long?

Late in the afternoon, Gryffin's horse stumbled.

She didn't fall, but her shrill, exhausted whinny pierced my ears and utterly broke my heart. Gryffin's pace this journey had finally caught up with her. Gryffin dismounted, and we made camp in that very spot that night.

I would've been grateful for the delay had it pushed the Equinox back any further. But of course it didn't, and Gryffin's tension was greater than ever. He paced the road, batting away mosquitoes. If it were up to him, we would have kept going, but Lucy was old. She huffed heavily, and her head drooped. After he'd finished his pacing, he stayed by her side, patting her shoulder and offering her fresh water, mumbling apology after apology. The following day, we kept our horses moving at a slow walk for Lucy's sake.

The towering city gates of Mareus loomed ahead of us just before dusk. Not a moment to spare. The Equinox was tomorrow.

But as darkness fell, firelight appeared in the sentry tower.

Gryffin cursed. "The Rebels have watchers posted."

In the dark, the moon just barely a sliver, it was unlikely that whoever was in the tower had seen us approaching. But the question hung in the muggy air. With the Rebels' eyes on the city gates, how were we going to get inside?

"I'll go," Zeke said.

My protest was immediate. "No."

"Rose." My name on his lips was both sweet as honey and hard as coal. "Finding my way into cities undetected is what I do. I'll be fine, and I'm the best chance we've got. You know it."

I wanted to argue, but I couldn't. He was a scout after all. Still, the old pang I felt anytime he'd left on one of his assignments returned, feeling like too-tightly laced stays.

Gryffin nodded his agreement. "We'll wait for you near the wall."

We slowed our horses to a halt a few hundred yards from the gate, far enough to remain undetected, and all three of them stomped their hooves and huffed loudly in the dark. Poor Lucy was almost wheezing. The glare in her dark eyes told us exactly how she felt about our journey. Gryffin dismounted and patted her neck. "I'm sorry, old girl. We're done. Don't worry."

*We're done.*

I laid a hand on Midas's neck. This was a goodbye I hadn't prepared myself for.

Zeke landed on the ground next to me quietly, and after patting Hugo's dappled cheek with a whispered thanks, he handed Hugo's reins to me. "Once I'm clear, I'll find a way to let you both through." He lifted my chin and kissed me. "Stay close. I'll see you soon."

He flashed a parting smile, and then he turned and jogged off. I had to keep my hand tightly clenched around Hugo's reins, for otherwise I would have reached out and grabbed Zeke's vest in a vise before he could disappear into the night ahead of us.

The ache in my chest only worsened once he was out of my sight. That years-old fear whispering, *Will I ever see him again?* But I had to trust. He knew how to get past those gates better than any of us. Right now, the rest of our quest relied on his success.

Which left me with Gryffin. That fact didn't help the ache in my chest, either.

We advanced as silently as we could to the foot of the huge wall, staying to the shadows along the marsh. There was a strip of solid, grassy ground at the wall's base, wide enough for a carriage, maybe two. This was where we would have to leave our horses, free to graze the grass and marsh forage.

We took care to stay a short distance from the city gates, and

Gryffin leaned back against the washed-out stone, arms crossed over his chest. I lingered by Midas. This was the first time Gryffin and I had been alone since before the wedding, and I didn't know where we stood. He hadn't even come to the ceremony. Any conversation between us this entire journey had been clipped, only held when necessary.

I twisted my wedding ring around on my finger.

The woman who had once met him under the guise of potential marriage has long since changed. He has long since changed, too.

Then his deep voice broke our silence. "I've been thinking about something."

I breathed out a sigh of relief. I was thinking he'd never talk to me again. But I wasn't sure if I wanted to know what he'd been thinking about. Still hesitant, I looked at him over Midas's back.

"We don't know what's going to happen when we break apart the relics," he said, looking down at the ground. "There could be a release of power so great that there could be an explosion. Or . . . there could be nothing."

Nothing.

An explosion meant death. Nothing meant a chance to live. Or something entirely different could happen. What we were doing was completely uncharted.

"Someone needs to break apart the relics, and someone else needs to survive long enough to put the relics back together again." He lifted his gaze to look at me. "I think that person should be you."

There was nothing but sincerity in his clear blue eyes. "Why?" I asked.

"Ezekiel surely won't do it," he said, a little smile on his face. It didn't escape me that he called Zeke by his name rather than *guard dog.* "He's going to spend his dying breath protecting you. And I can take the risk that comes with breaking apart the relics. You just need to stay safe long enough to bring them all back together again."

I wasn't ready to face what he was telling me. Instead, holding back tears, I stepped around Midas and scoffed. "'Just.' You make that sound easy."

"It won't be, by any means."

"Gryffin—"

"Rosemary." His voice still caressed my name, but this time, it was affectionate rather than romantic. "You deserve to be the one to walk away from this."

I tore my eyes away from him. "I don't think any of us are walking away."

"Probably not." He pushed himself off the wall. "But I've seen your strength and your willpower. If anyone could make things right again, it's you."

He was openly offering to take the risk of sacrifice. He, Zeke, and I had each done so in embarking on this mission in the first place, but here we were at the foot of our fate, after seeing just how strong Amicka could be.

Once again, I saw myself in him. We were both still willing to do whatever was necessary to bring strength to our people, even if that meant strength in death.

And here he was, not only giving me the chance to be the one to bring magic back to our land, but also the best chance of survival. I didn't believe for one moment that that chance was high, but still.

When I looked at him again, his face was pulled together in remorse. "I'm so sorry, Rosemary."

My chest tightened. "Gryffin, don't. You've already apologized."

"Haggard knows I can't ever apologize enough." He ran a hand over his face. "However little time we have left."

I stepped forward and put a hand on his shoulder. "Gryffin."

He let his hand drop from his face, and he looked at me, blue eyes full of sorrow.

"The action you're taking now is your apology," I said. "You're here. You're making sacrifices too. You *have* apologized enough." I let my hand fall from his shoulder. "Besides, it's . . . It's not only your choices that led us here."

He studied me for a long time as we stood there in the shadow of the stone wall. Then he said, "If I could end this life knowing I have your forgiveness, I would be happy."

My forgiveness. This man had done so much wrong. What he'd wanted all along was for not only his kingdom but for the entire Magian Peninsula to be lifted up, made stronger, but he'd had terrible influences. He understood that now. *I* understood that now.

We'd both lost things we cherished. Our reign, our kingdoms. Gryffin had lost his Talent, and I had all but lost Zeke. The difference here was I had gotten Zeke back, at least for a short while. And now Gryffin was doing everything in his power, even after losing all that he had, to make things right. He had nothing to gain from dying, yet he was still willing to make the sacrifice for everyone else of the Magian Peninsula. Gryffin was, I believed in essence, a good man.

He was still looking at me, hope in his eyes, and I offered him a small, sincere smile. "Yes, Gryffin. I forgive you." I did.

We fell silent, but the heaviness in the air that was always present between us felt a hair lighter.

Then, the quiet of the marsh gave way to muted voices. We both stiffened, and Gryffin turned on his heel, placing himself between me and the city gates a short distance away. There was a thud against the huge doors of the gate, and the muted voices rose to shouting.

My blood froze in my veins. What had happened? Did Zeke—?

A hand landed on my shoulder from behind me, and I spun around so quickly, sword in hand, that I almost sliced Zeke's fingers off.

"Hey, easy," he said, indignation coating his voice.

I dropped my sword and sprang into his arms. "Thank Haggard." I breathed him in, sage and leather. "With all that noise, I thought you'd been captured."

He smirked. "Are you still always this worried about me?" He burrowed his face into my hair, though surely it was as dirty as the bottom of my boots, and I felt his lips at my ear. "I always come back to you."

Too soon, he pulled us apart. "We have to move while they're still distracted. Come on."

I looked back at Midas one last time. He'd wandered off down the stretch of grass with Hugo and Lucy and was but a black shadow in the darkness of night, his head down, nibbling at the grass and tail lazily switching away the mosquitoes. I prayed he would stay safe there, always as content as he appeared to be now. Maybe one day he would even find his way home.

In that moment, he lifted his head, his big eyes finding me through the dark.

Would he sense when I was no longer with him in this world?

I whispered a goodbye, and he twitched an ear. Then he threw his big head and pawed at the ground. *Where are you going?*

I bit my lip against a sob as I turned away from my friend. I mustered what resilience I could as I shouldered my small pack, checking one last time for the spearhead, and followed Zeke in the dark with Gryffin at my heels.

Zeke led us down a ways to a door that blended in so well to the gray stone that anyone else would have missed it. Even its handle lay perfectly into an almost imperceptible indentation, and the door itself was so small that I had to duck a bit to go through without smacking my head on the stone wall above. Both Gryffin and Zeke had to stoop almost to a bow.

"How'd you find this door?" I asked.

Zeke shrugged. "A Rebel was sitting guard here so I knew there must have been something worth looking into. The locks on here were freckin' diabolical at one time, but they were pretty worn. Practically fell apart into a rusty mess in my hand. All it took to get the guard away was a bit of distraction."

"At the main gates?" Gryffin guessed.

He nodded, and his familiar proud smile returned. "I'd go running too if a brick came flying out of nowhere."

"And all undetected." I was in awe. I'd never actually seen Zeke work before aside from the smooth lies he'd told in Pruin so many months ago.

He waved a hand over his shoulder. "Nothing I haven't done before. I'll admit, it wasn't as easy as . . . before . . . the Silencing. But I still have the years of experience, and that's not easily forgotten when my very life has depended on it so many times."

I nodded. I knew I wouldn't forget the skills Yetta had taught me in the frozen woods anytime soon.

Beyond the small door, the streets of Mareus were silent and dark. How different they were now than when we'd first rode in, alight with banners and lively music, ready to celebrate the upcoming Solstice Day. Now, the once sparkling buildings were covered in grime and left in disrepair, boarded up and unlit, or even simply left gaping open to the elements. There were deep cracks in the stone streets, up the sides of stone buildings that seemed on the verge of tumbling.

The city had died with its king and queen.

Were there even any citizens still here? Something dark inside me told me no. Whether by choice or a Rebel's blade, not a soul aside from Amicka and her followers were still walking within these walls.

We sidestepped along the nearest building, Zeke taking the lead. I had a memory resurface in my head of silently picking our way through the streets of my own capitol when Gryffin's brother had invaded.

Zeke stopped in his tracks ahead of me. "What in the—"

I nudged his shoulder. "What?"

He stooped to the ground and picked something up. "I can't believe what I'm seeing." He turned back to us and handed us what he'd picked up. A wet sheet of parchment near tearing, and though the night was dark with hardly a moon to shine, it was easy to see the sketch of a man taking up most of the space. I took it from him and gasped.

The man in the sketch was Gryffin.

"What is it?" Gryffin took the parchment from me and held it close to his face. When he saw himself staring back at him, he leaned hard against the stone side of the building and read aloud what accompanied the sketch. "'Wanted alive. Reward: food rations for the winter.'" He squinted at the parchment and brought it closer to his face. "Food rations. Is that all I'm worth?"

Zeke reached around me and took the parchment back. "The point is they're looking for you. And that's not good for us." He turned and looked down the dark alleyway in front of us. "We'll need to be careful."

I wanted to ask the question burning through all our brains, but I knew it wouldn't be any help because we had no way of knowing.

Why was Amicka looking for Gryffin? And why couldn't she use her power to find him?

We slinked further into the city, further into the destruction. The closer we got to the castle, the more blackened everything became. A thick layer of soot caked the walls and streets, the cobblestone roads slick with ash and sea spray. It'd been just three months since the Rebels took over the city, but it looked like it'd been abandoned for years. Maybe it was the darkness of the night that made everything seem more shadowed, but any hint of light from the crescent moon was swallowed up by ruin. I struggled to wrap my head around why Amicka and the Rebels would just let it decay like that.

Speaking of. Where *were* the Rebels? We'd run into no one since entering the city. Aside from the guards at the gate entrance, where was everyone?

Zeke stopped short in front of me, and his breathing hitched. "Great Haggard."

I peeked around his shoulder, and in the silence, my gasp sounded loud to my ears.

The castle, Gildshoal, just a few blocks in front of us, was crumbling. The once gold spires—the ones still standing, anyway—were as black as everything else. Cracks climbed up the walls, and I could see directly into what I thought was the Great Hall. The white alabaster walls were bright against the black exterior, but even they were spotty with soot. I remembered the balls of smoke the Rebels had carried in their hands the day of their attack, and I was surprised the alabaster shined white at all.

As we stood there, there was a loud *crack*, and my eyes shot up to one of the remaining turrets. It shook, and then it began to buckle in on itself.

"Down!" I shouted, and we dove for cover into the nearest building that wasn't completely boarded up. Zeke hovered over the top of me, and Gryffin protected my side facing the street. Their sentiment was charming, but it made me claustrophobic. I would rather not have nearly four hundred pounds of men falling on top of me if this building collapsed too.

A thick cloud of dust and ash flooded through the street and invaded the doorway we'd crashed through, filling my nose and making my eyes sting. I coughed and sputtered as the dust settled around us, but only when the rumbling stopped did we dare move.

Zeke shook out his hair with a cough and peeked his head out the door, looking down the street. "No movement. I don't think that collapse was intentional. The whole castle must be too unstable to hold itself up anymore."

"Then it's too dangerous to venture near it," I said, brushing off my trousers. "We won't find Amicka or the relics in there. Let's go around."

Zeke nodded. "Hope we find *anyone* soon. This entire city has been unnerving."

"But where will we find Amicka?" Gryffin asked. "If not in the castle, then where?"

None of us knew the answer to that question. The only thing we could do was continue on through the streets.

Zeke still took the front, his scout ears best trained for coming across any sort of noise that could lead us in the right direction. We gave Gildshoal a wide berth, inching closer to the coast. It was somehow getting brighter around us, as if the moon were shining stronger than before. I could easily see down the deserted streets, the shattered windows and collapsing walls. It seemed the destruction was worst closest to the castle and the coast.

When the buildings parted and we got our first glimpse of the East Sea, it was suddenly clear where we needed to go.

Out in the ocean, on an island rising above the water's surface, a blue light glowed and pulsed with intensity, like a star in the sky too close for comfort. It enveloped everything around it—the rocky island from which it came as well as the one peering out from behind it, the boats sailing between the islands and the mainland, the waves slapping roughly against the shore—all bathed in blue.

The same blue that shined when the relics had been brought together on Solstice Day.

Zeke wouldn't recognize it—he'd been near dying at the time—but Gryffin and I shared a look. The relics were on that island, and maybe Amicka too.

"Look," Zeke said, bending down. "There are more of those flyers." In his hand were several pieces of parchment, all with Gryffins staring back at us.

Suddenly, muffled voices and screeching wagon wheels rounded the corner, and we ducked into the shadows.

I chanced a peek around Zeke's shoulder and saw a wagon pulled by a team of two great bay horses and manned by two Rebels in dark cloaks and red tunics, carrying piles of the flyers, creaking and rumbling as it turned down the main road through the city and out of sight.

Were they going to spread these flyers around the Peninsula? I still didn't understand why Amicka couldn't just find Gryffin herself.

We sneaked closer to the docks, where finally, it was bustling with people. Tethered boats were being loaded with crates upon crates of what must have been what they'd been collecting from us in the kingdoms. All our work and provisions, shipped to those blue islands. That had to be the Solan Islands, where the Rebels were probably staying.

"What are the odds of us being able to sneak onto one of those ships?" I asked halfheartedly.

Zeke shook his head. "One of us maybe, but not all three. And before you say anything, no, you are *not* going on your own," he added, looking pointedly at me.

I grumbled and crossed my arms. "I wasn't going to suggest that." Or maybe I was. But clearly not anymore. "Gryffin can't go unnoticed. His face is plastered all over the city."

Gryffin stood up straighter, and his blue eyes brightened. I'd seen that look before, his brain working through something. "No, I can't go unnoticed. So what if I go . . . completely in plain sight?"

Zeke and I jerked at the same time, looking at Gryffin as though he'd had a screw knocked loose.

But Gryffin spoke slowly, coming to terms with his own thoughts as he said them aloud. "You two could be under the guise of taking me to Amicka, turning me in. I could be your ticket on board."

Zeke crossed his arms. "What if they just take you and don't let us leave the shore?"

That was a valid point. Then who exactly would they let onto the ships, without question?

I knew who. The only people who would be on those ships in the first place. "We could disguise ourselves as Rebels."

Zeke and Gryffin both looked at me.

"We could disguise ourselves as Rebels," I repeated, more sincerely. "That's the only way we'd be let onto one of those ships."

"All right," Zeke said slowly, giving my idea a chance. "And how do you expect us to do that?"

The creaking and squealing of wagon wheels interrupted us again, and we ducked out of sight.

Again, the wooden wagon was drawn by two horses, two Rebels sitting on the bench. Flyers floated out of the back of the wagon as it bumped along the road. It rumbled past us slowly, the two Rebels laughing at something unknown to us.

Suddenly, seeing the opportunity, I looked at Zeke. This could be our only chance. He sighed in surrender and nodded, looking over my head at Gryffin. Gryffin nodded back, and I watched them both as they followed the wagon around the corner of the narrow street to the main road. I stayed a few steps behind, careful and quiet.

A horse's shrill bray filled the dead air, and then a thump against cobblestone. I hurried around the corner in time to see Zeke heaving one unconscious Rebel into an abandoned building. Gryffin was in the back of the halted wagon grappling with the other. Suddenly, the Rebel jumped out the back and landed hard on the cobblestone with a cry. He scrambled to find his footing and rushed toward the corner I was hiding behind, with Gryffin bounding after him.

I quickly unsheathed my sword and hid behind the corner of the building. Then, as I heard his footsteps nearly on top of me, I jumped out in front of him and pushed into him with all my might, a strained cry escaping my throat. He landed hard on the ground in front of me. Heart pounding in my ears, I hit him in the head with the hilt of my sword before he had a chance to get up. He slumped to the ground as Gryffin rounded the corner.

We were both huffing, and guilt immediately spread through my body. This man hadn't done anything, yet I'd clobbered him in the head. He wasn't dead, I reminded myself. Just . . . would have a headache the size of a horse. It was fine.

Through the guilt, I heard Gryffin breathlessly say, "Thank you."

"You're welcome," I answered, hands on my knees. I straightened as Zeke emerged with his Rebel's clothes in his hand. He threw them in my direction, and then he slapped one of the horses on its hind. The wagon lurched forward, continuing down the cobblestone road.

Zeke nodded in satisfaction. "That should buy us some time. But we'll need to hurry before they notice an unmanned wagon."

I nodded and ducked inside the nearest open door. Thankfully, it was empty just like the rest of the city. I tugged my dirty tunic over my head and, removing the spearhead from my belt, hastily stepped out of my trousers. I heard the men groaning outside as they worked to get the other Rebel's clothes free, and then Zeke appeared through the door just as I pulled the Rebel's telltale red tunic over my head and tucked it into the loose black trousers.

"I missed the best part," he said, feigning sadness. His wink made my heart sputter in my chest. Really? Even now, in the face of our doom, he had this effect on me?

"You did." I took a step toward him, closing the distance, and ran a finger down his bare arm. "Be quicker next time and maybe you'll catch a glimpse." I smirked and gave his forearm a quick squeeze. But underneath my joke was a painful misery. We would never get another moment like this again.

From the burning sorrow in Zeke's eyes, I knew he felt it too. He lifted my hand and brought it to his lips, kissing my finger upon which my golden ring rested.

From outside, Gryffin knocked loudly on the doorframe. "We don't have all night."

Zeke groaned and dropped my hand. "He may be the most knowledgeable of us all, but what I wouldn't do to actually turn him in, just to be rid of him." He yanked off his shirt, and I drank in every glimpse I was granted of his chest and toned abdomen before he tugged the red tunic over his head.

I slipped the spearhead underneath my tunic, between folds in the oversized fabric, and went outside. Gryffin had dragged the other man into the same abandoned building as the first Rebel. At the sight of me, he grimaced. "That Rebel red is too sinister for you." He handed me the black brimmed hat one of the Rebels had been wearing.

I took the hat from him and tucked my hair into it securely. "I'll take that as a compliment."

Zeke emerged from the open door in his own Rebel red with a look of disgust. "I don't know the last time this man bathed."

"What's our plan now?" Gryffin asked. "Waltz down to the docks?"

His tone was sarcastic, but I nodded. "That's the only way I see us taking you to Amicka."

Zeke touched me on the shoulder. "Let me do the talking, all right?"

For once, I didn't put up a fight. Getting us through a throng of Rebels wasn't a burden I wanted to carry, and he admittedly was better at lying than me, despite all the practice I'd had in Tarasyn.

Through the darkness, we carefully picked our way down the alleys and streets, following the pulsing blue glow back to the shoreline. At the docks, firelight flickered and danced against the ships awaiting clearance to leave. We stopped behind the final corner of the buildings before the city gave way to the sea.

Inhaling deeply, I turned to the men. "Now is as good a time as any." I looked at Gryffin. "Are you ready?"

"As I'll ever be," he answered quietly. "Being turned in as a wanted man to a known killer who also happens to be a powerful sorceress. It can only go so well."

I was beginning to notice that Gryffin became sardonic when he was nervous.

Zeke chimed in. "We don't know why she's looking for you. It did say 'wanted alive.' Maybe she won't kill you."

Gryffin glared at him through narrowed eyes. "Oh yes, that's likely."

I laid a hand on his arm. "We won't let her take you away. We need you. Don't quit fighting, all right?"

He took a breath and nodded. "I'll do what I can, Rosemary. Of course I will."

With a final nod, Zeke and I took a firm hold on each of Gryffin's arms. Apparently, a little too hard on Zeke's end. Gryffin hissed and sneered at Zeke. "Try not to get too much joy out of throwing me around."

Zeke smiled widely. "No guarantees."

I rolled my eyes at both of them. "Zeke, behave. Gryffin, toughen up. Now let's go."

We stepped out of the shadows of the building and strode toward the docks.

# CHAPTER TWENTY-TWO

I MADE MYSELF look as confident as I could, shoulders back and sure steps. My blood was racing so loudly in my ears that I couldn't hear the waves hitting the boats as we sauntered across the wooden boardwalk, all but dragging Gryffin between us. The bustle of the Rebels loading and unloading supplies kept everyone distracted long enough for us to make it to a gangplank bobbing up and down with the ship to which it was connected. Only then did a woman in red posted at the bridge's threshold with a parchment in her hand stop us.

She looked us up and down. "Authorized persons only. What's your purpose?"

Zeke held up the flyer and spoke in a stern tone. "We have the wanted man. Gryffin Danicio."

Gryffin pulled against us, almost slipping out of my grip before I regained hold and yanked him back. Zeke tightened his grip, and Gryffin sucked in a sharp breath through clenched teeth. "Found him wandering around the outskirts of Aridia, who the Haggard knows what he was doing there."

The woman looked at Zeke, then me. I thanked fate for the darkness of the night and shadows the brimmed hat cast over my face. I kept my lips pursed in a grim line.

"And which one of you gets the reward?"

We were silent for a moment, and then Zeke laughed darkly. "I made the capture. It's mine."

The woman's eyes settled on me, and there was a weight in the salty air as she gauged my reaction. So I lifted my head just enough to let the blue glow show my lips and flashed her a mischievous smile. "We'll see."

The woman's sudden grin was bright against the shadows. "I like you." She stepped aside and looked back down at her parchment. "Names for the ship record?"

Zeke was quick to answer. "Eryx and Lanra."

How did he come up with these names on the spot like that?

The woman wrote the names down on the parchment and nodded us forward without another glance. As we stepped onto the gangplank, Gryffin put up one last fight for show before Zeke elbowed him in the gut, garnering a groan from Gryffin and a glare from me. Once out of earshot of the woman, Zeke snickered. "I'll never miss an opportunity to hit you."

"That's not news to me, believe it or not," Gryffin said through a grimace.

I smacked their arms. "Hush, both of you." I found us a place to sit on some barrels that were tied tightly to the deck of the ship. The sloshing of the water against the sides of the ship almost distracted me from the pounding of my heart from our success, but it did little to take my mind off the increasing heat of the spearhead through the fabric against my skin. It was like it *knew* how close we were to the source of its power, though it held little in itself anymore.

Then, the boat lurched forward, and we were edging away from the pier.

As we made way into the channel, leaving the mainland behind us, our good humor died. There truly was no turning back now.

I shook my head, trying to focus. I felt the sting of the salt in my nose, the wind threatening to take my hat. Shipworkers bustled around us, commanding sails and tying off ropes thicker than my arm. The shriek of pulleys and the creaking wood of the hull dominated any sound and stifled conversation between the three of us. I would have found it hard to talk past the lump building in my throat anyway. The black outline of the Solan Islands grew nearer, and that meant time was dwindling. Time with Zeke. Time as a queen, providing strength for my people.

I tried to imagine my father in my place. Disguised as the enemy, hunkering low and hoping to remain undiscovered. But I couldn't. I couldn't imagine him this low, this *small.* He'd always had a confident power about him, a superiority that couldn't be disguised. What would he have done had he been dealt the hand I'd been given?

He would have stayed with his people back in an unorganized Lecevonia. He probably would have sent someone in his place on this doomed task, and he would have met his end with his people if it failed. He never would have given up the title of "king" as I had, to his last breath.

I hadn't done the same. I'd taken liberty in the stripping of my title, marrying Zeke and allowing myself freedoms I hadn't dared to consider before. I took on this challenge myself, knowing death awaited me at the end of it. I chose to leave my people without a queen.

Lecevonia was only as strong as its leader, as my father said. Knowing he wouldn't have made these same choices, I worried if my actions had made me stronger or weaker.

One thing was certain. If with Haggard's help this insane plan somehow succeeded, I would've made my father proud. And Lecevonia's leader would be strong. She would be Talented, which was more than I could offer.

Yes. Lecevonia was in good hands with Isabele.

The largest island loomed higher and higher. The pulsing blue glow choked out the stars in the black sky and, as we got closer, enveloped the ship, bathing the deck and all of us in blue. As I looked over at Zeke, it was almost as if I were seeing him in broad daylight. What time was it anyway?

"Hide your faces," Gryffin whispered gruffly. "These people may not recognize you, but Amicka surely will."

I tugged the brim of my hat lower. Would we see Amicka that soon? My heart thrummed in fear.

The sails above us turned, and the ship groaned and slowed until we jolted against the side of a dock. Gryffin nearly jumped off his barrel, and it wasn't until then that I realized his color looked terrible.

"Have you never sailed before?" I asked him.

He scoffed, though his breath was unsteady. "On what? The frozen rivers near Snowmont? Our port off the cliffs has been closed for centuries. It's not even on the maps anymore."

Zeke nudged Gryffin's boot with his own. "If you need to heave, do it onboard. Give these Rebels a nice gift to remember you by."

To my utter shock, Gryffin actually chuckled. Then he wiped a hand across his clammy forehead. "Please. Let's just get this over with."

Zeke stood, and I followed suit, pulling Gryffin up with me. We were among the first to cross the gangplank, and Gryffin's legs wobbled. Between the two of us, Zeke and I managed to keep him upright.

As we stepped off the dock and onto hard ground, the spearhead in the folds of my tunic suddenly felt blazing hot, burning against my waist.

"Agh!"

I released Gryffin's arm just long enough to fold more of the tunic's fabric between the spearhead and my skin. It helped, but it wouldn't be long before the burning would be unbearable. Zeke and Gryffin looked at me, searching for some explanation of my outburst, but I just shook my head. As long as we moved quickly, I'd be fine.

We climbed the stone steps hewn into the side of the island's cliff face, following others hauling goods from the ship. Gryffin's color returned to normal as we continued higher. Up ahead was a giant stone wall of cells, bars facing the sea stained green by the salty air. An old prison?

The steps led us through a dark doorway. A man in red with a parchment directed the flow as Rebels crossed the threshold. "Food to the left, wood and other goods to the right."

As we approached, Zeke squared his shoulders. "And wanted men?"

The man leaned back on his heels with a smile. "A holding cell for now. We will send word to the Sorceress. She'll be pleased."

I saw him write on his parchment the time of our arrival at two o'clock in the morning.

My heart skipped a beat. Past midnight. That meant today was—

He waved his hand toward an opening in the rock obscured by shadows, but with the blue glow streaming in through the cliffside doorway, I saw there were more stairs going up. Zeke nodded to the man and roughly pulled Gryffin forward toward the steps.

As soon as we were encased in shadow, we softened our hold on Gryffin's arms.

The spearhead had once again grown too hot, and I sucked in a breath through my teeth as I peeled the folds of fabric off my skin. I reached through the front and tried to touch it, but it singed my fingers.

Zeke stopped on the steps and reached for my arm. "What is it, Rose?"

"Adria's spearhead is growing hotter by the minute," I said. I felt my fingertips, tender from the heat. They were probably red, like I'd just grazed hot cast iron.

"Hm." Gryffin's voice sounded intrigued. Of course it did.

"Did you see that it's past midnight?" I asked.

Gryffin let a grave stillness hang in the muggy air before answering. "It's now the Equinox. We only have today to make this work."

That was when I noticed it.

A humming that I imagined had been there since we stepped foot on this island but was just now growing louder than my own thoughts. It reminded me of the hum of the relics when I'd had them in my possession.

"Do you hear it too?" Gryffin asked quietly.

What was it, and where was it coming from?

We continued up the stairs until the stairwell opened up before us. Balls of fire floated and acted as torchlight for the cavern, but they did little to stave off the damp chill. That blue light shined through the open bars that faced the sea, giving the whole room an ethereal glow.

We couldn't see anyone. We only heard the sounds of other prisoners moving within their cells. Coughs, rattling chains, and the screech of metal against stone.

"Dreary," Zeke muttered.

"You haven't been here for months," a gravelly voice said from the depths of one nearby cell. "Imagine how we feel."

That voice piqued a familiar thread in my mind.

Yetta!

Gryffin raced forward and fell into a crouch in front of her cell. I rushed in behind him, my hat falling to the ground.

Her long gray and silver hair hung limp around her, her once strong body now bony and pale in furs and leather that fit much too loosely. Her gray eyes still swirled like storm clouds.

"You're still alive," he said breathlessly. "How?"

But when she saw me, she crawled up to the bars, chain clinking. She ignored Gryffin's question and spoke directly to me. "You have the spearhead?"

The burning against my side was unbearable. "Yes."

"You and Ezekiel need to leave. Now!" She reached through the bars and pushed me, nearly toppling me over. "Go back to the stairwell and continue up. Follow the hum."

"But—Gryffin—"

"Go!"

Flustered, I scrambled to my feet and backed away. Gryffin looked at me with wide eyes, and I was sure I looked just as stunned as he did. Then I turned away and met Zeke at the prison block's entrance.

"Ezekiel." Gryffin's voice echoed against the damp stone.

Zeke straightened his shoulders and looked at him.

"Don't let her be the one to break the relics apart. You do it."

"Go!" Yetta shouted again.

There was no time to process seeing Yetta again or leaving Gryffin behind. That was never part of the plan. Who knew what would happen to him when Amicka saw him down there? I couldn't dwell on it. I just focused on moving one foot in front of the other, taking the stairs two at a time as I listened to the humming grow louder. Zeke followed closely behind. Yetta's urgency had my heart pounding in my ears.

As we continued to ascend, the blue glow that had been outside now infiltrated the keep and illuminated the stairwell, and the humming gradually transformed to the familiar voices I'd heard in my head for months while the relics were in my possession.

*Here we are.*

*Power.*

*Unstoppable.*

My legs were burning, but I pushed myself up the stairwell. The light was almost blinding and the voices were deafening when I collapsed over the top step. The spearhead blazed hotter than fire, and I couldn't take it anymore. I yanked the red Rebel tunic out of the waist of my trousers and shook the singed fabric until the spearhead fell to the ground. Tears rolled down my cheeks, and I couldn't hold back sounds of pain as I twisted to look at where the spearhead had rested in the folds of fabric, now ripped away so forcefully. A dark red and black patch of burned skin tattooed my waist like a brand, raw and freshly bleeding.

I was too scared to try to touch it. It hurt so acutely, like nothing I'd ever felt before, but I couldn't deal with it now.

We were in a room with a steep gabled ceiling. Huge floor-to-ceiling windows showed the ocean far below no matter which way I looked. At the center of the room, in its own swath of space about six feet off the ground, floated the source of the blinding blue light.

The relics of the Five Talented. They were still in their formation of a star.

Zeke stepped in behind me and helped me to my feet. His face was pinched in revulsion. "What the Haggard is that sound? It's making me want to rip out my eardrums."

I pointed toward the pulsing star in the middle of the room. "Them." Though *they* seemed inseparable now.

But that was what the spearhead was for, if we figured everything correctly.

"That thing is too hot to touch," I said, eyeing the relic on the floor warily. "We'll need to find a way we can use it without touching it."

Zeke and I looked around the room. It looked as though it'd been storage, but everything had been pushed to the perimeter to make room for the star. Wooden desks topped with rolled parchment and barrels of random objects haphazardly thrown together lined the walls. I took one direction while Zeke took the other. I saw Zeke pocket a few things out of the corner of my eye, including two daggers.

On the top of a desk, I found a roll of twine. Zeke met me back near the spearhead with a rod of wood about the length of his arm in his hand.

I wrapped the hem of the red tunic around my hand and, touching the spearhead as little as possible, quickly tied it to the tip of the rod, remembering the knots Yetta had taught me. It seemed like it'd work well at first, almost like a makeshift arrow. Then, the wood started to smoke. "No, no, no . . ." The heat of the spearhead burned right through the wood and twine, and it clattered to the floor.

Zeke swore under his breath. "We need something else."

We searched again. I wound around the room, but nothing seemed helpful. Then, on the floor under a cluster of barrels, I noticed boot tracks of smeared ash across the ground. "Zeke, help me move these." We pushed two barrels out of the way, and there was an old fireplace that certainly hadn't been used in decades. In the fireplace was an iron roasting spit suspended above the cold ashes.

I grabbed it off its stands and rushed back to the spearhead. If the spearhead was that hot, then maybe . . .

I laid one end of the spit against the spearhead, and slowly, the metal began to glow with heat. "Quick, find some wire!"

Zeke was at my side in a minute, holding out some sort of wire trap I'd only seen before in Port Della used for fishing. He broke the wooden frame and yanked the wire free, cutting his hand in the process.

"Zeke!"

He hissed and handed it to me. "It's steel," he said, shaking his injured hand. Blood droplets fell to the floor. "Hopefully it'll hold against the heat."

I quickly ripped a strip of singed fabric off the hem of my tunic and handed it to him for his hand. Then I wrapped the wire round and round the spearhead and the spit until it was thick and secured. We watched it for a few seconds, and this time, the spearhead stayed in its place.

"Thank Haggard," I said in relief.

Then I looked up at the star. Here we were with the source of Amicka's power, and we had in our hands the one thing that could take it away. I wished Gryffin were here to guide us through the next steps. This was the part he had volunteered to do. "What should I do? Stab it into the middle?"

Zeke took the makeshift spear from my hands. "You are going to go behind that barrel over there, and you are going to put the relics back together afterward." My protest was on the tip of my tongue, but he put a finger on my lips. Then he gently grabbed my wrist and pulled me toward him. "Even if this doesn't work—"

"It has to work."

"Even if this doesn't work," he said again over my words, "know that I will love you till my last breath. Whenever that last breath may be."

His words made my hands tighten into fists, holding onto his tunic in a death grip. I let my head fall to his heaving chest. "I love you too,

Zeke. I love you so much."

He lifted my chin to make me look at him, his brown eyes alight in the blue glare. His half-smile stilled my heart. "I know. Perhaps better than you do."

"I don't want this to be it."

"It might not be."

It might not be. There could be an explosion, or there could be nothing.

He gently pulled himself out of my grasp. It felt like a fresh wound. I ducked behind a barrel near the old fireplace, tears streaming.

How could I let him do this? My only answer was because the Magian Peninsula needed me to. I had to be strong and let him take this risk so that I could finish what we started. And I hated myself for it.

I peered over the top of the barrel and watched Zeke hoist the spear over his shoulder.

It was now or never.

He stood maybe five strides away from the star. After a deep inhale, he took two steps forward and thrust the spear with a yell, aiming straight for the point of contact in the center, where Vena's bow touched all the others.

There was a huge pulse of blue light through the room.

I watched as Zeke was thrown to the ground. The spear clattered to the floor next to him, and the pulsing blue star still floated as though unaffected.

"Zeke!" I was above him in an instant, and when he coughed, relief replaced all my fear.

"I—" He groaned and held his head. "I don't know what happened."

I helped him sit upright and took the spear myself. I went forward more cautiously than he had and lifted the spear, prodding the relics with the spearhead.

Nothing.

"How . . ." I reached forward, and when my hand touched the star, a jolt of electricity shot through me. I jumped back, all my nerves on fire.

"How is this possible?" Zeke whispered.

I didn't know. All I knew was that the relics couldn't be touched.

We'd been wrong.

Then a whirl of salty air swept through the room, and Zeke and I clung to each other as a suffocating presence appeared in the doorway.

# CHAPTER TWENTY-THREE

HER DARK HAIR was as wild as it'd been when I first saw her. She'd abandoned the furs and leather for a glittering red gown that hugged from her neck down to her hips, then descended to the floor in a loose skirt. The entire thing was studded with rubies. On her head was no longer a ring of antlers but a towering crown of black metal and ruby-tipped spires. Her eyes were the most horrifying, full of a burning red that had spread so much that the whites of her eyes were almost gone.

In her shadow stood Gryffin.

Disbelief and betrayal started to gather in my mind.

But then his clear blue eyes focused on me. Pleading. *Trust me,* they said.

Those were words that he has begged of me before. Though old wounds threatened to open anew, I kept the stabs of doubt at bay.

"How do you like this empire I've built?" Amicka raised her hands and gestured around her. "My Rebels are more provided for than they've ever been in their lives, and the people who belittled and ridiculed them are the ones suffering now."

"The Peninsula will not last if this keeps up," I shot back. "All of us will starve to death or be killed, and then what?"

"Then I'll build it up once more, and I'll use my power for the good of *my* people. The ones who never lost faith in me or the magic of this land."

Behind her, Gryffin's gaze shifted between me and the spear that had been abandoned on the floor. Slowly bending down, I took the spear in my hands.

Amicka had no fear. Why should she? She merely smiled and nodded her chin toward it. "An old friend, I see."

The blue light surrounding us was flickering uncontrollably. There was so much power in this one room. The voices had reached an unbearable volume, screaming in my ear. Zeke unsheathed the daggers he'd grabbed.

Gryffin's eyes flitted from the spear in my hand to the star. I looked at the pulsing relics, which looked more and more unstable the longer I looked.

"You want to bring that spear to me, Rosemary," Amicka said. Her voice sounded like she was speaking through heavy fog. Where had I heard that before? A familiar sensation swept through me, as if my mind were starting to stretch itself thin.

Why not give her the spear? We were powerless. *What was I thinking?* My feet began to take one sure step toward her.

Gryffin let out a roar and wrapped his arms around Amicka, tackling her to the ground. Zeke slid one of the daggers across the floor in his direction, and Gryffin snatched it up.

I understood then. My mental castle began to construct, just as it had against Gryffin and against the voices, stone by heavy stone laying themselves in a barricade. As my walls grew higher, that sensation of stretching lessened. Though Amicka wielded Gryffin's Talent now, my castle was stronger. When that last turret was standing tall, I was firmly within myself again, my mind snapped painfully back into place. I took a stumbling step backward, holding the spear close to my body.

Gryffin held the blade to Amicka's neck. "If you try to Persuade her again, I will slice your throat."

She yelled and, with a twist of her hand, blasted Gryffin away from her and into the wall behind them. He fell in a heap on the floor, but he still held on tightly to his dagger. Gasping, he rose again and rushed at Amicka, but she raised both hands, and a gale surged through the room. Gryffin was lifted into the air like he weighed nothing, and this time, he smashed into one of the windows, black glass shattering on top of him as he hit the floor.

I barely heard his unsteady voice over the wind. "The spearhead!"

Amicka spun back to me, gown and eyes blazing, and held out her hand. The spear turned so hot that I screamed, but I refused to let go. I looked at the star of relics again, the blue light it emitted now flickering in and out.

Weakening.

With Amicka here with the relics, there was too much power in this one room. Whatever barrier was around the relics was faltering.

*This* was what Gryffin had been silently trying to tell me. How did he know? Had Yetta told him that this would happen?

I took a step toward the star, but before I could get any further, Amicka sent a flare from her open hand into the floor in front of me. A cry escaped my lips as a cyclone of flames erupted before me, and the sheer heat had me hurtling backward, falling over a wooden desk behind me. The spear fell from my blistered hands, and my back radiated pain. I thought I smelled singed hair.

A shadow fell over me as the cyclone dissipated, and it was Zeke, dagger at the ready.

"I almost killed you once," Amicka said, red eyes seething. "Don't be a fool to think I will show you the same mercy this time."

"Zeke," I said, grabbing the back of his tunic. "She's too strong."

"I'm the pessimist, not you." He gritted his teeth and held his ground. "Get the spear!"

His words were suddenly cut off, and his feet left the ground. As he writhed in the air, white-hot marks began showing themselves across his throat, like a wire wrapped around his neck so tightly he couldn't even scream. In terror, my gaze darted around to find Amicka. She had her hand suspended, twisting at the wrist as though turning a key. By the second, those white-hot marks glowed with a stronger intensity. She let out a wild shriek. "Enough of this!" She closed her fist, and Zeke's eyes rolled back, his face purple.

Everything inside me screamed to make it stop, to do whatever Amicka wished. Anything to make her stop crushing Zeke's windpipe.

But I couldn't do that. Not like I had the last time I'd faced her. I'd given up everything we'd worked toward to save Zeke's life, and it had ruined everything.

This time, I needed to be stronger than that. For Zeke, for my people, and for the people of the Magian Peninsula.

Only one thing could make all of this stop.

I got to my feet, and Amicka dropped Zeke to the floor with a thud. I prayed he was still alive. She circled around to place herself between me and the wavering star of relics. To be so close to her source of power made her cheeks sallow, her steps heavier. From her blazing eyes fell teardrops of red, and I realized in horror that it was blood.

I picked up the searing hot spear, hissing against the pain.

"Do you know what you're doing?" she asked scathingly. "There's nothing left to fight for. Everyone who didn't believe will be reduced to bones and embers. My Rebels will be the new people of this land!"

Wind still roared through the room, and the more she spoke, the stronger it blew. One gust nearly flattened me to the floor again. I clamped my teeth together and used all my strength to stay upright. The star making a halo over Amicka's head began to grow dim, its power nearly exhausted as it all flowed into her body.

Blood streamed down her cheeks, her wild eyes wide. "I've won. I'm as powerful as the mages that once blessed this land. Because *I* never stopped believing that such power existed! *I* was the one brave enough to harness it all!"

I would be the one brave enough to try to stop her.

I lifted the spear over my shoulder and ran forward through the wind.

In Amicka's hand sparked a glowing orb of what could only be lightning. It zapped and popped, a promise of death to anyone it touched.

I just prayed I could do what needed to be done before she sent the orb barreling into my chest.

I aimed the spear above her head as she let the orb fly—straight into Gryffin, who had stumbled to place himself between me and the Sorceress.

My heart stuttered to a stop.

Petrified.

*He's going to spend his dying breath protecting you.*

No . . .

But there was no stopping the momentum of my body or the spear flying from my open fingers. It sailed over Gryffin. The star went dark, and the spear, no longer stopped by some invisible force, embedded itself into the center of the relics above Amicka's head.

My vision stayed clear just long enough for me to witness the nightmare of Gryffin falling to the floor. The air in my lungs shrieked out of me with the thud of his body.

Then, everything was blocked out by an explosion of light. All I saw was white, but I heard Amicka's scream, mingled with my own, and the crash of glass as every last window in the room shattered.

And the voices. They exploded too, to a volume I never fathomed.

Then I collapsed.

My vision was still white. White all around me. I neither saw nor felt anything except the silent sobs shaking through my absent body.

But I still heard.

*Rosemary.*

Without ever hearing this voice alone before, I recognized it as a voice of the relics, one of the voices that had always blended with the others.

"Rosemary," he said again. "You've been strong."

It was a man, powerful and steady like my father. That was when it dawned upon me that this was Equos.

"I . . ." I struggled to find my voice. What was happening? Was this what Amicka saw when she brought the relics together on the Solstice? "I did what was right. People were dying."

A new voice, a woman this time, deep like velvet. "What's a few less mouths to feed?"

I prickled at that. "Who are we to decide who lives and who dies?"

The woman chuckled breathily. "I've felt the pressure of a hungry kingdom in the Silver Mountains. Ruling is easier when there are fewer people to care for."

Viridi.

"But you did feed them, didn't you?" I asked. "You used your

Talent for your people, and you saved them."

She sounded pleased. "I stand corrected."

"You can do the same," another woman said, her voice lighter than Viridi's. It must've been Vena. "It's the Equinox. You can choose."

Her words confused me. "Choose what?"

A man, voice thick as oak, replied, "You can choose whether to harness the power yourself, as the last one did, or to disperse it throughout the land."

"Talents would arise again," said another man, younger than the others by the sound of his voice and breezy as the sea. "They would no longer be forgotten or ground down to nothing. A legend made true again."

An Awakening. The way it was meant to be.

"If you take it for yourself, you will be able to provide for your people," Equos said. "Not just the people of Lecevonia, but of all the kingdoms."

That was all I ever wanted. To provide for my people.

"You would be like a mage," Equos continued. "And you could use it for the good of everyone."

Viridi hummed her approval. "That is what any ruler would want."

"But there is a cost to so much power," Vena chimed in, her voice layered with warning. "You saw the last one's eyes. You must be careful with how you use your Talents. A human's body is not meant to harness such power."

"But think of all the good you could do while you wield that power!" Viridi said, speaking over her sister. "Can anyone else be trusted with it, Rosemary?"

Their words fought to overwhelm me. I still only saw white nothing, smelled or felt nothing, but my senses burned past their capacity. "How am I hearing you?"

"You broke our relics apart," Equos said. "Yet, they are called to be together. That is why we speak to you. It is your choice. Do we wield our power through you, strong and resolute? Or do we spread ourselves into the land, the plants and animals, the people of the Magian Peninsula, weaker but equal?"

I imagined my father as Equos, and that rooted me to this moment. What would he have done?

Lecevonia was only as strong as its leader. His voice rang clearly through my head. He'd instilled that thought into me, and it had carried me through many trials. Did I dare question this truth? The relics had called to *me*. If I chose to keep this power, I would be like a mage, and there would be no questioning the strength of my kingdom. No faulty lineage, no weakened link. It wouldn't matter. I would be powerful, and we would be safe. Forever. The weight of my reign that was perpetually on my shoulders wouldn't hurt me anymore because I would be strong enough to keep it lifted.

That was what my father would have done. I wanted to do it too. I wanted to know what it felt to be the one wielding the power rather than the one at its mercy, as I had been too many times.

But what of Isabele? Of Yetta? Of the young Hiddon girl Clementine? Weren't they also capable of good? What would Lecevonia become if its *people* were strong?

The white nothing surrounding me vanished, and in its place I saw a kingdom flourishing. Rebuilding with ease the towns and cities that Amicka had destroyed, crop fields and pastures healthy, prosperity alongside the other kingdoms because they would be strong too.

Lecevonia was not as strong as its leader. It was as strong as its people.

And its people needed a ruler who stood for what was best for them, not out of greed or even security, but out of compassion. Out of *sacrifice.*

After all, it was those actions out of sacrifice that had made the most difference. Sterling blocked Clara from the arrow that would have killed her. Thomas's death opened my eyes to Gryffin's Talent. Cassia and Xal gave their lives to help me in Tarasyn. I faced trial after trial in the frozen woods to return to my people. Zeke loved me so selflessly that he found strength in *my* strength. Gryffin . . . My sobs returned. He was why this choice in front of me was even possible.

Selflessness and sacrifice. That was where true strength lay.

The oppressive weight lifted off my shoulders. I didn't need to be strong for my people. Instead, I needed to make my people strong.

This was my truth.

Equos's deep voice was echoed by the others. "So be it."

# CHAPTER TWENTY-FOUR

THE VOICES GAVE way to the rush of sea breeze.

My entire body ached.

"She's alive," Yetta said from somewhere nearby. "Her mind is returning. I can feel it."

Yetta. My thoughts were murky, but I recognized her voice. She was okay.

"Rose?" Zeke's voice was soft and low, like how he used to wake me up in the inn during our time in Flecte. I found my breath, and I sighed.

"Rose!"

My eyelids fluttered open to find Zeke's brown eyes hovering over me. Was that a red fleck in his right one?

Zeke let out an exhale and lifted me gently, cradling my head to his chest. "Thank Haggard." His voice was hoarse, rattled by Amicka's stranglehold.

"Zeke." My voice sounded no better than his. I reached up to touch his neck, where painful red lines circled below his jaw. But he was alive. The coolness of relief spreading through me soothed my body's ache. It made my thoughts sharper.

A bony hand touched my shoulder. Yetta. I looked up and saw her smiling at me, though her gray eyes held sorrow.

"Gryffin," I said suddenly, and I mustered the strength to sit up and look around the room for him. But with dread in my heart, I already knew what I would find.

When I saw his body lying there, a sob choked out from my lungs.

Radiating from under his vest were thin white burns forked like lightning, and they spread across his body like lace in his veins. And his eyes, their blue as deep as the ocean with not a red fleck to be seen, stared lifelessly at the ceiling. I touched his cheek, still warm, and hoped to Haggard that by some miracle life would pour back into his eyes. That he could live to see the world forgive him. But he remained still, and another sob raked through me.

Behind him was what was left of Amicka. She'd been reduced to a pile of ash and rubies, glowing embers, and a shattered black crown.

Zeke followed my eyes. "I came to just as she began to crumble, the moment you broke the relics apart with the spear. The relics are gone too."

*Their magic dispersed across the land.* It'd worked.

Yet the only one who wasn't returning home was the one who would have celebrated the most.

I hadn't realized that my eyes had been drawn back to Gryffin until I was staring at him through my tears.

None of us were meant to survive this. I hadn't even thought to prepare myself for this goodbye. My heart felt too constricted, unable to beat properly.

Zeke took my hands and helped me to my feet. The burn on my waist throbbed as I straightened. My back felt bruised and beaten. But I ignored it all as I turned to Yetta, and I wrapped my arms around her as tightly as I could.

"I'm fine, I'm fine," she said dismissively. But she didn't let go of me either.

When we parted, the overcast look in her stormy eyes told me that at least one person shared in my grief.

I shook my head. "Why did you let yourself be taken, Yetta? You must've known Amicka was there in the woods."

"Of course I knew. But her mind was a dark place." A shadow fell over her weathered features. "She was prepared to have her Rebels of the Red Sun set fire to Viridi if I didn't comply. I couldn't let that happen."

I felt the trace of a smile on my lips. Once a queen, always a queen.

Yetta shot a glare to the pile of ashes and rubies on the floor. "Amicka took me for knowledge. I refused to give her anything of value until I saw my grandson alive. That was our bargain. She couldn't look for him herself without leaving the relics for too long a period, so it bought us some time."

No matter how many times she did it, Yetta left me in awe of her cleverness.

Zeke pushed my hair back from my face and cupped my cheek in his hand. "You wouldn't wake up. I was terrified, Rose." His eyes roved over my face, as though he were committing it to memory. "Where did you go?"

"I . . . I was with the Five Talented." I realized how crazy that sounded, but I pushed on. "They gave me a choice. Amicka had had a choice too when she brought the relics together on Solstice Day. I chose differently than her." I chose differently than my father. I chose differently than a lot of people probably would have.

Without Amicka, the Rebels were pliant. It wasn't hard for Zeke to persuade a few of them, through threats, to let the rest of the prisoners go and secure us passage off the island. Enlisting the help of more Rebels, we took Gryffin's body with us. It felt disrespectful to leave it up there in that tower. He deserved a proper Tarasynian burial, atop the tallest peaks of the Silver Mountains.

As we stepped onto the shores of mainland Loche in the rising sun, I heard the familiar hum. Well, felt more than heard, deep in my bones. The one that had been there all my life and just hadn't noticed until Amicka had taken it away. When I looked over at Zeke and Yetta, their looks of relief told me they felt it too.

That was the first moment I felt like we'd succeeded. The grass would return greener, the trees fuller. Lecevonia's horses strong, Somora's oaks and pines healthy. The Talented would reach their full potential and build back the kingdoms better than ever.

There would be peace again.

But many were no longer with us to enjoy it.

Zeke's scruff tickled my cheek. "Good morning."

I smiled at him. Sleep had left us long ago. Wrapped in the sheets of our bed, I lay with him as the sun just barely peeked through the window of our chambers. His hand trailed down my bare back and over my hips, always careful around the healing burn on my waist. Our castle healer may have been Talented, but she still needed practice. My burn had been too deep for her to Heal easily, and I would probably have the mark of the spearhead branded on me forever. A reminder of all I'd lost, and all I'd gained.

We'd been resting for two weeks now, and I'd been letting my advisors take care of things that needed to be done. Today I would make my first public appearance since being back home, but I refused to think about that until at least nine o'clock. Right now was for me and my husband.

"They're going to ask you, you know," I said, tracing circles on his shoulder. "If you're accepting the role as king-consort or not."

Our marriage was fortunately still valid in the laws of Lecevonia, even though my title of queen hadn't been mine at the time. My advisors had asked if I wanted a second coronation to reclaim it, but I thought that to be unnecessary. However unofficially, I'd been queen all along. I was too confused at the time to see that until now.

That left Zeke with a choice. Become my king-consort and have a seat on the council, have his voice count in decisions for our kingdom. Or decline the role and stay within the castle walls. As my husband, he was too much of a liability to continue scouting. Even with his Talent of stealth, which explained how he'd never been caught before, I couldn't take the chance. Diplomatic trips for him wouldn't have any weight without the title of king-consort, so truly, he'd simply be my husband. I just didn't know if that would be enough for him.

I hoped he'd take the role, to be by my side and rule with me in all ways. But if he chose not to, I'd have to respect that too. Politics had never been a desire for him.

"Can't we just stay here for the rest of our lives?" Zeke asked, nuzzling into my neck. "You're the queen after all. No one can tell you what to do."

I giggled as his hair tickled my chin, but I fought through the temptation and shook my head. The sun was rising too quickly. "Unfortunately, that's not how it works," I said, sliding out of bed. I wrapped a robe around myself and sat at my vanity, and in the mirror, Zeke followed. A fire lit in the pit of my stomach. The sight of my husband was something I would never grow tired of. He picked up one of my brushes and began combing it through my hair.

His red-flecked eyes met mine through the mirror. I'd gotten used to those eyes quicker than I thought I would. They were still my favorite shade of brown. "Do you feel ready?"

His question gave me no hesitation. The people of Lecevonia were my strength, and I was theirs. Realizing this, rather than shouldering it all on my own, gave me a freedom I hadn't known before. It was not something that tethered me down as I'd once believed. The freedom to make my own choices in the way I lived did not weaken me. In fact, I felt stronger for it. Like this morning, this life with Zeke.

Did I feel ready? I was born to rule. Royal expectations be damned. "Yes. More than ever."

He smiled at me through the mirror. Then he leaned down and pressed his warm lips to my jaw. "I'll call for Hazel."

My ever-faithful lady-in-waiting appeared in my mirror just minutes after Zeke left, and once she was through with me, I still felt safe in my own skin. My hair flowed in gleaming brown waves over my shoulders rather than a tight updo, and my green eyes, though fleckless, were bright and confident. The scar on my forehead was visible but barely, just another subtle reminder that I'd been through things that made me into who I was. The tawny embroidery that ran through the dark red of my dress made me look just as I felt—earthbound and strong. Resilient to whatever storms or quakes I was thrown.

Hazel turned toward my desk and opened the box that housed my crown. I hadn't worn it yet since I'd returned home. The swirling gold glinted in the warm light streaming in through the windows, and as she placed it atop my head, the weight felt no heavier than what I was capable of.

She fondly tucked a strand of my hair behind my ear and sighed. "You're ready, my queen."

With a deep breath, I stood and wrapped the old woman in my arms. As many times as she'd readied me for appearances, diplomatic meetings, and suitors, even my own wedding, this time felt different. I felt as though she and I finally got what we wanted—a confidence visible on the outside as well as in. I released her and smiled. "Thank you, Hazel. You know I wouldn't have gotten this far without you."

She huffed and waved off my remark, but a telltale sniffle told me how she really felt.

Zeke waited for me outside my door in a red and blue vest and black trousers, golden hair tousled in such a way that made my knees weak. With his half-smile, he took my hand and kissed it. "Your Majesty."

We walked the long hallway in comfortable and much-needed silence. I was to speak from the library's balcony, and the moment we entered the room, I was greeted not by the smell of ash, but by the rumbling chatter of the masses anticipating my arrival. My heart thumped louder in response.

Zeke paused when we were just out of sight of the people below. He untwined our arms and blew out a deep breath. "Your people await." He gave what looked like a bit of a sad smile and stepped back.

My brow furrowed, and I held my hand out to him. "Won't you come with me?"

"I . . . I'm not . . ." So strange to see Zeke without a word to say, looking so flustered with his hands nervously running along the front of his vest. Emotions warred in his eyes. "No," he finally said, taking another step back. "This moment is for you. Not me."

I felt my confusion cool into steel. "It could be for both of us."

"I'm not ready. I don't know. Not yet."

His confession punctured my heart with a surprised sting. But I nodded and turned away from him before he could see it in my eyes.

I'd support him, I reminded myself. Sacrificial love was how we'd gotten this far.

Pushing aside the hurt, I focused again on the thrum of thousands of people. I wouldn't wait any longer. Leaving Zeke behind, I stepped out into view on the balcony.

Their cheers roared through my veins. The courtyard below was packed with people and overflowed into the streets as far as I could see. These weren't just Lecevonians. These were also the refugees from Hiddon, and all those who'd fled the freeze of Tarasyn. All the people I'd pledged to help as well as I could without knowing how, just knowing that I couldn't let them die without trying to save them. Jerime, Renera, and Clementine were probably out there, somewhere, hopefully leaving everyone's feet properly on the ground. Out in the distance, there were fireworks like the ones I'd seen all those months ago in Tarasyn. But when these exploded in the morning sky, they released sweeping trails of red and blue smoke, the colors of Lecevonia's coat of arms. The colors of the other kingdoms followed, and the crowd cheered louder.

With a smile I raised my hand, and rolling like a slow wave in the sea, the crowd quieted from the courtyard to the streets. I lowered my hand.

"This is victory!" I shouted, which erupted another round of cheers. "With Amicka's defeat, we have found victory! No more threat of starvation, no more fear of destruction and death! With our resilience, we found peace. We made it through a time of darkness and came out stronger. All of us, stronger than ever!

"This is a new era. An era of magic that was seen by our ancestors and has now been reclaimed through our perseverance. Talents open a world of opportunity for us here in the Magian Peninsula. New skills, new capabilities, new limits to test. May we support one another and lift each other up.

"There will of course be much to learn. Things like where we each stand in this new time, what our roles are, and where our strengths lie for both the Talented and not. This *will* take time. However, we all have our part to play, and as for me, I begin by supporting you, the people of my kingdom. I am not Talented myself, but my strength draws from your wellbeing, and with the backing of the Crown, we will build our kingdom as well as the entirety of the Magian Peninsula into a place of peace and abundance! Hand in hand, all of us, we will thrive!"

My audience then broke out into cheers and chants, and my blood pounded in tune with their excitement. The rush still warmed my cheeks even as I waved and backed away from the edge of the balcony, back into the stillness of the library. I turned, expecting to see Zeke waiting for me, hopefully with a proud smile on his face.

Instead, I found Gryffin.

Or rather, the ghost of him that my mind often fabricated these past two weeks. I had been changed in part because of him. I was *alive* because of him. Gryffin would always have a place within me, as deep as my soul.

He leaned against one of the bookshelves, and he did have a proud smile on his face.

Then he was gone, and I could breathe again. In his wake was his scent of smoke and honey. It lingered on my tongue, bittersweet.

Shaken, I glanced around the library, looking for some sort of reprieve. Where was Zeke?

The doors opened and my heart leapt, but it wasn't him. My advisors strolled in one by one, each one looking pleased in their own way. Lord Clark with his wide smile, Lord Brock with a proud gaze. Lord Quince with tears in his eyes, sweet man, and Lord Castor with a funny little smirk of approval on his face.

"Your Majesty, your words were gloriously received!" Lord Clark took my hands in his and squeezed them proudly. "Your assurances of peace and prosperity are precisely what this kingdom needs to ensure unity and hope."

Lord Brock bowed his head deeply. "Yes, my queen. Your father would be very proud."

I truly hoped so, though I didn't need my father's praise as much as I once thought I did. "Thank you, all of you. It truly is the beginning of a new time, and we get to watch it happen." I looked over their shoulders. "Have any of you seen Ezekiel?"

They all exchanged a glance, and Lord Quince shook his head. "No, my queen. But, speaking of—"

"Has he decided on his role yet?" Lord Castor crossed his arms. "Things are changing quickly, and this isn't a decision he can sit on for much longer."

I agreed. But instead, I said, "Time is what he needs."

Lord Quince stepped up. "But, Your Majesty, we don't have time. Colonel Burnstead's scouts received word of Princess Avirine of Loche and her husband taking the throne, and Princess Lilyana of Hiddon—she's alive! Who knew?"

I hid my smile.

"Her coronation will be in the coming weeks, and we need to be sure to send a delegate. That's why we need Sir Ezekiel—"

"Nonsense. I'll go myself."

Lord Quince looked between me and Lord Brock, and Lord Brock stepped forward. "You're needed here, my queen. Everything is new."

"I'm going to go myself," I repeated. "She will need the support just as I did, crowned that young."

Lord Brock sighed. "Of course, Your Majesty. And Princess Kathryn—"

"I'll be going to her coronation too. Unquestionably. She's my friend."

Kathryn. However much they didn't get along, Gryffin's death left a sadness upon her heart. But she willingly stepped into her new role as Queen of Tarasyn. Her surviving brothers, Michael and Laris, had no interest in the Crown. The determination in her blue eyes, which were now flecked with red, reminded me so much of Gryffin. She would leave for home in a few days, with Celeste and the Tarasynians who wished to return in tow. And she, like Princess Lilyana, would need my support too, and I planned on giving it to her in whatever way I could.

There was silence throughout the library for a moment. Finally, Lord Castor huffed and turned away, and Lord Brock bowed his head. "As you wish. We'll make the arrangements. Please, Your Majesty, talk with your husband."

Pursing my lips, I breathed out stiffly through my nose and nodded. "Yes. I'll talk with him. I agree that he needs to think things through soon." The discomfort on his face when I'd reached for him to follow me out onto the balcony slid across my mind.

Of course I wanted him to choose what it ultimately meant to marry me and the role that entailed. But if he truly didn't feel as though he could . . . What kind of life would the alternative be for him?

Lord Clark cleared his throat. "One last piece of information, and then we'll leave you to your thoughts. We received word from Colonel Burnstead. He requests your blessing to step down from his position for a life of laity instead."

I cocked my head, surprised. "But he's done such a good job of it, ever since my father appointed him. Why?"

"Fatigue, Your Majesty." Lord Clark shrugged. "He wants to spend his time with his family. He did however emphasize the honor that he has felt serving you and your father through the years."

I'd never had a commanding officer ask to be decommissioned. I couldn't help but take it a bit personally, not wanting to serve under my rule any longer. But beneath the sting, I understood his longing for a slower life, one uninterrupted by war strategy and the weight of protecting the Crown. Hopefully, we wouldn't be dealing with war for a while.

Then an idea began to brew.

Perhaps his resignation was a good thing.

"I grant him my blessing," I finally said. "Though I'd like to speak with him at some point to thank him for his years of service."

Lord Clark smiled. "We'll send word. Try to rest, Your Majesty."

They each bowed and, without another word, left the library.

And not wanting to be alone with my thoughts, I followed them out, heading for the one place that came to mind.

The trees painted swaths of red and orange as Midas and I careened over the creek. With the cool air filling my lungs, I was more alive than ever before. The rush sent my hair standing, goosebumps budding along my arms and back.

When I had seen Midas, along with Lucy and Hugo, waiting in the marshes after our return from the Solan Islands, my heart had exploded with gratitude at their loyalty, and probably a bit of stubbornness. I'd thought I'd seen the last of my friend, but he'd proved me wrong. Now, as we pounded down the rocky path—the very same I'd met Gryffin on so long ago—he and I felt connected once more. His excitement and mine melded, our combined joy of freedom propelling Midas's hooves faster.

The drumming of another horse's hooves followed in our wake, and a small smile creeped across my face as I pushed Midas faster. The sound of the other horse soon faded. Midas and I flew over the trunk of a fallen tree—I'd have to remember to have that removed later—and made a sharp turn off the main path onto a stretch of dirt invisible to anyone who didn't know to look for it. Leaves the color of fire kicked up behind us, blazing in the wind we left behind.

Off the path, I saw where I wanted to go—a clearing near a bend in the creek, goldenrods waving in the patch of sun. I began pulling back on Midas's reins, and just outside the clearing, I hopped off his back. The tips of the goldenrods brushed his belly, leaving yellow streaks of pollen on his black fur. The creek reflected the sun's noon light, golden specks floating in the beams that broke through the trees.

I stretched my hands out on either side of me as I walked through the tiny meadow, listening to the rustling of Midas's movement through the long grass and flowers.

This was living to me.

The goldenrods, the blazing colors of the trees around me, the angle of the sun shortening the days, the chill chasing off the shadows of summer—I appreciated this autumn more than I ever had before. It rivaled with spring.

Arms wrapped around my waist.

I pushed down a gasp. I knew these arms. His Talent would forever surprise me.

I lifted my face and turned toward him, my nose nuzzling into his neck as I focused on my racing heart. "It's about time you caught up."

Zeke's chuckle rumbled in his chest. "I didn't realize I was late."

"Mhmm," I said. "Any time you aren't with me, you're late."

"Well then I suppose I'll never leave your side." He brought his lips down to mine and kissed me slowly. One of his hands crept up my neck and slid into my hair, holding me to him.

Okay. This was living to me, too.

When we parted, I sighed and took his hand in mine. "My advisors want an answer. I can't hold them off much longer. And . . ." I bit my lip, looking away from his red-flecked eyes. "I don't want to anymore. I need to know too."

His face darkened just slightly as he rubbed his thumb over the back of my hand. He rubbed his other hand through his hair.

"Can't we just continue like this?"

I shook my head. "You know you wouldn't be happy like this. Never able to leave the city without me."

He picked up a rock and threw it into the creek, disrupting the sun's beams. "But I'm not a statesman. How am I supposed to know the difference between a rightful tax and a lord with a legitimate complaint? A genuine request for help and a greedy hand grabbing for the kingdom's pockets?"

"For the record, I think you'd be quite good at it, considering how easily you call anyone's bluff." I furrowed my eyebrows. "But your role would deal with more than just the kingdom's money. You know that. It'd be diplomacy meetings, and trade agreements—"

"I know, Rose. It's just . . . it's not the life I had ever pictured for myself."

I studied him for a moment. An indecisiveness in his eyes told me there was more. "I'm sure that's true, but I don't think that's it."

A defensive flare of his nostrils. "Well, what else is there?"

"I don't think those things scare you. And you know, I think you'd actually like the challenge. You've never been one to step down from one, anyway."

He smirked. "Maybe. Being married to you is a challenge, and I don't regret that yet."

"It's a good thing I also don't mind challenges." I nudged him in the shoulder, fighting back a laugh. "Because being married to you is no waltz either."

He held a hand over his heart. "I'm a delight."

"Sure. Let's get Hazel's opinion on that."

His playful smirk fell into a grimace. "I'd rather not."

I took his hands in mine and looked him squarely in the eyes. "What's the true reason? Please just tell me."

Zeke's eyes bore into mine, bouncing back and forth beneath his furrowed eyebrows. "It's foolish."

"Foolish? Surely not." I put a hand on his cheek. "You can tell me."

Warring through some battle in his head, he finally threw his hands up in the air and let out a rough breath through pursed lips. "All right. What if . . . they don't approve of me?"

"Who?" I asked. "My advisors? They already approve of you."

"No. *Everyone.* The citizens, the castle workers, the rulers of other kingdoms! Knowing where I come from—"

"You're of a noble family!"

"But not royalty. Come on, Rose, don't you see? I'd love to stand by your side in all things. But if no one accepts me—"

"Of course they'll accept you." Thanks to Sterling, I was not fully royal either, and they accepted me just fine.

He shook his head at my words. "If no one accepts me, it'd be humiliating for you and for Lecevonia, and that's the last thing I want."

"Zeke." I took his face in my hands and turned it back toward me. I couldn't help but smile. My Zeke, usually so confident—if not *too* confident. "Of course everyone would approve of you. You had a role in stopping Amicka too. And even if that wasn't the case, it wouldn't matter. You're my husband, rightfully and lawfully. That is greater than any opinion someone may have."

Finally, his brown eyes softened as my words seemed to click, and he took a steady breath and nodded.

I let out my own sigh of relief. It wasn't his lack of wanting to serve the kingdom with me, but rather a bit of fear. To know that was what I had truly needed. I could live with that.

"I have an idea of a role you might enjoy more than king-consort," I told him. I supposed I didn't need one anyway.

His expression turned to one of inquisition.

I chose my words carefully, trying to keep my excitement at bay. "Colonel Burnstead is stepping down from his position. So, I'm offering it to you. As commanding officer of the kingdom's scouts, it can only go to someone I trust with every piece of myself. You'd stay nearby, as Colonel Burnstead did, organizing our scouts' assignments, and you'd know the goings on of the kingdom even before me, but you wouldn't be tied to the politics of it all. If nothing had changed, you'd have been one of the next in line for the position anyway."

Zeke's eyes widened. "Truly. Colonel of Scouts."

I nodded, hope rising. "And with your Talent and experience, I think it might be perfect. You don't have to decide this moment, but it does need to be soon—"

"I'll pass on it."

I froze.

Pass? I thought surely . . .

He laid a hand on my cheek. "You're right. I'm your husband. Scared or not, I *do* want to stand by your side in all things. Thank you for offering Colonel Burnstead's position to me, but I'll put on my big boy breeches and be brave." He pulled me close with one arm around my waist, the other drawing my face toward his. "There's no greater position than your husband. Seeing how brave you are all the time, becoming king-consort should have been an easy choice for me."

Pride and love for him swelled within me, and I stood on the tips of my toes to kiss him.

His acceptance completed what I had just barely dared to dream. When I'd first been crowned, and after so many failed suitors, I'd believed no marriage of mine could be filled with this much love. *Do what was right for the kingdom*, I always thought. Never, *Do what was right for me.*

Instead, I was living the life that was once impossible.

As Zeke's lips pressed against mine, so warm, their admiration and hunger matching my own, I dared to feel as though everything was as it should be. Zeke stood by my side. The hum of magic warmed the earth. I was Queen Rosemary Avelia, Reigning Sovereign of Lecevonia. I was unafraid, and I was happy.

Our kiss left me breathless, head swirling as Zeke broke away just enough to speak. "I'm yours. Always."

I nodded, never once doubting his words. "Always."

# EPILOGUE



*~THREE YEARS LATER~*
*ISABELE*

ROSE WORRIED AT her lower lip, hesitating at the door of the carriage. "Are you sure you'll be all right here? You'll keep the closest eye on Jem? He gets into things so quickly."

"He's nearly two! Of course he does." I hiked my little nephew up onto my hip. "He won't leave our sight. He'll be fine."

"Oh, the timing of this is just—"

"Just fine," I told her calmly. "I wish we could all go." Queen Lilyana and her soon-to-be husband were all anyone talked about these days—a come-back-from-the-dead queen and her lover who was no more than a baker. I glanced over at my husband Henry lifting chests into the carriage, tickled by the idea that Lilyana and I had both fallen for bakers. All strong arms and good souls, coming home smelling like fresh-baked bread every night. "And you're all right to travel?" I asked, for the third time.

Rose sighed and rubbed her round belly through her travel cloak. "Yes, Isa. My midwife and all the healers gave me the go-ahead. I'm just past the halfway mark, and the baby and I are both healthy." She looked at Jem on my hip, who was eyeing a bright red bird in a nearby forsythia tree. "It's just . . . such a long time away from him."

Zeke appeared from behind the carriage, having just loaded the last of their things. Since having children, his hair had gained a touch of silver, but none of us dared tell him. "It's three weeks," he told Rose. "We will be all right. He's going to have more fun here than on the road with us. You'll see." He ruffled the little boy's head of yellow curls. But after Zeke said what he did, he pursed his lips, suddenly appearing to be saddened by the thought. Those kinds of things never got past me. He leaned in and kissed Jem's head. "I love you, son. Your mama and I will be back by the month's end. I promise you."

Rose's lip quivered, but she somehow kept her voice steady as always. "I'll send a letter once we leave Bowsrock and head for Snowmont. Haggard forbid we get stuck by the first snowfall—"

"We won't, Rose." Zeke took her hand and held it tightly. "All will be well."

"The horses travel faster than ever now, you know," I reminded her. The return of the magic to the land had truly made our kingdom's horses stronger and faster. "And with the new paved roads I've heard about, it should be smooth travels for you."

That was everywhere these days. New ways of doing things. New roads and towns built by Talented architects, Firemakers keeping inns and homes warm through the winters, plentiful fields and greenhouses upkept by Greensows. So many had come to me to discover just what exactly their Talent was, and truly, no two Talents were just alike.

Rose and Zeke looked at one another, in a standoff it seemed, until Rose finally sighed again and reached for Jem, hugging him so tightly that he giggled and started to squirm. "Mama!"

She laughed and kissed him on his cheek. "I love you. So, so much."

He nuzzled his forehead to hers, just about making my heart melt. Once he started to wriggle again, she let him down on the ground.

I wrapped my arms around Rose and took one last look at her belly, with its amber aura surrounding it, and I smiled, wondering what wonders this little baby would bring to our world. "Give Celeste my love," I said, watching them climb into the carriage.

As the door closed behind them, Rose smiled through the open window. "Of course I will. I'm so excited to give her some spice wine and tiliarose from home. It's been three years now, and she still complains of the cold. You'd think Kathryn would have Eased that by now."

Kathryn's Talent was one of the first I identified since the Awakening, though I'd gotten it wrong at first. Eerily similar to her brother's Persuasion, she had the Talent of Ease. She could take the edge off the minds of others, so to speak. If her Talent hadn't been able to make Celeste entirely comfortable with the constant snow of Tarasyn by now, that spice wine was sure to do the trick.

I did love a nice glass of spice wine. The autumn breeze picked up just then, as if I needed any more convincing to open a bottle from the castle's cellar.

Rose and Zeke settled into their seats as the carriage took off. Henry and I waved from the stable's entryway until we could no longer see the cloud of dust that followed them.

I looked around the stable and found Jem picking at a nearby bale of hay, green eyes curious. I picked him up in my arms and held him close.

There was a time I thought I would never feel complete again.

When my Talent had been ripped out of me, so had my sense of self. But now, I still reveled in the feeling of wholeness. Much like what I saw in Rose with her little family. This life with Zeke was what my sister had dreamed of, as much as she dared to let herself think of it. It had felt impossible, too tied into her duty to become real. Now, I wondered if Rose felt the same way I did—whole, after being incomplete for so long.

My world was one of color now, auras of every shade in my view wherever I went, as vibrant as the new stained glass of the nerys lily we'd finally been able to replace in Hillstone's chapel. But here I focused on Jem, this little prince, and pictured his future where he'd grow in a land of magic, touched by enchantment every day.

After all, we all crave a little enchantment.

# of Reign and Embers

3

A Magian Peninsula Novel

# Family Trees of

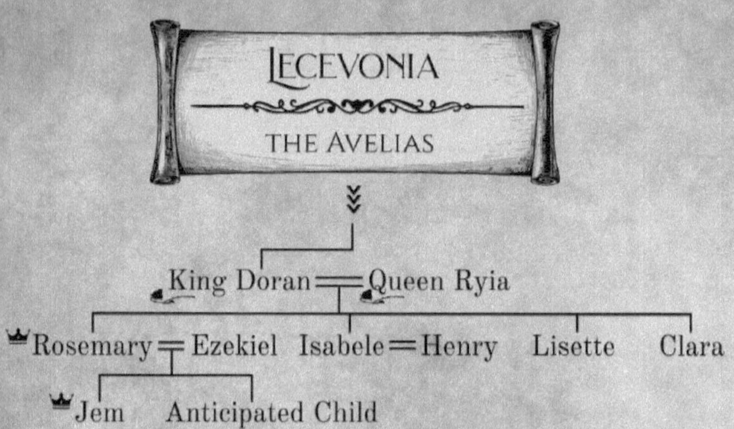


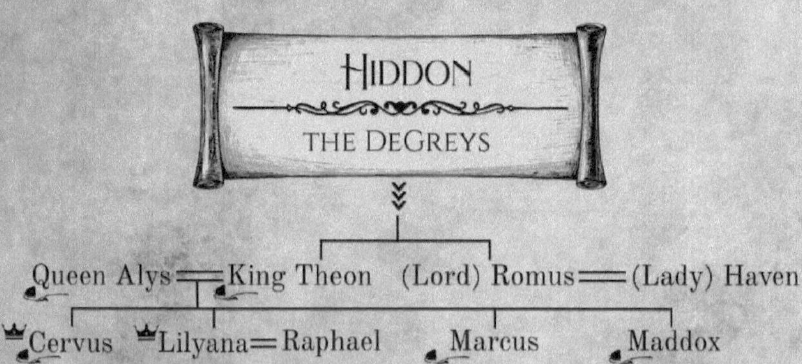


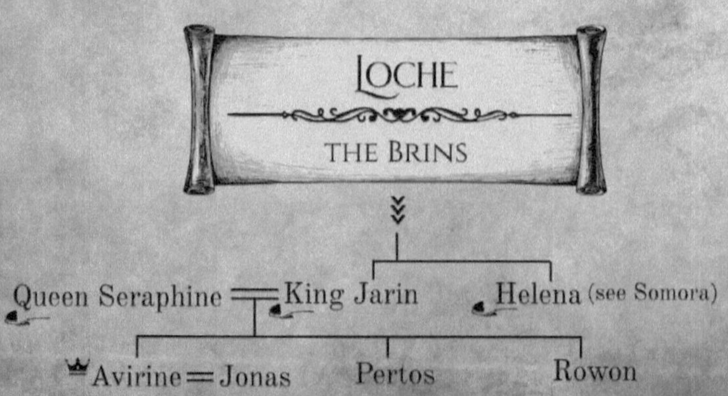

# THE FIVE KINGDOMS
## OF THE MAGIAN PENINSULA

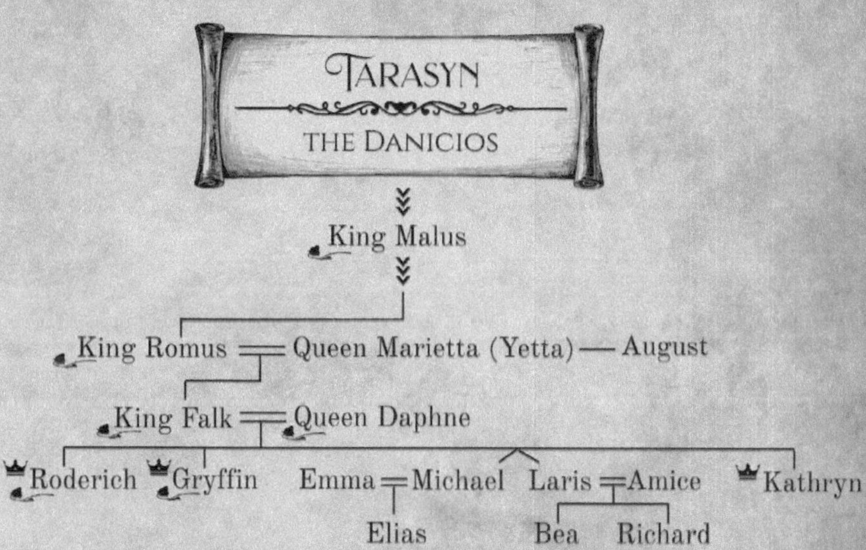


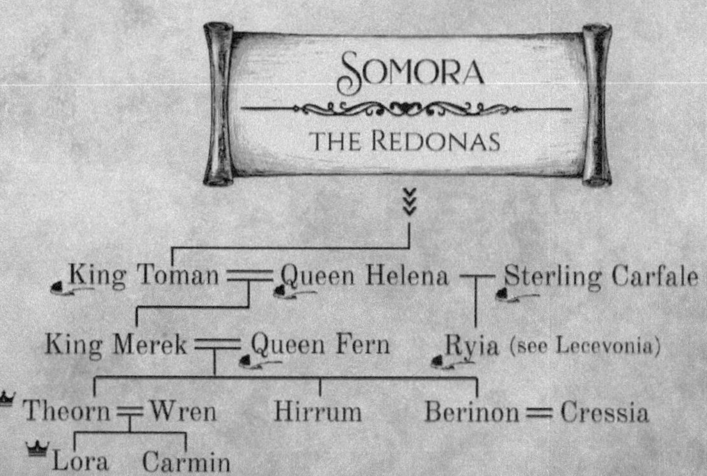


♛ = heir          ⚑ = deceased

# ACKNOWLEDGEMENTS

There was a period of time that I thought this book would not happen any time soon. Motherhood honestly hit me like a wrecking ball. Finding that balance and sense of importance that allowed me to give myself time and energy to write again felt impossible, until I did it with the help of people I hold so dearly to me.

Nick, thank you for being my rock, cheerleader, and partner in life every single day. You are the best husband to me and dad to our kiddos. Thank you for being willing (and offering) to solo-parent so that I can disappear into my writing hovel from time to time to get work done. You have always believed in me and my dream and have supported me every step of the way. Thank you for convincing me to keep writing!

Lori, thank you for putting the bug in Mom's ear that I seriously needed help with childcare to get the manuscript of this book finished. You put the fire under me again to get it done.

Mom, thank you for watching the kids that week so that I could write! Step 1 to completing this book was getting that first draft done, and that was possible because of you!

Mom and Dad, thank you both so much for, well, everything. Thank you for supporting my dream of being a writer and showing that support in so many different ways. You guys are amazing and have all of my love.

Rebecca, thank you for being my alpha reader, plot analyst, and number one fan. You have listened to me talk about this book for the past three years and have been right by my side (a phone call away) for this entire series. I love you!

Gee Gee, Amy, Hilary, Kristine, Vivian, Sam, Lauryn, Judye, Sophia, Laura, Jess, Karri, Vondie, Kathy, Sue, Matt, Misty, and to everyone else who has championed this series, I thank you so sincerely. Your support means the world.

To all of you who have waited so long for this book to be published, thank you for sticking by me! Your steadfastness helped me power through to the finish line, and you guys are truly why I told myself that I *needed* to get this book out into the world sooner rather than later.

Gina once again and Kaitlyn, thank you for making this book shine with your dragon-eye editing expertise. Your guidance and sharp attention to detail had a huge hand in making this book the best it can be.

Lena, thank you for creating another beautiful book cover to finish this series! It has been such a pleasure working with you, and your artistic Talent is a gift to the book world.

Thank you, reader, dearly. You picked up this series and gave it a chance. You followed Rosemary trial after trial, and you saw her reign triumphantly. Maybe you saw yourself in her struggles, maybe Zeke or Gryffin kept you going, or maybe you just thought the story was fun. Whatever your reason has been for seeing this through to the end, I treasure it. Truly, I write for you.

All thanks be to God, who has shown me the way through every battle and dark period I faced. In my most desperate times, I cried out to You, and You in some way, whether it be an easier tomorrow or a helping hand at just the right moment, gave me strength to see through to the light again. You have given me this gift of life and creativity, and I pray that I use it according to Your will.

To all fantasy lovers and book nerds out there, let's keep spreading love of the written word throughout the world! Books are where the mind makes magic.

IF YOU ENJOYED THIS BOOK, PLEASE CONSIDER LEAVING A REVIEW ON GOODREADS AND/OR THE WEBSITE OF PURCHASE.

Reviews are invaluable to authors. Reviews increase exposure of literary works you love and enable and encourage other readers to give this book a chance. Reviews also encourage the author to continue creating stories.

A review does not have be long, just a simple "I loved this story!" is great! Each and every review is important.

Thank you for your consideration in leaving a review.

# WORKS BY
# ASHLEY W. SLAUGHTER

## THE CROWNED CHRONICLES

*Of Legends and Roses,* Book One
Available Now at retailers everywhere

*Of Deceit and Snow,* Book Two
Available Now at retailers everywhere

*Of Reign and Embers,* Book Three
Available Now at retailers everywhere

## Short Story Anthologies

*Eumonia's Monody and Five Other Stories*
Available Now
Exclusive to Amazon and Kindle Unlimited
Read it for free on KU!

JOIN ASHLEY'S MAILING LIST FOR
EXCLUSIVE CONTENT, COVER
REVEALS, AND UPDATES!

(Don't worry, she won't spam you. She finds
sending emails to be intimidating.)

Visit Ashley's website to join:

https://www.ashleywslaughter.com

AWS
Writing

# ABOUT THE AUTHOR

Ashley W. Slaughter is an author, nature lover, wife, mom, and coffee/tea drinker. She received her bachelor's degree in Ecology and Evolutionary Biology from the University of Louisiana-Monroe in 2018, and between those rigorous biology courses, she took her favorite elective, Creative Writing. Writing has always been a passion of hers, as shown through her near-to-bursting manila folder of short stories she'd written throughout grade school. She began her publishing journey in 2021 with her debut award-winning novel, *Of Legends and Roses*. Ashley lives in south Louisiana, USA with her husband, sons, and three cats.

*"Books are where the mind makes magic."*